W9-ASP-724

FICTION
Andersen
L.

Andersen, Laura

The virgin's war

$16.00

DATE DUE

BY LAURA ANDERSEN

The Boleyn King Trilogy

The Boleyn King

The Boleyn Deceit

The Boleyn Reckoning

The Tudor Legacy Trilogy

The Virgin's Daughter

The Virgin's Spy

The Virgin's War

THE VIRGIN'S
WAR

THE VIRGIN'S WAR

A TUDOR LEGACY NOVEL

Laura Andersen

BALLANTINE BOOKS

NEW YORK

A Ballantine Books Trade Paperback Original

Copyright © 2016 by Laura Andersen
Reading group guide copyright © 2016 by Random House LLC

Published in the United States by Ballantine Books, an imprint of Random House, a division of Random House LLC, a Penguin Random House Company, New York.

BALLANTINE and the HOUSE colophon are registered trademarks of Random House LLC.
RANDOM HOUSE READER'S CIRCLE & Design is a registered trademark of Random House LLC.

Library of Congress Cataloging-in-Publication Data
Names: Andersen, Laura, author.
Title: The virgin's war : a Tudor legacy novel / Laura Andersen.
Description: New York : Ballantine Books, [2016] | Series: Tudor legacy
Identifiers: LCCN 2016007745 (print) | LCCN 2016013172 (ebook) |
ISBN 9780804179409 (softcover : acid-free paper) | ISBN 9780804179416 (ebook)
Subjects: LCSH: Elizabeth I, Queen of England, 1533-1603—Fiction. |
Great Britain—Kings and rulers—Succession—Fiction. | Great Britain—History—
Tudors, 1485-1603—Fiction. | Inheritance and succession—Fiction. | Queens—
Great Britain—Fiction. | BISAC: FICTION / Historical. | FICTION / Sagas. |
FICTION / Romance / Historical. | GSAFD: Historical fiction.
Classification: LCC PS3601.N437 V59 2016 (print) | LCC PS3601.N437 (ebook) |
DDC 813/.6—dc23
LC record available at http://lccn.loc.gov/2016007745

Printed in the United States of America on acid-free paper

randomhousereaderscircle.com

2 4 6 8 9 7 5 3 1

Book design by Caroline Cunningham

For Elizabeth Tudor

1533–1603

Princess, Lady, Scholar, Queen

With Respect and Great Affection

And with apologies to Mary I and Edward VI

Whose reigns (and/or lives) I so shamelessly edited

THE VIRGIN'S
WAR

PRELUDE

July 1577

Fifteen-year-old Pippa Courtenay woke to the blazing sun of a
late July day already smiling and practically floated out of
bed—before promptly falling earthbound under the onslaught of
humid heat. It hadn't rained for three weeks and each day the tem-
peratures seemed to climb higher. She would have to choose her
clothing with care today if she didn't want to melt before noon.

After the briefest hesitation, she threw caution to the wind and
decided to forgo a petticoat entirely. No one would know she wasn't
wearing one beneath her striped blue silk kirtle. Over that she laced
her lightest gown of white voile, delicately embroidered with jewel-
toned flowers and vines so lifelike they appeared to twine around
her as she walked. Her abundant honey-gold hair she plaited severely away from her face and off her neck, with the single black
streak she'd had since birth painting a curve back from her right
temple.

Then she tripped downstairs to Wynfield Mote's hall, humming
as she went. And when she entered the high-paneled lofty space, he
was waiting for her as promised: Matthew Harrington.

Eighteen, tall, broad, brown-haired and brown-eyed, Matthew gave her one of his rare smiles. "Shall we?" he asked.

Considering the unusual heat of this summer, they had decided on a breakfast picnic while the air was still breathable rather than openly liquid. For the same reason, they had decided to walk rather than punish horses with a ride. Their route was instinctive—eastward to the old church.

Pippa talked at an unusually rapid pace even for her. The words spilled out in a rush and burble of delight, dancing from topic to topic. It was such a pleasure to have Matthew home. For the last year he had been deep in his studies at Balliol College, Oxford, but two days earlier had returned to visit his parents. Edward and Carrie Harrington had served the Courtenays for more than twenty years, and Matthew was as much a part of the family as her siblings.

Pippa loved her family. But her older sister, Lucette, had been moody and difficult the last few years and now spent a great deal of time in London—ostensibly studying with Dr. Dee but more practically avoiding their parents. Her two brothers were training seriously with their father this summer and riding back and forth often to Tiverton Castle. Stephen, two years older, still thought of Pippa as a child, but even her own twin, Kit, had little time to spend with her. Matthew, though, could always be counted on.

She didn't set out to make the day momentous. She rarely set out to do anything—if Lucette invariably acted from principle, Pippa relied on instinct. Although most people found Matthew uncommunicative, with her he spoke freely. In and around and over her quicksilver voice, he told her wry stories about his college and tutors and fellow students, making her laugh in a manner no one else did. Not even Kit.

After the slow ramble, they reached the copse of beeches that looked down a hill onto the stone walls and spire of the old Norman church. She flung herself into the fragrant meadow grass at the trees' edge and leaned back on her elbows, staring up at the sky. Matthew lowered himself more cautiously to sit beside her and deftly handled the domestic details of laying out breakfast: ripe strawberries, early apples, fresh bread, and soft cheese. They took their time eating, letting their stories slowly wind down into companionable silence.

Eyes closed, Pippa lay down in the sweet-smelling, sun-warmed grass.

"Princess Anne is coming to Wynfield soon?" Matthew asked.

"Next week."

"And what trouble are the two of you planning to launch this time?" He corrected himself. "The three of you, I mean. Kit is the worst."

"Anabel's the worst," Pippa said drowsily. "Because *she* isn't afraid of my mother. You'll be here, won't you?"

"I've been invited to Theobalds for a month, to work with Lord Burghley's household. I can hardly say no to England's Lord High Treasurer."

Pippa's eyes flew open, the first shadow of the day crossing her sunny mood. "But I want you here!"

"What a pity I cannot learn the intricacies of English government from a fifteen-year-old girl."

He was deliberately baiting her, and she let herself rise to it. "Anabel is a fifteen-year-old girl," she pointed out caustically. "And before long she will be in a position to compose her own household and council. Shouldn't you be trying to please *her*?"

"The princess is far too practical to want advisors with no experience. Why do you think Lord Burghley is taking an interest in me? Because he believes it likely Princess Anne will draw me into her circle. He intends me to be an asset."

Pippa delivered a practiced pout—only halfheartedly, because pouting never worked on Matthew. Really, the only person it ever worked on was her father. When he merely continued to look steadily at her, Pippa huffed a gusty sigh and gave it up.

"I never could make you do what I wanted," she complained.

He made a sound between a laugh and a cough. "Do you think so?"

There was a queer note to his voice that made Pippa sit up and study him sharply. His face looked placid as always, but she caught the slightest quiver at the corner of his lips.

"Matthew?"

All her life Pippa had moved through the world with an awareness of shifting layers of meaning and feeling. Most often it was her twin whose emotions pressed in upon her, Kit who came to her in flashes of his present state. But just now the emotions were entirely her own. And in all that brilliant, beautiful day, there was only one thing she wanted.

So she took it.

Pippa leaned in so suddenly that Matthew startled back. But she gave him no chance to speak or wonder or think at all. She simply kissed him.

It was, of necessity, inexpert. Pippa was not in the habit of kissing the gentlemen of her acquaintance. She was attractive and wellborn and wealthy, but she also had a formidable father. Rumour had it Dominic Courtenay had nearly killed Brandon Dudley several years ago after discovering him in passionate concord with Lucette. Which meant Pippa would have to take the initiative with any man—and with no one more than the self-effacing Matthew.

Almost at once, as though sparked by the touch, Pippa felt Matthew's emotions blaze into life. His first instinct was pure physical response—his second, to pull away. But because she felt the resistance coming, she put her hands on the sides of his face to keep him engaged.

And once past his second instinct, Matthew let himself return her kiss. Having nothing to compare it to, Pippa had no idea if he was experienced or not. All she knew was that it was right. They fit perfectly, as she had always known they would.

Despite her curious double awareness, it was still a surprise when Matthew spoke. "I love you," he whispered in a suspiciously rough voice into her hair when they released each other to breathe. "I have always loved you, Philippa. But you already knew that, didn't you?"

She laughed breathlessly. "Why does everyone think I know everything?"

"Only the things that matter."

And just like that, like a candle being snuffed out, the brilliant day vanished and Pippa was wrapped in a dream or vision—a very specific one that had crept into her life so long ago it seemed to have always been with her. *Rushlight and fog, insistent hands and masked faces, melodious Spanish voices mixed with the unmistakable lilt of the Scots, the certain knowledge that she was dying . . .*

The vision had never frightened her—until now. Because for the first time, a new element was added to the familiar litany of her life's eventual end. *"Run, Philippa. Run now!" Matthew's voice. Matthew's beautiful, beloved voice, strained with fear and anger. But she could not run, because he was bleeding and if she left him he would die—*

Pippa gasped, the shock of it like falling into an icy Devon stream in winter. She came back to the hillside, the warm sun on her face and Matthew grasping her hands. "What's wrong?" he asked.

She slipped out of his hold and stood, still disoriented as to time and place. All she could do was escape as quickly as possible. "I don't always like what I know," she managed to reply. "And neither would you. Don't follow me, Matthew."

She ran away, knowing he would not override her. Matthew's restraint would always win out.

ONE

November 1584

1 November 1584
Middleham Castle

Dear Kit,

I confess to being unreasonably envious of you! Would you believe that it snowed here yesterday? Yes, it melted by morning, but when I think of you and Stephen in the temperate Loire Valley, I long to board the first ship that will take me away from Yorkshire.

And yes, I know, I am the one who counseled Anabel to take up residence this far north. But do you not remember Madalena's Moorish grandmother telling me that I am by nature contradictory? Who am I to gainsay such a wise woman?

I am not the only contradictory female in Yorkshire. I suppose you know from Anabel that Brandon Dudley and Nora Percy married suddenly last month. Not, despite what the gossips say, because there is a child coming too soon—no, for all its apparent suddenness, this wedding has been looming for some years. I am only surprised that they waited this *long. Nora is already thirty and has been in love with Brandon forever. But her mother did not approve—probably because Eleanor Percy hoped that one day her daughter would learn to be as cynical at manipulating men as she is herself.*

Although Eleanor's manipulations have not been notably successful lately. The Earl of Ormond proved willing to be her lover, but not her husband. And with the dangerous situation in Ireland, Ormond has finally broken with Eleanor for good and sent her back to England. She was not invited to her daughter's wedding.

Nor was the queen informed of the marriage in advance, despite Nora being her niece. Anabel is a little tense, awaiting her mother's response.

I wish you would write more often. To me, not just to Anabel. It has been surprisingly lonely being apart from all my siblings. At least you and Stephen are together, and Lucie has Julien.

Still, there is little time to indulge in self-pity in this household. Anabel is almost as ferocious a ruler as her mother, and Matthew—

Pippa Courtenay broke off writing. For a woman who had often been told she never lacked for things to say, she could not find the words to finish that sentence. How to explain her current tenuous relationship with Matthew Harrington, a man she had known since birth? At the age of fifteen, she had allowed herself one reckless moment with him—and had spent the last seven years ensuring they never again crossed the boundaries of simple friendship.

Twice in the last eighteen months she had attempted to explain to him the wisdom of that decision and persuade him to look for his future happiness elsewhere. It had not gone according to plan.

Which seemed to be the theme of the Courtenay family these last two years. After a bloody mess in Ireland, her older brother Stephen had spent five months confined to the Tower of London. He'd subsequently lost his title and estates as Earl of Somerset, then been unofficially banished from England. Now he and Kit—Pippa's twin—were training in France and serving with their father's old friend, Renaud LeClerc. And Lucie, though gloriously happy in her marriage to Renaud's son, Julien, had suffered three miscarriages in the last two years.

Hands came to rest on Pippa's shoulders and she gasped. The Princess of Wales said teasingly, "Run out of things for which to scold Kit? I can provide you a list if you need it."

"But then what will *you* write to him?"

Anabel took a seat next to Pippa, radiant in one of the soft-hued, luminous gowns meant to distinguish the princess from her royal mother's taste for richer jewel-toned colours. With a small, secret smile, she confided to Pippa, "Don't worry about me. I have no shortage of things to write to Kit."

No doubt. Pippa put aside her unfinished letter and deliberately changed the subject from emotional entanglements to something less fraught. Like politics. "How is the news from Dublin?"

Anabel pulled a face. "It continues disastrous. With the fall of Waterford, only Dublin and Cork are open to reinforcements, and that's presupposing we have any to send. No one thought the Spanish troops would remain in Ireland this long, but success breeds willingness and King Philip has had little difficulty rotating men in and out without losing the advantage."

King Philip being also Anabel's father. She had not referred to him as such, not even to Pippa, for two years. Not since the Spanish fleet had landed ten thousand soldiers to oppose English possession of Ireland. The Spanish king was the enemy now, or at least well on his way to becoming such.

"I suppose Mary Stuart continues to crow about it in her correspondence all over Europe," Pippa noted. After escaping English captivity several years before, the onetime Scots and French queen had added Spain to her list of royal titles with her marriage to King Philip. Even more than her husband, Mary violently opposed all English interests.

"Certainly, Mary cannot contain her satisfaction when writing to her oldest son. James's letters to me are three-quarters rants about his mother and one-quarter demands that England do something about Mary Stuart and Ireland. Not that he's offering any material help."

The courtship of King James VI of Scotland and England's Princess of Wales had thus far been conducted entirely on paper. Pippa couldn't help teasing, "Leaving no space for a single word in any of those letters about his most cherished bride-to-be?"

With simply the slant of her eyebrows and the curl of her lip, Anabel could switch from charming to haughty. Rather like her mother. "I am quite happy to escape fulsome and insincere compliments, I assure you. I am less happy when King James presumes to criticize England's queen and Parliament for not sending more aid to Ireland. In my last letter, I pointed out that Scotland is also a Protestant nation and perhaps they would be interested in lending money or men for the fight in Ireland. I imagine that will shut him up for a bit."

"This is quite the most amusing courtship I've ever witnessed," Pippa offered lightly.

"Just so long as James remains content with the courtship rather than pressing for a consummation of the treaty."

Anabel didn't have to add the obvious—that she continued to hope the marriage might never take place. Anabel was stubborn and passionate and hardheaded and romantic all in one. As long as she remained unwed, there existed the smallest hope that she might be allowed to marry the man she loved: Kit Courtenay.

Pippa sighed inwardly. *The course of true love never did run smooth. But this is beginning to be ridiculous. For all of us.*

"The Queen of England will not be kept waiting by a rebel Irish countess!" Elizabeth Tudor snapped. It really wasn't fair to snap at Burghley, who did no more than deliver the message that Eleanor FitzGerald was running late. But he'd had thirty years of serving royals and knew fairness was not to be expected.

That didn't mean her Treasury Secretary wouldn't offer his own retorts. "I could hardly burst into her bedchamber and drag her out half clothed," he said mildly.

"Oh, she's fully clothed, mark my words. This is a tactical move." Elizabeth, a princess since birth and a queen since she was twenty-five, knew all about tactical moves. She allowed her ruffled temper to smooth into glass. "Eleanor FitzGerald thinks she is announcing Ireland's independence. Truly independent rulers do not have to make such petty shows."

She caught the mordant humour in Francis Walsingham's eye at her pronouncement, but the Lord Secretary held his tongue. Like Burghley, Walsingham was present in order to intimidate the Irish countess as well as to provide Elizabeth with his experienced judgment after the encounter.

It was a further five minutes before the pages proclaimed the arrival of her ladyship, the Countess of Desmond. Arrived in England as emissary for the rebel earl, her husband, the only reason Elizabeth had agreed to meet with Eleanor FitzGerald was to impress upon the woman the might and power of the English court. Elizabeth had never been to Ireland, but she had read scores of accounts and knew that the Irish nobility—saving, perhaps, those such as her cousin, the Earl of Ormond—often lived in worse conditions than even her own middle-class merchants. Just because England was finding it difficult to fund a sufficient force of soldiers to beat back the Spanish didn't mean the Irish had any chance at all in the end. Indeed, without Spain's interference, the uprising would have long since been over.

A point Elizabeth did not hesitate to make when the tardy countess finally arrived and made her barely adequate curtsey. "I thought the entire point of Desmond's rebellion was resistance to foreign interference," the queen intoned. "We English have been part of Ireland for more than four hundred years, and yet we are accounted more foreign than the Spanish, who share no heritage with you at all?"

Twelve years younger than the queen, the thirty-nine-year-old

Eleanor was not easily frightened. Dressed soberly in a black gown that perhaps hinted at cultural mourning, the dark-eyed countess said stoutly, "The Spanish share our faith. And we have less quarrel with foreign soldiers who fight and then leave, than we do with men who seize our lands for their own and pretend they belong."

"As did the FitzGeralds," Elizabeth pointed out waspishly. "Not all that many generations ago."

"Long enough ago that we have earned the right to govern our own lands, and ensure our children can do the same," Eleanor blazed back. With two sons and four daughters, the countess had all the protective instincts of a mother. Perhaps even more than her husband's future, she wanted to ensure her children's.

At this point Lord Burghley intervened with his trademark logic. "If you believe the Spanish will allow you self-governance, then you are being willfully blind. It is just possible that King Philip is willing to commit troops merely for principle's sake, but Mary Stuart wants much more. Surely you have heard the rumours that their youngest son will be proclaimed Prince of Ireland in the coming year."

"He is two years old. We do not fear a child. Not the way we fear men who have determined the best way to rule Ireland is to murder every last Irish soul, thus leaving a clean slate for the English."

Elizabeth waved a hand in disdain. "I am not impressed by over-wrought melodrama. If you want the fighting in Ireland to stop, the answer is simple: evict the Spanish. When you have done that, then England and Ireland will have something to say to one another. Until then, go back to your husband. Tell him I have no place for traitors at my court. You will be escorted back to your ship tomorrow. My lady countess," she added pointedly.

The queen almost thought the woman would respond, for Eleanor had a very Irish glint in her eyes, but protocol prevailed. When Lady Desmond had left, Elizabeth looked at the one man in her government sure to have even more disdain for the countess than she herself. Burghley was a realist, but Francis Walsingham despised Catholics and the Spanish in equal measure. Long an advocate of a swift, harsh end to Ireland's rebellions, he was even more fiery now that the Irish were supported by Philip's troops.

"Well?" she asked her Lord Secretary pointedly.

Walsingham's hooded eyes had never grown easier to interpret. "The Spanish won't go. Not until they've made a serious play for Dublin."

"Dublin will never fall."

"Not in battle, but it might be starved into submission. If the Spanish decide to blockade the port—"

"Then they will be committing to open warfare against all our forces," Elizabeth snapped. "Philip isn't prepared for that."

"Yet." Walsingham let the syllable hang ominously, but said no more.

Elizabeth would like to have believed her Lord Secretary had learned discretion during his banishment from her court two years ago, but she doubted it. Walsingham was who he was and she valued him for it. Even if sometimes she wanted to kill him as well.

Of the two of them, Walsingham did not hold grudges. And though Elizabeth did, she knew the difference between wisdom and vanity. He had hurt her pride two years ago with his opposition to her proposed French marriage, but she could swallow pride for the greater good. Especially as there was no chance of that particular dispute resuming, for Francis, the young Duc d'Anjou, had died earlier this year of a tertian fever. It was just as well the queen had thought to take Anjou for herself and tied Anabel to James of Scotland, or else England would be doing some rapid maneuvering at this point.

"Keep an eye on the Netherlands," Elizabeth reminded Walsingham unnecessarily. "If Philip begins removing troops from the Low Countries, then we can begin to worry about Dublin and our own shores. For now, he is stretched thin on the ground."

Lord Burghley cleared his throat.

"Yes?" she prompted.

"Sir Walter Raleigh has been making quiet inquiries into the

Somerset estates. Raleigh would be most willing to buy Farleigh Hungerford from the crown. If the crown has decided to sell, that is."

"The crown has not so decided."

A long silence. "As long as it remains in crown control, Your Majesty, there are those who expect Stephen Courtenay will be reinstated to his titles."

"They can expect whatever they like. But I promise you one thing—as long as I live, Stephen Courtenay will never again be the Earl of Somerset. Spread that report, if you like."

It hurt her to say it, but not because she had second thoughts. Stephen had committed treason. Any other man in her kingdom would have paid for those crimes with his head. But Stephen was Minuette's son. So Stephen lived—but without title or lands or even his home. He had been in France for nineteen months now. As far as she was concerned, he could stay there indefinitely.

And if he helped keep his brother, Kit, out of England as well? All the better.

Maisie Sinclair had never been to Yorkshire before. Indeed, save for a precious few days two years ago visiting Stephen Courtenay in the Tower of London, she had not spent time in England at all. Despite her birth and childhood in Edinburgh, so close to the border that there always seemed to be alarms about whether the English were coming, Maisie's travels had taken her seemingly everywhere save her nearest neighbor. After her short-lived Irish marriage, Maisie had turned to the Continent. Since 1582 she had spent time in the Low Countries, Germany, Italy, and France. Now, at last, she was on her way home. Three and a half years after sailing from Scotland as the fifteen-year-old bride of an Irishman she'd never met, Maisie was prepared to make her play in Edinburgh.

But first, this visit to Yorkshire. Amidst her voluminous business correspondents was the household treasurer for Her Royal Highness Anne Isabella, Princess of Wales. Maisie's small but successful business interests had profited the princess in her investments, and the treasurer had issued an invitation to meet with him in person in the cathedral city of York. Maisie had considered for ten seconds—six seconds longer than it usually took her to make a decision—before sailing to Hull and riding the remainder of the way north.

She had not anticipated feeling nervous. *We are Sinclairs,* her grandfather had often drummed into her. *Sinclairs do not grovel before anyone.* But when Maisie approached the Treasurer's House in the shadow of York Minster and saw the royal banner of the Princess of Wales flying from the roofline, she very nearly turned on her heel and ran away. She had not been told that the princess herself would be here.

But her training held—all of her training, from her grandfather's hardheaded business principles to the nuns' strict codes of conduct—and probably no one noted the slight stutter in her step. One advantage of enormous skirts. She had with her a Flemish secretary she had hired in Bruges on the recommendation of one of her bankers and who had proven himself a dozen times over to be both astute and loyal. His name was Pieter Andries, and though she thought of him as a boy, he was a good ten years older than her. But where Maisie viewed the world without illusions and with the cynicism of a Scots banker, Pieter had a boundless faith in humanity. His wide-eyed joy in the world made Maisie watch out for him as though he were a naïve spaniel.

Pieter looked up at the banner and grinned. "This should be interesting."

So maybe he had learned her trick of cynical understatement during their time together.

They were met by pages and a soft-spoken, black-haired woman who introduced herself as Madalena Arias. She had the faintest of Spanish accents. "Mistress Sinclair," she said, for Maisie had insisted on returning to her maiden name after her brief marriage, "if you will follow me, Matthew Harrington is waiting for you in the recep-

tion hall. I hope you do not mind if Her Highness joins the meeting?"

It was a disingenuous question, but Maisie thought it well-
mannered of the woman to pretend to ask. "It will be an honour,"
she replied truthfully.

Pieter trailed behind her, looking suitably clerkly, and Maisie was
glad she had dressed with care. The shimmery mauve of her gown
was a unique dye done in the Low Countries, trimmed in lace as fine
as a spider's web at the collar and cuffs. Her hair was coiled in a
pearled snood attached to a small velvet cap, and her earrings were
tiny matching pearls. Perfectly correct and suitable for a wealthy
merchant's granddaughter.

When they entered the two-story hall with its black and white
checkered floor, Maisie's eyes went directly to the red-haired princess. She was unmistakable, not only from her well-known colouring
and elaborate gown, but from the indefinable air of power draped
around her. She was taller than Maisie—most everyone was—and
beautiful beyond merely the trappings of her dress and position. If
she had been a maid, she would still have been ravishing. But combined with her position, Anne Tudor would always command the
breathless attention of all who met her.

And she was as charming as she was gorgeous. "Maisie—may I call
you Maisie?—I hope you don't mind me sitting in. Matthew sings
your praises to such a degree that I simply had to meet you myself."

Maisie made a serviceable curtsey. "It is a great pleasure, Your
Highness."

An exceptionally tall man took a step forward. "Matthew Harrington," he said unnecessarily. "It is good of you to go out of your
way to come to York."

He spoke as he wrote, with economy and quiet strength. He had
the build to support his height, with dark brown eyes that assessed
her steadily.

"And this," Princess Anne said, drawing forward the other woman
present, "is someone most eager to meet you for herself. Philippa—"

"Courtenay," Maisie interrupted, then flushed. "I apologize, Your Highness. But she is very like her brother."

"Stephen?" Philippa Courtenay asked quizzically.

"I meant your twin, Christopher. I met him once in Ireland, on the way to my wedding. But yes, you do have something of Stephen about you as well."

The allure, she meant, but would never say. *The trick of looking at me with such focus that the rest of the world fades around the edges.* Anne Tudor might be the center of her world, but the Courtenays took self-possession to an entirely new level.

"I had hoped," Philippa Courtenay continued, "to have some talk with you of Stephen later. When you are finished with the business of high finance. He writes to you, I understand."

"He does."

"Why?"

This was not a woman to be parried with a soft answer. "Why me and not you, do you mean?" Maisie replied. "Because I was in Ireland. Those who have passed through trials together can understand one another in a manner others cannot."

To her surprise, Philippa smiled, genuine and open. "You will not mind if I ask you how to better understand my brother?"

"No, my lady."

Princess Anne had managed to subtly hold herself in the background, a skill Maisie imagined she didn't often employ, but now firmly took back the authority. "Let us sit and discuss my money. And when we are finished, I shall turn my dear Pippa loose on you. If you are as wise with words as you are with finance, that should be quite the conversation."

Maisie drew a slightly shaky breath and took the seat Matthew offered her. Discussing money was simple. It was the thought of discussing Stephen that made her pulse flutter.

The hour that followed was more exhilarating than any Maisie had spent in a long time. Despite her polite protestations, the young Princess of Wales had an astute business mind. She and Matthew

Harrington between them grilled her thoroughly, and by the end of the hour they had several new investments planned.

And then, with apparently artless ease, the princess took Matthew with her and left Maisie and Philippa Courtenay alone. Dressed in dove-grey damask, this youngest Courtenay daughter had her twin's good looks—sharp cheekbones and sharper eyes, hair like dark honey, save for a streak of glossy black that shone like Stephen's.

"Lady Philippa," Maisie said warily.

"Call me Pippa. Everyone does."

Since she couldn't quite bring herself to do that, Maisie simply nodded as though in agreement while silently vowing not to call her anything. And then she waited to be asked uncomfortable questions.

"Is Stephen ever going to recover from loving his Irish woman?"

Well, that was rather more uncomfortable than even she had bargained for. "It depends on how you define recovery."

A flash of amused respect from Lady Philippa. "I define it as not needing to turn to hard drink or easy women to salve his pain."

"Surely your twin can give you more accurate information than I can, seeing as how they are together in France."

"But Kit never met Ailis Kavanaugh. You were there. You watched it all happen. And before you tell me that you were far too simple and innocent to understand what was going on . . . don't bother. Your pose of childlike blandness does not fool me in the slightest."

It had been a long time since Maisie had met an adult who bothered to look behind the masks she wore. Stephen had been the last, and that only briefly and in flashes between his obsession with Ailis. It was something of a relief to shrug her shoulders and answer bluntly. "Your brother is not a man to be broken by anything save his own conscience. Stephen loved Ailis very much. But any chance they might have had vanished the moment her daughter died. It wasn't his lies or their different religions or political aims that ruined them—it was Stephen himself. He will never forgive himself for young Liadan's death. I think he believed that walking away from Ailis was his penance for the child's murder."

"That doesn't answer my question."

"Stephen will not take refuge in alcohol." Maisie didn't dare think about women. What did she know of how men eased their pain in that way? "He will not retreat from the path he has laid before himself—to serve where he can to the best of his ability. It is your queen's loss if it is not to be in England."

"That sounds rather cold."

"You asked for honesty, not comfort."

Lady Philippa smiled, but there was something sad to it. And piercing. She seemed to be looking deep into Maisie's own cold comforts as she said, "You are not wrong, but I do not think you see the whole of my brother. There is more to Stephen than duty, and a heart with room for more than one love. I do not think passion has finished with him quite yet."

In defiance of protocol, Maisie stood up first. She had no experience with passion and no desire to discuss it with this self-possessed young woman who also happened to be Stephen's sister. "My business is with numbers," she said with finality. "I shall leave passion and penance to those better equipped to recognize it."

Lady Philippa rose with a grace Maisie envied and her smile grew mischievous. "Thank you for your honesty, Mistress Sinclair. I will not forget it. Or you."

A promise, or a threat? Maisie couldn't decide which.

TWO

17 November 1584

Kit,

What have you been writing to Anabel lately? She is entirely too cheerful. It's making the household nervous. When Anabel is cheerful, she is apt
to be doing something reckless. I can only hope the recklessness is confined
to her letters. And yes, I know, I sound like a fidgety old maid. It's because
you're not here and Stephen's not here and Lucie and Julien have hardly
stirred from Compton Wynyates in a year. Her last miscarriage was so
far along that she had begun to hope. And when that hope was dashed yet
again . . . I am so worried about her and yet I cannot do anything!

We did have an interesting visitor while in York. Matthew has been
doing business on Anabel's behalf with Maisie Sinclair, the Scots widow
who was in the Kavanaugh household with Stephen. Her brother nominally runs the Sinclair family's main concerns out of Edinburgh, but she,
I suspect, is the true inheritor of her grandfather's genius. When she

agreed to meet with Matthew on her way back to Scotland, I persuaded Anabel to go along because I wanted to ask the girl about Stephen.

Maisie Sinclair was very defensive—not on her own behalf, but on Stephen's. I find that intriguing. She seems to think he is choosing to lose himself in duty in order to bury his unrequited love for Ailis Kavanaugh. What do you think? Does he talk about Ireland? Does he talk about the letters he sends and receives from Maisie? Does he ever say anything at all beyond work?

Write to me soon, and rather more fully than you are wont. It is not fair that Anabel gets all your words and I so few.

> *Your rather disgruntled sister,*
> *Pippa*

Kit couldn't decide whether to grin or grimace while reading Pippa's latest letter. He had never spent such a long time away from England and the many women who had formed the backbone of his home life. Although he missed much of it, he could not deny that life here at Chateau Blanclair was a particular kind of restful.

It was a household of men—Renaud, nearly sixty, had been widowed for some years and showed no interest in remarrying. His only daughter was married well, with three daughters of her own, but spent most of her time in Paris or on her husband's estates. And since the death of Renaud's eldest son and the departure of his second son to marriage in England, the only other resident family member was twelve-year-old Felix. Felix was his grandfather's heir and, between intensive tutoring, spent time learning the fine art of war. All in all, Blanclair was run rather like a soldiers' camp. In that atmosphere, Pippa's letters occasionally jarred on Kit.

But only for a moment. Then he was swept by a rush of bitter longing so strong his eyes stung and he had to breathe against it. What he wouldn't give to be with Pippa at this moment—because if he was with his twin, he would also be with Anabel.

Longing was abruptly cut off by a slap on the arm. "What are you moping about?" Stephen asked.

Irritation made him sharp. "Why is it that everywhere I go I'm followed by questions about your love life?"

Since Ireland, Stephen wasn't as easy to rile as he had once been. "I have no love life, brother, so the answers cannot possibly take long to compose."

"For a man with no love life, you have a multiplicity of women following your every move. Anabel went all the way to York to meet that Scots girl who has been writing to you since Ireland. And Pippa found her curiously unwilling to speak about you."

"If Anabel wanted to meet Maisie, it was for her business acumen," Stephen said evenly, the only sign of tension the slight twitch of his left eye. "And I highly doubt that anything in the letters we've exchanged is a tenth as inflammatory as what you've been writing to the Princess of Wales."

Kit grinned despite himself. "If I could cipher as well as you or Lucie, I could make them even more inflammatory."

Stephen rolled his eyes, but there was an affection behind the familiar gesture that Kit had never been aware of when he was young. Despite all he missed about England, he was glad to have spent this time in France with his brother.

"Come on," Stephen said. "Renaud has orders for us. A small sortie in the direction of Turin. Shouldn't take more than a month. We'll be back here by Christmas. And when spring comes, you should go home."

"We've talked about that."

"You can't wait for me forever, Kit."

"The queen will forgive you."

"I don't know that I care."

Kit narrowed his eyes. "You don't care if you're never allowed to go home again? Never to set foot on English soil? Of course you care. And of course Elizabeth will forgive you. It's not as though you killed anyone valuable."

"It's not who I killed," Stephen replied. "It's where and how. The queen can forgive much, but not insults to her authority. Even if I am allowed back to England, for what purpose? I have no interest in being decorative and useless."

"Like a younger son?" Kit shot back. "It's not all bad."

Kit forced his older brother to look at him, to acknowledge the hit, and finally Stephen let a smile ghost across his sharp-boned face. "We have the winter before us. Perhaps when spring comes I'll know what it is I want to do with my life."

In mid-November the entirety of Anabel's household at Middleham were uneasily wondering if the Princess of Wales intended to spend a second winter in the frozen North or might finally venture to the milder South. They had been out of Yorkshire twice in the last two years, but only to go to the princess's chief holdings in Wales. In all that time, they had come no nearer the queen's court than a hundred miles.

Anabel hadn't meant to avoid her mother's company this long. When she had taken Pippa's advice to go north and establish a strong royal presence nearer the Scots border, she hadn't considered all it might mean. Nor had she imagined how much she would enjoy the hard work of slowly weaving a disparate populace into closer ties to her own interests. With some of the strongest enclaves of Catholic recusant families settled in the North, the region had always been somewhat tenuous in its ties to the throne. And the North had long memories—a hundred years ago the people of Yorkshire had mourned the death of the royal usurper Richard III, and they still looked askance at the Tudors who had left his body on a battlefield.

But Anabel was not only a Tudor—she was also a Hapsburg, daughter of His Most Catholic Majesty Philip II of Spain. That impeccable bloodline went far with the recusants. Combined with her mother's gift for charming those she cared to charm, the Princess of Wales now found herself a little bemusedly with her own center of power. Not in open opposition to the queen's—but not precisely in concert with it, either.

All of that came into play over this one, outwardly simple decision: remain at Middleham for Christmas and the deep winter months or go to Greenwich for the traditional royal festivities. The gravity of the decision was underlaid by the fact that the royal invitation was not sent directly from mother to daughter, but through the official auspices of England's Lord High Treasurer, Lord Burghley.

Anabel considered it in concert with the closest of her advisors: her chaplain, her secretary, her treasurer, her master of horse, and her two chief ladies—Pippa and Madalena Arias. They met in the council chamber Anabel herself had decorated, at a polished table with the princess at the head in order to see the faces of her councilors. There were carpets on the floor in shades of apricot and summer green and a multitude of lamps lit early against the dull November sky.

"Well?" Anabel opened the matter for discussion. "How anxious are you all to return to the greater comforts of the civilized South?"

Her treasurer spoke first. "It is for you to say, Your Highness."

Trust Matthew Harrington to state the obvious without sounding obsequious.

"And it is for you all to advise me," Anabel said sweetly. "So—advise."

They spoke as their positions and characters demanded. The Spanish Madalena had been with Anabel since the princess was five, and provided a unique and Continental perspective on affairs. She spoke for the recusants. Would the Catholics who had begun to thaw toward Anabel be made openly hostile once again by her retreat to what some of them saw as the enemy's court?

"In that case, I should certainly go," Anabel said sharply. "I will not have anyone speak of the queen as the enemy of any of her people."

Madalena was not flustered. "Then your best choice is to continue acting as the intermediary. No one doubts your personal faith,

Your Highness, but by very virtue of your birth you give the Catholics hope."

"Hope that I will return England to Rome? That is a false hope that is best crushed at once."

"Hope that you will allow those who respect Rome to have a voice in the larger community."

The chaplain chimed in, a familiar refrain of disagreement with the Spanish lady. Edwin Littlefield had entered Anabel's service when she came north, having served before then in the household of the staunchly reformist Archbishop of York. "We cannot trust those whose allegiance to a foreign voice is stronger than their allegiance to their own queen."

"And how much is it England herself who forces that conflict, and not Rome?" Madalena urged quietly.

"It is the queen's fault that assassins are sent to kill her? That the Princess of Wales is under constant threat of violence? You are disingenuous if you do not accept that Rome and Spain together are behind those threats!" The chaplain could be easily roused.

"Rome and Spain, perhaps," Madalena acknowledged. "But not necessarily English Catholics. There are many who wish only to live in peace and be left to worship as their consciences dictate without disrupting the security of the state. They are the ones suffering under the queen's increasing punishments. Twenty pounds for not attending an Anglican service? None but the wealthiest can afford that."

Anabel struck the table with one hand to stop the familiar arguments. "Enough. I am looking for counsel, not rhetoric. Harrington, what do you think?"

If her council often reflected Anabel's own mercurial temper, then Matthew Harrington was the rock-solid exception. Though only twenty-five, he had the presence and gravity of a much older man. Like his father, who had stood by Dominic Courtenay through all manner of pain, Matthew brought absolute loyalty without sacrificing his own integrity. In the last two years, Anabel had begun to suspect that Matthew Harrington might be to her future what Lord Burghley was to her mother.

And, ironically, that Robert Cecil—Burghley's own son—would serve her more in the manner of Francis Walsingham. Like her mother's spymaster, Robert always seemed to know what was happening in the quietest corners of the world.

Matthew rarely offered his opinion without being asked, but always answered directly. "It would be wise to begin to make concrete offers to a few of the Catholic lords most likely to listen. The Council of the North will meet this spring—I would suggest you preside in person and use the opportunity to publicly show your desire to conciliate."

Christopher Hatton—her pragmatic secretary—leaned forward. "Won't that simply provide troublemakers with another wedge to drive between the queen and princess?"

It was the first time anyone had openly acknowledged the tension they had all felt; that the absence from her mother's court was beginning to be manipulated by those who wanted conflict.

Though Hatton had been addressing Matthew, it was Pippa who answered. "The troublemakers need an outlet, Your Highness. Better to be centered upon you, who can cope with it with grace and intelligence, than for us to have no entrée into that world. Would you rather they turn to young Anthony Babington or the Earl of Arundel?"

"No," Anabel said softly. "I would prefer to know what is happening in this kingdom beforehand, rather than be caught unawares. You think more definite approaches will be made to me by the Catholics this winter?"

"I think they have already begun. With King Philip's letter asking you to receive the Jesuit Tomás Navarro. Navarro is an experienced diplomat. He is coming as an envoy."

"Separate from Ambassador de Mendoza at my mother's court?" Anabel mused. "That is rather more than a mere approach. King

Philip is well aware that the queen will take offense, considering that any Jesuit in this country is liable to be executed."

"That is what the king wants. Not the execution of a priest, but to cause offense. To set you and the queen openly at odds. Your treasurer is right. Best to stay here this winter. Let them think you can be manipulated. Then perhaps we will learn something useful about Spain's future plans."

Anabel sighed. "All of which means I must send another coded letter to my mother lest she suspect me of truly conspiring against her." She meant it to sound teasing, but could see that her advisors picked up on her underlying nerves.

She met Pippa's eyes and wished they were alone. She tried to convey her question to her friend silently. *How long before the council begins to suspect what is really going on? And when do we take the risk of telling them?*

There was really no need to ask. For now, the answers remained the same for both questions: *I don't know.*

Philip II, King of Spain, moved through his palace of El Escorial followed by a sea of clerks and clerics. He listened as he walked. At the moment, it was his chief advisor, Cardinal Granvelle, who was speaking.

"The Pale has shrunk to little more than a protective boundary around Dublin itself," Granvelle reported. The Pale was that area of Ireland under direct English control. Despite centuries of colonization, the English had never completely subdued the whole of the country. Now, with Spanish troops and money running things, they were well and truly on the run.

Or, more accurately, under siege. "We will keep the English penned in over the winter," Philip said. "Use the time to consolidate control in the outer areas. Kilkenny continues to offer strong resistance under the Earl of Ormond."

"And come spring?" Nearing seventy, the Burgundian nobleman turned churchman considered it his right to speak openly, even critically at times. Between his bald forehead sloping back to a ring of white hair and his curly beard, Granvelle looked ever disapproving.

Philip smiled thinly. "You have been speaking with my queen. I can hear her eagerness for blood in your words."

"Her Majesty Queen Maria is truly committed to seeing Ireland freed of the taint of heresy."

"Her Majesty," Philip said frostily, "is truly committed to besting the English queen. I believe Maria will never be satisfied short of having Elizabeth in a prison of her own making."

"And you do not share that view?"

"I do not think it likely to come to pass. Maria's ambitions are too often fueled by her emotions rather than reality."

"And yours are not?"

Philip halted, and with practiced ease at reading their monarch, those attending his footsteps melted far enough away to give the two men at least an illusion of privacy.

"Say plainly what you mean," Philip commanded.

"My king, I say only what is being said in Rome—that you do not embrace your position as Defender of the Faith as wholeheartedly as you might. Some say that your will has been corrupted by your affections as a man."

"What do *you* say?"

Granvelle was not stupid. The cardinal had learned over long years how to balance on the edge of insult. "That one cannot separate the man from the king—or the woman from the queen. Queen Maria kindles a most human resentment against her cousin in England that ofttimes clouds her judgment. And Queen Elizabeth was not entirely a marriage of politics—for either of you. Even without your daughter binding you, I believe you would hesitate to destroy the English queen utterly."

"Destroy the queen, and I lose my daughter. And Anne is our best hope for England's future. Which is why we are sending Tomás Navarro to her household. Anne has an independent mind, and I mean to cultivate it in our own interests. Do not underestimate what miracles might be wrought by affection."

He turned away from Granvelle and continued pacing through the Courtyard of the King, startling into movement the hesitating flock of black-clad men. "As for Ireland," Philip measured his words with care, "come next spring we shall see what our ships might do to harry Dublin's port. Let us see how England copes supplying an outlying colony under fire. And Monsignor Cardinal? Don't ever assume that you know all of my plans."

Rather like his former wife in England, Philip excelled at playing the long game. Just now he was looking ahead, not merely to next summer, but to the next three or four summers. If all went well, by decade's end his daughter would rule England as a Catholic queen.

The French sortie along the Milanese border was accomplished swiftly and efficiently. Stephen had learned to appreciate such brief, sharp campaigns that involved neither honour nor passion. At least not on his part. It was just a job to him, one he performed with precision and skill and without raising any of the ghosts who lurked behind the scars of earlier—more personal—campaigns.

Ironically enough, Queen Elizabeth had done him a favour when she'd banished him from England after five months in the Tower of London. Had Stephen remained at home, with all the reminders of failure, he might have lost himself in solitude and alcohol as he had once before. But imprisonment imposed a certain discipline. He'd left the Tower leaner and clearer and ready to put the past behind. He'd at first resisted his family's plan to send him to Renaud LeClerc—especially the part about Kit coming with him like some sort of nursemaid—but there were times when his parents com-

bined forces and could not be gainsaid. So here they were, he and
Kit, twenty-one months after sailing from Dover, riding back to
Blanclair with Renaud LeClerc's handpicked men almost as though
they belonged.

The first one to greet them, coming down the lane on a dappled
grey horse meant for a much bigger rider, was Felix LeClerc, Renaud's grandson and heir. The twelve-year-old orphan had attached
himself to Stephen as though in replacement not only for his dead
father, but for his beloved Uncle Julien, who had married Stephen's
sister and moved to England.

"We feared you were going to miss Christmas!" Felix called as he
approached and expertly reined in the large horse. He had the height
of a young man, but when he grinned he looked like a child still.

Stephen was glad every time the boy grinned, for there was an
underlying solemnity often manifested in long periods of surly qui-
etness. Not surprising, considering Felix's losses.

"Christmas in France?" Stephen called back. "Never would we
miss the Christmas vigil and Yule log."

"Just as well, because a load of letters and parcels have come for
you both in the last week. If you hadn't returned, I should have had
to open them all myself."

Kit aimed a lighthearted slap at the boy's head as he rode up next
to him. Felix laughed and then the two were racing down the lane.
Stephen followed more slowly.

Once at the chateau, there was work to be done before anything
else. Horses to be cared for and baggage and remaining supplies and
weapons to be sorted. Stephen had had command of this particular
sortie—his French had become both more fluent and more collo-
quial in the last two years—and he executed every duty to comple-
tion before thinking of rest. The last duty was to report to Renaud
himself.

The official report was concise, and Renaud received it with only
one or two pertinent questions. Then he leaned back in his chair and
studied Stephen. Although Renaud was shorter and broader than

Dominic Courtenay, both men carried themselves like soldiers in every setting. And both had a knack for going to the heart of the matter. "That will see us through the winter. The question is, will you be with us when campaigning season returns in the spring?"

"I cannot begin to thank you for what you have done for me," Stephen said. "But after two years, it is time for me to decide what to do next. I cannot hide here forever."

"Commanding my men is hiding?"

"You know what I mean."

Renaud grunted. "I do. Frankly, I'm surprised you lasted this long. I thought your pride would have driven you away long before now."

"I suppose you know something about Courtenay pride."

"Pride—or stubbornness? Whatever you call it, you have coped well, Stephen. I think even your queen would be pleased."

"Not pleased enough to allow me back to England."

Only the French could manage that sardonic smile. "Probably not—at least not yet. But there is something freeing in being your own man. Where will that freedom take you next?"

"I had thought, perhaps, the Netherlands. Clearly they have need for soldiers."

"They have need for talented military captains—of which you are a very good specimen. I am sure you would be made more than welcome."

Stephen smiled a little. "You would not mind having trained a man just for him to go fight against Catholic soldiers?"

"Against *Spanish* soldiers," Renaud corrected. "I give my blessing on that if you want it. Better that than being drawn into the interminable Huguenot conflicts here."

"I thought you stayed out of matters of religion." The LeClerc household certainly appeared orthodox enough in their Catholic worship, though Stephen knew some of the servants were Huguenots, whom Renaud's late wife had hired to protect them and their families from the violence of the last decade.

"As you and your queen know perfectly well, religion is never free of ambition and politics. I prefer not to have my decisions made by anyone else's narrow interpretation of whichever religion they hold to."

"Well, I have no interest in throwing in my lot with the Huguenots. I've burned too many bridges with the doctrinaire Catholics already."

Renaud narrowed his eyes. "Because of Julien and Nicolas and what happened in England?"

"Because of Nightingale and Mary Stuart," Stephen allowed. It was all of a piece.

In the summer of 1580, French and Spanish Catholics had joined forces in an elaborate—and ultimately successful—attempt to rescue Mary Stuart from her English prison. It had been known as the Nightingale Plot. It was that plot that had drawn his sister Lucette into the heart of the LeClerc family, entangling her with both of Renaud's sons. The affair ended with violence and death in England. No matter how much had been kept quiet in the aftermath, there were those in Europe who knew enough to direct their Catholic vengeance at both the LeClercs and Stephen himself.

And one Catholic above all.

You have made an enemy today, Mary Stuart had said to Stephen as she left England's shores.

As though mentioning his sons had sent his mind in a specific direction, Renaud said abruptly, "It will be hard for Felix when you leave."

"I know. I'm sorry."

"The loss and sorrow is not of your making. And I understand why Julien cannot come to France. But, perhaps, when you leave in the spring, your brother might be willing to escort him to England for a time? I think Felix needs his uncle."

"I am sure Kit would gladly do so." And it would serve to ensure that Kit did not follow him into a war.

Renaud sighed, and Stephen could see the weight of the last years in his face. "We shall have you both for the winter, at least. I am glad. Charlotte is all that I could wish for in a daughter—but I confess that I miss both my sons."

After all the emotionally laden undertones, Stephen could finally be alone. He knew he needed a bath and a meal, but he was so tired and relieved to be without immediate responsibilities that he shut his door, pulled off his boots, and threw himself into a thickly padded chair in front of the fire. The small table at hand held the letters that had arrived in his absence.

Six from his parents—they wrote once a week without fail, though sometimes they arrived together in batches—and three from Pippa. There was only one from Lucie, and it hurt Stephen just to look at her handwriting. Her string of miscarriages had wounded her in a place he didn't know how to reach, and her letters to him had become almost painfully dutiful.

He laid aside his family's letters in favour of the last, addressed to him in the distinctive mix of merchants' scrawl and convent copperplate that announced Maisie Sinclair as thoroughly as her tiny frame or enormous mind.

He couldn't say when her letters had become so important to him. They started a few weeks after he'd left the Tower. Maisie wrote as she spoke—as though constantly engaged in a free-flowing conversation that made leaps from the philosophy of Erasmus to the science of Galileo to the wars of the Italian city-states to the price of alum on the open market. In the last year and a half she had written to him from Bruges and from Amsterdam, from Cologne and Rheims and Bohemia. She had ventured as far east as Krakow and as far south as Florence.

And though she was in motion and Stephen hardly stirred from Blanclair save for campaigns, he had come to understand that they were both learning to cope with the traumas they'd passed through in Ireland. Communicating with the only other outsider who had been part of the deaths and hollow victories of the Kavanaugh clan was a method of healing. Not as quick at inducing painlessness as the bottle, but less messy in the long run.

He had not heard from her since Kit's report of her visit to York. Stephen broke Maisie's seal—a fox, symbol of ingenuity and wit. Shortly after leaving England, she had sent him its match: a ruby-set pin in the shape of a fox. *This will ensure you aid any time you may need it from any of my men in Europe.*

He opened the letter and read with interest.

3 December 1584
Newcastle-upon-Tyne

Stephen,

Why did you never tell me how terrifying your youngest sister is? One would think that in private audience with the Princess of Wales— daughter of the most fearsome monarchs of our age—that Princess Anne would dominate. But it is the quiet ones one has to watch out for, I have found. Because once they start talking . . .

Well, never mind. It was a productive interlude from a business per- spective, so I must thank you for that. I would never have come to the at- tention of the princess if not for my acquaintance with you. My grandfather always told me that to be successful in business one needed not only financial assets but personal ones. I could hardly hope for a better asset than Princess Anne Isabella. With a significant degree of her busi- ness confided to my keeping, I at last have the position I have been waiting for to return to Edinburgh and challenge my brother.

An astute reader—and you are, if nothing else, astute—will notice that I am writing this from Newcastle more than two weeks after leaving York. If I am so ready for a challenge, you may ask, why have I not crossed the border yet?

I suppose if I knew that, I should not need to continue to write to you.

M. Sinclair

Stephen snorted with laughter. If Maisie was waiting for him to enlighten her actions, then she'd be waiting a long time. He couldn't even illuminate his own. Perhaps that was what they had in common.

He refolded the letter and reached for those from his family. As he shuffled through them, he discovered a small, square missive addressed in an anonymous hand he had begun to recognize. Though he knew what he would find, he still broke the plain seal and opened it to reveal the same thing he had found in every one of the ten similar dispatches he had received over the last six months: a meticulous ink sketch of a bird.

A nightingale.

THREE

The English court remained at Greenwich after Christmas, continuing the merriment into Twelfth Night and lightening the early darkness of January with masques and music and dancing. Amongst the guests this particular evening were Sir Francis Drake and his newly betrothed lady, Elizabeth Sydenham. More than twenty years younger than her famous affianced, she spent most of her time silent as Drake and Queen Elizabeth conversed.

With his trademark fervor, Drake extolled the beauties of Buckland Abbey, the grand manor he had bought with the fortune he'd made circumnavigating the globe. Elizabeth's own share of the prizes from that voyage had been equal to a single year's revenue for the crown; it meant she allowed Drake a certain freedom in conversing with her.

And she was not averse to his many stories about facing off against the Spanish. Drake's arrogance might border on being overfamiliar, but he was brilliant at sea. *El Draque,* the Spanish called him: the Dragon. After being separated from the others of his party during their circumnavigation, Drake and his single remaining ship, *The*

Golden Hind, had raided at leisure along the west coast of South America, taking upward of thirty thousand pounds from Valparaiso alone. With the looming threat from her former husband, Elizabeth knew that Drake's talents would soon be needed for more than exploration and unofficial piracy.

Drake broke off in the middle of recounting a scurrilous rumour about a Spanish captain in the Caribbean to say, "My, my! I had heard she was back from Ireland. I did not know she would be at court."

Even without looking, Elizabeth knew perfectly well whom he meant. Eleanor Percy Howard Gage Stafford (she had a gift for out-living husbands) drew male eyes wherever she went, no matter that she was nearing fifty. But then Eleanor had always had the trick of making the most of her assets. Women despised her, and men ... well, many of them despised Eleanor, too, but that rarely interfered with what they wanted from her.

Elizabeth Syndenham laid a possessive hand on Drake's sleeve as Eleanor drifted just out of range. Brazen as she was, she could not approach nearer unless directed to do so by the queen. With an inner sigh, Elizabeth did just that with the slightest wave of her hand. Not that she wanted to speak to Eleanor. But being queen meant doing any number of things one did not want to do.

"Your Majesty." Somehow, Eleanor managed to infuse the title with memories of thirty years ago, when she had been the king's lover and for a brief time wielded the influence of that position. It might have been even briefer—for William tired of her before long—save that Eleanor managed to give birth to a healthy daughter. William's recognition of Nora had ensured her mother's survival in a cutthroat world.

"Mistress Stafford," Elizabeth said icily. "Have you come to apologize for your daughter's hasty and ill-advised marriage?"

A rhetorical question, for she knew perfectly well that Eleanor had been taken far more by surprise than she herself had. Though the queen's displeasure was not entirely feigned—her pride instinctively revolted at the lack of protocol in Nora and Brandon Dudley's wedding—the marriage was not technically illegal. Just very ill-advised. She waited with something like pleasure for Eleanor to defend herself.

She should have known better; Eleanor always took the offensive. "To be sure, Your Majesty, I was greatly grieved. But being separated from my daughter for such a long time, I naturally trusted that her royal relatives would ensure Nora's perfect care and keeping."

Meaning: *Nora was in your daughter's household, so do not lay this at my feet.*

Eleanor, wisely or not, would always push to the next insult. "Naturally, I do not suspect Princess Anne of encouraging such disrespect."

Meaning: *Your daughter is almost openly defying you.*

"But of course, Her Highness has in her household those who might think themselves above such matters as the queen's permission. Philippa Courtenay's parents," Eleanor said delicately, "are hardly a model of respecting royal authority. Having lived with such latitude for so long, it is no wonder the Courtenay family feel themselves above protocol."

Over Eleanor's shoulder, Francis Drake listened with fascinated interest. And those nearest in the crowd, sensing the atmosphere, had begun to fall silent.

What Elizabeth would have given to have Minuette here just now, for no one had ever been able to oppose Eleanor as wittily and decisively as she had. The two women had a natural antipathy that had only been strengthened through years of enmity.

But this, Elizabeth reminded herself, was not a personal affair. Not wholly. It was a matter of kingdoms and religions and watching eyes. Elizabeth always made certain that such eyes would see only what she wanted them to see.

"Children may believe themselves beyond their parents' reach . . . but no one is beyond the queen's. Because I do not act in haste does not mean I do not act. And my responses are all the more effective for being measured." Elizabeth smiled, gracious and cold. "I do not consider Nora at fault in this matter, and I do believe her most sincerely attached to Brandon Dudley. They have prudently retired to his home at Kenilworth Castle, and I do not expect further difficulties from them."

Eleanor answered as though she been handed lines to read. "But you do expect further difficulties from . . . elsewhere?"

Meaning: *So it is true . . . the queen does not trust her daughter.*

As that silent thought passed from Eleanor to those watching, Elizabeth raised her hand in dismissal. "You have a house still at . . . somewhere near Kendal, isn't it? I am sure after the turmoils of Ireland, you will be glad to retire to a quiet life."

It was a pleasure to see the patches of colour betokening fury on Eleanor's face. But the woman had not survived as long as she had without learning how to submit when necessary. "As Your Majesty wishes."

Still, she would not be Eleanor without a parting shot. "Speaking of Ireland, your dear cousin Ormond sends his love."

Meaning: *I've been sleeping with your dear Black Tom, so don't count me out just yet.*

Elizabeth allowed Eleanor to curtsey and retreat, her own mouth tight to hold back words she must not say. As the crowd slowly began to pick up the threads of the evening, Francis Drake remarked, "It is a foolish woman who makes an enemy of you, Your Majesty."

"It is not only women who make that mistake," she replied grimly, satisfied that every word of what had occurred would soon be passed round the court with greedy pleasure. Spurring gossip was what she had intended with that unpleasant exchange. That it stung her pride to allow it was surely a small price to pay.

"Can't we forget chess?" Felix wheedled to Kit. "I'm bored. I've already done Latin and Greek and logic and mathematics today—wouldn't you rather be fighting than playing games?"

It had been a long winter already, with March still a few days off, and Kit quite sympathized with the boy's impatience at being shut up inside.

"You're too old to whine," Stephen said from his seat by the fire where he was writing a letter. "Besides, what do you think fighting is but an elaborate game? Chess teaches you military tactics."

"Then why aren't you playing with me?" Felix asked shrewdly.

Kit, sitting across from the board, laughed. "Stephen is awful at chess. Which might tell you something about the state of his military tactics." He ducked as his brother threw an embroidered pillow at him.

Felix remained unconvinced. "You can't tell me you'd rather play chess than fight."

Kit grinned, for there were parts of Felix that reminded him of himself when young. He had also been restless and easily bored. "Finish this game," he promised the boy, "and we'll practice throwing knives after."

"Don't spoil him," Stephen said over his shoulder.

That was a laugh. If anyone spoiled Felix, it was Stephen. Once it might have made Kit jealous, how devotedly the twelve-year-old hung on Stephen's every word and action. Felix liked Kit, but the boy worshipped Stephen. Since Kit had learned both to appreciate his brother and to be certain of his own skills in the last few years, it did not bite as it once might have.

For all his complaining, Felix was a good chess player. Kit was better. He made the boy work the length and width of the board before finally cornering his king. "Checkmate."

Felix bounced up, gladly conceding. "Knives," he demanded.

The house was quiet as they passed through. Renaud had been gone for nearly two weeks, on a visit whose purpose he had kept obscured from the household. With just the Courtenays and Felix in residence, much of the staff had been given leave, including the men-at-arms. Kit and Felix left the echoing corridors of the chateau and went to the armory to claim practice knives.

The arms master and Renaud's personal soldiers had traveled with him, so the only one to greet them was the previous arms master, a Scot named Duncan Murray. For more than a hundred years Scotsmen had come to France to fight—the King's Scots Archers were known all over Europe—and it was not unusual to come across them in unexpected places.

Murray was an old man now, seventy if he was a day, but despite his gnarled hands and slower step, he still looked strong as an ox. Gruff as ever, he studied Felix with care, inspecting his hands and arms, before choosing the knives for the boy.

"Want to watch?" Felix asked the old man.

"Watch what? The two of you showing off for each other? I had enough of that with your father and uncle. And your grandfather before that."

Felix's face darkened. "I am nothing like my father." He turned abruptly on his heel and stalked away, leaving Murray to shake his head and Kit to draw a deep breath and follow.

Felix was not inclined to talk. They took turns throwing the knives at the thick wooden plank scored with marks from previous throws. Kit gave a few pointers to Felix but otherwise kept his mouth shut.

It was Felix who finally broke the silence. "You knew my father."

In all Kit's time at Blanclair, Felix had never spoken directly of Nicolas LeClerc. The surprise of it knocked Kit off balance in more ways than one, and his next throw bit the wood wide of the target. "I met him," he replied cautiously. "Spent several days riding in his company."

Felix's throw was dead center. "Do you think I'm like him at all?"

The tall, lanky twelve-year-old anything like the fanatic, slightly mad, and wholly self-centered killer who had taken Kit's sister and the Princess of Wales hostage? What was he supposed to say to that?

"I know," the boy said, dropping his arm and turning to face Kit, "that I don't look like him. I look like my mother. Or so I'm told. I just meant . . ." He struggled for words, then flung his arms wide as if in appeal.

"I know what you meant," Kit said, and put his hands on the boy's shoulders. Slowly, Felix relaxed. "I think your father made choices. We all do. Often, we make the wrong ones. But I see no signs that you will make the kinds of choices he did—the kind that cause such destruction."

"The kind of choices that force your own brother to kill you?" Felix asked with brittle composure. "I suppose it's as well I'm an only child, so it cannot be put to the test."

Where was Stephen? Kit wondered. He was so much better at this sort of thing than he was. "Look, Felix, if you feel compelled to understand your father, why not ask your grandfather or uncle?"

"Grandfather does not care to be reminded. And Julien?" Felix shrugged. "Julien left."

As clear as though he'd shouted it, the last word of that statement hung in the air: *Julien left* me.

"You know that your grandfather's asked me to take you to England in the spring for a visit. It will be good for you to spend time with Julien and Lucette. I think they might have some of the answers you are looking for."

"I doubt it. And anyway, I'm not going to England."

"So eager to be relieved of my company?" Kit tried to tease.

"I do not want to see Julien or your sister. Why should I? She promised to marry my father. I thought that when they all came back, I would have a mother. But no one came back, save my uncle. And only long enough to ruin my life. Julien killed my father and Lucette married him as reward. Why would I want to see either of them?"

The words might have been adult—Kit suspected rehearsed many times—but the voice, already shaky, broke more than once. And there were tears standing in Felix's eyes.

Kit shivered, but from an instinct to treat the boy as he would have wished to be treated, he let the moment pass without pushing. Better to think on it and decide how best to approach Felix's pain. He tried not to feel that he was simply taking the coward's way out . . .

Without speaking, they gathered up the knives and returned to the stable yard that included the arms stores and blacksmith's space.

Murray did not come out to greet them, which was slightly strange. Despite his rough manner, the man was devoted to Felix LeClerc. The door to the armory was open. Kit stepped inside and froze.

He heard Felix on his heels, and keeping his voice light and steady, asked, "Felix, will you go get Stephen for me?"

The boy might be young and troubled, but he was quick. He melted away, and Kit hoped Stephen was smart enough to keep him from returning. Just in case, Kit stayed where he was in the door, to prevent the boy from seeing the body of Duncan Murray, faceup on the ground with a sword pinned through his heart.

When Felix ran into the study and told Stephen that Kit wished to see him, there was something in the brittle tone of voice that caught Stephen's ear. He rose straightaway from the letter he'd been finishing to Maisie and said, "What is it?"

The boy's face was pale beneath his shock of dark brown hair. "I don't know. Only he wouldn't let me pass into the armory."

In the field, one was accustomed to making rapid decisions. In this case, Stephen decided that leaving Felix alone in the house— feeling unwanted and useless—would do greater harm than whatever nastiness Kit had discovered. "Show me," he said, and was rewarded with a slight easing of Felix's tension.

When they entered the stable yard, Kit looked round from where he stood in the armory entry and even from across that distance, Stephen knew his brother meant to object to Felix's presence. He shook his head slightly, and it was enough. If the brothers had learned anything in the last two years, it was how to communicate with one another.

"Kit?" he asked as he crossed the yard, as calmly as though he were requesting a report from a junior officer.

With only the briefest hesitation, Kit said, "Duncan Murray is dead."

There was no need to specify it was unnatural—Kit would hardly be guarding the doorway if the man had had a fit or heart attack. "Let me see," Stephen ordered.

Kit stepped back to let Stephen pass, but kept Felix outside with him. Stephen squatted next to Murray's big body and touched the old man's forehead in respect.

Besides the short sword driven into his chest—one Stephen recognized as belonging to the Blanclair armory—Murray also had a bloody wound a little higher up. It was the kind of wound an arrow made, when pierced into flesh and then ripped free.

"Shot from cover first?" Stephen mused barely loud enough to hear himself. "And when Duncan dropped, the sword to finish the job. But why?"

Why, indeed, kill a man past the years of the kinds of passionate grudges that made men murder? Besides, those were usually committed in haste, and messily. This had been deliberate. Planned. Professional.

Stephen pulled the sword free, noting that the blood flowed sluggishly. He must have been killed just after Kit and Felix left with the knives. He squatted back down, hands searching for anything on or around Murray that might leave a clue. Surprisingly, there was a paper. Half shoved into his jerkin, it had only faint stains on the right edge where his heart's blood had met it. If Duncan had been carrying it before he was shot, it would have been much bloodier.

Stephen had to carry it to the open doorway for the fast-dying winter's light. An anonymous seal closed off the folded paper. And there, in the bottom left corner, something drawn in ink . . .

"Shit," Stephen pronounced clearly.

"What?" Kit asked.

He turned the back of the letter to his brother and pointed. It took Kit a minute to understand. "Is that—"

"A nightingale."

Their eyes met and decisions leaped from mind to mind. "Inside," Stephen said abruptly. "Now."

Felix protested. "What about Duncan? We're not just going to leave him there?"

"I will explain inside. Go with Kit." And, when Felix once more opened his mouth, Stephen again said sharply, "Now."

At some point Stephen had acquired his father's gift for infusing commands into single syllables. Kit and Felix vanished; his brother, Stephen was glad to see, with a hand on the dagger at his belt.

Stephen drew his own dagger and pulled a sword from the armory walls. Thus doubly armed, he drew a deep breath and set out to search.

Twilight was fast deepening, and both logic and Stephen's trained senses told him that whoever had been here had already faded away. He made a quick circuit of the inner walls, but to little purpose. Blanclair was not meant to be a defensive keep. It was a manor house. There were any of a dozen places an assassin could have crept into the grounds. And with most of the household as well as the men-at-arms away, the killer had risked little today.

Especially if he had been watching the house long enough to know how empty it was.

Stephen rounded the chateau walls once, then came in through the kitchen door and barred it behind him. The cook and scullery maid eyed him in surprise. "It's all right," he told them reassuringly. "Just closing things up early. You've no need to go outside again tonight?"

The cook knew better than to believe his assurances, but she simply answered, "No, my lord. We've all we need here."

"Good."

Next, Stephen found the steward. He gave a list of rapid orders that the man, though not a soldier, accepted without comment. One learned to do that in Renaud LeClerc's household.

Then he found Kit and Felix in the chamber he'd so recently left, his unfinished letter to Maisie still sitting on the table by the fire. Kit prowled the perimeter of the room, while Felix had dropped into a chair and sat apparently memorizing the pattern of the Turkish carpet at his feet.

Stephen set the sword down and returned his dagger to its sheath. Kit stopped moving and Felix looked up.

"Well?" Kit asked.

"Looks clear, but . . . ?" Stephen shrugged eloquently, and pulled out the letter from Murray's jerkin. "Let's see what message we've been left."

"'An eye for an eye,'" he read aloud. "'Nicolas LeClerc and Richard Laurent died martyrs in a righteous cause. Their blood demands recompense. This is the first.'"

At his father's name, Felix froze. Stephen felt the boy's eyes on him, demanding an explanation.

"So," Kit mused. "Someone Catholic. Maybe some of the Catholics Julien worked with have figured out he was never their man after all. Now they're coming after Blanclair since they can't reach him in England?"

"Maybe." But Stephen didn't believe it. This had a different feel. An overheated, manipulative, melodramatic feel. If he was right, then all of this was his fault.

Kit had learned to read him too well in the last months. "What?" he asked, eyes narrowing.

Stephen sighed, and darted a glance at Felix. But the boy had a right to know—to be honest, the most right. Blanclair was his home and he'd known Duncan Murray all his life.

"I would wager all of the property I no longer own that whoever killed Duncan was hired. And if we traced payment, I expect we'd find it in the form of Spanish gold."

Kit choked. "Mary Stuart?"

"Mary Stuart." Their eyes locked.

Felix looked between them. "The Spanish queen? Why?"

You have made an enemy, Mary Stuart had told Stephen.

I was always your enemy, lady. You just didn't have the wit to see it until now.

"I spent some months with her during her final months of English captivity." Stephen spoke carefully. "She was . . . unhappy when she learned that I had not been entirely honest with her."

"She hates him," Kit simplified. "Queen Mary thinks every man is hers to be charmed and those who resist must be punished for it."

"'This is the first,'" Felix quoted. "So who is the next?"

"I don't know." Stephen drew breath and let it out more shakily than he'd intended. "For tonight, we secure the house. All windows that can be are shuttered, all doors barred, and the remaining staff told not to go outdoors unless Kit or I are with them."

"And tomorrow?"

"Give Kit and me an hour, and we'll let you know."

Felix stood up, and with a sarcastic intonation so like his Uncle Julien that Stephen shivered, said, "I suppose I should keep my dagger with me."

"I suppose you should."

Stephen just prayed the boy wouldn't have to use it.

FOUR

The last day of February, Pippa set out from the Princess of Wales's court at Middleham to ride the short distance to Bolton Castle. Her visit was, officially, no more than social. Unofficially, she was Anabel's ambassador to the Catholic recusants. In the last two years she had been over most of the northern landscape—from Hexham south to Sheffield, and all along the Scots border from Berwick to Carlisle. She often traveled with Madalena, whose Spanish Catholic credentials carried weight despite the fact that she had been known to attend Anglican services with the princess.

On this particular visit, however—as ordered by Anabel—her companion was Matthew Harrington.

To be fair, Anabel had only resorted to ordering when Pippa would not be persuaded by softer words.

"Why so opposed?" Anabel had asked. "You're the one who wanted Matthew in my household in the first place!"

"For his abilities and his good sense," Pippa said with considerable exasperation. "Not to flirt with."

"That's a relief, because he's barely had more than ten words from you at a time since we came north. Why, Pippa?"

"Do not meddle with my privacy, Your Highness."

At that, Anabel's face had darkened with temper. But her eyes held a gleam of far-too-uncomfortable understanding. "The visit to Bolton Castle has nothing to do with your privacy. And as the Earl of Arundel is one of those likely to respond better to a man, then Matthew goes with you. Am I clear?"

So here they were, cantering uncomfortably across the frozen ground without a word exchanged until they reached Bolton Castle. The medieval structure was a perfect example of a rectangular castle and loomed over the surrounding landscape ominously. Inside the walls, though, all was warmth and welcome. The gatehouse guards drew back to allow Pippa, Matthew, and their eight men-at-arms to ride through the portcullis. They were met in the courtyard by grooms, one of whom Pippa allowed to hand her down from her mare.

"Lady Philippa!" It was Henry Scrope, tenth Baron Scrope of Bolton Castle, striding across the yard to greet them. "Such a pleasure to have you grace my home again." Pippa had always liked the baron, his humour and good sense a blessed counterpoint to the border violence he'd spent much of his life controlling. More than fifty years old, he was as vigorous as men twenty years younger, and still wore his hair long and swept straight back from his high forehead.

"The pleasure is mine, Lord Scrope. I believe you've met Matthew Harrington, household treasurer for the Princess of Wales?"

The men shook hands, then Scrope suggested, "Let us escape the weather and take refreshment in the upper solar."

In the solar awaited Scrope's quiet visitor, who had taken the trouble to travel north with only a handful of men and with neither banners nor livery: Philip Howard, son of the late fourth Duke of Norfolk, himself now the twentieth Earl of Arundel. Where Scrope was of an age with Philippa's parents, the Earl of Arundel was just five years older than herself. Slim and handsome, he greeted Philippa with courtesy.

"My lady, thank you for taking the trouble to ride to Bolton."

"I believe all the thanks are due to you, my lord. The burden of travel has been yours."

After five minutes of general courtesies and arranging seating with trays of delicacies laid to hand, they began their negotiations in earnest.

Pippa led the way. "Princess Anne respects your faith, as you know. She is aware of the burden imposed on the recusants and desires to meet with as many as possible to share their concerns."

"To what end, my lady?"

"Discussion is not an end in itself?"

"Discussion is nothing but a sop used to distract from the lack of real reform."

Scrope intervened. "They are serious, Arundel. Listen to what they offer."

"So there is something on offer?"

Matthew stepped in, for it was true that Arundel would take a man more seriously. In his calm, resonant voice, he said, "Her Highness is offering two seats on her privy council to those of the Catholic faith."

Stunned silence. Pippa had never seen the elegant Philip Howard so ruffled. He huffed a laugh, as though waiting for the joke to be revealed, but the rest of them merely looked steadily at him.

"You must be mad. Does the princess know what rash promises you are making in her name?"

"Listen to them, Philip," Scrope counseled. "What have you to lose?"

From his widow's peak of brown hair above a wide brow to the narrowing of his chin, Arundel looked darkly affronted. "My father lost his life to the present queen for his faith—why should I trust what her daughter's servants say?"

Matthew said sharply, "The Duke of Norfolk lost his life for attempting to kill Queen Elizabeth and put Mary Stuart on her throne. With himself as her husband."

"None of that is relevant," Pippa interposed, since Arundel looked ready to stalk out in offended pride. "Her Highness is entirely serious about this, Lord Arundel. She will be in York this spring for the Council of the North. From amongst those Catholic lords who attend her at that time, she will name two to her council."

"Why?"

"Because you need representation. If you do not have it, England will continue to split along religious lines. The Princess of Wales does not intend to come to her throne many years from now to rule only part of this people."

Arundel's expression remained wary. "The queen will never allow it."

"The queen is not here."

"Does Her Highness have men in mind?"

"Why do you think we are meeting with you?"

There was a long, considering silence before Arundel shook his head. "I am afraid I must refuse. I do not intend to be in the North this spring."

And now came their trump card. Very gently, Pippa said, "Because you intend to sail from England in April."

A slight flicker of the eyes, but the answer came pat. "I don't know what you mean."

"You need to take better care with your servants, Lord Arundel. One of them is not as loyal as you think. We are aware that you plan to flee to the Continent in the spring and leave England behind for good."

Arundel admitted to nothing. "Would not the queen be glad to see the Catholics gone?"

"Others may be able to flee unnoticed, but not Philip Howard. The queen will stop you; you must know that. If you try to leave England, you will be arrested and taken to the Tower. Would you

not rather have the chance to counsel Her Highness on the condition of Catholics in the realm?"

"You must consider it, man," Scrope intervened. "This offer will
never come from London. But Princess Anne is the daughter of His
Most Catholic Majesty, King Philip. One of her chief ladies is a
Spanish Catholic. The princess is the best chance we have of bringing a peaceful end to this religious conflict."

"Does Princess Anne intend to turn Catholic?"

"Princess Anne intends to heal the divide amongst her subjects."

"That is sophistry."

Pippa leaned forward and replied with all the intensity of which
she was capable. It was a great deal. "Then I shall speak plainly. England will never return to Rome. It is far too late. Even were a Catholic monarch able to obtain England's throne, they would not be
able to hold it. The sentiments of the people are too strongly opposed. That does not mean there cannot be a great deal done to ease
the suffering of English Catholics."

"How?"

"That is what the princess's privy council is meant to decide."

At long last Arundel gave a begrudging smile. "You present an
interesting proposition, Lady Philippa. You will not object to my
taking time to consider it?"

She was swept by relief, for she had been afraid of outright rejection. "If you must. We look forward to hearing from you shortly."

And that was that. They said their muted farewells and Baron
Scrope led them back to the courtyard. "You will not stay and let us
entertain you further?"

"Her Highness will be anxious to hear our report. And also,"
Philippa studied the iron sky, "it looks as though it's going to snow
again. Thank you, Lord Scrope."

As Philippa prepared to mount, Matthew neatly cut off the groom
waiting to help her. He offered his linked hands and said softly, "Well
done, my lady."

She paused. "I wish you wouldn't call me that."

"What should I call you?"

"There was a time when you called me Philippa."

He drew up to his full height, so that she had to raise her head quite far to see his expression. It was forbidding. But he never raised his voice. "And there was a time when you talked to me about things besides Princess Anne. When you are ready to confide in me again, I will call you by your name. My lady."

Then he bent once more and she allowed him to help her onto the horse.

The seven miles back to Middleham passed in frozen silence.

If their time in France had accomplished nothing else, it had taught the Courtenay brothers to work together. As Kit had learned to respect his brother, he thought that Stephen in turn had learned to trust him.

They needed all their combined talents in the aftermath of Duncan Murray's murder.

They sent couriers to track down Renaud. As the vicomte had not told them exactly where he was going—only in the vicinity of Poitiers—four couriers left to cover different routes, but each carrying the same message: *Come home.*

The next set of messages extended leave for the household servants. No sense having more civilians to worry about until they knew what was going on. The men-at-arms returned, however, and one week after burying Duncan Murray, Stephen summoned the men to present the current situation. Felix was also present; as the only LeClerc in residence, he could technically be said to be in charge.

Kit sat next to Stephen, where he could watch the room. His brother stood and spoke evenly and calmly, in a manner Kit had often heard their father do.

"You know of Duncan Murray's death, and the written threat that accompanied it. It was not, however, the first indication of . . . hostile attention. I had no reason before to suppose that attention was directed at anyone beyond me. Now that we know to what lengths our opponents will go, I am not prepared to simply sit and wait."

Coolly, calmly, as though discussing the weather, Stephen continued, "We've heard from three of the four couriers sent after the vicomte. Though they had not as yet located his present whereabouts, two of them reported that it appeared he had been summoned to meet privately with Henri of Navarre."

There was a murmur at this news, for Navarre was the de facto leader of the Huguenots in France. The French Protestants had suffered greatly ever since the St. Bartholomew's Day massacre in Paris twelve years ago. And with it looking increasingly unlikely that King Henri III would sire an heir, Henri of Navarre remained the nearest successor to the Catholic throne.

For a man as supposedly apolitical as Renaud LeClerc to meet with the Huguenot leader was indeed a surprise. Kit's first reaction to the news had been, *No wonder Renaud didn't tell anyone where exactly he was going*.

"One of the few things we can know for sure about Duncan Murray's killers is that they are committed Catholics and prepared to kill those even remotely attached to the Protestant cause. If they have been watching Blanclair, they might also have followed the vicomte to Henri of Navarre. The fourth courier is now three days late in reporting. That is possibly nothing serious. I do not like the possibility that I am wrong."

"And so?" asked the sergeant in command of the men-at-arms.

"And so, at daybreak tomorrow, Lord Christopher and I will ride in the direction taken by the missing courier in hopes of meeting either him or the Vicomte LeClerc along the road. Those of you here are charged with protecting the house in our absence."

The sergeant had another question. "What can we expect to see at Blanclair?"

"You should always expect to meet the worst."

"Are you taking any of the men with you?"

"Just my brother. We want to ride fast and without the appearance of undue alarm." Stephen hesitated, and looked swiftly to where Felix sat next to Kit. "And Felix will ride with us."

The three of them had argued about it long and loud—most of the loudness on the boy's part. The problem, Kit and Stephen agreed, was lack of information. They were guessing far more than was comfortable. Leave Felix behind or keep him under their direct protection—how were they to know which course was the right one?

Felix had finally announced that if the brothers left without him, he would simply ride out alone to follow. Since it would have meant confining the boy against his will to stop him, Stephen had been reluctantly persuaded.

It was Kit who had pointed out, "I doubt if Queen Mary intends to harm you, Stephen. At least not yet. She is targeting those around you. If we leave Felix behind, what if her men decide to target him?"

"And if Felix is a target on the road?"

"He'll have the two of us to stop it. She has lost the element of surprise. We're paying attention now."

But as the three of them mounted and prepared to ride out in the clear, frosty dawn next morning, Kit prayed silently, *Let us not be wrong.*

They had forced Felix to mount a smaller horse, so that he would sit lower than the brothers and could thus be more easily covered in case of threat. All three of them wore brigandines—Felix's a little large—and were well armed.

After the first two hours of tense riding, Kit felt himself relax slightly as the miles passed without incident. If anyone had been watching Blanclair, they had not troubled to follow. At least not close enough to be noticed.

Thanks to the depth of the cold, unusual for early March, the roads were tolerable and Felix was an uncomplaining and hardy traveler. By dint of changing horses several times and taking only brief rests, they reached Blois not long after sunset and secured a room for the three of them in one of the less respectable inns. It was

Kit's suggestion, meant to draw less attention to themselves by not announcing their identities.

While Stephen and Felix slept, Kit drank in the common room for several hours, accumulating a good deal of gossip. Some of it even to purpose. While they dressed next morning, he passed on what he'd heard.

"Renaud came through Blois three weeks ago. Stayed two nights, as though waiting for someone or something. There was a man last night who'd just come from Tours. He thinks Renaud was in conference with Navarre's men there. If Renaud is still in Tours, that's only forty miles. We can be there by dark."

"If he's still in Tours, then why haven't we heard back from the fourth courier?" Stephen asked quietly, when Felix had gone out of earshot to relieve himself.

"Ah, yes," Kit said reluctantly. "I asked around about local violence last night. I found there had been an anonymous body discovered on the riverbank just about the time you'd expect the Blanclair courier to have made it this far."

Stephen shut his eyes, then sighed and opened them. "All right. Seems we don't want to risk staying in Blois. But keep your eyes open and every sense alert today." In a grim undertone, he added, "I will not have another dead child on my conscience."

They were only ten miles out of Blois when they heard drumming hooves approaching from ahead, faster than the usual pace. Stephen drew his sword and urged his horse to the front, while Kit edged within arm's length of Felix, ready to snatch the boy's reins if they had to wheel round quickly.

Four men, riding hard. When they saw Stephen with sword drawn, they slowed. By the time faces could be seen, recognition had blossomed. They were Renaud's men, wearing his badge of scarlet and black. When the soldiers recognized Stephen and the others, they drew up sharply. "You heard?" one of them said.

Kit shot a look at Stephen but could only see his brother's back.

"Heard what?"

"The vicomte. He's dead."

Kit hissed in shock, but had the presence of mind to grab Felix's reins to keep him from darting his horse forward.

"You're lying!" Felix shouted as Stephen said over him, "What happened?"

"An assassination attempt on King Henri of Navarre. The king escaped unhurt, but Vicomte LeClerc was shot and killed in the melee. I'm sorry, monsieur," the soldier said to Felix. "It was pure bad luck."

Kit didn't think so. No doubt Catholic assassins were always happy to try and kill Navarre, but to miss him and just happen to shoot Renaud instead? He didn't like coincidences.

"How long ago?"

"Last night. The rest of the men are seeing to the necessities. We were sent ahead to warn Blanclair."

"Why warn us?" Felix asked, too shrewd by half even when traumatized. "If Navarre was the target?"

Stephen answered. "Because your grandfather went to some lengths to keep his visit to Navarre quiet. The Huguenots have many enemies. He wanted you kept clear of possible reprisals."

"Shall we escort you to Tours?" the soldier asked.

"No. We will see to ourselves. Continue on and let Blanclair know what has happened. Write to Madame Charlotte first of all."

"Yes, sir." The men were trained to obey, even if they thought their orders unwise. When they were out of sight, Stephen brought his horse round so the three of them could talk.

"We're not going to Tours, are we?" Felix asked. To Kit, the boy seemed to be all eyes, wide and fixed but dry. For now.

Kit and Stephen shared a long look, then Kit answered. "Stephen is right. Even if your grandfather's death was an unlucky accident, there are definitely assassins watching the area. The last thing he would want is to put you in immediate danger."

"What about *Tante* Charlotte?"

Stephen said, "She will be wise. I wrote to her before we left

Blanclair, laying out the situation. I do not think anyone will trouble her, not unless we draw attention back that way. The question is, where can we go to keep you safe?"

"Calais?" Kit mused.

"We'll be expected to head to our fellow English, which means we shouldn't. Nor should we go farther south into Huguenot territory. I suggest we make for Le Havre."

"And find a ship? Not easy if you intend to keep us anonymous. We haven't enough money to both hire a ship and hide our identities."

"There is a man in Le Havre who will help us, with very few questions asked. And I have all I need to pay him."

Kit raised a skeptical brow as Stephen pulled back his doublet and jerkin to reveal a ruby-set fox pin on his shirt. "Doesn't look terribly expensive," Kit said dismissively.

"It doesn't have to be. It only has to be unique. There is a man in Le Havre who will accept this pin as payment in full. He will help us with whatever we need."

"And who is this very accommodating man?"

Stephen smiled grimly. "Mariota Sinclair's business manager."

FIVE

After a winter spent profitably between Newcastle and York, Maisie Sinclair drew a metaphorical deep breath and, with a nicely judged amount of notice and fanfare, crossed the border and entered Scotland for the first time in four years. On a day of patchy April sun and squalls of freezing rain, she rode into Edinburgh and dismounted before her late grandfather's house in the Canongate.

If it had been left to her brother, no doubt the doors would have been locked against her. At the very least the household would have been caught surprised and unprepared for her arrival. But Robert, with all his resentments and dislike, was not solely in control of the Sinclair concerns. And so Maisie was met by well-dressed staff and smiling faces and the full complement of board members who endeavoured to keep Robert from destroying the company his grandfather had so carefully built.

"Maisie, lass, how you have grown in beauty." That was Andrew Boyd, his spare figure still upright and elegant despite his sixty years. He had been the late William Sinclair's partner since the age of twenty-five, and if anyone truly ran the concerns these days, it was Boyd.

She smiled, and tipped her cheek up to be kissed. "Well, you can hardly claim that I have grown in height."

As she accepted and returned the greetings of the staff and board, Maisie made silent notes about personalities and how likely they were to be on her side in the battle to come. She had expected to have the entire household staff in her corner, for Robert had always been a difficult person to please in any matter. From a child, her brother had been rude to the maids and condescending to the grooms and men-at-arms. But apparently Robert had turned his eye to the household staff when he inherited the business, and fully half of them were new to Maisie. It was easy to pick them out—they all had a slight air of slovenliness. And of the men-at-arms present, only a few were familiar. She did not like the look of the rest at all—hard and indifferent and cruel.

The board, however, had been largely beyond Robert's control. So Maisie was greeted with genuine affection even by those men who would likely oppose her ambitions simply because she was female. That was all right—she could deal with that sort of response. And she had the tacit support of the most important ones already; not only Andrew Boyd, but the four who had served longest with her grandfather. They knew where the brains had gone in this family.

Sulkily, Robert welcomed her home, his discontent plain. "Why did you stay away so long? We expected you to return soon after your husband's death."

"Did you? I must have missed your letter of condolence."

He might be completely unsuited for the task of running a large merchant concern, but Robert had his own native cunning. "You miss only what you do not want to see. Still, you are here now. We can begin to make plans for the next wedding."

"A wedding! Congratulations, Robert. I cannot wait to meet the . . . fortunate woman."

"You know I mean you. There are men aplenty interested in what money you can bring them. So many, that this time we can afford to place a higher price on you." With an ugly smile, he leaned in and said, more softly, "You see, sister, how I have learned this business. You are a commodity. All I have to do is find the highest bidder."

Despite expecting it, Maisie found herself shaken at the venom. But she was nothing if not always controlled. "I am no longer fifteen, Robert. I think you will be surprised by what price I command."

She turned away, and smiling brightly at Andrew Boyd, said, "Shall we go in? No doubt there is a meal prepared . . . and then we have much to discuss."

The discussions begun at table that day were not meant to force a confrontation, but to subtly shape the tone of the conversations to come. Everyone except Robert was eager to hear the stories from her travels, and Maisie knew precisely what to highlight in her recitations. Not just the prices and markets of various cities, but the personalities: gossip about who was sleeping with whom and whose son was being forced into an inconvenient marriage and whose brother was working for the opposition. There were stories of the continuing war in the Low Countries and French suspicion of Spain's increasing aggressiveness.

"Both Scotland and England should give thanks for the native enmity between France and Spain," Maisie concluded. "If ever they combined their might, our island would be hard-pressed to resist."

"Like Ireland?" Robert said nastily. He had been drinking a great deal.

She met his eyes steadily. "Yes. Very much like Ireland."

"You had no trouble opposing the English there."

Not all the English, she thought. But would never say. Stephen belonged to a separate part of her life, one she did not intend to share with anyone. He belonged to Cahir Castle and Oliver Dane and Liadan—and to Ailis Kavanaugh most of all.

Her first day back in Edinburgh ended in her bedchamber of old. Maisie was surprised and pleased to see it had not been altered in her absence and suspected she owed that to the housekeeper. The initial homecoming had gone well, she thought critically. She had expected nothing from Robert and so was unlikely to ever be disappointed. Andrew Boyd had been more than just welcoming—he had asked astute questions and, more critically, listened carefully to her answers. Of them all, Boyd knew the most about Maisie's personal business concerns in the last two years. And when he bid her goodnight, he added, "The board would like to see you in a few days. For a more formal accounting of your travels, and a discussion of your future."

Boyd, at least, did not mean a marriage. Or not only a marriage.

All in all, Maisie was highly pleased with herself. There was nothing she liked more than preparing perfectly and having that plan unfold as it should.

When she awoke in the morning, it was to be handed a letter just arrived from her factor in Le Havre, brought by ship from France, and suddenly her plans were—if not ruined—at least altered.

The Thistle will sail Friday, three weeks ahead of schedule. I have
filled what orders I could in the shortened time, but the primary cargo
will be three passengers: two men and a boy. One of the men carried a
ruby-studded fox, and thus I rendered all aid as previously ordered.

Maisie caught her breath. Only one man in the world possessed the ruby fox pin that was the twin of her own.

Stephen Courtenay was on his way to Scotland.

By the time their ship reached Edinburgh, Stephen's nerves had been at such a high pitch for such a long time that he had a permanent headache at the base of his skull. The journey from Blois to Le Havre was already a hazy memory, consisting mostly of fast riding, bad food, and sleep snatched a few hours at a time. They had traded their finer clothes for the rougher frieze of the countryside, but kept their weapons prominent. Felix proved tougher than Stephen had feared, especially after the devastating news of his grandfather's death. The boy had continued quiet, but made no serious objections about leaving France.

Either they had slipped their watchers or they were being allowed to leave. Stephen didn't much care which. Once in Le Havre, it was fairly easy to locate Maisie's factor, and producing the ruby fox provided instant aid. Maisie turned out to be majority owner of a ship called the *Thistle,* which providently was in port at the time. It had not intended to sail for several weeks, waiting for a cargo of spices from the Levant, but between Maisie's ruby fox and what remained of Stephen's money, they sailed from Le Havre less then seventy-two hours after arriving.

On April 21 the *Thistle* sailed into Leith, the chief port of Edinburgh. The captain disembarked and asked a few questions, then reported to his passengers.

"You sailed at the right time—Mistress Sinclair arrived in Edinburgh just this week. She's at her grandfather's house in the Canongate. I've sent a boy to let her know we're in port. Will you go straight to Edinburgh?"

"No," Stephen said. "It is for her to decide if she wants to see us. I assume there's an inn or two nearby?"

The captain directed them to an inn a quarter mile back from the water that was slightly shabby on the outside but warm and welcoming within. Between the three of them, they had only four packs and their weapons. But just knowing that he could now write to his family and receive help in a matter of days was a relief. For the first time since Duncan Murray's death, Stephen felt he could let go a little of his fierce sense of responsibility.

They bathed and changed into serviceable hose and leather doublets, then joined the crowd in the tavern. A mix of languages—from French to Flemish to a handful of people speaking Italian—wove together as expected in a merchant port. Bread, ale, and hearty stew woke the appetites of all. Even Felix began to lose the haunted look he'd had since Blanclair.

"What next?" Kit asked.

"We see about hiring horses for the two of you. Or, properly, borrowing money to hire you horses. I imagine we have some acquaintance in Edinburgh, and perhaps you can join a larger party heading south."

"I meant—what next with Mistress Sinclair?"

Stephen shrugged. "We'll see if she sends for me. I did make rather free with her name to get us here. She may be piqued."

"Why didn't you send a personal message to the Canongate? After all those letters you've written—"

"I will certainly write with apologies and a promise to repay Mistress Sinclair for the use of the *Thistle*," Stephen cut in austerely. "Though I suppose Father and Mother will have to bear that cost for now."

"Don't you like her?" It was Felix who asked, so plainly that Stephen could hardly shoot him down the same way he had Kit.

"Of course I like her. What has that to do with anything?"

Felix shrugged. "You don't seem very anxious to meet her again."

"It doesn't matter. Let's ask around, see if there are any English known to us in residence just now. At the least, we can go to the English ambassador. When he knows who you are, Kit, he'll fall over himself getting you back to England."

But Kit had stopped listening. He was looking over Stephen's shoulder and suddenly grinned.

"It seems Mistress Sinclair is quite anxious enough for the both of you. She just walked in."

Stephen froze where he was, half standing. Then, cursing himself for awkwardness, he straightened and turned.

His first impression was that Maisie had changed hardly at all from the last time he'd seen her, when she visited him in the Tower of London. She was still little, barely reaching his shoulder, and had the same pleasant expression that one had to decipher carefully to understand.

Her voice was also unchanged. "The brothers Courtenay. What a surprise to find you commandeering my ship. I little expected you to land on my doorstep the very moment I returned home."

Stephen flushed and could not immediately think of what to say. Kit, at his most engaging, rescued him. "Mistress Sinclair, how could we not be drawn to you as butterflies are drawn to the fairest blossoms?"

"You must be desperate if you're wasting your charm on me. And who is the third and handsomest member of your party?" She smiled at Felix.

Finally Stephen got a grip on himself. Noting the many eyes on them, curious and storing up gossip to spread around the port, he spoke softly. "Perhaps we might withdraw for a full accounting of our presence?"

The look she shot him was sharp with understanding and intelligence. But she might have been any mere Edinburgh hostess when she proclaimed, "You're coming with me. The Sinclair Company keeps a town house for visitors. I'll show you."

They walked the two miles from Leith to the Sinclair town house in Edinburgh. Maisie—who, one remembered, had been brilliant with a child in Ireland—took Felix as her companion and chattered to him all the way until even he was smiling.

Stephen and Kit walked behind, and Stephen was glad for his brother's unusual discretion in not prodding him with dozens of questions or comments. Other than shooting him a few curious glances, Kit left him alone.

They entered Edinburgh from the north, the castle rising on its stark crag to their right and the road continuing down to the Palace of Holyrood on their left. Following Maisie, they turned in that direction down the densely built road until abruptly she turned again, into a narrow close on their left.

The town house had a medieval feel, and Maisie informed Felix that parts of it were a century old. From outside, the ever-present dark grey stone gave it a forbidding aspect, but the interior was pleasantly updated. Maisie had clearly given orders before coming to the port, for the house was opened and aired and food and drink had been provided. After showing them to welcoming bedchambers, she neatly set Kit and Felix to entertaining themselves, then turned to Stephen.

"Let us withdraw, as you suggested, and you can give me a full accounting."

He had forgotten how intense her presence could be. It was an effect she had kept mostly muffled in Ireland, but now, secure in her home city, she practically radiated competence. No, something much more than mere competence—genius, perhaps.

Sitting across a table from her in an impersonal reception chamber, Stephen flashed back to his many meetings with Ailis in just such a manner. He'd had to guard himself carefully during those interviews. It was a hard habit to break.

"Tell me," Maisie said.

It was a long story, for Stephen began not in France, but with the details of his assignment to spy on Mary Stuart in the last months of her English imprisonment. He told Maisie about the Nightingale plot, about the Frenchmen who had embroiled Stephen's sister in the affair, and of the violence at Wynfield Mote that had not been sufficient to prevent the Scots queen from sailing away to become, in turn, the Spanish queen.

And how, last year, he had begun to receive anonymous missives containing no words—simply a drawing of a nightingale.

Maisie broke in then, with a question. "And you told no one?"

"No."

She did not ask him why. Perhaps she knew how much he had flayed himself for that error, wondering if Duncan Murray and Renaud LeClerc would still be alive if he had spoken earlier. Stephen finished the story with those deaths. Of their flight across France, he said little.

When he finished, he waited for her judgment. To his surprise, she asked another question. "Why me?"

"What do you mean?"

"Why put yourselves in the care of my factor? There are Englishmen aplenty in France. Surely the English ambassador in Paris would have conducted you to safety in far greater comfort."

"To England," Stephen pointed out. "Which I am forbidden."

"Please," she said derisively. "Queen Elizabeth would hardly have tossed you back to the wolves once you'd fled to her for help."

"I didn't want the queen's help."

"You mean you didn't—and don't—want *anyone's* help. So why mine?"

"Because you I trust."

At that she stilled, and Stephen had a chance to study her more closely than he yet had. He realized that despite his earlier impression, she had indeed changed in the interval since their last meeting more than two years ago. The bones of her face and brow had grown more defined, so that despite her youth, there was no longer anything of the child about her. One tended to think of her still as sixteen, though he supposed she must be nearly nineteen by now. Her mind had always been far ahead of her body, but it seemed the gap was narrowing. In Ireland, Stephen had grown used to seeing Maisie in well-cut but plain wool or linen. Today she was dressed in impeccable—if restrained—fashion: her skirts a subtle blue silk that shaded to mauve when she moved, an organza partlet rising from the bodice to encircle her throat, her hair contained in a velvet caul.

For a moment he remembered that hair falling free across her shoulders as she wept after Liadan's death. A flood of silver gilt that had altered her from schoolgirl to woman . . .

Mariota.

She coloured faintly as he stared at her, but said lightly enough, "Well, I shall see that your trust is not misplaced. I assume you intend your brother and young Felix LeClerc to ride south?"

"Yes. Perhaps Thomas Randolph—is Randolph back in Scotland

yet?—can arrange a party to conduct them at least as far as the Princess of Wales's court. If Anabel hasn't left the North since February?"

"The princess intends, I understand, to preside at the Council of the North in York next month. It is a simple enough matter to bring the two to her household. You need not even trouble the ambassador—I am sure someone on our board has business wanting in England."

"That would be . . . very generous."

"And you? Since your scruples are so firmly set against touching English soil until you are deliberately invited, what do you intend to do now, Stephen?"

He laughed. "Make my living. By the sword, since that is all I know. Once Kit and Felix are safely in England, I thought I'd sail to the Netherlands. They have plenty of military companies I could join."

She nodded. "I thought that might be it. I have been thinking, however."

When was she ever not thinking? Stephen wondered.

With a mischievous smile, Maisie said, "My mercenary company is currently in Scotland. Not fighting—not for the moment—but I thought it wise to have . . . *insurance* for my coming actions. I have established them thirty miles from Edinburgh, in a country estate called St. Adrian's. They are in want of a commanding officer."

She must have seen the instinctive pride that preceded a blunt refusal, for she quickly added, "Do not answer me now. There is time before the others are safely in English hands for you to consider. That is all I ask—payment for use of my ship, if you like. Consider it."

What else could he say? "I will consider it," he promised.

April in England was often temperamental—cold sunlight, fitful winds, sudden blasts of showers and occasional freezing rain. The changes in weather echoed the tenor of Elizabeth's court this early spring of 1585. With each day, campaigning season drew closer. Which meant decisions would soon have to be made. About Ireland, about the Netherlands, about—always and more than anything else in the world—Spain.

It was the topic Walsingham and Burghley returned to every single time they had the queen's attention. After all these years together, Elizabeth could have written the entire dialogue herself. That didn't stop them from having the conversation.

Walsingham was always the one pleading the cause of men and money for Ireland. "John Perrot is begging for more men, Your Majesty. So is Ormond. If we're going to land soldiers this spring, we'll have a very narrow window if the Spanish decide to harry our ships."

Burghley, as ever, was the voice of moderation. "Can Philip afford to spare ships for Ireland this year? The Netherlands is in ferment. He cannot continue to split his forces forever."

Elizabeth's role was to hit on the essentials. "Philip also cannot afford to lose face. Perhaps if there had been no child between us, he could have cut all ties to England. But pride will keep him meddling in our business. Pride—and Mary Stuart."

"Speaking of Princess Anne," Walsingham said darkly. "It is all but confirmed that Spain is sending an envoy to Her Highness in the North this spring. A Jesuit named Tomás Navarro. Do you intend to protest this flouting of your authority, not to mention the deliberate defiance of the law that prohibits Jesuits in England on pain of death?"

"We will protest. But lightly, Walsingham—there is no need to provide further fuel to Philip's self-righteous fury. He is trying to provoke me. I intend to be provoked only at a time and place of my choosing."

Burghley provided the final warning. "You can delay only a short time longer, Your Majesty. The delegation from the Netherlands is demanding an answer on a treaty of assistance. And if your Irish lords are demoralized by lack of aid, they may cut their losses and make whatever deal they can with the rebels. Dublin cannot hold out another season if the Spanish make a serious effort to take it."

Elizabeth sometimes thought that the entirety of her reign could be summed up by the warnings the men of her kingdom had given her. Once, she had thought it was her youth that prompted the overarching concern—but here she was, past the age of fifty (not that she liked to remember it), and more than twenty-five years a queen, and still there was a slight hesitation to trust her.

It was no wonder she lost her temper from time to time.

And yet . . . there were some bonds worth swallowing one's pride for. First and foremost, of course, her sacred bond to England. Her daughter. Both Burghley and Walsingham—though she had made the latter swallow his pride as often as she did.

And one other person. Someone for whom Elizabeth was prepared to make great concessions in order to repair the oldest of her relationships. She had not seen the Duke and Duchess of Exeter since Christmas 1582—when their eldest son had been imprisoned in the Tower for breaking Elizabeth's peace in Ireland. In that interval, they had confined themselves to their estates and not even written. It was the longest Elizabeth had ever gone without Minuette Courtenay near.

And so, finally, Elizabeth had—not summoned, but asked her friends to attend her at court.

They came as they always had, with little fanfare and less notice. Every other noble in England took pains to cultivate their opportunities, to assemble a circle of supporters, to flaunt their influence in the government or the court. In the earliest years of his title, Dominic Courtenay had been pressed and flattered by many who sought to benefit from his royal ties. But he'd always had a way of turning such people away without hardly having to speak a word. He might once have become the most powerful noble in England. Instead, his indifference was legendary and only his family—or duty—could stir him.

And always, the surest way to command Dominic Courtenay's aid was to persuade Minuette to speak to him. So it was the Duchess of Exeter alone who came to Elizabeth at Hampton Court, on a May afternoon of gentle sun and gorgeous blossoms. The queen had chosen the venue with care—for this palace had many memories for both of them. Not all good, but all of the sort that bound the women to one another forever.

In the years since her brother's death, Elizabeth had altered the decorations of the privy chamber that had once been William's. Even still, she imagined Minuette remembered the space well. She had spent many evenings there with the king when they were all young and thoughtless.

Elizabeth would never admit—even to herself—that she was a little frightened of meeting Minuette again. But she could not ignore the relief that came like a cool breeze when her friend entered as she always had, with no more than the usual polite curtsey. After an absence of more than two years, Elizabeth noted for the first time the signs of encroaching age in her friend: the lines around her eyes, a little fading of her rich honey-coloured hair, the slightest softening of her jawline. But Minuette's beauty had never been dependent on youth alone.

When Elizabeth beckoned her to stand, Minuette tilted her head and studied the queen carefully in return.

"Will I do?" Elizabeth asked, as she used to, seeking approval before a public appearance. For once, she was nervous that the rich purple of her gown and pearl-draped bodice were not sufficient to distract from her own fifty-one years.

But Minuette smiled, the artless, charming smile of their shared youth. "You do very well."

"I try to do well. But not always successfully." It was the nearest Elizabeth would ever come to apologizing.

Minuette's expression, wry but understanding, showed that she accepted the unspoken words. "What is it my queen desires of me today?"

"Your 'queen' desires your aid. Your *friend* would like to sit with you and discuss it beforehand."

If it was not—could never be—the same as before, that was a path they had already walked once in redefining their friendship after Elizabeth became queen. If only the two of them were allowed time and space, the ties that bound them would see them reconciled.

"Philip is sending a Jesuit priest named Tomás Navarro to join Anne's household as an ambassador. Oh, he is not titled that, of course—but it is plain. Spain believes the time is ripe to drive a wedge into the space between us. Philip wishes to force it so wide there can never be reconciliation."

"You could stop it—the Jesuit, at least. It would cause waves to refuse him access to the princess, but how much stormier can the sea become? I'll wager Philip expects you to stop it."

"Do you? I am not so certain. He knows my pride. He may very well be gambling that I will allow him to pass if only not to openly admit that Anne and I are divided."

"Will you allow him to pass?"

"I will. The Council of the North meets in May, presided over by Anne. Perhaps you have heard from Philippa?"

Minuette was always cautious in bringing her children into political discussions. But she could hardly fail to admit the obvious— that her daughter wrote to her. "We have heard something of it, yes. It seems an astute move, for Pippa writes that the North is grown increasingly supportive of Her Highness. And anything that strengthens people's ties to your daughter must strengthen your own."

"I am not sure it is wise for the public to come to that conclusion," Elizabeth remarked.

Minuette shook her head, but with an affectionate smile. "Ah, wheels within wheels, Your Majesty. That is a game at which both your parents excelled."

"But not my brother?"

They had so rarely spoken of William in twenty-five years. Yet Minuette hesitated only briefly. "Will never had your subtlety, Elizabeth. Nor your patience. He would never have been able to maintain peace the way you have. I imagine there are many Englishmen living who, all unknowingly, owe their lives to your reign.

"And now, I suppose that whatever spins at the very center of your many wheels is aimed at protecting as many of your subjects as possible," Minuette said decisively. "Am I to assume that you wish Dominic and me to participate in some of that wheel-spinning?"

"Are you amenable to my wishes?"

"War is coming, Elizabeth. We do not need you to tell us that. And as my children seem determined to be involved in so very many dangerous situations, what use is sitting at home and fretting?"

"Is that a yes?"

"A qualified yes. First, Dominic and I will hear the details of what you wish from our service. But unless it involves us assassinating political figures . . . we will serve our queen."

The relief this time was not a breeze, but a deluge of icy joy that left Elizabeth shaken. "Thank you. Let us not waste time—summon Dominic and we'll begin."

SIX

In late April the Princess of Wales and her private household traveled the forty-five miles from Middleham Castle to York. Anabel enjoyed every moment of the processional from the medieval walls through the beautiful town as the population cheered her arrival. Their destination was the Treasurer's House, once belonging to York Minster; now passed, since her grandfather's death, into private hands. Only steps from the gorgeous church for which York was famed, the house made an ideal base to begin her consolidation of the power of the North.

Much of Anabel's household and court would be quartered elsewhere in the city. Matthew Harrington had been inordinately busy in the preceding weeks making the physical arrangements. It was Anabel's task now to charm those citizens disobliged by her presence so that they considered only the honour of it, and not the cost.

Thanks to Maisie Sinclair's flair for business, Anabel's household was solvent and she could afford to pay for much of what they required. That alone helped ease their welcome, as did the reputation she had begun to acquire for a willingness to listen to the discontented Catholic recusants. There were surely many watching her arrive who, for the first time in years, had hope for their own futures.

The first days passed in a procession of banquets and official visits from the guilds of York and the chief officers of the town. These were occasions Anabel could handle with ease, while allowing a tiny part of her mind to fret about the silence that had fallen from France. It had been two months since she'd heard from Kit, and Pippa'd had nothing from either of her brothers. As she suspected her own mother had always done, Anabel covered her worry with work.

One week after arriving in York, Anabel received Tomás Navarro in the wide reception room of the Treasurer's House she used for official engagements. In the last year, she had forsaken using the royal coat of arms, with its white bordure denoting her as heir to England's throne; today the canopy of estate stretched above her seat bore three white feathers rising through a golden crown. This emblem of the Prince of Wales included an azure ribbon with the motto *Ich Dien.* I serve.

Reminded of that fact, Anabel cloaked herself in the Spanish hauteur inherited from her father and accepted the credentials the Jesuit priest offered. The credentials themselves were problematic, implying as they did that Spain considered Navarro an official envoy. Difficult, to say the least, considering that there was already an ambassador to England at the queen's court. Tomás Navarro did not look as though he were the slightest bit worried about causing difficulties. In his midthirties, the priest was slender and ascetic in his black robes, his clean-shaven face a picture of arrogant certainty. A man willing—and perhaps eager—to cause trouble.

Anabel did not falter. "You are most welcome, Father Navarro," she said in her flawless Spanish. She handed the written credentials to Madalena, who stood to one side of her throne with Pippa. "I trust your journey was not too troublesome."

The priest answered in Spanish, though no doubt he spoke acceptable English. He would want to highlight Anabel's attachment to Spain, weighted as it always must be with powerful undertones.

"It was no trouble, Your Highness, though any trouble would be worthwhile to be in your royal presence. Your father wishes only that the two of you could meet once more in person."

She smiled politely. "That is a worthy wish for any father—or daughter, for that matter. I trust you will be a fond advocate for him, and for me as well."

"I trust so, Your Highness."

"There will be entertainment, of course, but also work. If you care to join us tomorrow, we are meeting with the Lord Mayor and the city's guild leadership. Your counsel would be welcome."

"It is to counsel that I have come."

As if everyone here didn't already know that. What did Navarro think, that the people of England were stupid? Everyone knew that Navarro's presence at her court was a direct slap at the queen. It was up to her to use both his presence and the public's expectations to her own advantage.

Anabel drew a deep breath of released tension once Navarro was gone and she could retreat with her nearest advisors. In the closest thing to a privy chamber that the Treasurer's House could provide, she smiled wryly at Madalena, Pippa, Robert Cecil, and Matthew. Beneath her tightly laced pale blue bodice, she felt the flutters of her stomach absorbing the nerves she would not show.

"So it begins," she pronounced. "There's no drawing back now. From this day, the division between the queen's court and my own begins to widen."

"And next?" Pippa prompted. Her face had grown thinner over the last months, so that her jewel-green eyes looked very wide. That did not make it easier to interpret the expressions of said eyes.

"The Council of the North, attended by more Catholic nobles than have been gathered in one place for more than twenty years."

It was not the answer Pippa was waiting for. She eyed Anabel narrowly, until the princess sighed. "And yes, I shall write to James Stuart and suggest a meeting between us at the border this autumn."

"You needn't sound so mordant about it."

"And you needn't be so quick to remind me of my duty, particularly when your own emotional life is hardly a sterling example of success, Pippa!" Even as the words left her mouth, Anabel wished to recall them.

It would take far more than that to send Matthew Harrington fleeing, but he did flinch involuntarily, and Robert Cecil looked as though he longed to be anywhere else.

"I apologize," Anabel said winningly—to Matthew, not Pippa. "This is a conversation I believe Lady Philippa and I should continue privately."

She did not miss the long look Matthew directed at Pippa before he left. Pippa stared straight ahead, but Anabel could trace the slightest flush of her friend's throat.

"This is absurd!" Anabel exclaimed when the room had emptied. "If the two of you cannot come to an accommodation, I shall have to let one of you go. I can hardly concentrate on my responsibilities with you and Matthew actively ignoring each other."

"I thought we were discussing *your* emotional life, Your Highness."

"With James of Scotland? Emotion does not enter into it, only policy. You need have no fear that I will forget my responsibilities. And I suspect you are only focusing on my personal matters in order to avoid your own."

"If you wish me to leave, I shall of course oblige my princess."

"Pippa, stop being an idiot!"

They glared at one another, and for a moment Anabel had great sympathy for her mother. How many times had the queen come to these sorts of impasses with Minuette Courtenay? And which of them bent in the end in order to continue their friendship? The two women had not seen each other since Stephen's banishment more than two years ago. Was she really going to banish Pippa away in a similar fit of fury?

Finally, reluctantly, Anabel let her temper slip away. "I wish I knew what you were afraid of, Pippa. If you will not share, I cannot help you."

"No one can help."

Anabel never knew what might have followed this bleak statement, for at that moment there was an unusually aggressive knock at the door.

"Come!" she called irritably.

She had not expected to see Matthew again so quickly. His grim face was lighter than she'd seen in some time as he announced, "Visitors from the Sinclair Company, Your Highness."

"Did we have a meeting I'm not aware of?" she asked acidly.

"Their purpose is to deliver guests directly to your court from Edinburgh."

Despite herself, Anabel's heartbeat spiked. There was no chance that James Stuart himself had impulsively crossed the border, was there? What a mess that would be . . .

Then Matthew stepped aside to allow the small party behind him to enter. An older man who must be from the Sinclair board; a boy just entering his youth, tall and awkward; and then a man with hazel eyes and hair like sun-warmed honey, a laugh to rouse the dead, and sweetness to charm the birds from the trees.

She should be restrained. She should be formal. She should be the princess she had been raised to be. But Anabel was already across the room and in Kit's arms before any of that sensible advice penetrated.

"You're home," she said, happier than she had been in many long months.

"I'm home," he agreed.

30 April 1585
York

Your Most Gracious Majesty,

I have been formally received at your royal daughter's court in York. She is all that I would expect your child to be—intelligent, discreet, and

*farsighted. I am cautiously hopeful that she will indeed be amenable to
our dearest hopes. A princess of such gifts and ambition will always look to
wield her power.*

*Unexpectedly, one of our assets has presented himself at the perfect
time. Lord Christopher Courtenay arrived unannounced in York the very
day of my reception. The entire city is awash in rumours of their mutual
attraction. Rumours Her Highness has done little to squash. Not, of
course, that she behaves in other than the most proper of ways. But the
young lord is without doubt one of the strongest wedges into her life.*

*I have heard only the barest details of how Courtenay came to be so
suddenly returned to England, with the boy Felix LeClerc in his company.
It appears the French general, Vicomte Renaud LeClerc, is dead, in a violent manner unspecified, and both Courtenay sons fled France under
threat of their lives. The only other detail that I have heard whispered is
that there was a symbol connected to these attacks—a nightingale.*

*I offer this to Your Majesty's wisdom to decipher and follow as seems
best. Faithfully your servant in God,*

Tomás Navarro

Philip, by the grace of God King of Spain and the Netherlands,
ruler of an empire on which the sun never set, finished Navarro's
letter and, in a rare display of temper, ripped it to pieces before
throwing the remains into the fire. All of the good news passed on
from his daughter's court had been eclipsed by that single sentence
about nightingales.

But because he was a man whose passions were always ruled by
his will, he refrained from immediately confronting his wife. It was
not difficult, for Philip by nature preferred to take his time. Here at
El Escorial, his own purpose-built retreat, he had designed a private
suite next to the monastery church. Small and plain and difficult for
others to penetrate, the study and alcove bedchamber were Philip's
preferred environment. He would work for hours alone at his desk,
listening to the chanting of the Hours from the monks.

Since his divorce from Elizabeth, that work had centered increasingly on the Enterprise of England. His advisors had been counseling a military solution to England's heresy for twenty years—in the last four, Philip had begun to listen. It was hardly as simple as some wished to make it. When asked for a realistic estimate of what the Spanish fleet would require to defeat the English navy, Admiral de Bazan had provided a list that detailed five hundred ships and would cost nearly four million ducats.

As neither demand could possibly be met, Philip had asked the army in turn for their assessment. The Duke of Parma, leading the Spanish forces against the rebels in the Netherlands, claimed he could ferry an army of 35,000 across the Channel in one night. He did not provide an answer as to how the English were to be kept ignorant about such an army assembling near Dunkirk, nor how the barges could avoid the formidable English navy that would bar their way. Philip read the overoptimistic report, and in his habitual manner of commenting on what he read, wrote in the margins of Parma's letter, *Hardly possible!*

It was nearly a week after Navarro's letter before Philip traveled to the Alcazar of Segovia to, ostensibly, visit his sons and, actually, to confront his queen. Mary did not always keep residence with their young twins, but it was certainly politic of her to be with them now. Perhaps she had sensed Philip's simmering anger from afar. In any case, she took care that the two of them met in the royal nursery.

Philip knew how to wait, and he was genuinely glad to greet his sons: Charles, the elder by five minutes, and Alexander. Now three and a half, they were bright and cheerful, with the reddish hair of both their parents and a delight in life that lightened Philip's heart whenever he was with them.

After an hour with the boys, Philip and Mary withdrew. If she had any sense of what was coming, she hid it behind the royal facade that was her birthright. A queen from six days old, raised in exile in France at that wariest of courts, condemned by her own faults to more than a decade in confinement—Mary Stuart had learned her lessons in a hard school.

Philip had learned in a harder one.

"Maria," he asked in the quiet voice that everyone in his court knew to fear, "tell me about Nightingale and the assassination of Renaud LeClerc."

Mary might have a royal facade, but she had a desperately impulsive spirit and a fierce belief that whatever she did must be right. She did not bother to pretend ignorance. "You know all about Nightingale, as you were part of that plot yourself."

"Nightingale was accomplished five years ago, with your release from England, and it in no way involved the Vicomte LeClerc."

"It involved his son, Nicolas, who was martyred in the course of freeing me. Murdered viciously by his own brother, no less."

"Four years ago, and it is not Julien LeClerc who has been recently assassinated."

"Because he has retreated to England and taken refuge behind the skirts of your former wife!"

Philip studied her intently. "Let us not play games, Maria. It is not the LeClercs themselves who are the target of your furious vengeance. It is Stephen Courtenay. He hurt your pride and you want to hurt him in turn. Until very recently, Stephen Courtenay and his brother were in France with the Vicomte LeClerc. They fled after the man's death—perhaps to preserve their own lives? Tell me just one thing, Maria—did you, at any point, imply that this ridiculous plot of secret assassins had my personal approval?"

It was impossible for even the most self-centered of women to miss how very angry he was. "I do not need any man's approval to defend my own honour!"

"Not only is it dishonourable to kill a man who has never offered you harm, it is the sheerest folly. Spain is surrounded on almost every side by enemies. Our forces are split between Ireland and the Netherlands. England and your own rebellious Scotland are threatening to combine in a marriage that will lock you out of your home forever and steal my daughter from me. In all of that, the last thing we can afford is to make an active enemy of France!"

"France will not care."

"That the Vicomte LeClerc has been murdered? They care, Maria. Of course they care. Even if he has been less trusted by the current regime, he has royal ties. If ever his death is traced directly to Spain, they will demand redress."

He leaned forward and fixed her in his gaze. "And if that demand comes, I may very well offer them a redress they cannot dream of. I may offer them you."

She flushed, then paled—with fury, rather than fear. "I am a queen. I cannot be touched."

"Ask Elizabeth Tudor if that is true."

"What do you want from me?"

He could see how it pained her to ask, and he was glad of it. She should be pained by her foolishness. "I want you to remain in Segovia with our sons."

"For how long?"

"Until I say otherwise."

He expected her to press, to ask what would happen if she refused. But despite her tendency to act impulsively, she was not stupid. As she knew she would not like the answer, she did not ask.

"I am, of course, yours to command. In this." Her tone was not quite as conciliatory as her words.

No matter. Philip had what he wanted. Because of it, he offered the incentive for her to comply with grace. "If things go well in Ireland this summer, it would be useful for our troops to be visited by one of those for whom they are fighting. If Dublin can be taken and securely held, then you and Alejandro might profitably travel there for him to be introduced to his future subjects." He carefully did not indicate a time frame.

That both soothed her pride and flattered her vanity. Philip trusted that she would soon enough notice that he left orders behind him at the Alcazar: any letters she wrote were to come first to him, visitors or messengers denied private access to her, and if she tried to leave Segovia . . . she would be stopped. By force, if necessary.

Philip was not about to allow his present queen to wreck the plans he had for his previous queen.

It took Kit almost a full day to realize how very tense Pippa was. It should have taken him much less than that, but he had been wonderfully, joyously, distracted by his reunion with Anabel. She hardly let him out of her sight for hours, cancelling who knew how many appointments in favour of sitting with him and talking. Their words spilled over each other at first, both almost giddy at the relief of being able to talk rather than merely write, but it didn't take long to settle into the rhythm they had always had. Either Pippa or Madalena was present most of the time, but so quietly in the background they might as well have been alone.

Kit hardly even spared a thought for Felix until food was brought to them. "He's perfectly well," Madalena said in response to his ashamed questions. "Your sister has taken him in hand. And Matthew Harrington is talking business with Sir Andrew Boyd of the Sinclair Company."

"Did Boyd come merely to escort you?" Anabel asked.

"I believe he has some business to communicate from Mistress Sinclair to your household. I told him once we were here, we would be perfectly safe and he could transact his own concerns."

"So you are here to stay?"

"As long as you want me, in whatever position you choose. But first I must take Felix on to Compton Wynyates. He belongs with his uncle."

"He must be rather overwhelmed by the rapid disasters and changes in his life."

If he was, Felix had made little of it. Kit thought the boy had learned entirely too much from Stephen—his damnable self-control chief amongst those traits. Surely Julien and Lucette would know how to handle him. Felix had accepted the necessity of going to his uncle, though he seemed more resigned than pleased. Kit told himself it was only to be expected after his grandfather's death.

Anabel said, "You might as well press on quickly. Take Pippa with you."

He might have asked her why, but by then Anabel had moved to sit next to him on a stool hardly large enough for the both of them. He had to put his arm around her to hold her there, and when she laid her head on his shoulder, Kit was unable to think of anything else beyond the feel of her body next to his.

Two days after his arrival in York, Kit and Pippa took Felix and a contingent of Anabel's guards to make the 150-mile journey to Compton Wynyates. They had to go at some speed, for Anabel desired them to be back in time for the Council of the North. Felix, neatly engaged in conversation by some of the men, left Kit and Pippa to bring up the rear and talk.

For once, Kit was the one pressing his twin to speak. "What is wrong?" he asked gently.

That gentleness blew away into irritation the moment she widened her eyes and said with blank innocence, "Nothing whatsoever. Is something wrong with you?"

"No, you are not doing this, Pippa. Not to me. Talk or don't—but do not pretend I am someone else. You can be a brat elsewhere. With me you are honest . . . or you are nothing."

He felt her flinch, and then he felt much, much more. His hands slackened on the reins as he was hit by an enormous wave of emotion. From Pippa, all of it, all at once, two years' worth of fear and pain and worry launched at him like a weapon. She had never used their bond like this before, and it nearly staggered him.

Almost as quickly as it came, it abated to a more manageable level. As Kit regained a tighter grip of his horse, Pippa said, "Sorry. It seems I have missed you more than I knew."

"Next time bash me over the head with a rock, why don't you?" Kit answered wryly. "It would be softer." Then, more kindly, "Why will you not speak to Matthew?"

"I speak to Matthew every day. Just this morning you heard me."

He had grown too much to let her tease her way out of this. "Why have you not told him how you feel?"

She did not answer, not aloud. But Kit felt the brushing of her mind and he let himself reach for it. This time the emotion was focused and subtle, words mixed with thoughts and images. The brush of dank fog against his skin . . . the hiss of arrows in his ears . . . urgent voices . . . pain, low and sharp . . . *Run, Pippa. Run.*

"Pippa, what is it you see?" Kit asked urgently.

"This is for me alone."

"But it's keeping you from Matthew."

She urged her horse forward, and said over her shoulder, "All the better for him."

They stayed in Doncaster that night, and Kit wrote a letter to be dispatched straight back to Anabel's household.

Matthew,

> *I know that you are the very essence of reserve and respect. I know you would never make presumptions of any sort. Since I have none of those qualities, I take leave to say something presumptuous.*
>
> *If you love my sister, you must tell her so. Let me rephrase that— I know that you love Pippa. I also know that you are waiting for her to make the choice. In this matter, you are wrong. She will not come to you. You must go to her and break whatever fear is holding her silent. Her Highness has failed—I have failed—you are the only one who can reach her now.*

> C. *Courtenay*

SEVEN

Their brief visit to Compton Wynyates turned out to be even more fraught than Pippa had expected. It had been difficult enough to keep her secrets from Kit, with a twin's far too intimate knowledge. But Compton Wynyates, the beautiful house belonging to Lucie and Julien, had welcomed the Duke and Duchess of Exeter two days before the northern party rode in. Pippa sighed inwardly at the thought of meeting her parents and braced herself to tell more lies to more people.

The Courtenay reunion, however longed-for, took second place. They had sent a messenger ahead, so that the appearance of Kit and Felix had been anticipated. Pippa and her family held back while Julien crossed the open space to the horses in three long strides and pulled Felix into an enormous hug.

Pippa knew she wasn't the only one who noted Felix's stiffness as he spoke to his uncle. But the boy was well-bred and old enough to behave properly and greet Lucette with courtesy. Looking at her sister's face, Pippa knew Lucie had been expecting something warmer than courtesy. On their journey from York, Pippa had felt the tenor of Felix's anger and knew it was underlaid with grief. And why not? Whatever sins Nicolas LeClerc had committed, he'd been Felix's father. Understanding his father's crimes did not lessen the hurt. How was Felix supposed to respond to the uncle who'd killed his father and the woman who had betrayed him?

Compton Wynyates was as well-run as any Courtenay household, and quickly enough Felix and Julien had gone off together, the older man speaking in rapid French, and three of the four Courtenay children sat down with their parents in a sunny solar that had the stamp of Lucette all over it. Like Dr. Dee, with whom she had long studied, Lucie tended to collect a wealth of books and papers and objects that looked chaotic to an outsider but amidst which she moved with absolute ease.

"How is Stephen?" their mother asked, and Kit launched into the events of the last few months.

Dominic listened without comment to his son's account of Renaud's death, though his hand tightened reflexively. Did her father have any friends? Pippa wondered. She didn't think so. Only Renaud and Edward Harrington, Matthew's father, who had died in Ireland four years ago . . . and long before her birth, William Tudor. Now all three men were dead.

"Stephen won't come to England?" Lucette asked. Outwardly, she appeared unchanged: dark hair with glints of red, bright blue eyes, dressed in an understated gown of verdant green suitable for a woman of her class in her own home. But there was a tautness to her body and a discipline to her expressions that confirmed what Pippa had already known—the pain of multiple miscarriages had begun to wear down her sister in both body and soul.

"You know Stephen better than that," Kit answered wryly. "He will accept his banishment to the very letter. I doubt he'll ever set foot in England again unless specifically asked for by the queen."

As Stephen had written to everyone (Kit had brought the letters south with him), they soon left that topic and broached the unusual—for them—topic of politics.

Minuette took the lead. "Your father and I have agreed to be a visible presence at Elizabeth's court during this next year. He has refused a seat on the privy council, but has accepted command as Lieutenant General of the South. That puts us squarely into the queen's camp."

"As opposed to Anabel's camp?" Pippa asked.

"Precisely."

"How has Tomás Navarro's arrival as a Spanish envoy been received in London?"

"The people are surprised, but muted in their discontent. They are watching the queen to take their cues from her. As long as mother and daughter refrain from an absolute split, there is room to maneuver."

There would always be room to maneuver. No matter how closely the queen and princess danced to the edge of disaster, there would never be an absolute split. That was the entire point—two women, both clever and popular and talented, were seeing just how far they could push the limits of their authority. History was rife with examples of kings clashing with their crown prince heirs; to the point, sometimes, of facing each other in battle. But where was the precedent for a queen present and a queen future sharing the public sphere? It was no mistake that these two women were exploiting that natural question. It had been a forgone conclusion almost since Anabel was born.

Both royal women had been smart enough to recognize the coming struggle. And, in recognizing it, had possessed the wit to turn it to their own—and England's—advantage.

Now, nearly two years after its hazy inception, the plan hatched between queen and princess was taking on a life of its own. The Tudor women's intention had been to offer Philip and the Spanish a believable picture of Anabel as restless and discontented, stalking off to the North of England to soothe her wounded pride and evade the heavy controlling hand of her mother. A half-Spanish princess who allowed the English Catholic recusants a royal hearing they had often been lacking. A willful, steely minded girl who did not want to marry into Scotland if she could help it.

An emblem of hope for those Catholics who disliked and distrusted the current canny Tudor queen—and a prize figurehead for the Spanish to capture to their cause.

Of necessity, open communication between mother and daughter had been stilted and infrequent. The Spanish intelligence networks were fearsome, and there were Jesuits in England—besides Tomás Navarro—keeping watch on the queen and the princess. Ciphered letters could only help so far, and were too often a giveaway of the very plotting they wished to conceal. And now, with the situation ripe for exploitation, they must appear more than ever to be distant from one another.

Enter the Courtenays. With the royal family split, so they would apparently split along the same generational divide. Dominic and Minuette at court with the Tudor queen they had known all their lives; Pippa, and now Kit, attached to Anabel as they had been since birth.

And to navigate the space between camps? Lucette Courtenay LeClerc. Rumoured niece of the English queen, married to a Frenchman and former Catholic, known for her interest in scholarly pursuits and dislike of courtly games. Lucette had a correspondence nearly as wide as the queen; she could write to everyone and filter the necessary information between camps with greater ease than anyone else just now. That was the assignment on which Pippa had come.

The difficulty was in persuading her sister to care.

Lucette would not even agree to hear the proposition in its fullness that first day, insisting that Felix's comfort and welfare must necessarily come first. However, it was obvious to all within twenty-four hours that, whatever enthusiasm the boy had once had for Lucette, it was now tainted by abandonment and violent death. With

Kit anxious to leave and return to Anabel, Pippa more or less com-
mandeered her older sister after dinner the second night and dragged
her outdoors to talk.

"You cannot stay shut up here with nothing to do all day, Lucie.
Julien is worried about you."

"There is Felix. If I cannot manage to produce a child of my own,
why not help care for the son of the man I helped murder?"

The bitterness broke Pippa's heart, but she knew better than to
let it divert her. Lucie didn't need sympathy—she needed a purpose.
"Felix does not seem to want your care. Not at the moment."

"Tell me something less obvious, Pippa. Isn't that your specialty?
Tell me, dear sister, when you saw my French husband, did you see
any half-French children in our future?" Abruptly, Lucette stopped
walking and gripped Pippa above the elbow. Her voice was suddenly
frantic. "Tell me, please. Tell me my future is not to remain barren."

"Lucie—"

Lucette dropped her hand and swung away. "Never mind. I know
what you're going to say—it doesn't work like that."

If Pippa knew anything about her sister, it was Lucette's fierce
ability to set aside pain and do what she thought she must. For years,
that fierceness had kept her apart from their parents—particularly
Dominic. It was her gift and her curse: whatever emotional mael-
strom she might be drowning in, Lucette's mind would always demand that she *think*.

So it was no great surprise when she added, "Of course I will do
what I can to keep both sides informed. Letters find me very easily
here. But I won't leave Compton Wynyates. Not now."

Pippa watched Lucie walk away, her heart aching for her sister.
Why could not the happy remain happy? Lucette had passed through
much to make her beloved marriage, but that was not proof against
further heartache. At the moment, it seemed the daughters of the
family were destined for hurt, while the sons were better at living in
whatever moment they found themselves in. Kit could not see far
past his joy at being with Anabel again, and Stephen . . . Pippa knew

enough to have a good idea of what would happen for Stephen in Scotland. It made her smile now despite all the reasons for sorrow.

Lucette had never been one for much weeping, but when she left Pippa it was to retreat to one of the lesser-used wings of her too large house and cry alone. She had discovered many such spots over the last two years, for she did not want Julien to catch her in tears. His concern for her was heavy enough to bear as it was.

And that was a constant annoyance in the back of her mind— since when had avoiding Julien become something to be considered?

Perhaps Pippa had alerted Julien to their conversation, for she had not yet pulled herself together when her husband found her.

She only knew it when his hands settled on her shoulders from behind—gently, as though fearing she would pull away. He treated her with such delicate politeness these days. As though passion of any sort would break her.

Perhaps it would. And perhaps she didn't care.

She turned quickly in his grasp and pulled his head down to kiss her. For a few blessed moments he responded, but then he remembered and pulled away.

"Kissing will not hurt me," she told him.

"But what follows will. We must be wise, Lucie mine."

"If we must be wise, then you should not call me that."

They separated, several steps between them now. It was a matter weighing heavily on them these last four months, ever since the physician had advised that, for her health, Lucette should take measures to ensure she not become pregnant for at least a year.

It was a matter Julien avoided discussing. As he did now. "I think you should go north with Pippa and Kit."

"So eager to rid yourself of me?"

He was impossible to fight with these days—and perhaps that was what Lucette missed most of all. They had always sparred, from the very beginning, with a teasing tension that brought colour to her

life. Now he was so damnably courteous it was like being married to
a stranger.

"Felix is miserable and difficult," Julien answered reasonably.
"And not simply because of my father's death. He is ... troubled.
Angry. About Nicolas, about all of it."

"I know." The boy she'd known in France, who had treated her as
though she were the coming of an angel to brighten his life, had become an undeniably hostile stranger since his arrival the day before.

Going to Anabel's court would allow Julien time and space to
help Felix come to terms with the traumas of the last five years. And
it would certainly make her husband's insistence on celibacy easier
to maintain. How could she be expected to live chastely when everything about Julien seemed designed to draw her in? From the first
moment she'd met him again as an adult—tall and messily elegant,
wheat-coloured hair falling across his eyes, the cynical smile that hid
his gentleness—Lucette had wanted to touch him. In the five years
since, that had not changed.

If he would not let her touch him, then she might as well go
north. But she would not be happy about it. "I will go, since it seems
to be in everyone's best interests—except possibly mine."

"Lucie—"

"If I am to set out with my siblings tomorrow, I must give instructions as to packing now. Go tell Felix that he shall have you to
himself for a time."

She knew she was hurting Julien. The fact that he allowed her to
do so without protest only increased her need to lash out. Just as well
they separated, before her wish to hurt could do permanent damage.

Thinking the worst encounter behind her, Lucette forgot that
there was another man in her house at the moment who knew all too
well her instinct to push everyone away when she was hurting. As
she made up lists for the smooth running of Compton Wynyates
while she was gone—though her staff could very well have run the
entire estate without direction—she was interrupted by her father.

"Walk with me," Dominic half asked, half ordered.

With a sigh, Lucette agreed. Better to have this conversation away from the house. Not that she was sure what he wanted to talk about. Her failings, probably, being that they were so very obvious just now.

But he had a habit of neatly surprising her. Instead of asking about her health or Julien or the obvious tension in their home, her father mused, "Did you know there was a time that I left your mother? I don't mean the short separations of travel or of business necessity—I mean I left your mother and very nearly never went back."

She could not have been more stunned if he'd struck her in the head. "What?"

They skirted the perimeter of the formal garden and strolled silently across the turf edged with wildflowers before her father answered. "It was after Stephen's birth. He was meant to be born at Tiverton, but like you, he was in a hurry to get here. We were still at Wynfield Mote when he came. Once Christmas had passed and your mother was on her feet again and doing well, I traveled to Tiverton to ensure the estate and its people were not suffering from the deep cold.

"Or at least," he continued, "that was what I told myself. I may even have believed it—but your mother did not. I think she knew from the first."

"Knew what?"

"How very much Stephen's birth had shaken me."

"Stephen? But he was undoubtedly . . . I mean, there could be no question . . ."

"That he was my son?" Dominic asked with irony. "Of course. It was not logical. I understood that at the time. If I were going to be hurt by any child, it should have been you." He slid his gaze sideways to her. "I trust I no longer need to assure you that was never the case. From the first moment I laid eyes on you—all plump and fierce at a year old—I not only loved you absolutely but had not the slightest misgivings about my ability to do so."

Lucette shook her head. "I think Mother must be right. You think too much."

"Yes, well—I went to Tiverton in January and kept making excuses why I could not return to Wynfield. The weather, the servants, the state of the tenants' holdings . . . I exploited every single thing I could. Your mother did not press me. She continued to write, and I continued to reply in increasingly fewer words. Stephen's birth, it seemed, had opened every wound I'd accumulated for years. I had spent most of that time blaming no one but myself. And I was not wrong to do so. But that meant I had neglected to face the fact that I was also angry with others. With the king, of course, but also with Elizabeth for not restraining Will, and most painful of all, I was angry with your mother."

Lucette wasn't sure she wanted to hear any more. What use was it to discover that her parents' marriage had almost shipwrecked on the shoals of pain? If two such nearly perfect people could barely make things work, what chance had she and Julien?

Her father seemed to know precisely what to share and what to gloss over. "After six months, the cracks in our marriage began to be obvious to others. I knew I could not wallow any longer. I must learn to forgive . . . everyone. I just didn't know how to do it. And then I spent an afternoon helping a farmer repair the roof of his barn. He was an old man—seventy if he was a day—but still insisted on clambering up and down ladders and scampering at heights that made me uncomfortable. And he liked to talk."

He drew a breath and let it out, then smiled at Lucette. "For all my reputation, I seem to be talking quite a lot myself at the moment. I'll try to get to the point. The farmer had lost his wife the year before and he talked mostly about her. Not all of it complimentary, but with deep affection. And then he said something that made me pause. 'The young are too apt to confuse love and worship. God and saints and angels are meant for worshipping—people are meant for loving. In the good and the bad, so the Church tells us. But I think it matters more in the bad.'"

After that remarkable quote, her father fell silent and they walked together for a further ten minutes while her own mind fell surprisingly quiet. For no apparent reason, as she still didn't know how to reconcile love and grief and passion and fear.

Maybe she wasn't supposed to know. Maybe she was simply supposed to muddle through.

"Thank you," she said finally, and slipped her hand into her father's.

"Don't thank me," he said calmly. "Thank the farmer. Well, he's dead now, of course. But I made certain I would have cause every day to remember him."

"How?"

"His name was Christopher Wheeler."

"Ah," she said in a burst of amused understanding. "So that's where Kit's name came from."

"Yes." He tightened his fingers around her hand. "The only way to have a life without pain, my darling girl, is to also have a life without love. And that is no life at all."

By the time Maisie made her official bid to lead her grandfather's company, she was fairly certain that the entire city of Edinburgh knew what she intended. And half the ports of Europe as well. When a merchant and banking concern as large and wealthy as the Sinclair Company made a move to reorganize its leadership, people noticed. The board came together in full strength the second week of May to vote on whether to retain or dismiss Robert Sinclair as company head; at this point possibly the only person surprised by the entire affair was Robert himself.

Her brother shouted abuse at her for a while, until Stephen Courtenay took it upon himself to escort Robert out of the reception chamber of the Canongate house where she paced. Stomping feet and slamming doors followed in the wake of his departure.

"Thank you," Maisie said distractedly.

"If he weren't your brother, I would have silenced him in a more straightforward manner."

"Don't hold back for my sake." But her retorts were mechanical, for every beat of her heart was locked fast in the council room three streets away.

She was as sure as she could be that they would vote in her favour—which was not as sure as she would like. Her plans and presentations had been flawless. The company had steadily lost money and influence since her grandfather's death five years ago. Left to Robert, the Sinclair Company might well cease to exist within another ten years. Maisie knew she could change that. And if the board members allowed themselves to decide based on logic and sound business sense, then she would prevail. If, however, they allowed their conservative natures to dictate that a woman—particularly a young and unmarried woman—could not possibly run a concern of this size . . .

She had made her gamble. All that waited now was the fall of the dice.

"Mariota."

Stephen stepped into her path, putting a hand out to stop her restless pacing before she walked straight into him.

She blinked and looked up at him. Such a long ways she always had to look—it never failed to disconcert her. Then she smiled. "Am I making you uncomfortable? I apologize."

"No need."

"Stephen," she said, and impulsively reached for his hand. "Distract me. Tell me a story." Holding his hand, she pulled him to the carved wooden settle built into the wall next to the fireplace.

"What sort of story?" he asked warily.

"Tell me about growing up in a noble household. What was it like being raised as the son of the Duke of Exeter?"

"Those are two different requests," he said. "For I believe my family is not wholly representative of nobility."

"Do you miss it? Not your family, of course you miss them—your title, I meant. Do you miss being Lord Somerset, with all its position and responsibilities?"

"Sometimes. The responsibilities more than the position . . . or maybe that is simply what I want to believe of myself. All my life I knew who I was and where I belonged. Now?" He shrugged.

"Your title did not make you who you are, Stephen Courtenay. And you could belong wherever you cared to try."

"Like Scotland?" he half teased. "If so, one can only hope I make a better job of it than I did in Ireland."

His immediate future, as much as Maisie's, rested upon the board's decision. Stephen had promised her that if she were named head of her grandfather's company, he would take command of her mercenary force. If not, then he would go to the Netherlands.

At the thought of losing Stephen as well as her grandfather's company, Maisie jumped again to pace. This time he stopped her by encircling one of her wrists with his fingers. Keeping her thus lightly caught, he said nothing. He just looked at her.

She had seen that sort of focused look before, in Ireland. It had never been turned on her. It had always been the gorgeous, sensuous Ailis Kavanaugh who had captured Stephen's attention to such an intense degree.

Instantly, Maisie corrected herself. *This is not the same look at all. It's simply that I'm susceptible to any man who manages to actually see me.*

Well, perhaps not just any man.

"Mariota," he said softly. "If there were any justice in this world, you would not only be running the Sinclair Company already, but the whole of Scotland as well. I have never met a woman with the force of character to equal you—except perhaps Queen Elizabeth."

"Being the good Scot that I am, I'm not sure I take that as a compliment."

Stephen Courtenay had the most beautiful smile—perhaps because he so rarely bothered to produce it. Maisie's head spun a little and she remembered that she hadn't eaten today. Where his hand touched her wrist, she felt her skin burn. His hazel eyes didn't waver from hers.

Just when Maisie knew she couldn't stand another second of that charged silence, the door to the corridor was flung open. She snatched her hand away the moment Stephen released her. Maisie whirled round, expecting to see Robert returning to throw more tantrums.

It was not her brother. It was Andrew Boyd, and Maisie's heart began to flutter in an entirely different manner. Good heavens, she thought crossly. I'm turning into the epitome of feminine weakness.

There was no clue in Boyd's reticent Scots face. Maisie faced him, feeling Stephen rise to stand just behind her shoulder, and waited.

Still with that inscrutable air, Boyd said calmly, "Congratulations, Mistress Sinclair. The board of the Sinclair Company has agreed to pension off your brother, Robert, and to give his voting shares to yourself. Welcome to the business, Maisie lass." That last was said with genuine pleasure, and then Boyd had taken her hands in his and kissed her on the cheek as though she were his own granddaughter.

She could hardly breathe. Who knew that achieving what one wanted was almost as terrifying as failure?

"Well done, Mariota," Stephen said softly behind her.

Perhaps it was the relief, or the light-headedness from hunger, or sheer recklessness—in any case, Maisie turned and threw her arms around Stephen in a hug. It could have been exceedingly awkward, for he was so tall, but he bent to accommodate her and, her arms clasped around his neck, lifted her by the waist and twirled her in a triumphant embrace.

"I did it."

Maisie hardly knew she'd spoken aloud until Stephen replied, "I never doubted you for a moment. Whatever you want, you will find a way of having."

"And I want you next," she said recklessly, then blinked and cleared her throat. "To lead my soldiers, I mean. That was our agreement, was it not?"

"That was our agreement. I will not fail to keep my word." Stephen twisted his mouth in a wry smile. "And I shall thank the angels above that I don't have to go to the Netherlands. I don't speak Flemish at all well."

On May 14 the town of York shone brightly beneath a benign sun that seemed to promise only excellent things for the history-making day ahead. It began with a service at York Minster, which had been carefully designed to balance Catholic sensibilities with the Anglican service. The music was composed by William Byrd, well-known for his Catholic sentiments, and even Tomás Navarro unbent enough to compliment Anabel on that, though he declined to attend. She was in little doubt that the reports to her father on this day would be favorable.

After the service, Anabel processed from the Minster through the streets, taking a roundabout route to the Treasurer's House to allow the gathered citizens to see and cheer her. She admitted that it pleased her royal vanity to revel in the joy expressed at her appearance. One did not grow up Elizabeth Tudor's daughter without knowing how to exploit one's appearance for symbolism's sake. Today, Anabel had dressed in white to emphasize her youth and purity. As pearls had become in many ways her mother's emblem, Anabel had taken to adorning herself with diamonds. Restrained, and never vulgar, today they were in the ribbons that held her hair back from her forehead and sewn around the high neckline of her gown. At her throat was the enameled green panther Kit had given her, and on her hands she wore only the locket ring from her mother.

Her hair, which had grown back as thick and red as it had been before the scarlatina, fell loose to nearly her waist. A banner, her mother had always called their shared colouring—the banner of their royal Tudor blood.

The largest space in the Treasurer's House had been transformed into a royal council chamber. Anabel had a throne almost to rival her mother's—perfectly judged, as had been every other detail of this day—with the gorgeously embroidered colours of the Princess of Wales on the canopy above. She took her seat and rested her hands on the gilded and jeweled arms of her chair and coolly regarded the men and women offering obeisance.

There were two curved rows of chairs on each side, with plenty of space behind for the curious to crowd in. The men of Anabel's privy council took their places—Robert Cecil, Christopher Hatton, and Matthew Harrington chief amongst them—while the women she most counted on had to be content to stand. No matter. Madalena and Pippa would always be amongst the trusted voices she regarded, wherever they stood or sat.

When her council was seated, there were two empty chairs. Her secretary, Christopher Hatton, waited until the observers were silent before rising again to announce the names of those who would fill the empty seats.

The first had been a forgone conclusion for months, for no northern lord had been as accommodating and gracious to Anabel's presence than had Henry Scrope. The tenth baron was a canny choice for one of the Catholic seats on her council. He was sincere in his faith but not dogmatic in his dictates, and Anabel had high hopes of his good sense and counsel in the coming struggles. Also, as Warden of the West March, Lord Scrope commanded a significant military power in the North.

The second name had been up in the air almost to the last minute. Only four days ago had word arrived that Philip Howard would attend her in York, and he had personally come just yesterday. Anabel had insisted on meeting with him last night to force him to ac-

cept her offer face-to-face. Though she remained wary, it was no
doubt a great coup. As Earl of Arundel and titular head of the powerful Howard family, Philip Howard's name caused a great murmur
amongst those in the chamber.

Anabel shot a quick glance to Tomás Navarro and caught the
priest looking back at her speculatively. When their eyes met, he
smiled and inclined his head. It might have meant many things. She
hoped it meant he believed in the illusionary intentions she had
worked so hard to create.

She did not entirely trust the arrogant cast to Philip Howard's
face as he accepted his appointment and took his seat. It would not
do to forget, even for a moment, that both his father and his grandfather had been executed for treason to the crown. It was a precari-
ous path she was embarked upon, and she could not allow an
ambitious and devout nobleman to wreck it.

There was a hush after the two Catholics were seated, and all eyes
turned expectantly to the princess as her secretary also sat. No doubt
they expected a word of welcome or thanks. But Anabel had one more
appointment to announce, and this one she would do herself. Forget
appointing Catholics to her council—this would send the rumours
flying through England as thickly as bats speeding to their cave.

Anabel, at her most imperious, rose straight and tall. "It is our
intention to appoint a Lieutenant General of the Marches. Too long
has the post remained empty, keeping the wardens disorganized and
without proper royal support. And though it is our dearest wish to
be closely allied with Scotland, the protection and well-being of our
people must ever be our first concern."

This time the murmurs held a hint of excited alarm, for it was not
properly her right to appoint a lieutenant general. That belonged to
the queen. Thus, as planned, the Princess of Wales's announcement
could only be seen as an affront and an open challenge to her mother's power.

"Lord Christopher Courtenay." She spoke clearly and deliberately.

His name elicited far more than a murmur, but Anabel ignored it. She kept her eyes only on Kit, who approached with that easy grace he had always possessed, fulfilling at last his youthful promise of skill and strength. His dark gold hair and hazel eyes were set off by the chestnut silk of his doublet and hose. He had always had his mother's beauty, though his was entirely masculine. And like his mother—and Anabel herself—he knew how to use it to his advantage.

He knelt as Anabel spoke to him. "With this charge, serve well our people. Protect our borders and ensure our prosperity. We entrust you with our dearest hopes for this beautiful North of England."

His obeisance, like all else he did, was beautifully executed. She offered him her hand, to raise him up, but he kissed it first. Still at her feet, he looked up. Then, with the impudence she loved, Kit winked.

No turning back now. Anabel had launched her first shot in open defiance of England's ruling queen. What followed from this might well decide the course of the coming war.

EIGHT

15 May 1585
York

Mother,

The Council of the North has concluded its official business. You would be proud of Anabel; she conducted the proceedings with both gravity and charm. Like her own mother. I would not say that the men over whom she presided ever forgot that she is a woman—but she turned that to her advantage. The unofficial business looks to continue for several more days. The Earl of Arundel arrived just in time to publicly accept an appointment to Her Highness's council, thus continuing the Howard family tradition of committing oneself at the last possible moment. We shall hope the other Howard tradition of treason is not repeated.

Father Tomás Navarro cornered me in conversation at last night's festivities. He is young and intense and rather romantic in that austere Spanish way; pity he is a priest. In any case, he did not waste time trying

*to flirt with me. Instead, he questioned me rather closely about you and
Father and the queen. No doubt he is fully aware of my rumoured
relationship to Her Majesty—he seems to think that makes me more
disinterested than the others in York. And so I am. I find myself
impatient with Anabel's arrogance and Kit's adoration and Pippa's
distraction.*

*No doubt you are enjoying London precisely as much as I am enjoying
York.*

Lucette

3 June 1585
Scarborough

Mother,

*We are embarked on our Grand Tour of the North. Who knew how
much landscape is encompassed in Yorkshire and Cumbria and Lan-
cashire? I feel certain that by the end of the summer we will have seen
every single rock and vista and heather bush that exists. But of course, it is
not the landscape but its people who are the purpose of this royal progress.
For progress it is—in fact, if not in name.*

*Wherever we go, Anabel is received with the kind of attention and
rapture that I have previously seen commanded only by the queen. She
earns it, I admit, for she works long hours receiving people and listening
to their injuries and complaints. Pippa works even longer hours, for she
has been to all these places multiple times in the last two years to prepare
the way. Kit is only occasionally with us, as he does his work along the
border and ensures nothing will mar the coming meeting of Anabel and
the Scots king.*

Ironic, that last, isn't it?

Lucette

27 June 1585
Berwick

Mother,

The news of Elizabeth's condemnation of Kit's appointment has been
received rather coldly in the North. I would prefer it to have been discussed heatedly, for that argues the passion of a moment. But this cold-
ness? It will have to be handled carefully, or these two royal women may
find themselves seriously estranged. Like Edward II and his son . . .
though that was perhaps more rightly the fault of Edward III's mother.

Anabel has officially continued the ban on Catholic services, but she
turns a blind eye to the Masses conducted privately in her wake as we
travel. Tomás Navarro conducts many of the Masses himself, and takes
time to hear confessions and counsel gravely wherever we go. It certainly
has engendered goodwill.

To answer the rather pointed questions in your last four letters—and
that solely to keep you from coming north as you threatened—of course I
write to my husband. And he writes to me. Felix is adjusting as well as can
be expected, which I take it is not very well at all. I believe Julien had
hoped to have the situation better in hand so that he might come north to
see me. It is just as well he cannot. That is one strain too many to cope
with just now.

Lucette

"There can be no question," Elizabeth said in amusement, "that
Lucette is your daughter."

Minuette widened her eyes in that pretense of innocence Elizabeth knew so well. "Because she is clever?"

"Because she is insolent. How much of her attitude is assumed,
and how much real?"

"Far too real for my liking."

"Well, as you are always reminding me, one cannot force one's children into a state we desire. It is not as though I enjoy Anne's show of independence. All too easy to believe in her insults, so that at times I must remind myself of their purpose. And then I wonder— does my daughter begin to believe in her own acts? Can I trust her to do what she must when it comes to humbling her pride?"

"Because your own example of humility has been so evident over the years."

Oh, how Elizabeth had missed this! Having a friend who knew her well enough to dare to tease . . . that was a gift not to be over-looked. But, being who she was, her manner of giving thanks was astringent. "Perhaps I should ask your husband his advice. Except he has never managed to humble himself in his life—not even when it was a matter of saving yours."

Minuette eyed her narrowly but let it pass. "The point, Your Majesty, is that the North is turning out for your daughter. And the Spanish are watching every move closely. Just as they are watching you and your intentions with the Netherlands."

"Do you think if I refrain from making a treaty with the Netherlands that Philip will abandon his desire for war? No. If I refrain from aiding the Netherlands, then they fall to Spain, and Philip will have more troops and money to commit against England. A fight on multiple fronts is to our advantage—for now. I will not be drawn so far as to leave us unable to protect ourselves."

"And Ireland? If Dublin falls—"

"Dublin will not fall." Elizabeth spoke sharply.

"Because you wish it? I thought I was the one who believed that whatever I wished must come true."

"You and Will." Elizabeth had been thinking a fair amount about her brother lately. How would he have handled the Spanish threat? The only conclusion she had come to was that William would never have been married to Spain, and thus the fight would have been less personal. But surely it would still have been a fight. Spain and much of France were committed to violence to preserve the Catholic cause. England must lead the opposition or they would all gradually be choked to death by fanatics on both sides.

She shook herself out of the useless introspection. "Will you remain with the court while Dominic commands the South?"

"I would like to go with him when feasible—but yes, I will make the court my center while I am needed."

Impulsively, Elizabeth grasped Minuette by the hand. "You are always needed. That is your curse, my dearest friend—that so many people in so many places need you that you cannot possibly meet every need. I am grateful that this summer it is my turn to have you."

"It is good for me to have something to do. Otherwise I would merely fret. Why did no one ever tell me that mothering adults is exponentially more difficult than mothering children?"

"Why, indeed!" Elizabeth laughed in sympathy. "We shall simply both have to trust in the children we have raised. We will go to Nonsuch and sign the treaty for aid to the Netherlands—and our children will go to the Scots border to meet Anne's betrothed."

"And then?"

"And then we wait for Spain's violence to fall."

After more than two months of crisscrossing northern England, Pippa left Anabel and her court at Middleham Castle to enjoy a brief respite and herself pressed on northwest to Carlisle. In ten days' time the border town would play host to the first meeting of Her Royal Highness, Princess Anne Isabella, and His Majesty, King James VI of Scotland. Anabel had sent two of her household officials ahead to ensure the perfection of planning required for this visit.

Pippa, of course, being one. And Matthew Harrington the other. The first day was passed in silence, save for the necessary information required when riding forty miles in a rather isolated land-scape. Pippa was glad to reach the inn and shut the door on everyone. She was the only woman of the party, dressed for hard riding rather than fashion, and thus not requiring a maid. The tension had been so thick on the road that Pippa's entire body hurt with the weight of it. She didn't know whether to eat or sob or sleep.

In the end she did the first two and then settled down to attempt sleep last of all. Her eyes had just begun to be heavy when a firm knock sounded on her door. If she had been less strained, it would never have taken her by surprise. She had known the feel of Mat-thew Harrington almost before she had been old enough to recog-nize it. But she had worked so hard to keep him walled away—how could she deal with him when she was tired and afraid and unpre-pared?

She lay perfectly still, half hoping he would leave, but Matthew knew her almost as well as she knew him. "Philippa," he said in his deep, grave voice, "please let me in."

It was the "Philippa" that did it. She had ached to hear him call her by name again for so long. She rose and threw on a woolen robe over her shift and tied it. Then she drew a deep breath—meant to steady her, but in actuality simply making her light-headed—and opened the door.

She so rarely saw Matthew in anything other than impeccable order. Someone had once opined that he took such care in his ap-pearance to compensate for his less than illustrious birth. Pippa knew better. It was simply who he was. Like his father, Matthew set his own standards, and lived up to them unfailingly.

Tonight he was not impeccable. He had removed his doublet, and the fine wool jerkin was unlaced over his shirt. For an instant Pippa wondered if he knew what effect that had on her. But Matthew had never been one for devious manipulation.

"May I come in?" he asked.

Swallowing, she stepped back. It was not like him to even ap-proach the borders of impropriety. But now he entered her bedroom and closed the door on the two of them. Then he leaned against the door and studied her.

With anyone else she would have had a ready comment or quip to defuse the moment. Not with Matthew. She simply waited for him to say whatever he had come to say.

It was nothing that she had expected.

"Did you think I had forgotten, Philippa? In all my lifetime, I have never forgotten a single word you've said to me. For years I have allowed you to pretend that that summer morning at Wynfield Mote never happened. But pretending is getting us nowhere quickly."

If this was the conversation they were going to have, she needed to sit. Pippa lowered herself to the bed, trembling a little beneath her robe.

She did not bother to pretend she did not know what he was talking about. That would have been the final insult to both of them. "What has that to do with today?" she asked instead.

"It has everything to do with today, and tomorrow, and next year. Because in all the things you have said to me since then, I have finally begun to understand what it is you have *not* said."

"Don't."

"I remember every moment of that day, Philippa—including your silences."

I love you, Matthew had told her when she was fifteen. And she'd had only a moment to revel in the joy of it before the vision of disaster had swept her away and left her floundering in its wake. She had always been prepared to face her own life's end. She would never be prepared to face Matthew's.

He had allowed her to set the terms of their relationship since then, however much he disliked it. No more. Now Matthew leaned against her door, eyes alive with a passion that might have been desire or might have been anger. Or equally might have been both. And he was not waiting for her any longer.

"You saw something that day," he said evenly. "Something that made you walk away. Something that has kept you at one remove from me ever since. I have allowed you to keep me there, because I was afraid if I pushed, you would retreat even further."

He shoved himself away from the door. "No more, Philippa. What I said to you eight years ago is as true now as it was then— I love you. What can matter besides that?"

"Death matters. Love does not stop death."

"No more it does," he agreed. "But it makes the life before it worthwhile. You may be the seer, Philippa, able to decipher the heavens and its portents—but I can decipher you. You will die young. I have known that since you were fifteen."

For all his size, Matthew could step as delicately as a cat. He came near enough to touch, but didn't. Yet. She kept her head down, studying her own hands clasped tightly in her lap.

"I have been watching you." He knelt down so they were closer to the same level. "You are ill. Anabel and Madalena both know it. They thought it simply a product of too much work and too much stress. I thought so, too, for a time."

He lifted her chin with one hand, forcing her to meet his eyes. "I have spoken to the princess's physician, Philippa. He prevaricated, clearly at your bidding, but he is not a very good liar. He finally told me you have been coughing up blood for some time."

"Does anyone else know that?" she whispered.

"Madalena, I think. Everyone else is willing to believe what you are working so hard to show them."

"If you know so much, then you know why I've done what I have."

"No doubt you have told yourself it's for my own good. Keep me away, never let me get closer than friendship—in hopes that losing you might be more bearable.

"Philippa, if you die before me, there is no preparation beforehand that would make it anything less than devastating. All you accomplish by your stubbornness is to guarantee I have fewer sweet memories to hold to afterward."

He still didn't know everything. And she was suddenly too tired to lie any longer, even if only by omission. "What if you die first? Because of me?"

Surprise lit in his eyes, and then a slow comprehension. "So that's it—it's not your own death you fear. It's mine. Is that what you saw that day?"

"I will not lead you to an early death."

"Who is to say you can stop it? Doesn't Dr. Dee insist seers can only interpret fate, not control it?"

"I will not do it!"

"Do what? Listen to me, Philippa—you will certainly make your own choices. If you want to resist and pretend and lie to both of us, you can. But you do not make my choices. And I choose you. Every day."

She had never seen him so open. So vulnerable. In his face she could see it all—he had laid his heart before her and would let her walk over it if she chose. She had always known he was braver than she was.

It was impossible to know who moved first, but finally, after eight long years, they were kissing once more. Pippa couldn't think straight—couldn't think at all—drowning in this rush of mutual desire. Matthew had always been so familiar to her that she had only rarely seen him objectively as a man. But now she couldn't not see and feel it. She let her knees fall open so he could pull her against him, and his hands went to her hips, steadying her on the bed.

Her only clear thought for quite some time was: *Thank goodness there's no chance of Kit finding us like this.*

When reason slowly began to reassert itself, they drew apart a little. Not far—his forehead rested against hers and she could feel his breath on her lips. They were both breathing unevenly.

"Marry me, Philippa," he whispered.

"You must promise not to tell anyone else what the physician said."

He hesitated, but finally nodded. "I promise."

The river was crossed, the bridges burned . . . Philippa knew when and how to surrender. "Then I will marry you with laughter and joy, Matthew Harrington, for as long as is granted us."

"That," he pointed out softly, "is all anyone, seer or not, can ever promise."

For Stephen Courtenay, it was a summer of long hours and hard work, and he devoted all his considerable gifts and focus to making a success of the job Maisie had entrusted to him at St. Adrian's. The mercenary company he had briefly commanded three years ago in Ireland had not stayed entirely the same. Amongst the fighting men themselves, about half were new to Stephen. Of the officers, only the engineer and physician remained. It had been agreed that this summer would be spent in Scotland, training hard and knitting together the bonds necessary for a successful military company.

He often had cause to silently thank Renaud LeClerc for his time in France. It had been one thing to lead men from Tiverton or Somerset—men who were obliged to follow their liege lord because of his name. France had required Stephen to earn the respect and trust of men who did not care about his name or family, who cared only that he knew what he was doing and showed some respect for their lives as well as his own.

For two months he did not see Maisie, though they wrote to one another at least four times a week. As he reported on their progress, she wrote of her travails in consolidating her power. Her brother, Robert, was proving troublesome. No surprise. Stephen once offered to lead a group of St. Adrian's men to remind Robert of his limits, but Maisie gravely declined. Now that they were only thirty miles apart and their letters took only a day rather than weeks to reach each other, it was more than ever like being engaged in constant conversation. There were times when Stephen had to remind himself to write to anyone other than Maisie.

With his three siblings all now in the North, he kept up with their news almost as easily. Everyone in Scotland knew that the Princess of Wales and King James were finally set to meet in person in Carlisle. It was interesting to hear about this from the Scottish side— Stephen had always so naturally been attached to the English court that it was a little hard for him to hear Anabel, in particular, talked about as though she were simply a means to an end. But he kept his mouth shut. No need to make unnecessary enemies.

If he expected Scotland to be the nearest he would get to his family in the near future, Stephen was wrong. Ten days before the Carlisle conference, he was peremptorily summoned to Edinburgh by Maisie. "The king has requested it," she wrote. So Stephen handed command to his second, and with two dozen of his best men (as ordered by Maisie) he rode to Edinburgh. They stayed in the same town house where he and Kit had stayed on their arrival. Maisie sent all her orders by messenger, so Stephen was still a little in the dark when he met her outside Edinburgh's imposing castle the next morning.

She looked him up and down and nodded her head once in approval of his understated finery. Expensive cloth cut well, which proclaimed the wearer cared about his appearance without needing to impress anyone else. "Very soldierly," she said. "The king will like that."

"Why are we here?" he asked, as he had asked in writing more than once in the last three days.

She avoided answering just as neatly in person. "I imagine the king will tell us."

If Maisie were as uncertain as he was, she did not show it. He had never seen her dressed so finely—she might have passed at any court for a well-born daughter of the nobility. The gown of sky-blue damask suited her fairness, and the lace partlet and soft lace cuffs were beautiful without being ostentatious. As usual, she kept her abundant fair hair sleek and contained.

They were received in the overwhelming Great Hall of Edinburgh Castle, with its lofty hammer-beam roof and carved supports, amongst which were the thistles of Scotland. Stephen studied James Stuart with covert interest as the formalities were observed, wondering what Anabel would make of her intended husband. James was younger than the princess by four years, but he looked older than eighteen. There was a wary, almost careworn aspect to him that must have come from spending his childhood as a pawn fought over by various factions. He had his mother's colouring and sharp eyes, and Stephen reminded himself to take care. It would not do to forget that this was Mary Stuart's son.

Indeed, that was nearly the first thing James said. "I believe you knew my mother, Lord Stephen." Though he was no longer—and never again would be, Stephen knew—an English earl, he was still the son of a duke.

"For a short time, Your Majesty. At Tutbury." It also would not do to let James forget that Mary was no friend to England. Or to her son.

"Yes, my mother has written of you. In no very flattering terms. Since she describes me across Europe in much those same terms, I find myself disposed to like you."

James then turned his attention to Maisie, who would look at ease wherever she went precisely because she did not try to be other than herself. "And Mistress Sinclair, who has so neatly managed to upset every businessman in Scotland. I hear most of them now fear that the clever females of their families will run amok."

"If they are inclined to run amok, then they are not likely to make good merchants or bankers, Your Majesty."

"Quite. And I suppose I am hardly in a position to condemn clever females, seeing as I am about to meet my own very clever betrothed. That is why the both of you are here."

Stephen chanced a quick glance at Maisie. She looked inscrutable and unshockable as always.

"We leave Edinburgh tomorrow for Annan and Hoddom Castle. I will cross the border during the days to meet with Her Highness, but I will not spend the nights in England. The two of you will be part of my retinue."

Stephen would not have been more surprised if James had offered to make him an earl in Scotland. What did James Stuart care about him? But beneath the bewilderment was a sudden, aching need to see his family. His parents would not be there, of course, and he'd spent plenty of time with Kit recently. But his sisters? All at once Stephen wanted nothing more in the world than to see Lucie and Pippa.

"It will be an honour, Your Majesty." Maisie spoke without inflection.

"Yes, it will. An honour I could hardly refuse to offer, seeing as it has been requested by Princess Anne herself. In such strong terms that I suspect she may decline to meet with me in person if the two of you are not also present."

Stephen knew he must point out the obvious. "Queen Elizabeth has not invited me to return to England, Your Majesty."

"Queen Elizabeth will not be at Carlisle. I do not intend to leave you in England, Lord Stephen. I understand the force you are training at St. Adrian's is quite . . . valuable. I have no interest in their commander leaving us before they can be of service."

It was so easy to capitulate, because it was what he wanted. "Of course I will do as you wish, Your Majesty."

They were outside the castle before Stephen's head stopped spinning. He looked accusingly at Maisie. "This is your doing. You wrote to Anabel's court and suggested we be included in the Scots party. Why?"

She did not bother to deny the charge. "I have business to transact with Her Highness's household. Now that the assets of the Sinclair company are at my disposal, I can offer her greater opportunities for her investments."

"And you could cross the border yourself anytime you wanted to transact that business. Why Carlisle?"

She simply looked at him, and for once her face was not unreadable. It was alive with amusement and irritation and the sort of tolerant affection directed at small children slow to understand. "For your sake, Stephen."

NINE

Anabel rode into Carlisle in a burst of summer beauty that showed the borderlands at their best. Kit rode at her side; as Lieutenant General of the Marches, he was the commanding military officer for all the northern border. They were welcomed with good grace by the Warden of the West March—and new privy council member—Lord Scrope, with a pageant that served as a preview to the coming meeting between England and Scotland. Praises were sung, music was played, flowers were thrown, and at last Anabel was escorted to her suite of chambers and ordered everyone out except Pippa.

During the pageantry, Pippa had never been near enough to her princess for Anabel to guess how she might be feeling. Anabel knew she had been unhappy about being sent ahead to Carlisle with Matthew. It was Kit who suggested it, and now Anabel was curious as to how the two of them had fared.

She hardly needed to ask. The moment she turned Pippa to face her in the light streaming through the leaded glass, she knew. The sunlight was as nothing to the illumination in Pippa's face. Anabel caught her breath, then laughed triumphantly.

"It seems Carlisle is indeed the place for lovers to meet! I am so glad, Pippa."

"Glad enough to do something for me?"

"Whatever you like."

"Matthew and I want to get married."

"I can see that," Anabel said drily. "I cannot wait to throw you the most lavish wedding England has seen in years."

"On Thursday."

Anabel stared. "Thursday. As in three days from now?"

"Yes."

She was about to protest, to make all the arguments against it, but stopped herself. Pippa would have anticipated them all. "On one condition—that Kit and Lucette give their consent. If your parents are going to punish anyone for allowing this to happen without their knowledge, Pippa, I want their anger aimed at your siblings first."

It had been a long time since she'd seen Pippa smile so blindingly. "Agreed."

The joy of it was like a balm over the expected wariness and strain of the coming encounter. Anabel couldn't remember when she'd last been so anxious. Had her mother felt like this before meeting Philip of Spain? If so, she had never talked about it. Not that Elizabeth Tudor would ever willingly admit to weakness.

So Anabel didn't, either. Pippa was too radiantly happy to be as sensitive as usual, and what could Kit possibly say? That was one awkwardness too many even for them. Only Madalena, helping the princess dress on the day of James's arrival, had words of comfort.

As she adjusted the heavy folds of ivory silk that made up Anabel's overgown and sleeves, Madalena said in her low, melodious voice, "You have the heart of both a king and a queen, Your Highness. James Stuart will never be half the royal you are."

Anabel, to her own surprise, laughed. "Perhaps that will not be my opening statement to my future husband. But I will remember it." She stopped Madalena's adjustments with a hand. "Thank you, my friend."

She knew she looked as perfect as blood and wealth and style could make her. Beneath the ivory silk damask, a kirtle of the palest blush pink echoed the sarcenet foaming through her slashed sleeves. She wore diamonds in her hair and at her throat—a necklace alternating the diamond's pure light with cool blue sapphires. Anabel considered herself as free from vanity as possible for a princess born, but it was no sin to recognize the truth: she was beautiful. Any man would be glad to meet such a bride. She almost wondered if she should try to dim her beauty. She had no wish to inspire in James anything more than the cheerful acceptance of political necessity. The absolutely worst thing that could result from this meeting would be Scotland's insistence on setting a wedding date.

Like her mother, Anabel intended to keep her options as open as possible until the very last moment.

It had taken months of negotiation to arrange the ceremonies appropriate to a Scots king being received at an English border castle that had once held his own mother prisoner. Over hundreds of years, Carlisle Castle had been besieged by the Scots more often than any other English castle. All in all, a portentous site.

As the Scots had agreed to the symbolic submission of their king crossing the border, the princess's household had agreed to bear the costs. Anabel noted the evidence of money well spent as she paced through Carlisle Castle—from the inner bailey where she lodged in the Warden's Tower, through to the outer bailey where a viewing stand had been erected for herself and James to view the pageantry. Around and against the grey and red sandstone of the walls hung lush garlands of greenery twined with roses and thistles, and studded with plaques bearing her arms and those of Scotland. Separately— for she was in no rush to combine either their symbolism or their bodies.

Anabel sat on the viewing stand beneath her canopy of estate while everyone else stood to attention as the Scots party began to enter. As Lieutenant General of the North, Kit had joined Lord Scrope at the border crossing to greet the Scots. With Pippa, Mad-

alena, and Lucette to her left and Sir Christopher Hatton and Robert Cecil on her right, Anabel waited with a serene face to meet the
man she was betrothed to marry.

James drew the eyes of all the curious as the party entered the
bailey, dressed with a richness Anabel had known to expect from
reports. She made a rapid assessment as he crossed to the viewing
stand: the red hair and hazel eyes of his mother, but without Mary
Stuart's height or reported grace; nothing obvious from his elegant
Lennox father; a slightly awkward gait; a face of intelligence if not
warmth. Anabel rose at precisely the perfect moment to descend the
steps of the viewing stand and meet him face-to-face.

She could not avoid curtseying to a crowned king, but James
made the moment easy by instantly extending his hand to raise her.
Then, in his own—no doubt carefully calculated—show of defer-
ence, he kissed her hand.

"Your Majesty," she said, "welcome to England."

"I thank God and Your Highness for this gracious day."

He was not attractive. She had not expected it. But it was a shock
to stand so near to him with Kit just behind his shoulder—Kit,
whom all the world would find attractive.

She was introduced to the chief members of the king's train, and
in turn James met her own advisors. Then, as she placed her hand in
the crook of his arm to ascend the steps, James paused.

"I must not forget the gift I promised Your Highness," he told
her. "I believe your lieutenant general can bring them forward?"

There was the slightest emphasis on the title, just enough to make
Anabel's instincts sharpen. James did not like Christopher Courtenay. And as it seemed unlikely Kit had done something offensive in
the last hour, it could only be because of gossip James had heard.
Something to be careful of.

She let the thought go for the moment, because coming forward
was the little, clever Scots girl who had made Anabel so much money
in the recent past. Maisie Sinclair made a deep obeisance that encompassed both her king and the English princess. And at her shoul-

der, standing a head taller and as dark and watchful as he'd ever been, was Stephen Courtenay.

Anabel smiled with real pleasure. "Thank you, Your Majesty. This is a gift indeed."

She smiled up at the viewing stand, where Pippa and Lucette had had no idea that their brother was coming. Despite the difficulties inherent in the coming days, there would be at least a few pleasures.

If someone had designed an event specifically to undo Lucette's tightly wound control, they could have done no better than dropping Stephen in front of her without warning. She almost accused Pippa, standing next to her, but her sister's indrawn breath and blinding expression of joy eloquently assured Lucette that she had not known, either. It must have been Anabel, then.

It took all her years of control and inbred dignity to stand quietly through the ensuing hour of formal pageantry and welcome. She could feel her brother watching from where he stood below the viewing stand. As much as she had missed him, she was also terrified. If anyone could get to the heart of her troubles, it would be Stephen.

She had done the same for him, once, during a long winter at Farleigh Hungerford after Stephen's first foray into Ireland. He had come back from that broken, and she'd had to steel herself against emotion and set about putting him back together.

Turn about is fair play, a little voice whispered.

When the royals vanished inside for a meal with only Christopher Hatton and James's secretary, John Maitland, for company, Lucette was swept into reunion. Pippa, so extravagantly happy about her coming marriage with Matthew Harrington, threw her arms around Stephen and fired questions at him without pausing for breath. *How does it feel to be back in England? Are you making the men of the mercenary company properly afraid of you? When was the last time you ate and slept?*

Pippa's final question was directed to the quiet girl standing just outside their circle. "And how is your business proceeding, Maisie Sinclair?"

"Very well indeed. I am looking forward to speaking to Her Highness's treasurer now that I have greater assets at my command."

Her Highness's treasurer himself stood only a few paces off— Matthew having hardly been away from Pippa's side the last two days save for sleeping at night. And was that a smile when he bowed to the Sinclair girl? Who, despite her age and appearance, must be the shrewd businesswoman Lucette had heard so much about.

"At your convenience, Mistress Sinclair," Matthew said—with, indeed, a smile on his usually grave face.

"And you were right, I must confess," Pippa declared, linking her arm with Maisie's, "when we spoke in York last autumn. Here is my brother serving dutifully as you predicted he would in our last conversation. I am glad it is in Scotland, and under your command."

Lucette, despite her nerves, looked curiously from Pippa to Maisie to Stephen, who looked a little flushed—and not just from the heat of noonday.

"Come with me," Pippa said, encompassing Maisie, Kit, and Matthew effortlessly. "We'll take refreshment and talk about Scotland. Because, of course, I was also right in that conversation, Maisie Sinclair. Do you remember what I said to you?"

The little group passed out of earshot, and Lucette was left wondering what Pippa had said to the girl that could leave the air so charged between them months later.

Then Stephen stepped in front of her and she was forced to look at him. His eyes, those shifting green-gold hazel eyes of their mother, searched far too deeply. "I am sorry, Lucie," he said. "I know I said it in letters, but I am more sorry than you can know about your losses."

Not my losses, she silently corrected. My babies. Three she had failed now, failed to carry any longer than four months at the most.

He was wise enough not to say more on that subject. "I am also sorry that Felix was dropped so abruptly into your life again. Renaud had wanted him to come to England for a visit, but it should have been planned and prepared for, not spurred by further death and trauma."

"Felix hates me now," she found herself saying, and realized that here was an additional pain she had not yet acknowledged.

"He does not know what he feels. Surely you can understand the terror and confusion of having your world turned upside down in an instant."

With the Tudor rose necklace given you by the queen, she knew he meant. The necklace that had spurred the revelation of her shaky paternal heritage, kept from her far too long by her parents. In the wake of that trauma, Lucette had cut herself off emotionally from both her parents—but from her father most of all. Only when she had gone to France and met Julien had she been able to understand her parents' choices.

"Let us hope that Felix does not take as long to forgive as I did." She almost smiled when she said it.

"Will you spend the winter with the princess? It must be hard for Julien to be separated from you."

This time she did smile. The practiced court smile that would not fool her brother for an instant, but put an effective end to his prying. "Why worry about winter when we have so few days at present to enjoy one another's company? Come along, and you can tell me about Scotland and how on earth you came to be commanding a mercenary company belonging to a girl younger than even Kit and Pippa."

She managed to keep herself bright and attentive and closed off for the rest of the day. But when she escaped to the chamber she shared with Pippa (thankfully alone just now, for Pippa continued to circle between Anabel and Matthew every waking hour), she found a letter from her husband waiting for her.

Lucie mine,

Am I permitted to call you that with the barrier of two hundred miles between us? I am sure you will let me know if not.

Help, Lucie. I need you. Felix needs you—or at least, he needs some-one or something other than me. I do not know what to do for him. He is angry and confused and does not seem certain of who he is anymore. You and I have both had to come to terms with having our pasts shaken up and rearranged into a new picture—but you did it when you were much nearer Felix's age. I was already an adult when I had to face the past . . . and I had you to help me.

I know that you are needed in the North. I have no wish to supersede the claims of your family and your princess. But might you come home for a little? Or might I come north with Felix? Not to the princess's household—but near enough to see you?

What a melancholy note I have struck in this letter! It is not as bad as all that. Nothing can be wholly catastrophic as long as you breathe on this earth. That will very nearly be joy enough for me to the end of my days.

Though I would not mind being asked to kiss you again someday . . .

Julien

James Stuart might not have been the most physically prepossessing man of Anabel's acquaintance, but in person she quickly warmed to the deep intellect and scholarly interests that had previously been confined to his letters. If she had only to deal with his conversation, they might do very well.

Fortunately, James did not seem terribly interested in her person—certainly not as much as he was in her kingdom. That made their conferences slightly less awkward.

But only slightly.

"Your Highness," prodded the king's secretary, John Maitland, "is it your intention to continue to promote the cause of Papists at your court and in your policies?"

"It is my intention to serve and defend the people of England. All of them."

"Your mother has learned necessary caution concerning Papists over her lifetime, seeing as every assassin who has attempted her life has been Catholic."

"A logical fallacy, my lord. That every assassin has been Catholic does not mean that every Catholic is an assassin."

It was interesting that in the most charged moments, James always conceded the field of argument to Maitland. Anabel refused to be thus put off, so she spoke directly to James. "Surely Your Majesty would protest any attempt on my part to dictate Scottish policy. I am not clear why it should be Scotland's prerogative to instruct me on how to govern my council and household."

Intelligence, and possibly wry amusement, flickered in his normally flat eyes. "I expect the prerogative springs from our future marriage."

"As I understand the terms of the betrothal, the question of union is between the two of us personally, not our crowns. A union of country would fall to any child we might have in future."

"And that might work, if we were monarchs of distant countries— like England and Spain, say? But Scotland is quite rightly concerned about being swallowed up by English interests. We are a Protestant nation, Your Highness. I will only wed a woman of the same sentiments."

Did he have any idea how tempting that implied offer was? What would he do if she took him at his word and promptly became Catholic simply to avoid marrying him?

She smiled with deadly sweetness. "England is not a Catholic nation. But as long as there are English Catholics, I will not suffer their rights of life and liberty to be forfeited to their conscience. As my mother once wisely said—I will not make windows into men's souls."

James did not have the requisite sense of humour to parry her strokes lightly. His face darkened, but he managed civility at least. "I imagine this is a subject we will return to more than once in the next year. Perhaps we should leave it for now in the hands of our capable diplomats."

The next year. For that had been the purpose of this border meeting—to finally set a wedding date. Both sides had at last agreed to August 30, just over a year from now. Anabel had tried to push for two more years, but the tide was against her. She was already twenty-three. James's advisors wanted her wedded and bedded and with child as soon as possible, for then the alliance would be unbreakable without the kind of violence with which Spain now threatened England.

Tomás Navarro was displeased, as he was bound to be. Anabel wondered to what lengths Spain's displeasure would push them. Far enough, one hoped, to provide England an edge in the coming war. Keep them unbalanced and guessing about her intentions, and Spain might be caught the slightest bit unprepared.

But the priest confined his immediate queries to Ireland in a private conference with Anabel. "Do I understand that you will not ask Scotland for aid against the Irish Catholics and Spanish soldiers supporting them?"

"I will not." Because there was no point. James would never agree.

"That is good. I am certain that Your Highness desires peace. But it will not be to anyone's benefit to have a peaceful earthly life spent in heresy, only to be in torment eternally. I trust Your Highness keeps ever in mind the souls of your people."

"They are not my people, not wholly," she reminded him. "That belongs to my mother."

"Only so long as the people wish it."

It was the most dangerous thing Navarro had said yet. Anabel allowed him to leave without further discussion, but his warning echoed as she spent the next two hours riding with Kit and several of James's household. The king himself had declined the invitation, preferring to pore over some manuscripts brought here from Oxford for his pleasure.

When they returned, James was waiting in the outer bailey to greet her. Anabel did not see him at first. Only when Kit had swung her down from her horse, his hands lingering ever so slightly at her waist, did she realize they were being watched. She stepped neatly out of Kit's touch, intending to approach James, but the king merely bowed his head in acknowledgment and walked away.

That last evening there was music and dancing and wine enough to soften even the sternest border faces who had been bred from their cradles to be enemies. Not too much wine, though, for the Scots party still needed to cross the border before they slept. Anabel was careful to dance with Kit only once, moving from him to Stephen to a reluctant Matthew Harrington, and at last to James.

When the dance ended, James asked softly, "Might I seek a moment of privacy to speak to you? It is unlikely we shall meet again until our wedding."

"Yes, of course." Anabel felt all eyes on them as they left the hall for a quiet chamber nearby with painted ceiling and a wealth of Turkish carpets beneath their feet. No doubt both her council and James's were quietly fretting at the thought of these two royals conducting their own negotiations, but so be it. One could not run a marriage entirely at one remove.

But it was not negotiation James had in mind. She briefly wondered if he meant to kiss her, to begin to approach the intimacy required of husband and wife. But if nothing else, James was not an especially sensual man. Unique to a Scots king by the name of James, he had no bastard children and possibly was as much a virgin as Anabel.

He did not kiss her. Instead, he asked, "What precisely is the nature of your relationship with Lord Christopher Courtenay?"

Immediately she wanted to snap at him in affronted dignity, but she could not allow him even that much sign of personal displeasure. If she had been a woman only, then she could have indulged in any sort of temper. But she was a princess, walking a dangerous path between competing powers that would tear her to pieces the instant she slipped.

Striking what she hoped was the perfect balance of innocence and hauteur, Anabel said, "He is Lieutenant General of the Marches."

"An appointment properly belonging to the queen. And yet she does not object—or at least, not loudly enough to insist on his removal. Why, I wonder?"

"Because he will fulfill the task admirably."

"Because he is a Courtenay," James said flatly. "That, I imagine, is why your mother has not insisted on removing him. She has her own Courtenays to worry about in the South. And surely that is why you have appointed him. Not because of his talents, but because of his close connection to yourself."

"I am hardly likely to surround myself entirely with strangers. No more than you are. I remember Esmé Stewart."

His face darkened at the reference to his onetime favorite, disgraced and dead two years ago from the attacks of nobles who had not liked the French-born favorite. James himself had been imprisoned for a time in that upheaval. But he would not be deflected. "I am not given, I hope, to irrational jealousy. But nor will I be insulted. You must step carefully, Your Highness. Women are apt to prize passion over prudence—a lesson I learned before I could even talk. Do not make my mother's mistakes."

Almost she asked him if those mistakes included Mary Stuart's disastrous marriage to James's father, Lord Darnley. But she bit her tongue. He had more likely been referring to the even more disastrous and ill-considered elopement with Bothwell that had led directly to Mary's abdication and imprisonment in England.

She softened her response. "I would be ashamed to think evil of Your Majesty's friendships. And would hope that the man who trusts me with marriage might offer the same courtesy."

"So long as the loyalty of spouses remains paramount."

He was clever, this Stuart king. He would not shout or rail or even directly say what he meant. But that didn't make it any less clear. *I will be watching,* he meant. *I may not care for your heart, but that does not leave it free. The moment you cross the line with Christopher Courtenay, you will find yourself friendless in Scotland.*

If Robert Dudley had lived, she wondered, would Philip of Spain have delivered something of the same message to Elizabeth?

But Robert had not lived. And if her mother had always cared more for a dead man than her living husband, she had managed her marriage successfully enough so that when it broke down, it was for reasons of policy and not personalities.

Anabel knew she would have to learn to do the same. Unless . . .

Unless she got very lucky and fortune took a hand in the future that was still so rocky.

TEN

On Thursday, 19 August 1585, Philippa Courtenay and Matthew Harrington were married in Carlisle Cathedral, beneath the barrel-vaulted ceiling and the gorgeous East Window shining coloured light through its ornamental tracery. Anabel had forced Pippa into an elaborate gown of the princess's own: apricot silk velvet and damask decorated with golden beads along the shoulders and narrow cuffs. Her radiant face was framed by a lace collar stiffened high behind her honey-gold hair, the distinctive black streak twisted back and highlighted by an ivory comb set with moonstones. Matthew's stalwart frame and subdued finery, by contrast, acted like an anchor to keep his otherworldly bride tethered to the earth.

Despite the elaborate backdrop, the wedding was a quiet affair. Other than Anabel's chaplain, who performed the service, only the Princess of Wales and Pippa's three siblings were in attendance.

"Wilt thou have this woman to thy wedded wife . . ." intoned Edwin Littlefield. "Wilt thou love her, comfort her, honour and keep her, in sickness and in health?"

Despite her best intentions, Anabel found her gaze focused on

Kit. *Can I really do it?* she asked herself. *Can I stand before a priest next year and make these vows to a king I have no intention of loving?*

"And forsaking all others, keep thee only to her, so long as you both shall live?"

Kit's eyes flickered to hers. *Forsaking all others.* His face was stripped of its usual good humour. For a heartbeat, Carlisle Cathedral melted away and she could see nothing but the man she must forsake for England.

As Littlefield pronounced the benediction, Anabel echoed the words as a silent prayer of her own for this man who loved her: *God the Father, God the Son, God the Holy Ghost, bless, preserve, and keep you, the Lord mercifully with his favour look upon you.*

Robert Cecil and Madalena Arias had organized a fine supper for after the wedding in the Warden's Tower of Carlisle Castle. The members of Anabel's privy council and her ladies, all of whom had cause to like and respect both Pippa and Matthew, attended and offered toasts of congratulations. Lord Scrope attended as well, with the chief of his March command.

Pippa sat securely between her husband and her twin. With her left hand clasped in Matthew's, she turned to Kit and asked, "Well?"

He grinned. "Very well, from what I can see. Your frantic edge has gone."

It had indeed, something that surprised Pippa a little—and almost made her sad. What if she hadn't been so afraid all this time? Could she have had this peace much earlier? Even her body had responded. The coughing fits had eased this last week, so that she almost felt healthy.

Matthew leaned in and whispered in her ear, "Why were you so insistent on having Maisie Sinclair at this supper?"

Pippa turned quick enough to catch her cheek against his rough jaw and was momentarily distracted by the sensation. Attuned to her responses, Matthew held her there for a moment. She gave a breathy laugh and answered. "Cannot you guess why I wanted Maisie here—not just tonight, but in Carlisle itself? I thought you understood me better than anyone."

Matthew shifted a bit to look into her eyes. His were dancing in a manner that made Pippa giddy. "I just wanted to know if you would admit to matchmaking."

Reluctantly, she tore her gaze away from her husband to where Maisie Sinclair sat next to Stephen in close conversation. "Matchmaking would imply I set things in motion. They have done that themselves—I only want to help them recognize it."

Stephen and Maisie were close, she judged. Close to recognizing that what they had was not mere friendship.

How could she not want that for all the world? Now that her own friendship had turned the corner to the love she'd always been afraid of, Pippa thought everyone should be as happy.

She was not afraid anymore. Once she made a decision, she did not look back. She was Matthew's wife, for however long God gave them. As Matthew had said, that was all anyone could hope for. And she meant to revel in every moment given her.

Fortunately, Anabel was kind enough to retire early from the feast, freeing the newlyweds to retreat before their desire overcame their manners.

Pippa had asked Lucette alone to attend her. As the sisters left the Warden's Tower, Pippa noted Kit moving next to Matthew. Her twin had an unusually forbidding expression on his face. "What do you think he's saying?"

Lucette rolled her eyes. "Some variation of what Stephen said to Julien—'Hurt my sister and I'll kill you,' that sort of thing."

"You *have* been hurt," Pippa noted. Even on the edge of her wedding night, she could not turn off the impulse to help.

"But not by Julien," Lucette answered slowly. "It is only that he is the nearest to me, so he is the one to absorb my hurt."

Then they were at the bedchamber set aside for the newlyweds, and Pippa allowed herself to be absorbed in the process of removing the elaborate and heavy gown Anabel had insisted upon and changing into a whisper-fine cambric chemise with blackwork at the cuffs and neckline and a thin silk robe tied with ribbons. Lucette unpinned her sister's hair and brushed it until it lay in a heavy golden weight around her shoulders.

Pippa grasped Lucette's hand, resting on her shoulder. She could see her sister's face in the mirror. "'A fine cambric shift. And a bed.' You recommended the state to me, as I recall. Were you at all uncertain?"

"I'm afraid I am far too earthly a woman to indulge in hesitation. I wanted Julien every bit as much as he wanted me." Lucette bent and kissed the top of Pippa's head. "But if you are hesitant, no one safer to take your worries to than Matthew."

But when her sister had gone and her husband entered, Pippa discovered she had no thought of nerves. Only the wish to be in his arms and never, ever to leave them.

Maisie Sinclair had been somewhat surprised when the Scots left the border and she remained in England. She was even more surprised that Stephen agreed to remain as well. Of course, Stephen would hardly miss his sister's wedding. And it was flattering to be asked to join the wedding supper, except that Maisie didn't believe in wasting time being flattered. Better by far to know why things were being done.

She thought she understood Lady Philippa Courtenay—now Philippa Harrington—to some degree. It had been there in her teasing remarks to Maisie when they'd met again at Carlisle Castle.

I was also right in that conversation, Maisie Sinclair. Do you remember what I said to you?

Maisie never forget anything. Philippa had said: *There is more to Stephen than duty, and a heart with room for more than one love. I do not think passion has finished with him quite yet.*

So Philippa was matchmaking. Why? Maisie wondered. And how could his sister imagine that Stephen would ever look twice at a plain Scotswoman when he had the memory of Ailis Kavanaugh in his heart? Stephen had walked away from Ailis, but that didn't mean he wouldn't be searching for another gorgeous beauty, all fire and passion, to match him.

Of course, Philippa had never met Ailis. Perhaps the woman thought Stephen's work in Scotland had something more personal to it than professional. Even clever women can be wrong on occasion, Maisie mused.

Stephen kept her entertained throughout supper. It had been a less profitable visit than Maisie might have hoped, seeing that the Princess of Wales was engaged with the king and Matthew Harrington could hardly take his eyes off Philippa. She had been accorded a meeting with Robert Cecil, the princess's secretary, and met several times with Madalena Arias. Maisie had also spent one illuminating afternoon with Stephen's older sister, Lucette. The dark-haired beauty—with the blue eyes, some said, of the late English king—was not as unsettling as Philippa, but she had a formidable intelligence. Though her studies had been largely academic, Lucette was quick to question Maisie about her business, and not only followed the discussion but asked some truly insightful questions.

When the sisters withdrew from the hall at the end of the wedding banquet, Maisie tracked Stephen's gaze to where his brother sat in close conversation with Matthew. Stephen chuckled softly.

"What?" she asked.

"Matthew is being subjected to various warnings. It was my task with Lucie's husband, Julien. Now it's Kit's turn. It's what brothers do."

"Not my brother."

Stephen's sharp eyes turned to her. "Your brother never even met Finian Kavanaugh, did he?"

She shook her head. "Even if he had cared to—which he never

would have—I can't imagine that Robert would have intimidated a
man forty years older than himself. Especially an Irishman. Luckily
for me, Finian was kind enough."

"Kind enough that you do not find the thought of marrying again
distasteful?"

"Why would I marry again? As a wealthy widow, I control my
own future."

"Mariota, you will always control your own future. Of that I have
no doubt."

Every time he called her by her given name, it made uncomfortable things happen to her heartbeat. Fortunately for her peace, a
page appeared behind the two of them and, bowing, presented a
message to Stephen.

The seal was unmistakably royal.

Stephen broke it open where they sat and after a moment said,
surprisingly, "It's for both of us." He handed it to Maisie to read
herself.

13 August 1585
Whitehall Palace

*Lord Stephen Courtenay is commanded to Her Majesty's presence at
court as soon as can be arranged. He is to bring with him Mariota Sinclair of Edinburgh. We have business to discuss between the three of us.*

HRH Elizabeth

Maisie raised her eyebrows in surprised query. Stephen was wearing his particularly blank face that told most people so little. But she
was not most people. Maisie had learned to read the tiny twitches of
jawline and eye that revealed his uneasiness.

"I would wager," she said brightly, "that it will take your queen
less than five minutes to offer to buy my military company for England's use. Well, probably not buy it. Probably she will want it for

nothing. Do you think you are likely to be swayed by her patriotic arguments?"

His lips twitched with definite amusement. "It doesn't matter, does it? The company is yours. I will do what you tell me."

And there was that damned irregular heartbeat again. *Stop it, Maisie* scolded herself. *Confine yourself to the things you do well and leave romance to the beauties.*

When news reached London of Philippa Courtenay's precipitate marriage to a man whose birth could only be considered less exalted than hers, the rumours began flying of how soon a baby would be born. Elizabeth stopped what she could in her own circle by freezing disapproval. Minuette seemed untroubled by the gossip, though Elizabeth thought Dominic was likely furious at such idle discussions of his daughter's virtue. But despite Minuette's acceptance of the marriage, and their sincere approval of Matthew, Elizabeth knew how much her friend was hurt and surprised that they had not been told beforehand.

So when Stephen Courtenay reached London, Elizabeth allowed him to spend an entire day with his parents in their house on the Strand before summoning him to court. Let him tell stories of Pippa and Matthew to ease his parents' concern. But once Stephen arrived at Whitehall, she ensured that the pageantry was fully in place. She received Stephen and Mistress Sinclair in the throne room, made more impressive by the absence of a crowd. Only Burghley was with her. She had not even considered bringing Walsingham into this meeting—Stephen had little cause to feel fondly about her spymaster. And vice versa. In fact, Walsingham had opposed this particular idea of hers from the beginning.

Stephen entered with the kind of indifferent grace his father possessed in spades. He made the appropriate genuflections, as did the woman at his side. Elizabeth studied Mariota Sinclair in the time it took the two of them to advance the length of the room. Dressed exquisitely in a silver and black brocade that Elizabeth envied, the slender girl carried herself well despite her lack of height. She was obviously fair, though her hair was severely parted and almost entirely contained in a black velvet hood. As young as Maisie Sinclair was, Elizabeth recognized a kindred spark of intelligence and self-possession in her face.

Yes, she thought, this is a woman to have on my side.

First, though, to deal with Stephen. Elizabeth was prepared for coolness from the man she had banished from England for acts verging on treason. But Stephen possessed his mother's warmth as well as his father's pride, and his smile rested nicely between wryness and familiarity.

"Your Majesty," he said. "Allow me to apologize personally for all my offenses committed. I live only to serve as best I may in future."

This was why she had refused to see Stephen Courtenay after he'd killed a man inside her own palace—because she had known that any member of the Courtenay family would be able to disarm her fury in a heartbeat.

Balanced between chilly pride and gracious forgiveness, Elizabeth replied tartly, "Words are all well and good, but of no value without deeds to back them up."

"Do I expect that you are going to offer me a chance to prove myself with my deeds?"

For all his eerie resemblance to Dominic, Stephen had the edge of Minuette's insubordination. Elizabeth narrowed her eyes. "Since you know so much, would you like to tell me what that offer is—or shall we proceed directly to your answer?"

There was a laugh, hastily disguised as a cough, from the Sinclair girl. It made Elizabeth like the chit better—not that she would give her the satisfaction of knowing it.

Stephen's lips quirked as well. "I would never presume to speak for you, Your Majesty."

"Quite. Well then, let us proceed directly to business. But it is not with you I wish to transact it—it is with Mistress Sinclair."

She liked the girl even better for not flinching when the Queen of England turned the full force of her attention on her. "Your Majesty," she said politely. She did not hurry to assure Elizabeth that she would do whatever was wanted.

"I understand that you are in possession of a mercenary company. Personal possession, I mean—for you formed it before taking control of your grandfather's business. Indeed, I believe that very company took the field against one of my captains in Ireland."

Stephen did not react outwardly, but even without looking at him, Elizabeth could feel his anger. That wasn't really the point of this discussion, so she continued smoothly. "I believe that company is under your personal command, not subject to your board's approval?"

"It is under my command."

"I would like to hire it for a specific mission this autumn."

Under her breath, the girl murmured something that sounded like "two minutes." More audibly, she asked, "In the Netherlands, Your Majesty?"

Elizabeth tipped her head thoughtfully. "No, though I did consider it. But I already have good men in the Netherlands. What I need is a relatively small and very mobile force for . . . somewhere else."

"Where?" It was Stephen who asked bluntly, as though he knew already what the answer was.

Elizabeth met his uncompromising gaze. "Ireland."

Swift and insolent came his answer. "No."

"It is not for you to answer, Lord Stephen. You may command the force, but it is at Mistress Sinclair's disposal."

"I can hardly send a force without a commander." Maisie might be young, but she spoke with a nearly royal hauteur. "And I cannot compel any man to serve."

"But I can," Elizabeth replied.

"One Englishman, perhaps. But not the entirety of a company resident in Scotland."

Oh yes, this girl was good.

Elizabeth was better. "Scotland is quite willing to give me what I want just now, with my daughter's marriage not yet finalized. King James is amenable to pressure."

"Be that as it may, I cannot be bought, Your Majesty. I will disband my company before I allow it to be used against my will."

"Mariota, listen." Stephen touched the fierce girl on the arm, and spoke to her as though no one else was present. Elizabeth shot a surprised look at Burghley and saw that he was watching the pair with the same interest she felt.

"Do not make any rash statements on my account," Stephen told the girl. "I am tired of having sacrifices made on my behalf. I will pay for my own sins."

"You have paid! There is nothing left for you in Ireland."

"I think we both know that is not true."

There were undercurrents here that Elizabeth did not entirely grasp. She didn't have to. She merely had to manipulate them. "Perhaps," she broke in mildly, "if we explain the nature of the mission?" She turned to Lord Burghley and waved to him to proceed.

He wasted no words. "Spain intends to make a concerted push to capture Dublin in time for Mary Stuart to land there—before winter, if it can be managed. We want to prevent that."

"She intends to bring her younger son?" Stephen scowled.

"To view his future kingdom—yes."

"Then she'll be disappointed, for the Irish will never recognize a foreign monarch."

Elizabeth let that insubordination pass, for whatever Stephen might imply, she was not a foreign monarch. Ireland was as much English as anything else. More to the point, it was certainly not Spanish.

"We are not asking you to launch into battle beyond Dublin," Burghley said. "We only want to secure the integrity of the city against a Spanish landing. Your company is well-qualified to help accomplish that."

There was silence, longer than Elizabeth would have liked, but the queen recognized the internal and silent considerations in both of the young people before her. Ireland did not hold pleasant memories for either of them. Elizabeth didn't know the whole of what had happened there three years ago, but she knew that much.

They seemed able to communicate merely with their eyes, for not a word had been spoken between them when Mistress Sinclair said abruptly, "If Lord Stephen is willing to command the force, then I am willing to negotiate with your government for its use. For a fixed amount of time, of course—I do not make open-ended contracts."

"I would expect no less of William Sinclair's granddaughter."

Beneath Elizabeth's satisfaction at accomplishing what she'd wished ran a decidedly feminine curiosity about the nature of the relationship before her. She would have to ask Minuette what she thought of her oldest son and this decidedly bold young Scotswoman.

ELEVEN

29 *August 1585*
London

And so both my daughters are married.

30 *August 1585*
London

*If I were interested in presenting myself in the best possible light, no doubt
I would record only how happy the news of Pippa's marriage has made me,
how delighted I am that she has found happiness, that wedding Matthew
is the fulfillment of years of hope.*

*Every single one of those statements is true. But they are not the whole
truth. I have also wept for her choice to wed so quickly and so far from us.
Though I am grateful my other children were with her, I am angry that
Dominic and I were not.*

*Except that anger is not the true emotion. It is fear. Because I know
my daughter, and if I do not wholly understand the gifts she walks with, I*

*do know how they inform her choices. If she wed in such haste, it is
for a reason. I do not like what my fear whispers of what that reason
might be.*

*7 September 1585
Dover Castle*

*To distract myself, I have come to Dover with Dominic. I will remain in
the castle for a week or two while he rides back and forth along the coast.
Though the season will soon pass when a naval assault is likely, my husband will ensure that whatever is in his control is perfectly prepared.*

*Chief amongst the things we cannot control being, of course, our chil-
dren. It was so much simpler when the most I had to fear was illness or
accident or the likelihood of Kit throwing himself off the battlements in
an ill-judged attempt to keep up with Stephen. Now, even more than their
bodies, I fear for their happiness. Lucie is wrapped in self-imposed isola-
tion, Kit is in love with a princess set to marry another, and Stephen . . .
Oh, Elizabeth! How could you send Stephen back to Ireland?*

*My only consolation in that last is that Maisie Sinclair has insisted
that she will accompany her troops to Dublin. From the moment I met
her, I was impressed by her practicality. It is a trait not to be undervalued,
especially by those likely to get themselves into trouble over esoteric matters. Maisie, I believe, will keep Stephen grounded.*

Much in the way Dominic has always done for me.

Philip received the reports of his daughter's meeting with the
Scots king in contemplative silence. He wished he had heard directly
from Anne, but she wrote only very occasionally these days and al-
ways with the strictest formality. It was Navarro who wrote from
Carlisle instead, with a stiff bias against the Calvinist counselors
King James surrounded himself with:

*Is it proper for an Infanta of Spain to tie herself to the most flagrant here-
tic? The Infanta Anne has a wise heart, Your Majesty, and is open to the*

appeals of the faithful amongst her people. Should we not encourage her to consider a husband who would promote such instincts rather than crush them?

Navarro did not know Anne as well as Philip did. "Infanta" was a courtesy title to her, nothing more, for she was as English as her mother. That meant stubborn and suspicious and insular—but it also meant pragmatism and a willingness to negotiate for the things she most wanted.

And Philip would safely wager an entire shipload's worth of silver from the New World that marriage to James of Scotland was not what Anne truly wanted. Navarro might wish to promote a Catholic marriage, but the priest was being deliberately naïve. There were no French royals available at the moment, and England would never wed Anne to a mere Italian count, which left only Spain. England would revolt if another Tudor woman tried to wed a Spaniard.

There were one or two Catholic possibilities amongst her own Englishmen, but Philip did not even bother envisioning such a thing. Both Anne and Elizabeth had good reason to look to Scotland, and his daughter would not break such a necessary match lightly.

The first time Philip had traveled to England—during the late king's reign, when Elizabeth herself was only Princess of Wales— Philip had met a man named Robert Dudley. It had not been hard to guess why the young lord did not like Philip, and subsequent inquiries had confirmed how close he and Elizabeth were. Robert Dudley had been one of the casualties of William Tudor's violent end. But what, Philip wondered now, if Robert had lived? It would have been politically disastrous for Elizabeth to marry the fifth son of an attainted and executed traitor. Philip did not think she would have married her beloved Robin. But she might conceivably have refused to marry anyone else. She was just stubborn enough to do so.

Philip knew—had known for several years—that his daughter was in love with Christopher Courtenay. And by all reports, Christopher was equally in love with her. On paper, not the best match. Christopher was the younger son of the Duke of Exeter—though now that his brother had been stripped of his titles by Elizabeth, it was possible the boy would inherit. Nor was he Catholic, but his family was not noticeably fanatic in their Protestant sentiments. And Philip knew something that not many people did—that Dominic and Min-uette Courtenay had been married by a Catholic priest.

It was as well to keep all this information in mind, he mused. When he next wrote to Navarro, he might begin to steer him in an unexpected direction. One that would make his daughter sit up and take notice.

But before his daughter, Philip must deal with his wife.

He had allowed Mary to leave Segovia after several months, and she gave no sign that she had considered herself confined in any way. But she had been a touch less arrogant in their most recent dealings.

The arrogance revived the moment Philip told her something she did not wish to hear. In this case, that her long-planned visit to Ire-land was cancelled.

"We cannot disappoint our supporters!" she railed. "The faithful of Ireland need a symbol to fight for."

"Alexander is not even four years old. I will not risk one of my sons on the open seas with a less than certain reception waiting on the other end. Dublin has not fallen yet. There will be an intense push this autumn and I do not want him anywhere near that."

"Then send me."

Philip was only half surprised at the suggestion. Mary Stuart's physical bravery had never been a question, and she had always been driven to head directly for the things she wanted. Just now, she wanted Ireland. Not for the country itself or even its faithful Catho-lics, but as a symbol to fling in Elizabeth Tudor's face. *You cannot keep hold of your own territories,* Mary wanted to proclaim, *any more than you could keep me in prison.*

"To what purpose?" Philip asked reasonably. "You cannot go near Dublin."

"Then I will land at Waterford. The Earl of Desmond would surely be willing to meet me there."

The Earl of Desmond was surely willing to take Spanish money and men, but Philip knew the man would not be thrilled at an imperious foreign queen appearing in person to demand her due. But such was the position of the beggar—the things Desmond wanted must be paid for. Usually at the cost of swallowed pride.

Philip calculated while his wife watched with undisguised impatience. She had never learned to value the time he took before making decisions. To a woman accustomed to acting on impulse, his caution was an irritation.

"I will consider it," he said finally. "But you would sail on one of my warships, not a royal one. And you would be under the command of a military officer. For your safety."

"Of course," she agreed generously.

There was one more matter to broach. "May I ask you, Maria, what you have heard of the meeting of your son and my daughter?"

She sniffed, not being overly endowed with maternal sentiment for the son from whom she'd been separated as an infant. "I have heard that Anne is lovely and James is awkward. No doubt once they are wed, she will move to swallow up Scotland as her mother has tried to do with Ireland. If James cannot oppose his wife, then he may find himself in the same position I did—ousted by his own lords and sent running for the English border. Perhaps then my people will remember how I always held Scotland's independence sacrosanct."

Except for the garrisons of French troops both you and your mother used freely, Philip thought sardonically. If Scotland rid itself of James, it would not be to invite Mary back to the crown of her birth.

But that threat might make an intriguing line to play upon in the web surrounding his daughter's marriage.

———

In the weeks after the Scots visit, Kit threw himself into his new command with almost manic energy. There might be peace between England and Scotland, but the borderlands were a place—and a law—unto themselves. Men raided freely in both directions, one generation after another, and the complexity of familial enmity was enough to make a drunkard out of a monk. There was no shortage of demands upon the March wardens of England.

Up at dawn, in bed long after sunset, hours in between spent on horseback, Kit was frustrated when he finally flung himself into bed only to then stay awake staring up at the ceiling of whatever chamber he happened to be in. As lieutenant general, he nominally commanded all three Marches along the border and he ranged freely from Lord Hunsdon in Berwick to Lord Scrope in Carlisle.

He stayed away from Anabel for more than a month. Though they wrote one another almost daily, there was a constraint to their exchanges. Kit didn't know how meeting James had affected Anabel—for Kit, dealing with the living, physical man had provoked a restless urge to outpace the future. Knowing that Anabel must marry was one thing. Counting down to a specific day was entirely different.

Besides, being in Anabel's household would have meant being in the presence of Pippa and Matthew's unequaled joy every day. That was a bit much to ask him to endure just now.

But in late September, Kit received a summons from the Princess of Wales using all of her names and titles to attend a council at Middleham. He finished up a planned scouting ride with Scrope's men out of Carlisle, then rode south through a landscape of burnished heather and rocky vales and vast skies.

Middleham impressed Kit with the careful restoration of the medieval castle. Anabel had a feel for the past and the ability to enhance its beauties while updating its inconveniences. She had not, however, completely made it over into a manor. Like the other great castles of the North, Middleham retained its fortress feel. If called upon, it would be able to withstand a siege.

Kit had the uncomfortable feeling it might have to.

He found Anabel in a giddy, slightly dangerous mood. She was waiting for him in the courtyard—not with royal politeness, but more as a woman welcoming her absent lover. Little things—how she held on to his fingers when he kissed her hand, the way she met his eyes with a smile that acknowledged no one else, the subtle adjusting of her position so she seemed always to be turned to him. Though Kit was glad of it—what man didn't want the woman he loved to be so anxious to see him?—the part of him that had grown up in the last few years warned that it was a bad idea. He knew what James of Scotland had said to Anabel before he left. And from his own journeys through the borderlands, Kit knew that the Scots king was not the only one watching the Princess of Wales's personal relationships.

There had been only wisps of rumours in most places, like stray cloud drifts that moved so fast one could hardly pin them down. But in Dumfries those wisps had coalesced into an ugly scene. Kit had crossed into Scotland by invitation from Lord Maxwell, Scotland's West March warden. He took with him a contingent of men from Carlisle Castle, and military matters had gone well enough. Maxwell was a canny, worldly man unlikely to be moved by sentiment but very willing to come to practical arrangements.

The Carlisle men had been drinking with their Scots counterparts. When Kit crossed the courtyard after supper, he heard boisterous laughter and the kind of drunken noise that had never particularly appealed to him. He meant to skirt it all, since it did not sound anything more than normal high spirits, but then several phrases caught his ear.

Faithless in bed means faithless in war . . . it's not heads women rule with . . . weak and silly girl . . . Anne . . .

Kit could move swift and silent when he chose. That night he opted only for swift. Heads snapped round at his march, and men took a step back when they saw Kit with his hand resting on the hilt of his sword.

The ringleader—fortunately a Carlisle man, as Kit didn't suppose

Maxwell would appreciate an Englishman meddling with his household—held his ground, either because he was brave or because he was too drunk to notice the danger. He even hurled another insult. "And here's her lapdog to yip at my feet."

"Shut your mouth and walk away," Kit warned.

"For you? I don't think so." The man slurred the words and his steps forward were unsteady. But his expression was alight with malice. "You're no more than a jumped-up younger son of a traitor. Like your father, your only real talent lies in seducing the right women. Why else would yon silly princess send a boy to do a man's job?"

"That is treason," Kit said softly.

"I'm not afraid of you, any more than I'm afraid of your Tudor whore."

It wasn't his sword Kit drew. Swift as a snake, his left hand snatched the dagger at his back. In almost the same movement, he flipped it round and struck the drunken man with its hilt full across his face. And in case that wasn't enough, he struck again until the man went down.

And when they reached Carlisle, he went to Lord Scrope and demanded the man be thrown in a cell until he'd learned to keep his mouth shut.

He hadn't meant to tell Anabel, but gossip flew faster than even men could ride. The moment they were alone, she said tartly, "Been fighting, have you? I hear you broke a man's jaw in Dumfries."

"Did you hear why?"

She shrugged. "More or less. I appreciate your instincts, but I am meant to be binding the North to me, not alienating them."

"In that case, it might be best if I retire from the North. I'm doing your reputation no favours."

"Those who oppose me will always find a reason to justify their opinion."

"That doesn't mean we need to hand them reasons."

"I'm not sending you away," she said flatly. "At this point, it would only lend credence to such malicious talk. I won't have it said that I fear idle words. Perhaps you could bring yourself to flirt with my women?"

"You want me to flirt with my sister?" Kit asked with elaborate patience.

"You know what I mean."

If she would not acknowledge uncomfortable facts, he would have to force her into it. "I also know that this situation is not sustainable," Kit said. "What do you intend to do when you are married, Your Highness? Make me your lapdog in truth? I do not think your Scottish husband will allow that."

"Are you jealous?"

"Damn right I'm jealous!" He struggled to get himself under control. "But that doesn't matter. What matters is your reputation and your ability to rule. I am compromising that. It must end."

"What must end? Speaking to me? Serving at my command? What are we doing that is so unforgivable? Although . . ." Her eyes turned soft. She stepped within his reach and tipped her chin up consideringly. "If I'm going to be judged and convicted, Kit, shouldn't I at least have the pleasure of the sin beforehand?"

She kissed him before he could move, and then he didn't want to. For a few blessed moments his body concurred with her assessment and he very much wanted the pleasure. But that cursed sense of responsibility that his family had inculcated in him without his ever being aware did not completely desert him. "Anabel," he murmured against her cheek. "You know better."

She breathed out a mild oath and, slowly, released her hold on him. "I will make you a bargain," she finally offered. "I will refrain from dragging you into openly compromising positions if you will remain in my councils. Not for my sake alone. I truly believe your voice is valuable."

He was helpless to refuse her. "Then you shall have it. As long as you require."

———

Fortunately for Anabel, she excelled at putting aside personal issues and dealing with the public necessities of her position. She thought very few would be able to read any of the ruffled emotions behind the serene face with which she swept into her council chamber at Middleham. The men were on their feet, bowing, as she settled herself at the top of the circling chairs and waved them back into their seats. For conferences such as this, Anabel tended to keep to neutral palettes and severe lines in her dress; today's gown of dove grey velvet had close-fitting sleeves and a high-cut square neckline edged with an inch of silver bullion. *I have a serious mind,* such a gown declared, *and am not to be put off with flattering words.*

"Sir Christopher," she said to her chief minister and secretary, seated to her right. "We have had word from the queen's court at Nonsuch?"

It was a rhetorical question, for it had all been discussed beforehand in smaller, less formal groups. But this was for posterity, with clerks taking careful notes of all that was said.

Christopher Hatton answered in his normal, equable fashion. "The treaty was signed with the Netherlands on the tenth of August. The queen has agreed to provide more than seven thousand troops and to bear almost a quarter of the annual cost of the war. Philip Sidney has been appointed governor of Flushing and Sir William Pelham will command the English troops."

"In return?" Anabel asked drily. "For I well know the queen gives nothing without ample return."

"In return, the towns of Brill and Flushing will be ceded to English control, to be garrisoned at our own cost. Also, two seats on the Council of State and the title of Governor General of the Netherlands. That last," Hatton added drily, "the queen has declined."

Nicely judged, Anabel thought in admiration. No one negotiated better than her mother, or knew to the precise detail what could be safely bartered. But her public position of defiance allowed no more than a raised eyebrow and a cool, "Interesting. That could argue the queen does not trust any of her men to hold such a position."

Only Tomás Navarro looked pleased with that assessment. The Jesuit was allowed to attend her privy council meetings, without being allowed a formal position. A way of controlling the information that flowed to King Philip.

"England must recognize," Navarro said in his precise and accented English, "the futility of opposition in the Netherlands. The queen would do well to leave the rebels to His Majesty, who knows so much better what his people need."

In her opinion, the Flemish could hardly be reasonably called the people of a Spanish king, no matter that King Philip's grandfather had been archduke of that territory. But Anabel merely smiled noncommittally and asked Robert Cecil, "And Ireland?"

"Stephen Courtenay has embarked from Dumbarton with the St. Adrian's company of mercenaries. Their task is to strengthen English forces in Dublin and, if possible, push back against the rebels and expand the size of the Pale."

"At least I trust Stephen to do his work efficiently and without undue severity. He has no interest in religion or politics—only in doing his job well."

"A man with no interest in religion is a man scarcely to be trusted," Navarro stated.

Anabel turned on him the false smile and steely gaze learned at her mother's knee. "This council is not called upon to trust him. Dublin is the queen's concern."

"And your concern?" Give Navarro credit—he had no fear of plain speaking.

"The security and unity of the North." Anabel paused for effect, for not everyone on her council had heard the news that followed next. "Which is why I will be meeting with Her Majesty at Kenilworth in November. To impress upon her the value of the work we have been doing here. And to remind her that no part of her kingdom can be safely ignored."

It was for far more than that, of course. Those few who knew the entirety of the ambitious plan hatched almost three years ago knew that this was a precious opportunity for mother and daughter to consult in privacy and adjust their plans as necessary. News passed through ciphers and at second- or thirdhand could not replace two quick minds working in concert.

There was a murmur from her council, not distinct enough for words or loud enough for excitement, but Anabel was reasonably pleased. "In the next weeks before we leave Middleham, I expect every detail of our work in the North to be documented in perfect order. Matthew," she nodded at her treasurer, "and Lady Philippa will be making the rounds of the great houses and towns to remind everyone of our commitments—and theirs. And to note any concerns we should bring before Her Majesty."

"Will the members of this council be invited to Kenilworth Castle?" Philip Howard wanted to know. It was only the second time the Earl of Arundel had come north since accepting a place on Anabel's council. And she still found it difficult to read him.

"But of course."

"All of your council members?"

"Do say, Lord Arundel, if you are not happy with the idea."

He could almost match her for sardonic smiles—then again, he was a Howard. "I can conceive of no greater pleasure."

I'll bet, she thought grimly. Arundel was going to take a great deal of pleasure in facing down her mother. And almost as much pleasure in setting queen and princess against one another.

It was only when the council had dispersed that Anabel was cornered by Pippa. "Will you bring Kit south with you?"

"You have heard what happened at Dumfries," Anabel replied with resignation.

"I imagine there are peasants in Germany who have by now heard what happened at Dumfries."

"You're going to tell me not to bring him south."

Pippa hesitated. "No. I know better than to try and give you orders."

"I may not take orders from you, my friend, but I will take advice." Anabel looked wistfully at her. "Pippa, can you not tell me . . ."

"What?"

"Do I marry James next summer?"

"I don't know, Anabel. There are limits to my knowledge. I cannot see beyond—"

She broke off so suddenly it startled Anabel. "Beyond what?"

Pippa's expression closed off, something rare in her friend. "I can tell you the same thing I told you several years ago—you will marry of your own choice. That is all I know."

"'All' you know?" Anabel didn't believe that for a moment. But no one ever succeeded in forcing Pippa to share things she didn't want to. So Anabel shrugged and said, "Back to the original issue. Will it be politically devastating to have Kit come south with us in November?"

"It may feed gossip, but so would leaving him behind. People will find the stories they wish to tell. It may not be wise, but it will not break any of your plans."

The princess smiled. "Then I am willing to be unwise."

TWELVE

The only saving grace of being back in Ireland was that Stephen was kept so busy he hardly had the time or energy to fret about it. Partly it was his own doing—he drove his men harder than ever, throwing the company into sorties designed to push back the ever-encroaching rebels. There were Spanish soldiers aplenty around Dublin, in numbers that argued they might be thin on the ground elsewhere in Ireland.

It was a fact confirmed by Thomas Butler when the Earl of Ormond took to the sea to slip into Dublin by water. The earl stayed at Dublin Castle, where Stephen was also officially quartered with the Lord Deputy. Unofficially, he spent most of his time with his officers and men quartered outside the city, as he disliked the official attention being paid him merely because of his family name.

But Ormond was worth coming to the castle for. If for no other reason than that Stephen owed the man both thanks and apology for the last time they had seen one another. When Stephen had used the earl's dagger to kill a man in Queen Elizabeth's own palace.

Ormond waved the apology away. "You were young and passionate. Those are things we well understand in Ireland. I must say, though, I did not expect to ever see you here again."

"You and me both."

"You've come with good men, at least. The Lord Deputy is grateful."

Stephen merely grunted. Sir John Perrot was an entertaining man, but what little time Stephen had that was not spent in the field or training, he preferred to spend with Maisie. Perrot was not his first choice for company.

Ormond laughed and said, "If Dublin is not to your liking, how about returning to Leinster with me? It's where the rest of the Spanish are concentrated—trying to push me into the sea."

"My orders are Dublin and the Pale," Stephen said woodenly.

"And you have always shown yourself so quick to follow orders." It was said without malice. "Well, I can't say I'm surprised. And as long as you're pushing back the Pale up here, you're keeping troops from being used against me. If we hold them this winter, I doubt they'll have the stomach for another push. Especially not with my dear cousin, the queen, practically daring King Philip to come against England itself."

Maisie invited the earl to dinner before he left Dublin, and Stephen was relieved to have Tom Butler's attention turned on someone other than himself. She had taken a house and kept up a constant flow of business matters with the aid of her Flemish secretary, Pieter Andries. Though Stephen had been initially surprised at her insistence on coming to Ireland with him, he was grateful. It helped to have a touchstone whenever a scent or a storm or an accent pulled at his memories.

At dinner, Maisie controlled the conversation effortlessly, telling stories of her travels and making Ormond laugh. Then he managed to edge in a reminiscence of his own.

"Such a slip of girl you were, the first time I saw you. I thought a mistake had been made, and a child had been sent to wed old Finian Kavanaugh."

The name made Stephen flinch, and even Maisie seemed momentarily shocked. She managed to redirect the earl—who appeared to know exactly what she was doing but humoured her—and the rest of the evening passed without further awkwardness.

Stephen was just letting out a sigh of relief after Ormond's departure when Maisie said abruptly to him, "We should talk about it."

"About what?" Though he knew perfectly well. He had learned to understand the way her mind worked, to a degree. And he had been expecting this ever since Queen Elizabeth had made her uncomfortable demand.

Maisie seated herself with the kind of elegant flourish familiar to Stephen from a lifetime of highborn women. But her face was fierce and focused. "Have you made inquiries about Ailis since we arrived?"

It was the first time her name had been spoken between them in three years. The air shivered, and when Stephen blinked, he had the sudden sense of seeing everything more clearly.

"No. Have you?"

"Yes."

The breath caught in his throat. "And I suppose you want to tell me?"

She merely regarded him, the candlelight sliding across the angles of her face, her grey eyes alternately bright and shadowed.

Stephen sat down abruptly and dropped his head into his hands. "Tell me."

"Diarmid mac Briain changed his name to Kavanaugh when he married Ailis three years ago. For the sake of the clan." That, of course, Stephen had already known. Maisie herself had delivered the news when visiting him in the Tower of London after his arrest. Even then it had been no surprise. From the first week in Ailis's household, Stephen had known that the captain of the guard was in love with her. No, Diarmid would have had no qualms in changing his name if it brought him Ailis.

Maisie continued with more recent news. "The Kavanaughs continue to operate against those English left in Munster, primarily from Blackcastle. Ailis is the recognized strategist. The Earl of Desmond has trusted them in large part to hold the west while he and his men push against the coasts and the Pale."

He knew Maisie so well that he caught the slight undercurrent of reluctance in her recital. "What else?"

She did not look at him as she answered. "Diarmid and Ailis have children. A two-year-old son and one-year-old daughter."

Behind Stephen's closed eyes images swam. Ailis leaning in to kiss him, black hair against her bare shoulders. Diarmid backhanding the English spy across the face in disgust. Ailis's daughter, Liadan—inquisitive and generous and clever and brave and young. So very, very young.

And dead.

He felt hands against his, gently tugging, and he allowed Maisie to pull them away from his face. She knelt at his feet, her usually neutral expression wiped away by a distress equal to his.

"I'm sorry," she whispered. "I'm sorry you came back here. I'm sorry I didn't do more to stop it. I'm sorry you have to be reminded of what you've lost. Stephen, I'm so dreadfully sorry."

He said nothing; her rare vulnerability had touched another chord in him. A memory of an awful night. They had ridden miles, the two of them, carrying Liadan's little, broken body back to her mother. Stephen had found Maisie later that evening, weeping alone on the floor for a girl she had loved like her own. Her hair had been loose, a flood of silver-gilt fairness that lit up the darkness as surely as her irrepressibly brilliant mind.

And just like that, as Stephen recalled that night of sorrows, something deep within his soul clicked and tumbled loose.

For three years he had been celibate in mind as well as body. Ailis had broken his heart as thoroughly as he had ruined her life. After Ailis, Stephen would not take thoughtless comfort any longer, and a banished and disinherited nobleman was hardly a good catch on the marriage market. If he'd cared to contemplate marriage.

Maisie had been the perfect harbor. A relationship entirely intellectual that revived his interest in the world without encroaching on any of the painful memories of physical desire. For three years she had not been entirely real.

But in this moment there was nothing more real in the world than this girl—woman—so near to him that he could see the beat of blood beneath the fragile skin of her throat. Stephen had a nearly overwhelming urge to press his lips to that spot.

He sat back so hastily that Maisie almost fell over. He caught her and, apologizing, raised them both to standing. In that position he had to look quite a ways down to see her face. Her hands were still in his.

She looked wary. "If you would like to write to Ailis, I could find a way to get a letter to her."

Ailis had momentarily fled his mind. "That would be disastrous," he said, with less melancholy than he'd felt a moment before. "The best I can offer Ailis is to stay well away from her. We both understood that when we parted."

She withdrew her hands and he let his own drop, feeling foolish and oddly lonely.

"Mariota." It was the name he almost always called her, ever since he'd had to use it to break through her despair and save her life. She'd told him then that no one except her grandfather had ever called her Mariota.

Stephen didn't feel much like her grandfather tonight.

He cleared his throat and tried again, aware that he should retreat and clear his head, not frighten the poor, unsuspecting woman with incoherent babbling. "You do not have to worry about me. In this, the queen was quite right—though I probably won't tell her so. I needed to return to Ireland. I think you did, too. And I think we will both be the better for it once we are allowed to leave here and return to our lives."

Her expression had settled into wry forbearance. "As to that, I have had word from London that our company may depart Dublin

on or after November fifteenth. At least, that is when we will cease
to be paid, and I have no interest in remaining here voluntarily.
Have you?"

He shook his head. He had no interest in being anywhere that
Maisie wasn't. But how could he possibly tell her that? She considered him a friend, a trusted employee, almost a brother. He would
simply have to learn to swallow down this sudden impulse to throw
himself at her feet and declare his love.

24 October 1585

Julien,

> *The princess heads south soon in advance of her meeting with the*
> *queen. She does not require me for counsel at Kenilworth—not while she*
> *has Kit, Pippa, and Matthew—so I may as well come home.*

Lucette

> *P.S. That sounds dreadfully cold and awkward, doesn't it? I'm sorry. I*
> *do want to see you. I want to see you so badly I have a hard time thinking*
> *straight. It's a little irritating, actually. When have people ever had to re-*
> *peat themselves to me? When have I not been the quickest mind in the*
> *conversation? Never, that's when. But now I do spend all day distracted*
> *and all night restless. I have lost the trick of sleeping alone.*
>   *Am I still your Lucie mine?*

29 October 1585

If you have to ask, then I have failed you. Lucie mine—my heart, my
love, my light—wherever you are is home. I will count the hours until we
are together again.

Julien

Lucette refused her siblings' offers to ride with her to Compton
Wynyates. But she could not refuse Anabel's insistence on a detachment of guards to accompany her, so it was with three dozen armed
men that Lucette returned to the home of her married life. There
was perhaps no prettier aspect in England than the one revealed as
she crested the hill and looked down at her home. Red brick, tall
chimneys, dormer windows, and decorative castellations—she had
not realized how attached she had grown to this spot until now.

An outrider had gone ahead to warn the house, so it was not a
surprise to find people waiting as she rode through the arched entry
into the courtyard. She would always notice her husband first—most
people would, for he was taller than almost anyone she'd ever met
and he was far too attractive for his own good. He was already moving when she saw him, and by the time she reined in her horse, Julien
stood ready at her side.

"Welcome home, Lucie mine," he said softly enough that only she
could hear. She reached for his waiting hands, and he not so much
lifted her down as pulled her into his arms.

The reprieve lasted only a moment, for there were others watching. Most noticeably Felix. Who wasn't watching so much as glowering. Though the boy did not much resemble his uncle, the forbidding
expression he turned on her now was one with which Lucette had
grown familiar during the months she fell in love with Julien.

She didn't think Felix's glowering betokened the same end.

Julien dropped his hands and allowed Lucette to walk ahead of
him to the boy, who now topped her by more than an inch. "Felix,
how is it possible that you have grown again in so short a space?" she
asked.

His face was blankly polite. "Madame."

At her side, Julien asked sharply, "Is that how you speak to your
aunt?"

In tight and careful English, Felix replied, "Charlotte is my aunt. This is how I speak to the woman who pretended to love my father only to betray him."

"Felix!" Julien's hand shot out to grab the boy, but he whirled and left in a not entirely dignified escape.

Lucette stopped Julien when he made to follow. "Let him go. It is for Felix and me to work this out between us."

For though his face had been expressionless, his eyes had not. They were the eyes of a boy, in some ways still a child, who had lost mother and father and grandmother and grandfather and was stranded now in a foreign country. With the uncle he'd worshipped— before he'd murdered the boy's father. And with his uncle's wife, who had once agreed to become Felix's stepmother.

What a mess Nicolas LeClerc had made, of more lives than his own.

Not that she could claim to be doing much better at the moment. But in her time apart from Julien, Lucette had done a lot of thinking.

As though his mind marched with hers in every thought, Julien said, "And us? Are we to work this out between us?"

"We should withdraw. I do not think it a conversation for the courtyard."

Julien would likely have retreated to the library or a similar neutral space. But it was Lucette who chose, and she led him straight to their private chambers. She faced him in the small and elegant reception room, very aware of the bed looming behind the doors to her right.

She did not bother to sit. "It has been almost ten months now, Julien."

"I know it. To the day."

"So tell me—what happens two months from now?"

His voice tinged with cautious amusement, Julien said, "That feels like a trick question."

"In two months, with the approval of the physicians we have

agreed to heed—or you, at least, have agreed to heed—we resume the fullness of our marriage. Unless," she asked stingingly, "these months of marital celibacy have inclined you to look elsewhere?"

His face darkened and she was glad of it. Glad to rouse any emotion in him at all, even fury.

"I'll assume that is a no," she conceded. "Then you will be eager, no doubt, to have release once more. And then what? What if I once again fall pregnant and once again lose the child? What if the cycle continues on and on? Must we spend the next twenty years in either feast or famine?"

"Better that than to lose you."

"I have no wish to die, Julien, believe me. But I cannot live like this. Can you? Are you so resigned to long periods of absolute celibacy?"

She read the answer in the tightening of his shoulders and the way his eyes slanted away from hers. "What do you want from me, Lucie? It is your life."

"Yes, it is *my* life! So I should have some say in how it is lived. What do I want? I want this! Talk to me—tease me—argue with me—touch me. I will not break."

"Not from a touch."

"Are you so afraid of losing control? I trust you, Julien. It need not be all or nothing. Neither of us wants to refer to Nicolas, but surely we have both considered the same thing. I have been a wife long enough now to have a very good idea of what your brother once offered me as a husband."

Nicolas, who had been not only vicious and twisted and murderous—but who had been castrated just before the birth of his only son.

Of course there would be affection and even—how do I say this delicately?— pleasure. There is more than one way for men and women to experience pleasure. So Nicolas had said when he'd asked Lucette to marry him. And if Lucette had only been able to guess at some of those ways then, she had much clearer ideas now.

"Julien, why are you so afraid?" she asked. "I am sure you know as much as Nicolas did of women. No, that's not true. You know far more than he ever did, because he never considered women individually unless they could do something for him. But I am your wife, Julien. Why are you so content to keep your distance?"

"Content?" he choked. "You think me content? Ask the household about my short temper. Or the groomsmen about how hard I ride the horses. I nearly whipped Felix for insolence the other day . . . and I love that boy as though he were my own."

He did not touch her, but he did close the gap between them a little. "Can you not see how I am shaking for you? There is no contentment without your love, Lucie mine."

"Then let me give it."

"As you say—I am afraid."

"Why?"

"Because I seem to remember making a vehement, rather drunken speech to you one night about Nic's selfishness and how I would be much the better husband for you because I was a man whole and entire."

"And you're still trying to prove it after all this time? Nicolas is dead, Julien. He can only hurt us if we let him. To be a man whole and entire rests on much more than a single instinctive action— though, I warn you, I quite like that as well. But if you want me to obey the doctors, then we must find an accommodation."

She rested her palms against his chest, remembering the feel of his skin rather than the texture of fabric. "Let me be brave for the both of us," she whispered. "Let me love you. And show me how you love me in return."

They didn't make it to the bedchamber for some time. Neither of them cared.

THIRTEEN

I n the third week of November, Elizabeth awaited the arrival of
her daughter at Kenilworth Castle in an unusual state of nerves.
It had been nearly two years since she and Anne had been in the
same city, let alone the same room. Unfortunately, the initial meeting had to take place in public. Or, perhaps after all, fortunately—
for Elizabeth did not care to betray how much she had missed her
daughter. Even to her.

The setting could not have been more magnificent: the great hall
built two hundred years ago by John of Gaunt, Duke of Lancaster,
had soaring perpendicular lines of stone offset with windows and a
hammer-beam ceiling so impressively constructed that it allowed the
entire open space to be unsupported by pillars. Elizabeth had presented Kenilworth to Brandon Dudley when she made him Earl of
Leicester in 1580, and he had outdone himself to host this royal gathering. His wife, Nora, had truly come into her own now that she was
independent of her difficult mother, so that Kenilworth sparkled with
laughter and music and spirited conversation. There had been a mo-

ment or two this day when Elizabeth looked at her warm and lively
niece and silently said to her brother: *You would be proud of her, Will.*

Elizabeth had commanded an audience of courtiers, scholars, and
government officials to attend her at Kenilworth—an array of her
strongest supporters. Including, naturally, Dominic and Minuette
Courtenay. Though she conceded that they were here less for their
queen than to see their own children.

From where she stood in the great hall—herself adorned and polished and decorated to the highest degree—she heard the arriving
clatter of horses and murmurs of welcome from Lord Burghley. Elizabeth had long perfected the ability to remain still and composed
under any strain. But she could feel the faint tremor in her hands
and clasped them before her to mask it.

Lord Burghley appeared at the top of the elaborate steps, Anne at
his side. There were others behind her, but Elizabeth had eyes only
for her daughter. They'd been separated for almost two years, but it
might have been ten from the leaps Anabel had made in authority
and poise. They were disturbingly like rival queens facing one another across an expanse of polished chessboard, each assessing the
other's strengths and weaknesses.

Elizabeth had chosen a royal purple gown buttoned high to a
two-inch pleated ruff circling her slim throat. The sleeves were
close-fitted and the skirt split at the waist to flaunt a kirtle heavily
embroidered with gold thread. Atop the curls and twists of one of
her many wigs rested a diadem of pearls and gold.

In contrast, Anabel had dressed head to toe in black. The mourn-
ful colour and severe lines were as good as a public announcement: *I
stand with Spain.* Not that women all over Europe hadn't copied
Spain's fashions for decades, but somehow Anabel wore the gown in
such a way as to highlight her differences with England's queen. In
contrast to her mother's careful styling, Anabel's red-gold hair was
dressed in soft plaits, emphasizing the waves and gloss of her youth.
She wore not a single jewel.

With exquisite care, the Princess of Wales crossed the hall and made her obeisance. "Your Majesty."

There was politeness but no warmth to her voice. Although Elizabeth had expected as much, it stung a little. And made it easier to steady herself against the unexpectedly strong maternal pull.

"Let me see you." Elizabeth surveyed Anne carefully and critically. "I suppose the North has agreed with you. It is good of you to stir yourself long enough to attend on your queen."

"I was not aware I had a choice in the matter."

Oh, she was good. It was almost like hearing herself coolly oppose her brother. "There is always a choice." Elizabeth delivered it as a warning. "I am pleased with this one." Leaving no doubt that there were other choices with which she was less pleased.

There was a flash from Anne, a moment's amusement passed between them, then she stepped slightly aside to allow the others of her train to greet the queen. The first—insultingly—was Philip's meddling Jesuit, Tomás Navarro. It took no pretense for Elizabeth to eye him icily. And his contempt was certainly real enough. They had a cat amongst the pigeons here. Pray they had belled him sufficiently to give them warning.

Elizabeth acknowledged the others with hardly a pause, only giving Christopher an assessing gaze that he returned without flinching. But after him was his sister, and Elizabeth had certain things to say to Philippa Courtenay.

Primarily concerning the fact that she was now Philippa Harrington. "Well," Elizabeth noted drily, "no one could claim that marriage does not suit you. Three months a wife now, and still admirably . . . slender." It did no harm to point out to the gossips that there was no too-early baby in the mix here.

But there was impudence in the girl's hasty marriage, and Elizabeth would not let that pass. "It grieved us to realize how lightly you hold your queen's and your family's affections. To marry without word . . . was not wise."

Matthew Harrington, so like his quiet father, stood protectively next to his wife. He was not a man to be cowed by any authority, particularly not in defense of the woman he loved. "When has love ever marched with wisdom?" he asked. "Your Majesty," he added belatedly.

Elizabeth smiled. Those who knew her would know rightly how to read the warning there. "Admirably put. And as it stands, I have forgone my right of chastisement. That belongs to Lord Exeter. And Philippa's mother."

Every eye in the hall turned to Dominic, who stood stony-faced as only he could. On the other side of Minuette stood Carrie Harrington, neat as a wren in her gown of blue wool, eyeing her son with mingled affection and exasperation.

If Elizabeth had been Matthew Harrington, she would have felt more than a qualm at the sight.

It was a relief to move through the remaining necessary courtesies as quickly as possible and then retreat. Alone, for queen and princess needed to be marked keeping their distance from one another. There would be a few opportunities for private communication, but not immediately. Let Anne's household mingle with hers without the pressure of the queen's presence, so that curiosity might be assuaged on both sides.

And to confirm, to those suspicious eyes here and in Spain, that the gulf between the Tudor royals was widening to an almost unbreachable impasse. Everything depended on Philip believing that Anabel could be manipulated by Spain.

Walsingham came after her. "That went well."

She smiled fondly. "Only you would define that iciness as going well."

"It served its purpose."

"So it did. Tomás Navarro looked insufferably pleased with himself. So did Ambassador de Mendoza. You'll watch them, of course. But they'll be expecting that. It is their attitudes that will tell us more than their words. I suspect Navarro might be the sort of Jesuit to make enemies even amongst his own kind."

"I agree."

"Give me an hour to rest, Walsingham. Let it be seen as weakness, I don't mind. Not in a good cause, at least."

"And then?" he asked.

"And then," she repeated, slowly. "Send Christopher Courtenay to me. Philippa I could chastise publicly. Christopher requires more delicate handling."

Elizabeth could be delicate when she chose. That didn't mean she wouldn't also be implacable.

Christopher entered the queen's presence with a wariness unusual to him. She guessed that behind his elegant obeisance he was calculating whether he had done anything particularly reprehensible lately.

"Rumour preceded your coming, Lord Christopher. Even in the South we are hearing idle gossip about you and the Princess of Wales. It must stop."

He had become skilled at control, but he was not a master like his father. She saw the flinch of instinctive defiance. "I cannot stop rumours, Your Majesty. Surely that is a lesson I learned from you?"

"Don't play clever with me," she snapped. "I will not have my daughter's reputation dragged through the mud for the sake of a charming tongue. Already my court has received subtle complaints from Scotland about your behaviour during their visit."

"Are you ordering me to leave her service, Your Majesty?"

She smiled coldly. "You would like that, wouldn't you? So you could blame me. No, Kit"—and noted another flinch at her familiarity—"*you* must do this. I know my daughter. She is capable of wrecking all we have been working so hard to achieve out of sheer perversity.

"And also," Elizabeth conceded, "from the strength of her affections. I do not lightly discount what either of you feel. But the time for indulgence is past. I will sacrifice anything for the sake of England. And so must Anabel."

"What do you want of me?" he asked in a low voice.

"To make it easy for her. You are surrounded by beautiful women here. Take advantage of it. Not enough to cause a riot, but enough to still a few tongues. As long as you look at no one but my daughter, those who would split this kingdom in two have leverage. Turn your eyes elsewhere—and make Anabel believe it."

Christopher Courtenay must always have known his days were numbered. "Yes, Your Majesty."

Over the course of the next week at Kenilworth Castle, Kit applied himself to the task of womanizing. He couldn't decide what made it more uncomfortable—Anabel's presence or his parents'. He judged that at least his parents weren't likely to try and kill him because of it.

It wasn't that he didn't know how to talk to women. He'd always had a reputation for teasing charm and a lightness of heart that drew people to him. Though it had been tempered in the last years, it wasn't too difficult to remember how to flirt. And there were plenty of women willing to let him practice.

But he was older now. At twenty-three, most women expected more from him than flirtatious words or multiple dances. Almost at once it was clear that all Kit needed to do was start the matter. The women would finish it for him.

He let himself enjoy it. It wasn't so difficult—just stop paying attention to the critical voices in his head and let his instincts guide him. He was young and healthy and, unlike probably most men his age, a virgin. At last it was beginning to weigh on him.

Lettice Wixom quickly showed herself the most determined of those competing for his attention. The daughter of a prominent member of Parliament, Lettice was nineteen and merry and buxom. She'd been married at seventeen to an elderly Midlands landowner who had conveniently died after six months, leaving his young widow a wealthy woman looking for pleasure.

She promptly latched onto Kit to give it to her. He thought himself in control of the situation, until their fourth night at Kenilworth when she neatly managed to cut him away from the crowds and maneuvered him into an empty section of the loggia that led to the formal gardens. It was no hardship to kiss her, and if his conscience burned a bit at the thought of Anabel, it was not so difficult to submerge it in her warmth.

Her hands were skilled and far more experienced than his own. But he was a fast learner. Her giggles gave way to sighs of pleasure and at last she whispered, "I know a quiet way through the back of the castle. I have a private room," she teased.

A little breathlessly, he said, "I don't think that's wise. Surely someone would notice."

"My father was half drunk before we came out here. And he doesn't care."

"Mine does."

"Afraid of your father?" She breathed into his ear, her hands busy with the buttons of his jerkin.

"My mother, more like." Despite his words, he kept her pulled against him, hands encircling the corseted waist. His mouth trailed from her lips to the line of her jaw and farther down. He knew there were reasons this was a bad idea, but they were rapidly flying from his head. Any moment now she could simply crook her finger and he would follow her without thought.

"They might be glad to have the gossip dispelled," Lettice said. "And for certain, the queen will."

He stilled. "What gossip?"

"That you're sleeping with the princess."

For all that Kit knew such things were being murmured in shadows and corners, to hear it thus lightly spoken of shocked the desire right out of him. He stepped away from Lettice so sharply that her hands were left hanging in midair. He might have found her surprised expression comical if he wasn't suddenly, thoroughly furious.

"If you were a man, I would strike you for that. In point of fact, I have done so. No one speaks of Her Royal Highness in such terms."

"I didn't mean anything by it. Heavens, do you think I care? I know what it is to be sold off into a marriage not of your choosing. Why should she not take her pleasures where she can?"

His hand had actually raised of its own accord, and Kit forced himself to drop it without slapping her. "Go. Now. And keep your mouth shut."

His temper might have been disastrous with another woman, resulting in either tears or tantrum. But Lettice was not easily insulted. "You know where to find me when you want me. You might think me a foolish girl, but I am not wrong when I tell you the best thing you could do to serve Her Highness is to flaunt your presence in other women's beds."

Kit was the one who stalked away, leaving the girl bemused and probably pitying behind him. If he'd been somewhere familiar, he'd have known where to go to be alone. But at Kenilworth, from sheer bad luck, he entered through what he thought was an unattended door into a side corridor only to walk straight into his sister.

On second thought, knowing Pippa, it probably wasn't luck of any kind.

Without a word between them, Kit shut his eyes and swore under his breath. Then he opened them. "Where is she?" he asked.

"I'll take you."

She did not lead him to Anabel's privy chamber or bedchamber. Instead, he followed her to a quiet room, kept discreetly away from the bulk of the guests. Pippa's room, he knew at once. Well, Pippa and Matthew's.

Of course there was a bed in here, but Kit had never felt less like kissing Anabel than he did now. She stood at the window, her back to him, and waited until Pippa had left to stand guard before saying, "I always thought Lettice Wixom an uncommonly silly girl. But then, I suppose it is not her conversation that attracts you."

"You told me to flirt," he said. "Do you not remember it?"

"That was not flirting. If I hadn't sent Pippa to find you when I did, would she have had to look in Lettice's bed?"

"No," he flared back at her, and that finally made her turn and face him. "Pippa found me coming back to the castle. Alone."

He could see the whiteness of her face outlined like the smooth edges of a marble statue. But her eyes were not any sort of remote mask. Fury, fear, hurt . . . it cut through Kit's anger like a dagger.

"What," he asked helplessly, "do you want from me, Anabel?"

"What do I want? Or what am I allowed to have?"

"My point exactly."

They held like that for a few painful moments. Kit had the sense of a tipping point being reached. This could not hold forever. But he had hoped for a little longer.

"Come here," he said softly, and offered her his hand. She took it and allowed him to pull her to a bench. They sat together, touching nowhere but their hands. The bleakness of her expression told him that she had already anticipated his words. But they still needed to be said.

"There is nothing useful for me to do at Kenilworth," he announced. "The best thing I can do for you and England is to fulfill my responsibilities as Lieutenant General of the Marches. I'll leave for the border in the morning."

"Do you wish to be released from that responsibility?" she asked distantly.

"What do I wish . . . or what am I allowed to have?"

It had the desired effect of making her laugh a little. But her blue eyes were serious when she said, "If you ask it of me, I will release you from my service. I am certain the queen would offer you an equal appointment."

"I've put in a lot of effort along the border. I think I can serve well there. But I will not come to your household unless necessary."

"Fair enough. That should please even the most stringent of my critics."

"Anabel, we should speak of what comes after. After the plotting, after the coming war . . . after the wedding."

"Are you saying that your loyalty to me extends thus far and no farther?"

"I'm saying that your husband may have strong opinions about me." Especially if James knew how the amber and dark rose scent of Anabel's perfume led Kit to imagine locking the door and making use of the bed behind them.

"It matters not. James of Scotland will run neither my household nor my court."

"It *will* matter. You know it will." If only because Kit didn't know if he was selfless enough to serve near Anabel once she was another man's wife.

"I am not a fool, Kit. I know that one day you will marry as well. And when I think of that, I believe I know how you feel about James Stuart. I don't know which I would prefer—that you marry a woman you can love, or that you marry one who will never give you what I could in friendship and devotion. That is selfish, I know it."

"Not so selfish," he murmured. He wanted to pull her closer, to rest her head on his shoulder. Instead, he traced patterns on her hand with his thumb while he spoke. "I've no doubt James Stuart is a good man. I do not wish you a life of misery. But the thought of him being allowed to kiss you . . . to touch you . . . that your nights will be given to anyone not me?"

Kit shrugged, the words painful to pronounce. "When I consider that, I understand why you were angry with me tonight. And I would like to vow that I, at least, will never marry."

"That is hardly practical. Nor would I expect it. You are young, Kit. I would not condemn you to a lonely life.

"But could I ask you one thing?" she added wistfully. "A request, and not a royal one. Will you promise not to marry until after I do? I know we need to distance ourselves. I know it would be wise for you to be seen courting another woman. But I do not know if I will be strong enough to do what I must without hope. You are my hope,

Kit. Always and forever. Even if it is a lost hope . . . will you let me keep it as long as I can?"

He could not hold himself apart any longer. He leaned in and touched his forehead to hers. It was easier to speak without looking at her just now. "I swear it," he whispered. "And no matter where I am or what I am doing . . . I will carry you with me, *mi corazon.* Always."

As their time at Kenilworth Castle drew to a close, Anabel made a polite, if remote, farewell to her mother. The queen departed first, to spend one night with the Duke and Duchess of Exeter at nearby Wynfield Mote. Kit had already left for the Marches, leaving behind a buzz of gossip that confirmed the wisdom of his departure. Anabel had always known how to conduct herself with propriety, but it was noticeably harder to do so when her soul was rubbed raw.

In the early afternoon after her mother's departure, Anabel very publicly withdrew to her private chambers. Her ladies let it be known that she had a debilitating headache and had no wish to be disturbed. A short time later Philippa Courtenay Harrington left Kenilworth Castle as well, following her parents home with her husband Matthew in tow. They would return in time to accompany Anabel tomorrow on her departure north.

Three miles outside of Kenilworth, Matthew shot an oblique glance at the woman riding beside him. "Are you well, Your Highness?"

"Don't call me that," Anabel shot back. "For anyone watching just now, I am your loving wife."

At least, she certainly hoped so. The point was for Anabel and her mother to be able to speak freely without fear of watching eyes. It was important that they maintain the illusion of distance and a severe difference of opinion as to the ruling of England. It was Pippa who had come up with the idea of she and Anabel switching places—

and if it was Pippa's idea, it argued that the plan would be successful. Once retired behind closed doors at Kenilworth, the princess had changed from her gown of heavy black silk into a chestnut-coloured one belonging to Pippa, with a dark brown safeguard as an overskirt to protect the gown while riding. Madalena had plaited and hidden Anabel's distinctive hair beneath a tight linen wimple and the folds of a heavy hooded cloak, and the princess had departed unremarked with Matthew at her side.

They covered the distance to Wynfield Mote in cold and silence and it was a relief to see the lights of the manor house that had given Anabel more hours of warmth and joy than any royal palace. She and Matthew crossed the moat to the interior courtyard, where they were met by Dominic Courtenay and ushered out of the cold.

Only once inside Wynfield's enclosing walls did Anabel throw back her hood and consign her cloak into Carrie Harrington's waiting hands. Then Matthew vanished with his mother and Dominic asked her, "Ready?"

"It is good of you to take these risks, my lord."

He raised skeptical brows. "Risky to welcome both my present and future queens into my home? Most men would give their right hand for such an honour." He looked wryly down at his own missing left hand and, surprisingly, smiled.

"But you are not most men, Lord Exeter. And my thanks to you are not as the thanks I offer to others."

Still smiling, a little sadly, Dominic leaned over and kissed her on the cheek. "Let's get you to your mother so we can get you safely on your way back. I know my daughter—Pippa will find it difficult to stay confined to a single chamber while pretending to be you."

The queen greeted her in the study situated at one corner of the quadrangular house. The fire was lit and the space small enough for a coziness unusual in the chambers inhabited by royalty. Elizabeth Tudor could never appear less than royal, but in this house she looked softer than elsewhere.

"Any difficulties?" she asked as Dominic ushered Anabel in and then closed the door on the two women.

Anabel shook her head. "Not on our part. And I don't anticipate anyone breaking into my chamber at Kenilworth to confirm I'm the one in my bed. As long as I can slip back in without being stopped, all will be well."

"And if you cannot?"

"Then I let it be thought I summoned Kit to Wynfield Mote to meet me away from prying eyes," she replied airily.

Elizabeth made a skeptical sound. "Let us hope it does not come to that. So, to business."

"Tomás Navarro has been writing secretly to Philip Howard and other influential Catholics. Fortunately for me, the Earl of Arundel trusts my intentions more than he does those of a Spanish priest. For now. It is when Arundel stops passing on those letters that it will be time to worry."

"We cannot afford to wait out this winter. Every day must prepare us for war. With the concentration of Spanish troops along the Irish coast, our months are numbered before they are headed to our shores."

"How do you suggest I prepare the North without alienating Navarro and risking my new bonds with the Catholics?" Anabel asked.

"By playing on every Englishman's overriding prejudice—the suspicion of foreigners. It should not be difficult to provide Navarro an opportunity to overreach himself. I suspect his first move will be to co-opt your cooperation. I don't know how, but I promise you, at some point he will approach you with a deal the Spanish think will ensure your compliance."

"Do I accept that deal?"

"That will be for you to decide," Elizabeth said. "We both know that our chances of defeating Spain rise with each month—each day—we can preserve the fiction of our estrangement. The longer we can wait to spring the trap, the better."

"The trap only works if the North is convinced of Spain's perfidy.

It cannot be merely a religious war. It must be seen as a fight for England's survival."

"And so it is. Do not ever make the mistake of forgetting that. You will know how to frame it, Anne. I trust your instincts." Elizabeth drew a deep breath and let it out in a sigh. "And if the Spanish are not so easily accommodating as to provide a reason for the North to revolt, then create one."

"You are confident in your preparations in the South?"

"With Dominic leading the way? We are confident enough. Which is to say, in any fight we will almost certainly be outnumbered in terms of trained soldiers. But only if the Spanish can land. I trust our navy to ensure that does not happen. It will be up to you and your Wardens of the Marches to protect the northern ports. And your relationship with James Stuart should provide any extra men you need."

"So it should."

Her mother glanced at her sharply. "You are discontented?"

"No more than any royal woman unable to choose."

Elizabeth waited, but when Anabel declined to elaborate, she shook her head. "None of this will matter if we fall to Spain. How much choice will you be allowed with the Inquisition in force amongst our people? Who might you be forced to marry in that case? It will hardly matter, because the Spanish will ensure whoever it is will take England's crown matrimonial and reign as king in your place. Is that what you wish—to be nothing more than a figurehead?"

"I assume you do not actually require an answer."

"No. I think we are finished. Let's get you and Matthew returned before anyone does take it into their head to check personally on your health."

Neither of them was much for sentiment, so Anabel was a little surprised when her mother walked out with her to bid farewell. But it was just as well, because there was the sound of running feet and then Dominic was at the door of the Great Hall, Minuette two steps behind him.

Elizabeth looked swiftly between them. "What is wrong?"

"Word from Carlisle. The garrison received a message from Lord Maxwell, in the Scots West March, about an unexpected landing at Dumbarton."

"Who?" the queen barked.

"Against all odds and expectations, Mary Stuart has landed in Scotland."

FOURTEEN

Maisie received the first notice of disaster three days before departing Dublin. Long accustomed to keeping her own counsel, she swallowed against the shock of the letter from Edinburgh and awaited further news. It came swiftly—by the time they boarded ship she had received eight letters in all. Each, unfortunately, elaborating on the same theme.

In your absence, your brother Robert is making a serious play for the Sinclair Company.

It wasn't that she was shocked by Robert's attempt. But she had never dreamed that he might be successful. How easily he would be able to subvert men who she believed trusted her. It seemed her sex was a bigger obstacle than she'd feared. Success wasn't enough. She would always be second choice because she was female.

Andrew Boyd was still on her side. Several of the warning letters had come from him. And three other members of the board still held with Boyd. If her brother had been the extent of the threat, Maisie would have been confident in her ability to handle it. But Robert, either with shrewd advice or through his own cunning, had gone to the king.

Maisie cursed colourfully when she received that news—a string of dockside words that would have confirmed the bad opinion of many about women who meddled in business. Because King James, from an excess of caution as well as an inborn distrust of ambitious women, had sided with Robert.

No matter what the king thought, however, he could not simply hand over the company to Robert or override the decisions of the company's board. But he could—and apparently had—put pressure on the board. Robert had not argued directly for her removal. Rather, he had pointed out her youth, her innate fragility as a female, her susceptibility to sentiment, the fact that—at only nineteen—surely she would marry again. Which meant unscrupulous men wishing to marry her simply to get their hands on the Sinclair Company.

Would it not be wise, Robert had proposed to the king, to require her to marry *before* she could wield such control? That would allow the board to consider her future husband as a critical factor in determining her leadership. And so the king had decreed: if Maisie Sinclair wished to be considered a fit leader, she must marry.

Robert did not expect her to, of course. He knew her stubbornness enough to guess that she would rather keep her pride and abandon both their grandfather's company and, perhaps, Scotland. And so she would have to do. If the king could not be brought to change his mind—and Boyd wrote that he did not consider it likely at this point—what choice would Maisie have but to leave before she could be thrown out?

But she did not want to leave Scotland. She could take the mercenaries, they belonged entirely to her—but their commander? Stephen was needed where war was most likely to break out. Without her, surely he would return to England and take up the place the queen wished for him.

Maisie would have preferred to remain on deck in the open air as they sailed out of Dublin into the Irish Sea, but late November was not kind. Though the winds were favorable, there were bursts of sleet and the deck was slippery underfoot. So she sat in her tiny cabin and pondered what she would do when they landed.

A knock sounded and she sighed. "Come in," she called.

"What's wrong?" Stephen asked straight out.

"What makes you think something is wrong?"

He stared for a moment, then abruptly sat down next to her on the edge of the narrow bed. For all her vaunted self-possession, Maisie found it difficult to be in such close quarters. Stephen's hand came up to her face, and she waited dizzily for him to touch her. But he didn't, quite. Instead, he sketched the air above her cheek. "When you are angry, your eyes become the grey of the North Sea in storm."

She handed him the latest letter from Andrew Boyd wordlessly, and waited for him to read it. She knew every word by heart.

King James commands your presence at court as soon as you reach Edin-burgh. He will tell you that you are temporarily suspended from the Sin-clair board, subject to making a respectable marriage. I'm sorry, lass. I do not think he will be moved from this point.

Bless him, Stephen did not waste time in outrage or surprise. "I can think of three responses," he said.

"First?"

"I march your mercenaries into Edinburgh and persuade the king to change his mind."

Despite herself, Maisie grinned. "Tempting but impractical. Unless you are looking to be banished from every European nation one after the other. Second?"

"I march your mercenaries against Robert and persuade him to renounce his claims and banish himself from Scotland."

"Persuade?"

"Perhaps with a shade more violence behind it." He said it with a disconcerting relish.

"And third?"

"You comply."

Maisie's eyebrows shot up so far she could almost feel them against her hairline. "By marrying some greedy stranger the king or my brother proposes?"

"By marrying me."

The silence was tangible, and Maisie felt as though something heavy had landed on her chest. She could hardly draw breath to speak.

"Also highly impractical," she managed, with what she hoped was amusement.

"But tempting?" Those hazel eyes of his slid across her face and she looked away.

Not for anything would she reveal just how tempting. "I can manage. There is no need to offer yourself as sacrifice."

"It would be no sacrifice." He spoke as though deliberating which words to choose so there would be no misunderstanding. "Surely such a clever woman recognizes how important you have become to me."

Important. Not quite the same thing as loved. "Your family and your queen would be horrified."

"I think you underestimate my family. And the queen cannot have it both ways—if I am no longer one of her nobles, then she can have no say in my personal life."

"Marry me and you will never be restored to your title."

He smiled grimly. "All the more reason. I do not want it."

"Stephen—"

"Mariota, you need not be afraid. If it helps, consider this simply an extension of our friendship. There need be no personal awkwardness. The marriage would be for you to define. I would never press you for . . . well . . ."

No more he would, more's the pity for her. "Yes, I see," she found herself saying despite her better judgment. "May I have time to consider it?"

"To weigh the benefits and drawbacks? I would expect no less of you."

He stood as abruptly as he'd done everything else in this astonishing conversation. Maisie stayed where she was, watching him covertly, his height and elegance and the straight lines of his back and shoulders. There was an awful lot to notice in just the two seconds before he reached the door.

Then Stephen paused, and she got to her feet, wondering wryly if he had come to his senses and was about to get himself out of a situation he'd never intended to wander into.

He looked back at her, a slanting glance over his shoulder. "There is no one else I could envision marrying. Not after Ireland."

Because of Ailis, he surely meant. *Because I will never love again as I loved her, but you could forgive me that and live with what is left.*

Could she live with what was left? Stephen would never love her, not as he had loved Ailis. And not as Maisie herself loved him. He would be kind, for he was incapable of being other than that. Clearly he was not interested in her body, but she believed that their minds did connect.

It was far more than Maisie had ever expected to have. She just didn't know if it was enough.

After his abrupt proposal to Maisie, Stephen took himself equally abruptly out of her way. He could hardly believe what he'd said and was afraid if he stayed any longer his matter-of-fact logic would give way to an outpouring of sentiment that would surely frighten her. Fortunately, the seas proved troublesome and every hand was needed to effect the difficult crossing. They had to put in at Belfast for two days and at the Isle of Arran for three. It was easy in those conditions to maintain a distance of cordiality and politeness.

But the first week of December the skies cleared, and finally their ship began the tricky navigation through the western peninsula to the mouth of the River Clyde and the port of Dumbarton. It was only then that Maisie approached him.

"We should speak before we land," she announced. There was no indication of what she meant to say. With heart beating irregularly, Stephen followed her to her cabin.

Neither of them sat. Stephen leaned against the closed door, hoping he looked more cool than he felt. Maisie faced him with an expression that gave nothing away.

She had only to speak two words. "I agree."

The relief that swept him kept him against the door, this time for support rather than effect. He had to swallow against his first reaction, which was to smile broadly and take her in his arms. He could not frighten the bird just when it had flown into his hand.

"I'm glad," he said, striving for the practical tone she would expect.

"On one condition," she added.

He cocked his head curiously.

Maisie looked away as she stated her condition. "That we marry before reaching Edinburgh. King James may not entirely approve of an Englishman, and I will not risk anyone else meddling in the arrangement we have come to. Better to confront them all with a fait accompli."

"Agreed."

"Your parents won't mind?" she asked. "I mean, of course they will mind, they've already had one child marry without notice this year and I am hardly the wife they would choose for you. I suppose I mean, will they ever forgive me?"

That brought him away from the door with a jolt. She sounded so . . . uncertain. He took her cold hands in his. "There is no need for forgiveness. We will do what we must to protect your company and yourself. And when we have secured your position in Edinburgh, we will ride south and explain it to my parents."

Stephen wanted to smooth her hair, to cup her chin in his hands, make some gesture of affection. He refrained. "They will love you, Mariota. Rather more than they love me, I expect. You have nothing to fear."

"I appreciate what you are giving up, Stephen. I do. I will make no demands on you. You must consider yourself free in every important respect."

That was not encouraging. "Demands?"

She blushed, a subtle wash of colour across her cheekbones. "You surely must want children. Title or not, you are the oldest son in an important family. It will be expected of you. I have no objection . . . that is . . ."

Stephen had to drop his eyes, certain Maisie would mark his disappointment. She was hardly throwing herself at him, was she? Not very flattering. But perhaps, in time, she would come to love him the same way he loved her. Soul and body.

Or perhaps not. "I have no objection to bearing your children," she continued firmly. "I also have no objection to how you choose to meet any other . . . needs you might have. I am quite certain you will be discreet."

After that extraordinary speech, what on earth was he supposed to answer? Tell her she had misread him completely? Confess that for months now, without even being aware of it, he had not been able to envision any woman in his bed but her? Maisie needed him in order to protect her place in the company. That was all.

He had promised her that the marriage would be hers to define. And Stephen was, if nothing else, a man of his word. "That you will allow me to help you is quite satisfaction enough. Children need not be a question between us. Certainly not now."

But as he pressed a chaste kiss to her cheek to seal their bargain,

Stephen felt as though the children the two of them might have were haunting him forlornly. Dark like him, or moonlight pale like Maisie? Her brains, of course, and her courage. He was twenty-six years old—he'd never especially thought about children. Until now, when the woman he loved seemed prepared to bargain for them simply as an offering to his pride.

Not the ideal way to begin a marriage. But for all that, Stephen could not bring himself to regret it.

The Spanish court passed Christmas at El Escorial, the beautiful palace wrought almost entirely from King Philip's imagination. The only thorn in the season was the continuing silence as to Mary Stuart's current whereabouts. She must have left Waterford by now, even with the worst of seas. She could not mean to spend all winter in Ireland, not with Spanish troops concentrating along the east coast in preparation for supporting the English invasion. There would be, at least, no shortage of ships and soldiers able to defend her, but no commander wanted a royal woman to protect in such a delicate situation—and certainly not a woman as politically dangerous as Mary. Philip told himself the ships escorting her back to Spain would have had to sail quite far south in order to avoid drawing too near England's coast, thus causing the delays . . . but he was grateful that he had not given in to her pleas to send Alexander with her.

Christmas with children was enchanting, and Philip took great pleasure in the time he spent with his sons. His time with Anne had been so circumscribed by distance and cirumstance that he had few memories of playing with her. He'd had another child once, though . . . a boy who, even at the age of four, had been dangerously willful. Independence was a trait to be cultivated, but reckless violence was not. Carlos had given far more hours of heartache than he ever had of joy, and his death almost twenty years ago had not been greatly regretted. But every now and then, when Philip saw a flicker of familiarity in the tilt of Charles's head or the high pitch of Alex-

ander's chatter, he recognized the cost of being a king first and foremost. Before even a father.

Anne had written to him, a rarity that he marked down to Christmas goodwill. She had said nothing of Ireland or the Netherlands,
nothing of her mother, nothing of religion. So many topics were
banned between them that her letter had been little more than polite inquiries about her half brothers' health and gossip from her
own household. Philip had shaken his head when he learned of
Philippa Courtenay's hasty wedding to a man not of her class, but
Anne was clearly touched by the romance of it. Though she had
added, in words as tart as her mother's: *She's a braver girl than I, to run
the risk of offending the Duke of Exeter. But then, some fathers are prone to
forgive their daughters any manner of sins.*

Not like you, ran the unwritten corollary.

The correspondence from Tomás Navarro was more revealing.
The priest's letters from Kenilworth Castle arrived in a bundle on
the second day of 1586, and Philip read them alone. One had to sort
through the Jesuit's prejudices, but otherwise his reports were concise and clear.

*The queen and the princess were not more than civil to one another in pub-
lic . . . spent no time speaking privately . . . When the queen expressed dissatis-
faction with the attendance of the Earl of Arundel, the princess forbore to
listen . . . the princess quarreled with Lord Christopher Courtenay and he
rode back to the Scots border on his own . . . they say there was a woman in
it . . .*

About damn time, Philip thought in a rare burst of profanity.
He'd begun to fear that Christopher Courtenay was that rarest of
creatures—a man so devoted to a single woman that he could not be
swayed by any temptation. When the Courtenays had visited Spain
several years ago, Philip had gone so far as to offer the boy a Spanish
bride. And when the Duke of Exeter declined on his son's behalf,
Philip had waited fatalistically for his daughter to make an enormous error.

He should have trusted her. Anabel not only had his own moral character, but Elizabeth's strong pragmatic streak. That didn't mean he wasn't grateful for whomever the unknown woman was who had finally persuaded the strong-minded Christopher Courtenay from the path of hopeless devotion.

On the other hand . . . this might be just the crack in Anne's certainty that could be profitably exploited for her own good. Philip took his ponderings to Mass at his private chapel in El Escorial. While the monks sang service, their voices floating from behind the sail vaults of the church, Philip sought the will of God. For his daughter. For England. For the souls of all the people wandering so far from the paths of light.

And when Mass was finished, Philip knew what he would do next.

Not only for Anne's sake. This was more than a matter of battle plans and troop movements. This was a crusade. And one did not launch a crusade without meticulous and wide-ranging preparation.

After Mass, Philip retired to his private study and the hours of daily and solitary work ahead of him. He loathed traveling and, other than to England four times during his marriage, had not been out of Castile in twenty years. To compensate for his lack of personal presence, his governors and generals and advisors abroad sent long, detailed reports almost daily.

These *consultas* formed the basis of his control of the far-flung Spanish Empire. His soldiers in Ireland had been disentangled from Irish engagements and held themselves ready to support the Enterprise of England. Philip had allotted five hundred soldiers to bolster the Earl of Desmond in holding what they had gained from England. Frankly, Philip didn't much care if Desmond held on. Not politically, at least. And as for religion—well, all he need do was defeat England and Ireland would be preserved.

The news from the Netherlands was less encouraging. The rebels had been fighting for fifteen years and showed a continuing reckless disregard for Spain's strength or God's truth. His nephew, Alessandro Farnese, had been Governor-General there since 1578, following in the footsteps of his mother, Margaret of Parma. Margaret, Philip's illegitimate half sister, had served him well enough in her time, but he never trusted anyone wholly. Not even his own blood.

But the month's most shocking news did not come in the form of a *consulta*. It was hand-delivered from a courier who was covered in sweat and grime from his desperate ride to El Escorial. Clearly he had known the significance of his message, if not its details. The details were shocking and desperate enough to make even Philip lose his control and exclaim aloud.

Mary Stuart, Queen of Spain, being overtaken in the Irish Sea, has been forced into harbor at Dumbarton, Scotland. It is not yet known if she will be welcomed by her former subjects, or if resentments against her still run high enough for her liberty to be constrained.

He had warned her this Irish venture was a bad idea. But though Philip would protest furiously any affront to his pride and his queen, he could not bring himself to be personally enraged. He had always known Mary was her own worst enemy. Perhaps the Scots would do him a favour.

3 January 1586
Wynfield Mote

After the tense and intentionally difficult council at Kenilworth Castle between Elizabeth and Anabel, Dominic and I remained at Wynfield for Christmas. I consider myself accustomed now to the absence of our grown children, but Christmas is difficult without them. There are so many memories here of excited faces and high voices and bare feet dashing across cold floors in play. Or, sometimes, fighting. And not just Kit and Stephen. Pippa was always a peacemaker, but Lucie could more than hold her own against her brothers, and she never hesitated to use her lofty superiority as the oldest to remind them so.

It is much quieter now. And yet, there is still the heart of my happi-

ness, for Dominic has always been the foundation of our lives. Mourning for the past is tempered, as always, by the security of his love.

We will remain here until the weather breaks or until events force us back into the world. It will no doubt be sooner than we would wish.

12 January 1586
Wynfield Mote

Thankfully, Lucie has begun writing to us again—as her parents, not as the queen's supporters. And although she has never entirely regained the lightheartedness of her childhood, I can detect once more the laughter and sparkle beneath her dry wit. It can mean only one thing—she has made her peace with Julien. That is one less worry in the troubles to come.

As for Pippa, she is keeping her own counsel more than she usually does. Her reticence might be nothing more than being wrapped up in her new husband, but I doubt it. Does she not understand that my imagination supplies much worse scenarios than whatever the truth is? One day my children will be parents and then perhaps they will begin to comprehend.

Kit writes short missives sent from his constant travels along the border. I know better than to expect personal outpourings from him. And Stephen has sent only one letter since he left for Ireland.

Time to shut the door on the outside world, even that of our children. Those who think passion must necessarily die with age . . . well, they are not married to Dominic. Or me.

15 January 1586
Wynfield Mote

So much for the closed doors. A messenger arrived from Kit in the North, riding as though the devil were on his heels. We expected more news about Mary Stuart and her enforced stay in Dumbarton while King James decides what is to be done with her. But the news was much more shocking

*than that. For though the messenger was sent through the Warden of the
West March, the message itself was from Stephen.*

On January 2, I married Mariota Sinclair. I apologize for the
shock. We intend to come south as soon as can be arranged.

*I hardly know what to think. Are we such frightening parents that
half of our children dared not risk coming to us in advance of marriage?
Or even wish our presence at such a moment? Dominic and I may have
married in secret, but there were hardly any adults we might have asked!
Only Dominic's mother, who like as not would not have known her son in
any case.*

*Where I was the one most upset to miss Pippa's wedding, Dominic has
taken Stephen's secrecy much more to heart. It is hard for him, missing his
sons. Perhaps because he always found it more difficult to tell them how
he felt.*

> *22 January 1586*
> *Wynfield Mote*

*We are riding tomorrow to Compton Wynyates to spend a week with Lu-
cette and Julien. If the weather holds, Pippa and Matthew intend to join
us. I don't know which topics will be the most delicate—political or personal.*

*After that, Elizabeth wants us back in London. Spring will be here
before we know it. We must be prepared for whatever comes.*

FIFTEEN

The Sinclair mercenary company spent nearly a month in Dumbarton after reaching the Scottish port in December. Officially, to ensure against reckless action before someone in authority could give orders as to what to do with Mary Stuart. With a complement of Spanish officers from the unlucky ship under uneasy confinement as well, the governor was glad to have additional military support, and Stephen was happy enough to offer help. It couldn't hurt to do anything that might dispose King James to gratitude just now.

Behind his professional demeanor, Stephen was savagely glad that Mary Stuart was once more under threat of confinement. She deserved that and more for the deaths of Renaud LeClerc and Duncan Murray.

The delay in Dumbarton gave Stephen and Maisie time for their banns to be posted the required three Sundays in the local parish of the Church of Scotland. Stephen spent nearly every day of that wait certain that Maisie would change her mind. But soon enough, on a day of high winds and freezing snow, the two of them stood before a

Calvinist priest and made their vows. The marriage service of the Scots church was not as appealing or musical to Stephen's ear as that of Elizabeth's prayer book, but the essentials were the same. Perhaps a little more dwelling on the physical nature of their vows—ironic, Stephen thought, for a church that seemed to find such relations distasteful.

One body, one flesh, one blood ... the husband has no more right or power over his own body, but the wife ... and therefore to avoid fornication every man ought to have his own wife ... and they twain shall be one flesh, so that they are no more two but are one flesh ...

Stephen preferred the Church of England service, which dwelt with rather more tolerance—even joy—on the union of husband and wife. *With this ring I thee wed, with my body I thee worship ...*

Just as well to have the sterner version, since there was little chance of him being allowed to worship Maisie in that particular manner. If his bride was at all worried about the service's command to keep each other from harlots—after she had given him carte blanche to seek them out—she gave no sign of it. From the subdued wardrobe she'd taken to Dublin, Maisie had chosen a gown of wintergreen more suited to a sermon than a wedding. But her hair was dressed less severely than normal, and the silver gilt fairness was a celebration of its own.

She allowed him a brief kiss after they were pronounced man and wife, but other than the pearl ring he'd purchased in Dumbarton for her to wear, their relationship resumed its normal businesslike course without disruption. Maisie wrote and received letters— taking care not to announce her marriage to Edinburgh; she preferred to do that in person—and Stephen trained his men as much as possible in the January weather and sent a brief notice to his parents of the wedding.

At last, a royal clerk arrived with instructions from King James.

As you are in Dumbarton with a military company under your command, we desire you to protect and guard our mother, Mary Stuart, from

*Dumbarton to Blackness Castle near Linlithgow. We trust you to keep
the journey swift and quiet, as it would not do to cause Her Majesty trouble along the way. Keep her apart from the people; there will be royal
guards to provide discreet shelter and aid along the way.*

*We urge you to remember her feminine nature, her false charm, her
perversity in acting from impulse. Do not be swayed.*

That was hardly likely, Stephen thought grimly. In fact, he would
wager the Scots king knew perfectly well the history between his
mother and Stephen Courtenay. During the last months of her imprisonment in England, Mary had welcomed him into her household and shown every sign of liking him. Then she had recklessly
and carelessly put both Anabel and Lucette in grave danger, and Stephen had revealed himself in the aftermath to be Walsingham's
agent.

I was always your enemy, lady. Never more so than now, with the
murders of two innocent men sacrificed to her pride. No, Stephen
would not be susceptible to Mary Stuart's charms. Which argued
that this would be a particularly unpleasant journey across Scotland
in the snows and biting winds of winter.

He was not wrong.

At first Queen Mary flat-out refused to leave Dumbarton with
Stephen. Or, as she called him haughtily to his face, "a false-tongued
heretic with the heart of a serpent."

When he informed her that her assent was not required, she
switched tactics and decided she wanted nothing more than to see
her son, and treated Stephen and his company as a royal escort of
honour. If Maisie had not also been traveling with them, Stephen
would have lost his temper before the first day was scarcely begun.
But Maisie's dry wit and mordant sense of humour pulled him back
from the edge of rage and outright insubordination.

It took eight miserable days to cross Scotland. He grudgingly admitted that it must be painful for Queen Mary to return to the landscape of her nation, despite the fact that she had spent far more of

her life outside Scotland than within it. She became quieter the closer they drew to Edinburgh. On the last day, as they approached Linlithgow, she clearly expected that palace to be her destination.

When they passed it by, she sent a guard for Stephen. With a sigh and a curse for King James, who had cravenly left this final announcement to an Englishman, Stephen halted the company. He dismounted to speak to the queen.

"Why are we not entering Linlithgow?" she demanded imperiously. "It is nearly nightfall and we must recover before going on to Edinburgh."

"We are not going to Edinburgh."

"Has my son come to meet me? If so, surely it is at Linlithgow Palace. He knows it would mean much to meet him again where I myself was born."

Mary Stuart had indeed been born at Linlithgow in December 1542, and it was there just six days later that word had come of her father's death and her new role as Queen of Scotland. A significant place. Too significant to allow Mary entrance.

"The king is in Edinburgh," Stephen said curtly. "He has prepared quarters for you at Blackness Castle until such time as decisions are made as to your meeting."

"Blackness!"

Well might she look horrified, for Blackness Castle was best known in this century as a state prison. Cardinal Beaton, the Earl of Angus . . . Blackness was not a comforting destination for a woman whose last months in Scotland had been spent either as a prisoner or on the run from her own subjects.

But she had no choice. And say what you like about Mary Stuart, she was undeniably royal in her bearing. She made no further protest. It was an enormous relief for Stephen to lead the queen's carriage and a small party of his men—and Maisie—onto the spit of land that jutted into the Firth of Forth. There, Blackness Castle perched forbiddingly.

It was known colloquially as "the ship that never sailed," for the castle was shaped to fit its site, with north and south towers like a stem and stern and a central tower called the mainmast. Designed primarily as an artillery fortification to protect the royal port from the English, the castle was not intended as a pleasure spot. Stephen shivered as they passed through the curtain wall and rushed through the ceremony of handing Mary over to John Maitland, King James's principal secretary. The queen did not deign to thank him for the escort.

Maitland invited Stephen to remain for the night, but he declined with almost offensive quickness. "You don't mind?" he asked Maisie as they remounted in the cold.

Her small frame swallowed up in fur-lined cloak and gloves, she peered at him like a little owl from the depths of her hood. "If you had agreed to stay at Blackness, I would have gone on without you."

He laughed. "I sent the sergeant to secure us chambers at an inn. I'd prefer to avoid royal residences as much as possible."

"Hopefully the king will allow us to continue to do so."

"Are you worried?" he asked. "I don't think King James is the sort to lightly break a marriage. All we have to do is convince him this works to his advantage."

"Right." Maisie smiled wanly. "That's all we have to do."

At the last moment, Pippa almost begged off going to Compton Wynyates. Matthew would have approved. She could truthfully have claimed illness, though she had been better in the five months of her marriage than she had for a long time.

That didn't mean she was well. The coughing fits might be in abeyance, but it was temporary. Each day she felt a little more tired, a little more unfocused, a little less pulled together. And each day, her moments of not-quite-thereness grew more frequent. Throughout her life she'd mostly been able to control them, or at least to deflect away the attention of others, but that control was slipping.

When her vision grew dark around the edges and the voices of those present went mute—not once, but five or six times a day—it was difficult to pretend all was perfectly well. Matthew was the first to notice. He must have had a word with Anabel because the princess began keeping Pippa at her side as much as possible.

Matthew never forced her to talk, but he remarked as they rode into Compton Wynyates, "It will be a relief to be away from Navarro. I don't like the way he looks at you."

It was not jealousy speaking. No one could interpret Navarro's interest in Pippa as sexual. He was not the handsome priest bound to vows of chastity while secretly burning for a woman he could not have. No—Navarro eyed her as a predator would its next meal.

Three months ago Navarro had stopped her on an empty staircase at Middleham and asked about the black streak in her golden hair.

"My father is black-haired," she had answered. "My mother told me it grew from the spot where he kissed my head when I was born."

"To bear such a mark from birth is not a blessing," Navarro had pronounced stonily. "It is a curse."

Bruja. He had not spoken the word, but Pippa had heard it loudly at the time—and every time he'd looked at her since.

Witch.

Lucette met them outdoors, her face glowing with the cold and her eyes lit up with pleasure. Though Pippa had been fairly confident of her sister's healing, seeing confirmation of her regained happiness was an enormous relief.

"What fun we are going to have!" Lucette announced, laughing, as she pulled Pippa into the warm and welcoming hall. "Mother and Father are already here and she has been writing to Kit in Carlisle, asking him to come and drag Stephen with him. It seems she wants the whole family together."

Pippa's vision grew black and she heard what had become almost second nature to her this last year: a mix of Scots and Spanish voices, talking above and around her. But this time she could decipher a few of the words. *Send for her family. They will want to say goodbye.*

Her husband had grown quick to recognize her spells, and it was his hand on her elbow that brought her back to the surroundings of Lucette's hall. Her sister had not missed the moment—her sharp gaze made that clear—but she did not choose to pursue it just now.

"Fun, indeed!" Pippa said brightly, returning to the subject at hand. "Father has always had an equable temper—at least where we are concerned—but we have certainly tried it severely this last year. How do you suppose Mother is soothing him?"

Lucette arched an eyebrow, a trick remarkably like Queen Elizabeth. "In this matter," she said darkly, "it is the other way round. Mother has opinions, and she is determined to share them. I do not envy Stephen."

Pippa thought of her older brother and the young Scots woman, of the way the air tightened between them as though the very elements of the earth were conspiring to bind them together. "I think," she said, "that Stephen is fully as opinionated. He will apologize for hurting her, but never for his choice of partner. Rather like Mother, in fact."

"I wouldn't say that to her," Lucette warned.

"I won't have to. Mother will see it for herself."

Unfortunately, Minuette Courtenay could see all manner of things for herself. Including her younger daughter's increasingly fragile control. She was wise enough not to confront her directly. Instead, she began by asking Pippa about Anabel's state of mind.

"She is so young," her mother mused. "It is a dreadful burden Elizabeth has laid on her."

"I think it was fully as much Anabel's idea as the queen's."

"But when we are young, we often cannot see the full cost of what we choose." Minuette hesitated, those hazel eyes nearly identical to Kit's, fixed on Pippa's green ones. "You, of course, are an exception. You see far more than I do. Far more than I would like."

"If you are asking me if I have seen the outcome—I have not. If John Dee cannot prophesy the end of this war, it is hardly likely that I could."

"Then what is it you do see, Philippa?" her mother asked gently. "What is it that troubles you enough to put shadows beneath your eyes and lines of care on your face? Why does Matthew track your every move as though afraid you will break—or vanish?"

"I see pain," Pippa answered unwillingly, picking her way with care over the difficult landscape of this conversation. "But that is hardly a surprise. One cannot have war without pain. Especially not a war within a family. For all her logic and apparent indifference, Anabel hates exploiting her relationship to her father. And she hates even more being exploited by him."

"My darling girl." Minuette bit her lip, clearly considering how far to press. "I love Anabel and I love England. But not as I love you. Will you not tell me?"

Pippa looked straight into her mother's face and lied. "There is nothing to tell."

It was simpler after that to just avoid her family. Pippa thought she had found an isolated section of the vast house—not as large as Tiverton Castle, though enormous compared to Wynfield Mote— but soon found another person who had fled from too much familial intimacy.

"Hello, Felix." She spoke softly, as one would to a horse about to bolt. She had not forgotten how haunted he'd looked upon his arrival in England last spring. But the expression he turned on her now was, if not that of an entirely lighthearted child, at least considerably eased.

"My lady," he said in very good English. In the manner of fourteen-year-old boys, he had shot up even more, and was clearly on the way to matching his Uncle Julien's remarkable height. And despite being too thin as yet, his brown hair and eyes were attractive.

"Pippa," she corrected him. "You look much happier since last I saw you." Never let it be said that she was afraid to speak bluntly. She was only oblique about her own feelings, not those of others. "You have come to terms with your uncle?"

"Yes." Felix blinked and cleared his throat. "I suppose I should apologize to you as well. For my father's wickedness in your home."

"It is not your responsibility, Felix. And what your father wrought did by far the most damage to you. It is I who am sorry, for all of it. I cannot envision living in the world without my parents. And, of course, your grandfather. Renaud LeClerc was a very good man." She studied the boy, showing in the bones and the eyes and the height a hint of the man he himself would be. "Will you return to France?"

"No. Not this year. We will wait until matters are decided between England and Spain. My uncle and Lucette have said they will travel with me when I wish. But I intend to make this my home until I am old enough to run Blanclair."

"Good. That is good." She felt tears prick and blinked rapidly to clear them.

"My lady . . . Pippa?" Felix said hesitantly. "Why are you sad?"

Because I like this world and I like you and I wish I could see you become a man worthy of Blanclair . . .

"It is the travel," she said dismissively. "I think I will rest for a while."

And though it had been a device to escape, once Pippa retreated to bed, she almost instantly fell asleep.

It didn't take long for word of Kit and Anabel's argument at Kenilworth to make its way to the Marches of England. If Kit had thought it difficult enduring the sidelong glances and whispers that followed when he was in Anabel's good graces, he soon found this was even worse. As though every word of speculation merely confirmed his own misery.

So he threw himself into work—a remedy he'd never considered when he was younger. What had happened to the careless, jealous younger son? The boy who knew he could never be as good as his father or brother, so why even try? It seemed that, after all, his father's streak of duty and honour had been painted across Kit's soul.

There was no shortage of duty along the border. Reivers, for generations a source of mischief on both sides of the national boundary, did not stop their raiding and thieving whatever the formal understanding between England and Scotland. They were a law unto themselves, and the job of the wardens on both sides was to keep disorder from blowing into catastrophe.

Kit had a decent working relationship with the Scottish Lord Maxwell, but halfway through February the man was abruptly released from service and a new Warden of the West March of Scotland appointed—a warden with a superbly trained mercenary force at his command. Kit rode with officers of the Carlisle garrison to meet his brother at Dumfries.

"How on earth did you manage this?" Kit asked Stephen. "Won't the queen protest your service to a foreign power?"

"I'm not serving a foreign power—I am following orders from the woman who commands my service."

"Your wife," Kit said flatly. He'd been astonished to hear of Stephen's sudden, surprising marriage to a girl so much younger and so different from the women he'd watched his brother attend to over the years. He'd always sought for beauty, and Maisie Sinclair was not beautiful. Interesting, yes. Clever, no question. And yet Kit was quite certain his brother had not married for the sake of a clever mind.

Stephen refused to elaborate on the subject. "King James had to pull Maxwell off the border because of his noted Catholicism and open sympathy for Mary Stuart. The king's eye is on the longer view—not reivers, not thieves, but Spanish soldiers. With his mother in his hands, he thinks that the Spanish will have nearly as much interest in attacking Scotland as England, and the last thing the king can afford is one of his own wardens joining the Spanish. You and I are meant to prevent that."

The rest of their time at Dumfries was taken up with official matters. When Kit realized that he was keeping up with his brother in matters of policy and military tactics—that he even gave Stephen pause on occasion—he felt undeniably proud. Even when his older brother said caustically, "It's because of how well I trained you."

When they walked out together for Kit and the Carlisle men to ride back across the border, Stephen said abruptly, "I am sorry you've had to separate yourself from Anabel. It must hurt, having to lie to everyone about your feelings."

"How do you know I'm lying?"

Stephen eyed him sidelong. "Please."

"As long as Anabel can bring herself to believe it."

"She won't. You know that. Only in the heat of temper would she ever manage to believe you don't love her. But she will play the game as well as you. I'm just sorry it has to be that way."

"Don't be too sorry. You have your own troubles ahead."

Stephen grinned. "But at least I have the wife of my choosing."

"Do you?" Kit asked curiously.

Though his grin widened, still Stephen declined to be provoked. "Keep working hard, little brother. You'll have to, to keep up with me."

After returning to Carlisle, Kit headed east for his usual rounds of the Middle March. He expected only the normal course of business—low supplies, requisition difficulties, lack of ready money—but upon arriving in Tynedale, he was met with the news that he had a visitor waiting for him from the Princess of Wales.

It couldn't be Pippa, or the man would have said so. But Kit hoped for some kind of personal news.

Unfortunately, it was perhaps the last person he wanted to meet—Tomás Navarro. Kit stopped short on the threshold, then moved warily into the chamber.

"What can I do for you?" Kit asked in Spanish, taking a seat not too close, where he could keep a watchful eye on the priest.

Perhaps the only thing Navarro respected in Kit was his ability to speak Spanish. He answered in the same language. "I come with a message."

"From Her Highness?" What on earth would Anabel be doing, sending this unfriendly, judgmental Jesuit as a messenger?

"From His Majesty, King Philip."

That rocked Kit back into his chair. He was surprised enough to have to think carefully about translating his reply into Spanish. "I was not aware His Majesty could have anything to communicate to me."

"He wishes to express his gratitude for your loyalty and devotion to his daughter. He recognizes the difficulty of your personal position and respects your willingness to serve without reward. Other than to please God and Holy Church, His Majesty has no greater wish than to see his daughter happy in her duty."

"I have never doubted His Majesty's intentions." A nicely ambiguous reply for an ambiguous message, though he hardly had the patience for it. In this respect, Kit was very much his father's son. He did not like evasion and dissimulation and all the other subtle attendants of politics. Why could royals and diplomats never speak plainly?

"His Majesty is writing to his daughter with a proposal," Navarro said delicately. "When she receives it, she will undoubtedly send for you. It would please His Majesty greatly if you would use your influence to persuade her to accept his offer."

"You're not going to tell me what that offer is?"

"I am not."

"Do you know?"

"I do." His face darkened. "And for myself, I do not approve."

Interesting. "Royal masters do not wait upon our approval."

Navarro rose. Every now and then, in his controlled and elegant movements, Kit was reminded of the man within the cassock. Early thirties, lithe and fit, a man who would not be out of place on the battlefield. Perhaps the priest saw the Church as just that.

"I will not stay," Navarro announced. "I expect I will see you before long."

"It was good of you to trouble yourself on such a disagreeable errand. If it were up to you to counsel Her Highness, I wonder what you would advise?" Kit didn't mind harassing the man. But he was not expecting the violence of his reply.

"I would tell her one or two token Catholic lords on her council are not sufficient," Navarro spat vehemently. "I would tell her that allowing Mass to be said avails her little if she will not submit her own soul to the sacraments. I would tell her that opposing her mother is not the same as turning to her father. I would tell her to beware a man who appeals to the worst aspects of a woman's character."

This was more than Kit had bargained for.

Navarro hadn't finished. "And I would tell her that she is harboring more than heretics in her household. 'Though shalt not suffer a witch to live.' If England is to be cleansed, it must begin at home."

"I hope you are not implying what I think you are," Kit said, soft and dangerous. He realized he was gripping his dagger hilt.

Navarro's eyes flicked from that to Kit's face. But he did not back down. "Nothing is more dangerous than a servant of Satan who appears in the guise of a beautiful woman, mingling friendship with heresy."

"Stay away from my sister. If you threaten her—"

"I am under orders, the same as you. His Majesty, King Philip, is unaccountably fond of both you and your sister. I will not touch either of you."

Navarro turned away, but not without a parting shot as he walked out: "I will not have to. I trust God will do it for me."

SIXTEEN

24 February 1586
El Escorial, Spain

Her Royal Highness Anne Isabella, Infanta of Spain and Princess of
Wales,

Mi cielita. How I wish I could speak to you in person. I trust you
will believe that, however stiff my words, my heart is poured out in true
affection for you.

I am not cruel, whatever the most stiff-necked of the English believe. I
am seeking earnestly every day to both do my duty and please my family.
As to the duty—you know war is coming. I could not stop it even if I
wished to. And I do not wish to. "Spare the rod and spoil the child." But it
need not destroy you. You are young, my daughter, and beloved by your
people. Your recent actions have shown your wisdom as well as your te-
nacity in doing what you feel is right.

I believe the people of England desire a righteous ruler. I have no de-

*sire for bloodshed. Far better to cut short violence—something you are in
a position to achieve.*

   *I will be plain, mi cielita. With your support in the North of England,
the coming war could be considerably shortened. Your people will shed less
blood, and your mother may be brought to see wisdom short of her own
death. In return for your support of this righteous cause, I will see to it
that your marriage will be of your own choice. I think we both know
whom that choice would be.*

   *I commend to you Tomás Navarro as a faithful counselor. Trust his
guidance and both of us may achieve all that we desire. And trust I am always your loving father.*

Philip

Anabel thought herself a subtle and imaginative woman, with a
healthy skepticism bestowed by both her clever parents. But never
could she have imagined that her father would tempt her to treason
by offering Kit Courtenay as her husband.

It was enough to take her breath away. For all of a full minute she
allowed herself to consider that future: Queen Anne, young and beloved and wise, with Kit beside her every day and every night.

After that wistful minute of fantasy, Anabel deliberately took
those images and folded them away in a tiny corner of her heart as
she tore her father's letter to pieces. Then she tidied away the out-
ward evidence of her anger, composed herself to what she needed
Spain to see, and summoned Tomás Navarro.

"You know what His Majesty wrote to me, I understand?"

"I do. What shall I tell him?"

"I am quite capable of writing to my father without your aid.
That is not why I sent for you. What I need from you are specifics
of what is wanted from me."

He hesitated, as well he might. Navarro was not a stupid man and
he had no cause to trust her the way her father did. Anabel knew
they were poised on the precipice of the crisis: Had the last two

years of studied royal tension been for nothing? Or had she sufficiently played the part of a disaffected daughter ready to be lured
away by pretty promises?

The great advantage was that she was royal and Navarro was not.
He might have a degree of latitude in his work, being so far from his
masters in Spain, but both his mind and his heart demanded obedience to those masters. And they all—king and priests—wanted Anabel on their side.

Navarro leaned in, hands clasped, his handsome face sculpted by
good bones and strong opinions. "Neutrality," he said bluntly. "That
is all Spain asks of you. Neutrality to allow Spanish troops to accomplish what must be done quickly. The swifter the battle, the less
bloody the costs."

"And . . . afterward?" Let him think her hesitant to name her
mother, a feminine shrinking from the hard facts of what would happen to Elizabeth Tudor. Navarro might be fanatic enough to believe
that England's queen would capitulate short of death—but Philip of
Spain knew better than that. Her father knew her mother must die.

Navarro spread his hands wide, as though himself offering her
the world. "England has a queen willing to rule in partnership with
Holy Church."

How deluded they all were! And how willfully they misread the
tenor of the English. Even the most fanatic Catholics—a fraction of
the minority—would hesitate to allow the Pope and Spain to dictate
English policy once more.

"If I am to be neutral, then I must know when and where such
will be called for. It would hardly do for me to be sitting in the very
path of your march and be widely seen to do nothing about it. Few
of the English could forgive that. I must appear to be too far away
and too weak to offer effective aid. England will only accept me if
they believe I have done what was possible to protect them."

Tell me, she silently willed. *Tell me when and where your men are landing. Tell me what we need to know to stop you once and for all.*

"You will have warning."

"How much warning?"

"You understand that precise dates will not be decided until shortly before. So much depends on the weather and the tides. You should expect perhaps two weeks' notice."

"And my . . . acquiescence will spare the North?"

"There will be some troops landed here. For your safety, of course."

Anabel had never been so grateful for her training in controlling her reactions. She was as sure as she could be that Navarro saw only her assessing, disinterested gaze. "It goes without saying that not a word of this escapes this room. If it does, I shall know whom to punish."

He rose and bowed. "As it pleases Your Highness."

She didn't believe that for a moment. Anabel felt fairly confident that she could defy her father even to his face and he would not hurt her. But Navarro? He would need to be carefully watched without alarming him, and locked away at the last moment to prevent him from wrecking all their hopes.

One thing at least she could be grateful for. If Kit were the lure to bring her to the Spanish trap, then summoning him fulfilled her purposes perfectly. Also, there was an undeniable thrill of nerves at finally being within sight of the end. Spain would have to attack this year. At most, this would all be over in a matter of months.

The King of Scotland was not amused when informed of Mariota Sinclair's wedding. In the end, Maisie was fairly certain that the only reason James Stuart didn't order the dissolution of her marriage was the fact that Stephen Courtenay was a close friend to the Princess of Wales. James needed to tread with care in that direction in order to make his own coming marriage successful.

And it didn't hurt that Maisie owned—and Stephen commanded—a highly trained and deadly force of mercenaries.

With the grudging approval of King James, the condition set for

Maisie to keep control of the company had been met. Andrew Boyd greeted the news with real relief. The other board members were warier, waiting to see if she would exact punishment for what might be seen as their betrayal. But Maisie needed only to punish the troublemaker—Robert.

She had declined to take her husband with her to that interview. Actually, it was less an interview and more two people talking at cross-purposes to one another. But Maisie had always had the greater patience and the loudest voice when it counted. She made it plain to Robert that his allowance would continue only so long as he ceased making mischief for her in Edinburgh. He glared at her thunderously as she departed, but she trusted he would drown his anger in wine and brothels rather than risk losing any money.

With that settled, Maisie turned to the trickier business of establishing her marriage in public eyes. Stephen officially moved into the Edinburgh house, but they maintained separate bedrooms. Maisie knew at some point they would have to make the pretense of sharing a bed, but she shied away from that conversation. The last thing she thought she could endure was Stephen taking her for form's sake—or worse, from pity. So she kept him at one remove, and was grateful when the king appointed him to serve as Warden of the West March.

Then came the letter from his parents. One week after the Courtenays' formal congratulations—stiff with surprise behind the kindness—the newlyweds rode for England.

The Duke and Duchess of Exeter came all the way north to Carlisle, both to see Stephen and for a formal accounting of English military readiness in the North. Maisie drew a breath of relief when she and Stephen were able to slip into Carlisle Castle without encountering his parents publicly. The Courtenays excelled at tact.

After seeing her settled, Stephen left to find them. He'd been gone only a few minutes when someone knocked on the door. Maisie opened it to discover Dominic Courtenay.

He wore dark colours over the snowy white cuffs and collar of his shirt, with an obvious indifference to how the blues and blacks suited him. Maisie had met him briefly during her stay in London at the queen's summons, but she'd never had the full force of Lord Exeter's focus turned on her. She had thought Stephen was intense—he was a child compared to his father.

She stood frozen for so long in her tangle of thoughts that he had finally to ask, "May I come in?"

Maisie stepped back hastily and let him enter. He shut the door on the two of them and, clearly grasping her surprise, led her to a seat. He sat across from her, his hand resting lightly in his lap as he leaned forward and studied her. "Welcome to the Courtenay family," he said, kindly enough.

"Thank you, my lord."

His faint smile was so like his son's it tugged at her heart. "I have never warmed to titles. Please, call me Dominic." He hesitated, then added, "Perhaps, someday, Father?"

"That is very generous. I know how we must have pained you. I swear, it was not done with the intention of causing pain. It seemed—"

"Necessary. I understand that. Better than you know. I did not come here for apologies. My wife is scolding Stephen—if there is any blame here, we consider it to be entirely his—but we are both very glad he has chosen so well."

"That is kind of you." She had to forcibly stop herself from adding "my lord" to every phrase. "I can hardly be what you had in mind for your son."

"What I have always had in mind was a woman he loved."

How was she supposed to respond to that? Surely Stephen didn't want her telling his father that their marriage was primarily a matter of convenience. Why was she so damned uncomfortable? She could coolly manage any number of businessmen and merchants and even mercenaries . . . but this man was entirely different. He looked at her as though he could see right to the heart of the secrets she was keeping from his son.

"Well," Dominic said, with a gentleness she had not anticipated, "no doubt Stephen is beside himself wondering what I'm saying to you. Why don't we go put him out of his misery? My wife has arranged for a private meal, just the four of us."

And that was hardly likely to ease her nerves.

14 March 1586
Carlisle Castle

I expected to be quite sharp with Stephen in our first conversation, but he disarmed me almost instantly with the light in his eyes. Oh, he apologized well enough. And I am sure he meant it. But the happiness is too deeply rooted to override even his guilt.

Mariota Sinclair is quite an enchanting daughter-in-law. I used to worry about the sorts of women who would wish to marry the sons of a duke. I do not think I would have much patience for vapidity or coquetry. I should have trusted my sons. Stephen always appreciated beauty, and a casual observer might suppose Maisie to be an exception to that rule. I am not a casual observer, nor is Dominic. I could tell at once how taken my husband was with her.

And Stephen? I have never seen my son both so certain and so vulnerable at the same time. After dinner, when we had bid them good-night, I asked Dominic, "Is it only me?"

He shook his head. "You could cut the tension between them with a dagger." Then he laid his hand on the curve of my neck and kissed me lingeringly. "A tension that we both remember well."

Yes, indeed. The tension of unfulfilled desire. The question is—why? They are married. And clearly they are each of them desperately in love with the other. So why are they also so clearly keeping out of each other's way? It can only be that they do not know how the other feels. As a mother—perhaps simply as a woman—the temptation to force the issue is extreme. Which my husband recognized at once.

"Leave them be," he warned me, at some point between kisses and the shedding of clothes. "They will come to it themselves, and it will be all the sweeter."

All these years of marriage—and still I hate it when Dominic is right!

In mid-March, Kit was back in the West March helping to police a hot trod. Having had nearly a thousand cattle lifted by a band of Maxwells, the English Grahams sent a hundred armed men into the Annan Valley to trace and reclaim their property in the six days allowed them by border law. Such trods were meant to be reported to—and policed by—the local wardens, though most families managed to forget that step. But this time Lord Scrope had been alerted, and he sent his captain to ride with Kit and enough of the garrison to keep order. The men rode with the Grahams through the many folds of Scottish hills and valleys where reivers had been hiding stolen herds for generations.

As an exercise it had much to recommend it in preparing for war. If the Spanish tried to take England from the North, their disciplined troops would be at a severe disadvantage against borderers who knew how to fight in highly mobile, smaller groups that could come at them in ambushes through a landscape foreign to the invaders. It also had a great deal to recommend it as a way to relieve stress, and allowed Kit to simply do what he was good at rather than fret about all the things he couldn't control.

They managed to find both Maxwells and cattle on the fifth day. Though Kit didn't have major experience on the border, the Captain of Carlisle did. Kit watched Captain Bell, listened to his questioning of both Maxwells and Grahams, and knew that something was not right. He instinctively kept his mouth shut and let Bell organize the return across the border. They stayed with the Grahams until the family was safely back into Cumberland, then led the garrison back to the castle.

When he and Captain Bell were alone, Kit asked abruptly, "What is it?"

The man was experienced enough not to waste time in pleasantries or false protestations of humility. "I doubt it was Maxwells alone who planned this raid."

"Why?"

Bell grimaced. "Not any one thing I can put my finger on. Instinct, more than anything. They led us a merry chase, but they know that landscape well enough to keep from being found at all. It was like a game—far more than usual, I mean. Did you not note how cheerfully they surrendered the animals? I'm not saying I wanted fighting, but in fifteen years, never have I seen such an easy end. Not with Maxwells and Grahams involved."

"If not the Maxwells . . . who?"

"Could be one of the other families, shifting blame, but border families scorn hiding their mischief. They're proud of it, rather. I'd sooner believe this was a feint, meant to draw our attention to Annandale just now."

Kit inhaled sharply. "Draw our eyes while . . . what? If I've learned anything about reivers, it's their practicality. They know the English Marches are stronger than they've been in years."

"They also know that war with Spain is looming, and that English strength is being hoarded for that fight."

"Still doesn't explain a halfhearted raid. There's been no word of other violence in the West March?"

"Not yet. I've sent word all along the border. What worries me is not open violence."

Kit had reached the same point in his thinking. "If not immediate violence . . . Lord Maxwell recently had his wardenship revoked by King James for suspicion of his loyalty. Do we know Maxwell's present location?"

"Perceptive. No, we do not. And none of the Maxwell men were talking."

"You think the raid was designed to allow Lord Maxwell—a noted Catholic—to . . . what?"

"Mary Stuart is still in hold at Blackness Castle. If it were me, I would ensure King James is alerted to Lord Maxwell's disappear-ance."

"No more soft speaking," Kit said flatly. "You have another reason for suspicion. What did you find?"

Bell pulled out a fragment of paper and tossed it on the table. Kit didn't even have to read the words to know what the trouble was. All he needed to see was that the words were written in Spanish.

"Spanish orders?" he hazarded. The fragment held only partial sentences, the rest ripped away, and only a few at that. Kit found himself supplying any missing letters as he read: [re]*frain from open violence . . . keep the garrisons bus*[y] *. . . in hold at Lakehill H*[ouse] *. . .* [pay]*ment in full when she is fre*[e].

Lakehill House? Why did he recognize that name? He ran through all he'd learned of the recusant families in the North and came up blank. But still the name fretted at him even as he asked Bell, "I presume the man who held this fragment has been arrested?"

"We didn't find it on a man," Bell said evenly. "It was in a pack that no one claimed."

And I could hardly detain all of the Maxwells with just our small force from the garrison, ran the captain's unspoken defense.

Kit left it at that. This was not Bell's responsibility. It was the warden who answered to the queen. Or, in this case, the Princess of Wales. It was Kit's job to know what to do next.

"Damn it," he said softly. He stowed the fragment in the pouch at his belt. "This goes no further than this room," he ordered. "Under-stood?"

"Understood. You'll be heading to Middleham?"

"Yes. Once I send a courier to my brother. As current Warden of the West March, he can deal most quickly with King James. Also, Stephen has some experience with Mary Stuart. He will take any possibility of a rescue attempt seriously."

Royalty thrived on secrets and conspiracies. There were, Kit de-cided mordantly, entirely too many kings and queens and princesses in this whole affair for his liking. Give him a plain, honest enemy on the battlefield any day.

Since Christmas, Philip had felt a rising sense of urgency, as though each day that did not see the Enterprise of England launched was a day closer to failure. He had always been cautious, prone to remarking that "Time and I are two," but now nothing could be accomplished quickly enough for him. It was God, he knew. Having brought him to this point of destiny, God needed him to launch into action.

God did not seem to care about complications. After weeks of exchanging letters with Admiral de Bazan in Lisbon, where he had been preparing the armada, Philip received word that Bazan had collapsed from illness. He could not possibly command the armada this year.

Working unexpectedly fast, Philip immediately appointed Don Alonso, the Duke of Medina Sidonia, to take charge of the fleet. The duke had kept the king's peace in Andalusia, overseen defenses against pirates (many of them English), fulfilled his responsibilities with a mildness that would not offend his immediate subordinates, and, most importantly to Philip, was a man of impeccable moral character and a devoted son of the Church.

He was also humble, a fact that Philip would have appreciated more if it didn't lead the duke to reply with a polite demurral.

My health is not equal to such a voyage, Medina Sidonia wrote, *for I know by experience of the little I have been at sea that I am always seasick and always catch cold . . . Since I have had no experience either of the sea or of war, I cannot feel that I ought to command so important an enterprise.*

When Philip replied sharply, Medina Sidonia capitulated and at once took himself to the port of Lisbon. Philip knew the preparations were not perfect. Admiral de Bazan had written often, lamenting that he did not have enough ships, enough money, enough men

(Bazan had scoured prisons, hospitals, and fields around Lisbon to make up his crews), and, always, not enough time.

Philip was finished with excuses. Only with the greatest reluctance did he accept that the armada could not be ready to sail in March—possibly not in April—and when Medina Sidonia pleaded the paucity of heavy guns amongst the ships, Philip and his war council managed to find the money to send him. But he would not agree to demobilize the men to any degree, insisting that they remain on ship while in harbor so as to be prepared for immediate action.

And always—always—he was watching the English navy. They had greater numbers, though smaller ships, and they were fast. They could form and reform at sea in a day, or dash back into port without warning. The greatest advantage the Spanish possessed was surprise. The sooner they could launch, the better.

No, Philip corrected himself, our greatest asset is not surprise. It is Anne.

For he had on his desk, amidst the reports and cost sheets and lists of ships' repairs, a letter from his daughter. The most personal letter to him she had composed in years.

Father,

I thank you for your very kind letter of last month. I was, as I'm sure you can imagine, considerably taken aback by your offer. I know how deeply you have wished me to marry a good Catholic. That you would be willing to consider Christopher Courtenay . . . it argues a care for my happiness I did not expect.

Tomás Navarro has been most assiduous in your service. And as I have immersed myself outside of London, I have found a great faith and deep devotion in many English Catholics that humbles me. If there is aught I can do to ease their burdens . . . I have spent much time in prayer pondering what God would have me do.

I do not want war. But if war must come, then I will do whatever lies in my power to ensure it ends quickly.

HRH Anne Isabella

It was as close as his cautious, clever daughter could safely go in a written communiqué. Reading between the words, Philip felt confident that northern England would be easily taken, leaving the bulk of his forces to seize London and the South.

Spain could not have hoped for more.

SEVENTEEN

"What will you do now?"

Anabel studied the fragment of Spanish orders in her hand, the red haze of anger slowly fading from her eyes, until finally Kit's question penetrated her awareness.

Her first instinct was to drag Tomás Navarro before her and let fly her fury at Spain's damned interfering ways. If Spain had paid the Maxwells to provide a distracting raid, it pointed straight at the Jesuit in northern England who would gladly see Mary Stuart freed to wreak havoc in Scotland. How dare a foreigner meddle so brazenly? How dare he complacently assume he could do what he liked and she would simply swallow it?

"Anabel," said Kit, warning in his voice.

"I know!" She rubbed her forehead. "I know," she said more moderately. "This is a time for diplomacy, not temper. But I will not forget . . . nor forgive."

He nodded. "So again I ask—now what?"

"Now I invent an errand that will take Navarro away from Middleham for a time so I can convene a council without his presence.

You will report this to them. And then those I trust most will give me their advice."

It was not a full council, of course, that convened the next morning in Anabel's privy chamber. Arundel was rarely there, in any case, but Lord Scrope could have easily made it if asked. But considering that she expected some delicate and possibly inflammatory discussion about the Catholics, better keep him away. Better keep all the northern, sectarian interests away, in favour of those trained to take a wider view. In the end it was those few whom Anabel trusted completely: Sir Christopher Hatton, her secretary; Robert Cecil, her Master of Horse; her chaplain, Edwin Littlefield; Matthew Harrington, treasurer; Pippa and Madalena, whom Anabel would never consent to leave out where at all possible. And Kit.

Once Kit had made his dispassionate report on the hot trod and the suspicion of Spanish payment to the Maxwells for their cattle raid—and possibly a rescue attempt of Mary Stuart—Christopher Hatton led the queries. At forty-six he was the oldest member of Anabel's inner circle by more than ten years. Unusually, he rarely used that fact to claim superiority. Which made Anabel more willing to grant it to him. He had served in important government posts in London for twenty years before being released to the Princess of Wales's household. His only real fault was how little he liked the North.

"You've alerted King James?" Hatton asked Kit.

"Through my brother, Stephen. I also had the Captain of Carlisle send out inquiries to the other marches about suspicious people. Which, I grant you, is not all that easy to separate from the usual borderers."

"Any word back?"

Kit shook his head. "Nothing yet. Most of the garrisons report everything as normal. But then it would be, if we believe Lord Maxwell will use only his own people for any rescue attempt."

"Spanish agents would be highly noticeable in the borders," Hatton noted drily. "This isn't London. And frankly, there are plenty of

Spanish who might be happy to never see Mary Stuart again. She tends to bring trouble wherever she goes."

"Trouble," Madalena pointed out, "could be precisely what is wanted just now. We know the armada will launch in the coming weeks. What better way to distract Scotland and northern England than the Catholic Queen Mary running loose stirring up dissent?"

"The problem of Mary Stuart is for Scotland and King James to handle," Anabel said flatly. "No one could be more wary of the woman than those Scottish lords who drove her out twenty years ago. There is nothing we can do about that."

"Perhaps it is time to bring everything into the open," Littlefield said. The chaplain had always been the one most uneasy about Anabel's deception with her mother.

Her reply was swift. "No. It is too early. I will not waste the last two years by panicking so near to the end. The sacrifices we have all made must be worth it."

"Then we simply wait?" Hatton asked.

"Did I say so? What we do is deploy our less obvious weapons." Anabel smiled. "Why do you think we have spent so much effort seducing the North? For precisely a situation like this. Now our chief seductress will reap the benefits of her efforts."

She heard Matthew Harrington shift in his seat. Was he going to protest openly? she wondered. If he meant to, his wife forestalled him.

"I don't think I've ever been called a seductress before," Pippa said with just the right touch of amusement. "I'll begin making the rounds tomorrow. Surely, if there is anything to know, someone in one of the northern Catholic households will have heard. Even if it's only a whisper."

"Which means someone might go to serious lengths to prevent you learning it," Matthew pointed out. In a matter of just a few words, he managed to sound both worried and threatening.

"Of course you will go with your wife," Anabel said. "And the point is not to flush anyone out. I trust you both to be discreet and not raise any alarms. All I want is information. The decisions are not in your hands."

Pippa laid a hand on Matthew's arm in restraint. "Of course, Your Highness."

"Don't spook anyone," she warned Pippa. "Be charming and subtle and naïve."

It was at this moment that Kit said suddenly, and apropos of nothing, "Lakehill House!"

Everyone turned to him. Even Pippa, who looked nearly as startled as everyone else.

"Do you have something to add?" Anabel asked.

"I knew I'd heard that name. Now I know why I couldn't remember. It's in the North, true, not far from Kendal, but it's little more than a farm with no significant ties to any northern power."

Everyone else continued to look blank, but Pippa said, "Of course. How could I not have seen that at once?" Her words were little more than a murmur, as though asking herself.

"Kit?" Anabel prompted.

"Lakehill House," he announced, "was given by the crown some thirty years ago to the youngest son of the Duke of Norfolk, Giles Howard. When he died, it remained the property of his widow. Eleanor Percy."

At once, Anabel grasped the meaning. Eleanor Percy: mistress of the late King of England; mother of the king's daughter, Nora; the woman who had held Dominic Courtenay prisoner at the king's command at . . . yes . . . Lakehill House.

Christopher Hatton asked skeptically, "Why would Eleanor Percy mix herself up in all of this? She has no morals, I'll grant you that, but she's never made trouble beyond breaking up other marriages."

"Perhaps she simply hasn't had the chance," Anabel answered. "But in the recent past the Earl of Ormond has sent her back from Ireland, the queen commanded her to remain away from court at—

as Kit pointed out—little more than an isolated farm . . . My mother once told me not to underestimate Eleanor's ability to cause trouble."

"Also," Pippa said drily, "Eleanor Percy hates no one on this earth more than she hates Minuette Wyatt Courtenay. Until now our family has kept to ourselves except when under the queen's direct protection at court. No longer. Kit and I are in the North, Stephen is in Scotland, my parents are far out of reach in the South . . . yes, Eleanor might go far to cause Minuette's children trouble."

"This is not trouble," Christopher Hatton pointed out to Anabel. "This is treason."

The Tudor smile could never have been mistaken for warm. "I can think of no more suitable response than for Minuette Courtenay's son to arrest Eleanor on charges of treason. Go to Lakehill House, Kit. Travel quiet and swift so she won't see you coming. Then throw her in the deepest cell you can find."

The council chamber emptied swiftly after that. Kit did not wait even to say goodbye—he would be halfway to Kendal by dark. But when Pippa moved to join Matthew, Anabel stopped her with a touch to the wrist. She could feel the fineness of Pippa's bones and marked the increasing sharpness of her friend's cheekbones. Caught in stillness, there was a pallor to her skin that Anabel had not noticed before.

"Are you sure you're well enough to do this, Pippa? It's a lot of ground to cover in the next weeks," she said with concern. "You're not . . . I mean . . . You've been married seven months. I have no wish to jeopardize your health."

"I am not with child," Pippa assured her. "It will pass, Anabel. Better for me to work through it. Let me be useful. That is all I wish."

"You will let me know if the strain is too great? Or no, of course you will not. But Matthew will. I will not have you suffer in my service, Pippa."

"If I suffer, I assure you it will not be from too great service. That I promise."

Anabel did not find that as reassuring as she'd hoped.

The mood in London was rather like that of a cat mincing across hot stones: edgy and irritable. In late March, Elizabeth settled in at Whitehall, turning the usual seat of her government into a functioning war council as well. Although Walsingham was Lord Secretary, in this crisis she deputized Lord Burghley to stretch his role as treasurer to oversee England's civil government until further notice. That left Walsingham free to exploit his truest talents at working in the shadows and bringing her the information she craved.

Of course, that didn't stop him from exploiting his second great talent as well—that of annoying her with his freely offered opinions.

"Why is the Spanish ambassador still in London?" he groused.

"Because Mendoza is useful," she snapped back.

"Not any longer. We have learned all we can from his coded communications with Philip. And he knows it. Even he is openly wondering what you intend to do with him when the battles begin."

"Perhaps I will execute him."

"That is hardly helpful."

"But wouldn't it make you feel better, Walsingham? You cannot lay hands on Philip, no matter how this war turns out. Wouldn't you like to punish as many of his trusted servants as possible?"

She was only partly teasing. She herself would find it satisfying to wipe the smugness from Mendoza's eyes. It was the smugness she loathed—the superiority of self-righteousness that made her want to snap and snarl in a man's face. Or, better yet, smile coldly while she won the game in which they thought she was too slow—and too female—even to compete.

"The only issue now," Walsingham said with greater than normal patience, "is whether we manage to expel Mendoza before he is formally recalled by Philip. Don't lose the opportunity to make a statement, Your Majesty. Send for Mendoza and give him a personal message for the Spanish king. I guarantee all of Europe will be watching for it."

"It is not all of Europe that matters. It is my people."

"Your people are only awaiting your word."

"Which is why I have been hesitant to give it. I do not want merchants and honest men and women to be punished for the sins of others. I will not have London turn on those Spanish who reside here honestly. Is that clear, Walsingham?"

"We will do what we can. But war, of necessity, breeds chaos."

"Not in London."

She trapped his gaze until he nodded, his dark eyes grave. "We will do our best. Other than Mendoza, the immediate aspect to consider is the security of Calais. I've no doubt the French will take their chance to seize it while we are engaged with Spain. The question is—how far will you go to hold on?"

The queen had thought long and hard about the threat to Calais. Its loss thirty years before had been a personal scar whose pain Elizabeth had never anticipated. And when Spanish troops had in turn liberated it from the French—and Philip offered its return to her as a betrothal gift—it had been very nearly the deciding factor in her acceptance of the marriage. She did not want to lose Calais again.

But she could afford to lose Calais. She could not afford to lose England.

"I will send no further strength to the garrison. They must hold with what they have. And if the French move against them in force, I do not want a needless slaughter. Better far to retreat and retrieve what strength we can back across the Channel."

Walsingham knew how difficult that was for her. One of his lesser gifts was knowing when to be hard and when to be gentle. Now he offered a great kindness. "The mark of a true monarch, Your Majesty, is the ability to make wise decisions in the most difficult of times. You have always been unusually clear-sighted. Calais may be a luxury we cannot afford to keep. But its loss, if it comes, will not be in vain. I promise you that."

She spared him one grateful glance, then moved on briskly. "Lord Exeter's reports from the South are consistent in their summary: our ships and sailors are prepared and spoiling for a fight. Drake has been importuning me to let him strike the Spanish ships in harbor at Lisbon."

What Drake had actually written from Plymouth was more than importunate; it had verged on a lecture. *The advantage of time and place in all martial actions is half a victory; which being lost is irrecoverable . . . Wherefore, if Your Majesty will command me with those ships which are here already, and the rest follow with all possible expedition, I hold it, in my poor opinion, the surest and best course.*

Walsingham had seen that letter, and all the same reports. "But the preparation of our troops on the ground is thin and uneven. If the Spanish are able to land troops—"

"They won't."

"If they do?"

"Then I trust that my people will fight harder for their homes and families and freedom than Spanish soldiers will fight for either conquest or money."

What protest could Walsingham make? They couldn't conjure an army from thin air. She had stouthearted, honest men who despised the thought of foreign invaders. She had excellent commanders. She had faith.

It would simply have to be enough.

On a Wednesday morning in April, Maisie—unusually—had no meetings to attend and decided to spend the day at home. Stephen had been out in the Western March with their men for the last two weeks, and it was a release of tension to not be keyed up at every moment waiting for their paths to cross. She sent Pieter Andries off to the warehouse in Leith for inventory, and took the opportunity to wash her hair and dry it before the fire in the reception chamber mostly used for guests. It was a lovely, old-fashioned room with painted walls and a box-beamed ceiling. For once, she discarded the piles of correspondence that always awaited her and chose instead a book of French poetry.

She should have known that such relaxation was a mistake. When the door to the chamber was flung open with enough force to strike the wall, she jumped from the settee on which she'd been curled up. Her book fell to the floor as she stared uncomprehending at Robert.

Her brother was more disheveled than she'd ever seen him, which was saying something. She'd long known him as a drunkard, but she'd never seen this particular light in his eyes. It made her uncomfortably aware that she was in dishabille—a brocade, silver-worked robe over her fine linen smock, not even any slippers. She would have felt considerably better armored in petticoat and kirtle, bodice and heavy sleeves.

"Robert," she said warily. "May I help you?"

"Help me? Since when, dear sister, are you worried about helping me?" Though his voice was slurred, his movements were sharp.

"I will not speak to you when you are drunk. And I will not speak to you at all about business matters. If you have concerns about your allowance, you may take it up with the board."

It was surprisingly difficult to feel authoritative in bare feet. Robert crossed the stretch of floor between them and studied her.

"Bitch."

The insult was as vivid as a blow and rocked her back equally. "You'd better go, Robert," she said evenly. "I will not listen to this."

But as she attempted to move around him to the door—to summon the servants—his hand shot out and grabbed her by the arm. Hard.

"You're not going anywhere, little sister. Do you think I'm afraid of your feeble maids and clerks? They don't even know I'm here. I let myself in."

"I think you are afraid of my husband. As you should be."

"Your husband," he spat, "is not in Edinburgh. And his only interest in you is in restoring his fortunes. I can pay him off as well as you can. But you . . . oh, I will make you pay for your insolence. Thinking you can order me around just because Grandfather was taken by your wit and your fawning. I am the oldest. This business belongs to me. You will not take it."

"You are hurting me, Robert."

"Good." His grip moved to her shoulder, both hands now holding her caged before him. "I mean to hurt you. I mean to humiliate you. I should have done it years ago before you had time to become this . . . unnatural creature."

She twisted in his grasp, but all she accomplished was to make him shake her until her head hurt. She opened her mouth to yell for the servants and Robert clamped a hand over her mouth.

All her life, Maisie had been taught by her grandfather that she was clever and talented and that her mind made her the equal of any man. It was a shock to be so forcibly reminded that, despite whatever talents she possessed, she was too small to effectively defend herself. She clawed and kicked but accomplished little except tearing open the ribbons that tied her robe. Robert in his rage backhanded her so that she fell, stunned, to the carpet.

Then he was on her, both hands circling her throat while his weight kept her pinned down. He's gone mad, she thought through the swimming of her head, followed instantly by, I'm going to die.

His weight was pulled off her so suddenly that she choked and was momentarily blinded by the release of pressure. Slowly, her vision cleared enough to recognize the man who had turned his own violence back on Robert.

Stephen had come home.

———

After more than two weeks on the border and riding two hundred miles in the last thirty-six hours, Stephen couldn't decide which he wanted most—a bath, food, or his wife.

My wife. It was getting harder, keeping away from her. Every night they spent under the same roof he found himself severely tempted to take advantage of her good nature and claim he wanted children. He wanted to believe he refrained because he was a good man—but he knew it was mostly his pride. He did not want to be taken out of pity. He loved her too much for that to be endurable.

Still, his tiredness was lifted by pleasure when he turned his horse over to a groom in the open yard a block away from the house. He let himself in and, aware of his travel-stained clothing and almost two weeks' growth of beard, made for the stairs to clean up before seeking out Maisie. She was likely out in the city, in any case, tending to business.

He was three steps up the front stairs when he heard a crash from behind the closed door of the reception chamber. With a hand on his sword hilt, Stephen ran lightly down and opened the door, trying not to look too threatening in case it was simply a clumsy servant upsetting something breakable.

It took him a precious few seconds to comprehend the tableau before him. Two bodies on the floor, clearly struggling, a man's back stretched over a much smaller form with little bare feet . . . Stephen had already moved forward to intervene when he saw the spill of silver-gilt hair spread across the Ottoman carpet.

He stopped thinking then. He did not take time to draw his sword, but flung himself at the man and jerked him off so hard the assailant's feet left the ground. When he saw it was Robert Sinclair, his rage, if possible, intensified. He didn't need weapons. He'd learned to fight dirty from his brother-in-law Julien, and Stephen took vicious pleasure in hurting Robert now.

The man folded almost at once, and the only thing that stopped Stephen from beating him into unconsciousness was the desire to get him out of sight. With his fist clenched in Robert's filthy doublet, Stephen pulled him near enough to choke on the fumes of cheap wine.

"You have three days to leave Scotland. Take any ship you like to any port you choose . . . but if you ever set foot in this country again, I will kill you."

The man might be vicious, but he had the instincts of an animal primed for survival. He knew Stephen meant it. Twisting Robert's arm behind his back, Stephen marched him across the parlour then out the front door. With a shove, he pushed him down the stairs and left him in a huddle on the ground.

Returning to the parlour, he hesitated over whether to summon a servant to help Maisie. She had gotten to her feet, looking more blank than he'd ever seen her. She caught his eye and read his indecision.

"Don't call anyone. Not yet. Please."

He swallowed, and closed the door behind him. "Are you all right?"

Why did people ask that at such times? Of course she was not all right. From halfway across the room he could see the marks on her throat where bruises would blossom, a long scratch across one cheek. Her robe had been ripped open and the ribbons torn from their seams. It hung off one shoulder, the shift beneath grubby where her brother had put his hands.

Stephen swallowed again and had to force himself to stillness. If he let himself move, he didn't know what he might do.

Maisie moved, instead. And as she came nearer, he saw that the blankness was merely a thin mask over her fear. And fury. "Such a fool," she said bitterly. "I should have known better. What was I thinking?"

"It is my fault," he argued. "I should not have left you alone in Edinburgh. I just never dreamed . . ." His hand moved of its own accord and lightly touched the welt next to her eye. That was when Stephen realized she was shaking.

He pulled her into an embrace, meant only to comfort and ground her. To allow her to gather her considerable reserves of strength and then return to her preferred distance. The kind of comfort he had offered in Ireland after Liadan's death, the first time he had seen that flood of pale hair loose about her shoulders . . .

"Stephen," she whispered.

He drew back just enough to see her face, and waited for whatever she meant to say or ask. He was stopped by the expression in her eyes.

And then she kissed him.

She couldn't have reached him if he hadn't bent down to meet her. For a few heartbeats he kept careful control, trying to discern the mixed motives behind her gesture. He would not take advantage of her. He had been down that road before, and it ended every time in blood and guilt.

"Stephen," she kept saying, every time she freed her mouth enough to speak. "Stephen, please."

With all his force of will, Stephen finally held her off from him just enough to ask, "Is this merely turmoil? Because, God help me, I would take you even if it were, but I could not bear for you to regret it after."

"Regret?" She choked on a laugh, partly a sob. "I love you, Stephen. For so long. Did you not know that?"

He stared at her, almost as shocked as he'd been when he walked into the parlour. "Truly?"

"I would not burden you with it, for I knew you could never want me the same way. I am not Ailis. How could you content yourself with me after women like her?"

There were no more words after that, or at least no more than a few broken syllables. Why tell Maisie she was wrong when he could show her just how wrong? Stephen bent to kiss her in earnest now, and in their mutual eagerness they stumbled across the floor. There was a window with a deep ledge, and Stephen lifted her onto it the more easily to reach her.

Always before in his life, there had been a bed, even if only a pallet inside a tent. But neither of them had the patience to delay more than was absolutely necessary. He pushed the ruined robe down to her elbows, holding her there, and kissed everywhere he could reach. When she moved to free her arms, it was to pull them out of her brocade sleeves altogether so that there was only her gossamer shift covering her, the fabric outlining the body beneath so clearly that Stephen groaned with several years' worth of frustrated desire. He thought he managed to say her name.

Then her hands were at his waist, undoing buckles and laces and pulling him nearer, and his own hands found the hem of her shift and slid it up, and then he could not have composed a coherent thought if the entire world were on fire and he was needed to save it.

Afterward, they were both too deliciously boneless with pleasure to stay upright. He lifted her from the window ledge and slid down with his back to the wall, legs stretched out long. Maisie curled up next to him, her bright head resting on his chest.

"That," she said dreamily, "was nothing at all like Finian."

Indignation flared. "I should hope not," he said. "Finian Kavanaugh was an old man."

Her laughter rang like church bells across a once-frozen landscape. "You called me Maisie," she added.

"Did I? I suppose at the moment I could not spare breath for the extra syllables. Mariota." He kissed the top of her head, one hand winding a length of her thick hair around his palm. "Why did you never tell me? All these weeks of marriage, when we might have been doing *this*?"

"You never gave any sign that you would care to have me in your bed. Which," she added with laughter, "I suppose you haven't as yet."

"I kept my distance for your sake! Because one moment you were agreeing to marry me and the next you were matter-of-factly assuring me I was free to sleep with any other woman I liked as long as I was discreet. 'I have no objection to bearing your children,'" he quoted. "What the devil was I supposed to think?"

"Did you really suffer for it? I thought . . . from what I understand, men's desires are easily satisfied with almost any woman."

"Are you asking me if I've been satisfying myself elsewhere? Because I have not. I have not done so since I left Ireland. And certainly not once I landed in Edinburgh last year and laid eyes on you again."

"Why?"

He tried to think how to explain it. It hardly seemed the time to turn delicate now. "What you said about men and satisfaction . . . it is true enough that lust is a hunger that can be met rather easily. I have had my share of such careless encounters when I was younger. But desire? Desire is wound around and shot through with love, so that only the one desired can satisfy it. I had long since fallen in love with your mind and your heart, Mariota. Once I realized how much I desired your body as well, it was far too late for any other woman to suffice. Only you.

"And that is why I asked you to marry me. In hopes that one day we might meet in the middle." He looked around them wryly, at their disheveled clothes and her discarded robe. "This was rather more than I expected." With the lightest touch, he traced her cheekbone and down her throat. "Or dared hope."

"I suppose I was rather forward."

"And thank heaven for it, for I'd never have had the nerve. Come." He shifted and stood, pulling her with him. Then he swung her up and she twined her arms around his neck. He carried her to the door, her light weight in his arms both warm and arousing.

"Wait," she said. "Won't we shock the servants?"

"You have the best trained servants in all Scotland." He laughed softly. "And we were not exactly silent. I'll wager they are all of them as discreetly far out of earshot as they can get without leaving the house."

"Where are we going?"

"Where do you think? We are going, my wife, to a proper bed. And I do not plan to leave it for some hours. We have weeks to make up for."

EIGHTEEN

Kit had never seen a more depressing view than Lakehill House. True, the whole of the North could appear bleak and barren to those accustomed to more flagrant beauty, but he'd learned to appreciate the stripped-down nature of both the landscape and its people. Eleanor Percy had clearly not even tried. Her farmland was scraggly and unkempt, the farmers resentful and suspicious, and the manor house itself looked fitting to an engraving of hell.

It did not help his opinion any that he kept imagining his father here, brought secretly from the Tower after a feigned execution, chained up for the king's vengeance until Elizabeth became queen and Dominic Courtenay emerged from Lakehill House missing his left hand. It was not a story told within their family. The Courtenay children had to piece it together over the years from gossip. And when approached, the queen had been willing to lay out only the bare facts.

The last time Kit had seen Eleanor Percy, they'd both been guests of the Earl of Ormond in Ireland. The woman had clearly been angling for the earl at the time, and despite his noted toughness of mind, Ormond had succumbed sufficiently to install Eleanor at Kilkenny for two years. Kit wondered if being cast off since had humbled her at all.

It hadn't. When summoned by Kit's abrupt commands to her slovenly steward, Eleanor Percy wafted into the dark hall dressed for court. Everything about her proclaimed charm and availability— from the low-cut square neckline of her wine velvet gown to the delicate curls of her golden hair. Only when she drew closer did Kit note the slight stiffness of that hair, denoting an expensive wig. He imagined she kept the chamber shadowy in order to hide the betraying signs of age in her face.

"Lord Christopher!" she trilled. "What a surprise. Though not as surprising as your recent rise in the world. Your brother's disgrace is certainly working to your advantage. Or is it," she said with a confidential smile, "that you have learned the trick of pleasing a certain young royal? And here I thought you despised me, but you seem to be following in my steps. What will they call you, I wonder, when the princess seeks your bed rather than her husband's?"

She uttered the insults secure in the knowledge that a gentleman— and the Courtenays were undoubtedly gentlemen—would never lay a hand on her. It was a close run thing, though, and Kit had to deliberately loosen his hands to keep from slapping her.

He had a better weapon at his command.

"Eleanor Percy Howard Gage Stafford." He used every name she had ever possessed to ensure all was done in proper form. "You are under arrest, charged with high treason. You will be taken from here to a prison of Her Highness's choosing to languish at her pleasure. You have fifteen minutes to gather any personal items you might require. You will not be allowed servants to attend you."

Silence, broken by Eleanor's voice trying valiantly to convey amusement. "My dear Lord Christopher, you have run mad."

"We have evidence," he said tonelessly. "And I expect we will uncover somewhere here the gold you are storing to pay England's enemies."

It was Eleanor who ran a little mad then. She flew at Kit without warning, managing to score his cheek with her fingernails before he could get a grip on her. It was like trying to subdue a wildcat. She hissed and spat and shouted obscenities.

"I should have killed him when I had the chance! Dominic Courtenay and his little whore ... she was no better than me ... I never tried to pass off another man's child as my husband's ... Bitch, she'll pay for this ..."

Kit did have to slap her at last, though he admitted enjoying it more than he should have. It served to stop the stream of filthy accusations, and then he waited, holding her upper arms pinned tight, while Eleanor brought herself under nominal control.

She couldn't quite manage to sound easy. "You will never have enough evidence of this ridiculous charge to even try me, let alone punish me."

He leaned in slightly, to impress upon her his words, not knowing how much he resembled his grim father. "You have been playing games with royalty," he said softly. "Royalty does not require evidence."

Pippa spent six weeks crossing the length and breadth of England's North with her husband. Matthew was the official emissary from the Princess of Wales's household, visiting as her treasurer on assignment to assess the various households' financial and practical readiness for war. Unofficially, Pippa had the more critical task of assessing levels of commitment and possible conspiracies.

It was exhausting. She had worn her gift lightly through her life, so deeply was it woven into her awareness. When she was little, she'd thought everyone experienced the world the way she did. She was ten before John Dee recognized her gifts and subtly began to orient her perspective in order to use it. But recognized or not, it had always simply been part of who she was, and as often as not it was outside her command.

"God speaks when it is necessary," Dr. Dee had long ago advised. "Which is not the same thing as speaking when we *think* it is necessary."

There were times when Pippa wished she was the witch Tomás Navarro thought her to be. Then she could control events. She could be like the Willow Witches of northern tales, three sisters who had destroyed kingdoms and punished faithless men with spells of great power. During this most recent exhaustive tour of the North, she and Matthew had passed a ruined medieval tower that legend claimed had been home to the sisters. Witch Willow, the tower was called, and though Pippa suspected the name had come from the suggestive shape of a nearby ancient tree, she still wished for one moment that she could call down a spell of her own to blast Tomás Navarro and the Spanish threat out of England once and for all.

God, stars, visions, dreams, uncanny knowledge . . . Pippa had grown accustomed to the caprice of her gift. But never had it weighed on her as it had this last year.

The physical effects were rapidly becoming the most difficult to conceal. The weakness and coughing and frequent fevers of her illness were exacerbated by the pressure of too much knowledge, especially when that included other people's secrets. As she and Matthew passed from town to town and household to household, Pippa grew steadily more fatigued, making it difficult to sort through multiple impressions of secrecy to pinpoint which ones mattered.

They knew that the Cholmeley family had a Catholic priest in residence, for Anabel had given tacit approval for them to hold Mass within the household itself. That had, naturally, been pressed to its limits, and his services frequently had more than sixty in attendance. But there was no evidence that their involvement with the Spanish went any deeper, certainly not to the point of treason. And they showed no evasion when pressed for their preparations to help defend northern Yorkshire.

York was simpler; the city was unlikely to throw open its gates to welcome a Spanish army unless Anabel herself was present and ordered it. And even then they might well demur. Cities of that size had complicated relationships with sovereigns. Their sympathies might be split where religion was concerned, but the first concern of any city and its merchant guilds was the stability of trade and livelihoods. Pippa found practical people so much easier to deal with than idealists.

By the time they finished up their rounds by meeting with Lord Scrope at Bolton Castle, Matthew had begun to watch Pippa more closely than ever, and she suspected he was one incident away from pulling her out of public affairs. But Pippa knew how critical Lord Scrope's support was for Anabel. They had played a delicate game with these Catholic lords—allowing them greater latitude in order to gain their loyalties. Loyalties that might turn in a heartbeat if they felt themselves manipulated and betrayed. Anabel's gamble—and the queen's—was that their deepest loyalties were to England and their own security first. Would they sacrifice their sovereignty and the safety of their country simply to have a ruler of the same religion? The time was rapidly approaching—perhaps only weeks—before Anabel would have to make plain her absolute loyalty to her mother in order to fight the Spanish. Success in that fight would depend in large measure on how valiantly the northern Catholics came to her side, even at personal cost to themselves.

So Pippa kept herself and her traitorous body under iron control as she and Matthew met with Lord Scrope. She liked the man, one of those individualists the Marches of England seemed to produce, and was fairly confident of his support. But it would not do to make a misstep.

He and Matthew discussed military readiness and matters of supplies in both food and arms for the spring and summer, and then it was Pippa's turn.

As Warden of the West March, Lord Scrope had been informed by his Captain of Carlisle of the Maxwells' lackadaisical cattle raid and the possibility of it having been meant merely as a distraction. The borders were a network of complex relationships and grudges, and Scrope spent some time going down those torturous paths in trying to understand it.

"Might it," Pippa finally asked directly, "have been directed from outside the Marches itself?"

"You mean Spain."

"I don't mean France," she answered wryly.

He gave her a quick, distracted smile. "No. If you are asking me if I have specific and personal knowledge of such an attempt by the Spanish to divert us along the borders, I do not. If you are asking me if I think it likely . . . perhaps rather more likely than not."

They had kept back word of Eleanor Percy's arrest, made easier by her isolated position both geographically and socially. Surely whoever had employed her had noted she was gone, but they had also kept the news quiet. To what purpose?

"Lady Philippa," Lord Scrope said, "it is no secret that the Spanish are already sending out ships to engage with and assess the strength of England's navy. They intend an invasion. Does Her Highness believe the northern border vulnerable to welcoming Spanish troops?"

So much for evasion. But this was precisely why Anabel had sent Pippa—that she might judge in the instant how to proceed with specific men. "Should she believe that?"

He was silent for a long time, gazing down at his linked hands. Pippa sat perfectly still, feeling the whirl of his emotions without being certain which would prevail. Religion or country? Faith or freedom? Loyalty or treason? Next to her, she could feel Matthew's stability anchoring her as always.

When Lord Scrope looked up and met her eyes, Pippa knew the tipping point had been reached.

"I knew the last King Henry—William, as he preferred to be called by his friends. I was never that, exactly, but we were of an age and I spent enough time at court to have a passing acquaintance with him. I never knew a man so quick, so clever, so certain to know his own mind. It was an . . . intoxicating mixture."

Pippa could not possibly guess where he was going with this, but instinct kept her quiet.

"But for all his gifts, for all the hopes England invested in him after the tumult of his parents' marriage, William was a disastrous king. He had his father's temper and his mother's suspicions, and his own reckless impulsiveness where your mother, Lady Philippa, was concerned—and I tell you that England has seen no better day for a century than the day Elizabeth Tudor came to the throne. I say that as a faithful son of Holy Church. This queen has done almost the impossible: preserved peace for nearly a generation. Catholic I may be, but I have no desire to see wrought in England the violence done in France in the name of my faith."

"Violence may come without our desiring it. How we meet it matters a great deal."

Lord Scrope asked bluntly: "Princess Anne has no intention of aiding the Spanish in taking northern England, does she?"

"What do *you* intend?" She could not take the risk of confirming anything to a man who might, whatever her instincts, be prepared to spring that secret before Anabel was ready for it.

"I understand your reticence, Lady Philippa. I am not a fool. Any child of Queen Elizabeth and King Philip will have a subtle intelligence and a stubborn sense of righteousness. Princess Anne is not a woman to make decisions solely for her own gain. The Spanish might be willing to believe she would sell her mother for a crown of her own, but I am not."

"What do your fellow Catholics believe?"

"Which side will they come down on, do you mean? I cannot make predictions. Every man must choose as his conscience dictates. I will say that the borders, at least, are the home of men and women whose greatest pride is in their independence. They may not like London's rule—but far less would they like Spain's. For the rest of the North?" He shrugged. "I can't tell you what religion will drive people to do."

"Can you tell us what you will do?"

"I think you already know, Lady Philippa. If the Spanish land in the North, I will march every man at my command to oppose them."

Pippa was swept with relief so strong that it openly shook her. She felt Matthew's hand on her arm, steadying her. "Her Highness— and Her Majesty—are honoured to have your service. May we ask that this discussion remain entirely private until such time as the matter is brought into the open?"

"You have my word—but that does not mean it will not be discussed. Some of my fellows see only what they want to see. But others are near as canny as I am, and with long experience of the wiliness of Tudor minds. I am surely not the only one to guess the truth."

"I will take that message to Her Highness," Pippa said. "Thank you, my lord." It was time to stand up, but she was not entirely steady on her feet. As though all the strain of the last year, intensified by these weeks of working to see beyond the surface of things, had suddenly slipped through her controls and landed heavily on her body.

"Philippa?"

She could hear Matthew, but dimly, as though from a distance. Her vision was spiraling into an image so familiar to her now it held no terrors. *Rushlight and fog, insistent hands and masked faces, melodious Spanish voices mixed with the unmistakable lilt of the Scots, the certain knowledge that she was dying . . .*

The last thing she felt was her body slipping through Matthew's grasp.

When she awoke, it was dark and she was in an unfamiliar bed. The disorientation swirled for a precious few seconds, until she heard a woman say, "She's rousing, sir."

And blessedly, there was Matthew, his normally placid face twisted with worry and a touch of anger. "How long has this been coming on?" he asked directly.

She looked over his shoulder, at the Bolton Castle maid attending her, and Matthew understood at once. "You may go," he told the girl, with an abruptness he hardly ever used.

When they were alone, Pippa answered. "Long enough for me to husband my resources so that I might finish this particular task. And I have. Lord Scrope was our last assignment."

"And what has it cost? Are you trying to kill yourself out of some misguided notion that dying in Anabel's service is your fate? Do you *want* to die, Philippa?"

"How can you ask me that?"

"Because I see no sign of you trying to avoid it!"

She inhaled sharply, and her husband dropped his head into his hands. "I'm sorry," he said, muffled and broken in a way she'd never heard before.

"You knew this when you married me, Matthew. You told me you understood."

"Understanding is not quite the same as facing it."

She sat up and pulled his hands away so he would look at her. "No, it is not." Her head was heavy with fatigue and her eyes pained from holding back tears. "Do you think I do not care? Do you think me reconciled? I am not. I do not want to die, Matthew! I want to live with you until we are old—I want to have your children—I want to be at peace. But I cannot change what will come. No one can. The only difference is that I can *see* it coming."

And then the tears were not simply threatening, but engulfing her. Matthew climbed onto the bed and pulled her into his arms. She wept for some time, and knew he did, too. But he did not fail her, as she had known he would not. When the storm had gentled, her husband was once more prepared to be the rock she needed him to be.

"I do not suppose," he asked gently, "that you would retire from court life if I asked you to?"

"Are you asking me to?"

He cupped her chin in his large, square hand. For all her life, Matthew's brown eyes had been one of her favorite sights. Even distressed, they steadied her. "No. I will not make you refuse me. You are right, Philippa, I came into this with my eyes wide open. It is not fair to you to change my mind now. Wherever you are, I will be. Whatever you do, I will help you bear it. On one condition."

"Which is?"

"You *allow* me to help you. Tell me what you need. To keep people away from you? To guard your time and privacy so that you can keep your strength for whatever is coming? And Philippa, sweetheart?"

He kept her chin turned to him, staring directly into her eyes. "Do not try to protect me. Whatever it is you fear for me, you must put it aside. Because the only thing I fear is failing you. Promise me."

Already she could feel the pressure lifting, the constant drag on her body shifting just enough for her to breathe easier than she had in weeks. She leaned forward and kissed her husband, determined to not worry so much about the future that she lost the present. "I promise, husband."

The last day of April an exhausted, sweat-stained courier was, most unusually, brought directly into the queen's presence, Lord Burghley at his side. The three gold cups on his badge marked him as one of the Earl of Ormond's men, and Elizabeth shot a sharp look at her treasurer as she took the sealed message. But if Burghley had been apprised beforehand, he gave nothing away.

She broke the seal and read. Ormond, a distant cousin, had addressed her with a greater than usual familiarity even for him. But propriety, or the lack thereof, was the last thing on Elizabeth's mind when she read his news.

Cork has been retaken. Some of the remaining Spanish soldiers and ships are concentrated in Waterford, clearly intending to gamble on reaching England. The remainder of the ships and men set sail last week, we do not know where. The Irish rebels are rapidly falling back to the lines we held before the Spanish interference.

But even that news was not what caught Elizabeth by the throat, seizing the words so that she had to try twice to read it aloud to Burghley: "'Desmond is taken and is in my hands at Kilkenny Castle. I await instructions.'"

Elizabeth was certainly not one for praying to saints, but just now she felt like blessing St. Brigid herself. With the Earl of Desmond in English custody, the rebellion would collapse. Ireland might be only a side battle of this conflict, but it was important to her and to her people. News of Ormond's success would bolster confidence in their coming fight with the Spanish.

More practically, Ireland would stop begging her for the men and money she needed here in England.

"Our thanks to my dear cousin," Elizabeth told the kneeling messenger. "My household will see that you are rested and refreshed from your faithful and difficult travels." She sent him away with a waiting page and turned jubilantly to Burghley.

"Publish this widely and loudly. And summon Walsingham. He will be delighted at this success."

Lord Burghley did not look as though he entirely found this a success. He had always been the voice for negotiation and conciliation in Ireland.

"Cheer up," she told him. "Without Desmond, the rebellion will fall to pieces. We will have the whole of the country by the end of the year."

He was not mad enough to contradict her at this rare moment of good news, but she read the caution in his eyes and knew the arguments he would make.

Ireland can never be predicted or trusted. Religion plays merry hell with practicality. We cannot depend on logic to believe we have won.

All true enough, Elizabeth granted when forced to listen to it later that week in council. But along with her understanding of hard political realities, she also possessed in large measure her father's gift for public relations. She knew how to choose information, how to highlight what she wished and shadow what she didn't, how to in-spire a population to devotion and pride and ferocity.

It proved the perfect opportunity to expel Ambassador de Men-doza from England. She had a final, stormy interview with the man, then told him to go back to Philip and assure the Spanish king that, just as Ireland had been freed, so England would never be enslaved. After Mendoza left London, Elizabeth convened her council with a clear message: make all the arguments you like in this chamber, but when you leave it is *my* message that you carry. Ireland is our first victory. The first victory, but not the last.

And to set her seal upon it, a special service was held at St. Paul's in celebration and gratitude. Elizabeth loved such occasions, and this was no exception. Dressed in heavy and elaborate cloth-of-gold studded with pearls and moonstones, a six-inch cartridge pleated ruff, and a fall of stiff gauze from her shoulders that elevated her from queen to legend. Her appearance was as important a part of her reign as her policies—the people wanted a fairy queen, a Glori-ana of more than earthly beauty and intelligence. She was heartened by the thunderous cheers of the crowds lining the streets, a reminder that her people loved her. That her people would fight for her.

Further evidence of that was provided in the next two weeks. As the bulk of the Spanish fleet continued its frantic preparations in Lisbon, a small number took to sea to test the English navy and scout what weaknesses might be revealed.

There were not many, save for the fact that England's best sailors were not yet at sea but still preparing their commands. Drake and Raleigh could have easily turned the Spanish feints, but it was more important that they and their men and ships be prepared for the critical encounters to come. And so the Spanish effected a surprise attack on Penzance. It was a lightning strike, for they could never hope to hold a position with only fifty men, and certainly not with the bulk of the English fleet less than eighty miles away. But they pillaged and burned, rather in the manner of the northern border reivers, and left an uneasy film of fear behind when they fled. And, most devastating of all, Calais fell to the French eager to exploit England's crisis.

In the aftermath, there were those of the queen's advisors who pressed for the arrest of anyone who showed even the slightest attachment to the old religion. Walsingham, as always, warned of sinister conspiracies, and even the sensible Lord Burghley fretted about the "secret treasons of the mind and heart." Elizabeth would not be moved. Jesuits and seminary priests might be treated as agents of an enemy power. And the queen conceded the necessity of placing the leading, most powerful, Catholic recusants under protective custody, sequestering their arms and horses. Further, she would not go.

Dominic Courtenay came to court after surveying the damage done by the Spanish raids, riding fast and hard and without his wife. Once the necessities of business were concluded—quickly and efficiently, as Dominic handled all things—Elizabeth indulged a more personal curiosity.

"Where is Minuette?" Her friend could often be persuaded to come to court without her husband, but rarely the other way around.

"At Tiverton, raising both troops and morale. Military leadership is thin on the ground, Your Majesty. She might be our best choice for the west country. With Kit in the North and Stephen in Scotland?" He shrugged. "There aren't a lot of Courtenays to go around my family lands."

"There is no need for Stephen to continue to sulk in Scotland. I have written to tell him so. He is needed here, wherever you think he should command."

"With his company of mercenaries in tow?"

"I certainly hope so. This marriage of his should bring some reward."

She waited for Dominic to protest that cynical statement, but he could stick to the point when necessary. "I am sure Stephen will serve. Whether he brings the mercenaries with him is a matter for his wife and the Scottish king."

"As James Stuart does not seem in any hurry to provide more than token assistance to us at this point, he had damned well better release those mercenaries. Or I may tear up the marriage treaty myself."

"For now," Dominic said, "I have asked Julien to take a command with my men. The central counties are not in immediate danger—and if the Spanish get as far as Oxford, we have greater problems than who is commanding where. Lucette intends to go to Kenilworth and keep Nora Dudley company. Also, it's a convenient spot from which to gather and send out information between North and South."

"And your wife?"

"She insists on returning to the south coast," he said wryly. "I have tried to persuade her to stay with you, but she is . . . stubborn. She insists on coming to Dover."

"Just as well, for I intend to make a tour of the coast later this month. I'll take Minuette with me, if you want greater security for her."

"By traveling with the heretic queen who has been the target of Catholic assassins as long as she's been on the throne? That is very secure, Your Majesty." But his lips turned up at one corner as he spoke. "I suppose your council has already tried to persuade you from going about in public?"

"They have, so don't bother. I have never been afraid of my people—I will not begin now."

"And if an assassin gets lucky? They must be trying harder than they ever have before to kill you. Whatever they may think or guess of the Princess of Wales's intentions, no doubt they consider she would be a queen far easier to manipulate."

"Then it is as well for England that they are entirely wrong. I do not intend to die, Dominic. But if I do, it will not be cowering in security while men die at my command. And I trust that Anne would revenge me nicely."

In this week of surprises, Dominic delivered one more—he

laughed softly. "Do you ever wonder if this war would have to be fought if only William had lived?"

It was the first time in almost thirty years that she had heard Dominic speak her brother's name. She would not show how it moved her. "Perhaps not this war. But we both know that is solely because there would have been more wars fought more frequently. I have not been a perfect ruler—I do not believe there is such a creature. But I believe—I have to believe—that I have done as well as any ruler could have with the circumstances I was given."

There were occasions—few and far between—when someone looked at Elizabeth as though they really saw her. Not her crown, not her throne, not the trappings of power . . . herself alone. Elizabeth Tudor. Minuette was the most frequent, and sometimes both Burghley and Walsingham achieved it. But to see that look from Dominic—a man whom she both liked and respected, a man who in his last extremity had clung to loyalty as a lifeline, a man who did not lightly offer affection or praise—made her feel like the girl she had not been for decades.

"You will not die, Elizabeth," he told her. "Nor will England fall. Not while I have breath in my body to defend both, I swear it."

His promise was almost as encouraging as the two hundred ships guarding England's shores.

Once Pippa and Matthew returned to Middleham, the council met to discuss their reports of military readiness and apparent Northern ignorance of any attempt to free Mary Stuart in Scotland. In private, they passed on the news of Lord Scrope's shrewd guesses about Anabel's true intentions as well as his promise of armed support.

Kit watched Anabel, knowing the relief behind her serene acceptance of that fact. "It is time to see for myself the readiness of what standing forces we have along the border. There have been several lightning raids along the south coast, but it is the Duke of Parma who worries me. It is his army in the Netherlands that will embark in those Spanish ships now preparing to sail—and with Calais retaken by France, Spain has another easy port near Parma. And while our navy is protecting the English Channel, what of the missing ships from Ireland? There are twenty unaccounted for. What if they sailed north from Ireland?"

"To come directly at Scotland? No." Hatton answered his own question. "You're not afraid of them hitting Scotland—you think those ships are sailing *around* Scotland to come at us from the north. Where the English navy most conveniently is not."

"It's how Mary Stuart was smuggled out of Scotland when she was a child," Anabel reminded him. "With ships heading in the other direction, but still. We know the waters north of Scotland can be navigated. What are the chances that the missing Spanish ships are bringing troops to land at Berwick or Newcastle or even Hull?"

Kit broke in. "I suppose this is why you want a tour of the coast and the East March. You consider them most vulnerable."

"Even discounting the missing ships out of Ireland, the Duke of Parma could conceivably scrape together enough ships to carry part of his army from Flanders. Not enough to oppose the full force of England's navy in the most direct crossing—but what if he decides to gamble on finding open water north and launches against us?"

That possibility hung in the air with a weight no one could shake. Kit could have sworn he felt the threat of Parma's troops beating inside his chest. And the danger of it all was that, in trying to be prepared for every possibility, they could end up unprepared for whatever actually happened.

As Anabel gave her household orders, preparatory to departing on their tour of defenses, Kit pulled Matthew aside. "How is Pippa?"

"Can you not tell?"

Kit grimaced. "I was hoping you would tell me different." His brother-in-law simply looked at him, and Kit sighed. "I know. Sorry."

Matthew offered only this: "If you want to know more than you can already feel or guess, you'll have to ask her."

But that was a conversation Kit shied away from. He knew Pippa was not well. He could feel the faint drag of illness in himself and knew it was his twin, trying hard to shield him from the worst but not entirely able to hide. What worried Kit was what else she might be hiding more successfully.

Once Pippa would have sought Kit out, either to reassure or, more likely, scold him into focusing on his own life. But she stayed with Anabel for several hours after the council broke up and then went straight to bed. Kit had not the heart to disturb her, so he left a note before he left with Anabel the next morning.

Pippa

The success of this war does not depend solely on you. Quit behaving as though it does. You will do Anabel no good if you are too sick to get out of bed. And I'm sure Matthew prefers to have you on your feet. I expect to see you rested and returned to full sarcasm on my return.

Kit

Despite his personal worries and the stress of looming war, Kit enjoyed traveling with Anabel. The princess was cheered resoundingly wherever they went, from town to tiny village, and she took care to spend hours meeting personally with as many people as could be managed. They moved from Middleham down to York, where the city leaders had already taken a distinct liking for Anabel herself as well as a healthy respect for her leadership skills. She had skillfully led the Council of the North, either in person or in correspondence, and was now reaping its benefits.

From York they went farther south, to the port of Kingston upon Hull, where they heard intelligence reports from the Netherlands. The Duke of Parma, who had led Spain's armies against the Flemish for the last seven years, was charged with assembling the land forces needed for an English invasion. There had been some discussion in

London, Kit knew, about trying to disrupt Parma with the forces they had supporting the Flemish rebels, but that was scotched in favour of using what time and money they possessed in preparing England itself. The most encouraging aspect of the current intelligence reports was that Parma was irritated about having to feed an army that was doing nothing much at the moment but eating and waiting.

After Hull, Kit led the royal train along the coastline heading north. They called at every town and estate of even minor significance along the way. Just weeks behind Pippa's journey, Kit could see the value of his sister's work every day. Even the wariest Catholics who had most cause to dislike London—such as those families with ties to the Pilgrimage of Grace fifty years before—had been softened by Pippa's attentions and Anabel's concessions. Northerners might be suspicious and wary, but they were also highly practical. The fact that the princess had two Catholics on her council went a long way in assuring the disaffected that she, at the very least, would listen to them.

At Newcastle, the primary northern fortress of England, they stayed five days. Anabel, as president of the Council of the North, spent two days hearing cases and dispensing justice. The position had long been held by members of the royal family—often the direct heir to the throne—but she was the first woman to do so, and Kit knew it weighed on her. But she let the strain show only in flashes, and only in private.

Then it was on to Berwick, that northernmost English town that had changed hands with Scotland more times than could be counted. There they were met by the Warden of the East March, Henry Carey, Lord Hunsdon. First cousin to Queen Elizabeth through their mothers, Hunsdon had long been a stalwart military support to the queen. He had come to Berwick almost twenty years ago as governor, and was instrumental in squashing the Rising of the North soon after. He had continued to rise from position to position, as much by his successes as by his blood, and spent much of his time now down south.

But with the Spanish threat, he had been named Captain General of the Queen's Forces in the North, and thus, in important ways, he was Kit's superior officer.

Hunsdon received Anabel fondly. In his late fifties, he had the long, narrow Boleyn face of his cousin and the erect and vigorous air of a lifetime soldier. With the princess, he walked the precise line between the personal and the professional. And when she assured him, with only Kit and Hunsdon's second in command in attendance, that their hopes were to lure Spain into sending a portion of their fleet against the North, he was quick to grasp why.

"A tactic your grandmother might well have conceived," he said admiringly. He had been Anne Boleyn's ward for much of his childhood and it was his aunt who had provided him the education that launched his career. "Do you think you have sufficiently misled the Spanish into believing you will do nothing to actively hinder their armies?"

"One can never say for certain," Anabel answered. "It is to be hoped that this visit is being viewed as my attempt to discover which men can be trusted and which would need to be removed. I need hardly say that you are considered by the Spanish the chief obstacle to any devious plan of mine against my mother."

"I am honoured," he answered drily.

From Berwick, she had been invited by King James to cross the border and meet with him a little west at Melrose. In the event, she once again refused to cross the border. She phrased it kindly enough—*I will come to Scotland as a bride comes to her husband*—but Kit knew how it would rankle with James.

It did not keep the Scottish king from coming to Berwick himself.

James Stuart arrived at Berwick under apparent cover of disguise. It was one of those convenient fictions—everyone knew who he was, but they all agreed to pretend not to, outside the castle, in order to avoid both formalities and hostilities. The king did not come unattended. With him were Alexander Home, Warden of Scotland's East March, and also, as Kit had hoped, Stephen Courtenay and several of his officers from the St. Adrian's company.

Excluded from the official meetings, Kit and Stephen were meant to discuss the unofficial matters. They took to the castle ramparts high above in order to do so in private. From there they had a spectacular view of the town, protected by its own recently built ramparts. The ingenious construction used earth to back the stone walls, allowing for greater absorption of artillery fire. Berwick Castle itself sat outside the ramparts, connected to the town by a bridge that led to a gated entrance. The air was still and heavy with moisture, and sharp enough even in the summer to necessitate cloaks.

"Is James going to offer Anabel any help?" Kit asked bluntly.

"I don't know. You don't suppose he fully trusts me, do you? I'm English. Just as King James is courting Anabel to protect his own interests, he's courting me because Maisie owns St. Adrian's. He wants her company."

"Will he get it?"

"That is up to her."

Kit rolled his eyes. "You two don't talk?"

With a perfectly straight face, his brother replied, "I have better things to do with my wife than talk about war. I'm sure you can imagine."

"I think I prefer not to." Kit choked back a laugh. Now that he looked closely, his normally straitlaced, disciplined older brother had a look of unusual mischief in his eyes. So Pippa had been right—Stephen had married for love. Not that his twin would be surprised by that. She was always faintly offended when others were astonished at her being right.

Kit cleared his throat. "Your happiness aside, it is a matter of some concern to both the queen and Anabel that England secure the use of St. Adrian's this year."

"I do have some tactical reasoning left to me. You know that, St.

Adrian's or not, the queen has asked me to return to England to take a command. I have agreed."

"Good. You're needed." It was a long time now since Kit had thought every compliment given to his brother was necessarily a criticism of himself. "And your wife? This wife you enjoy so much you have no time to talk—why did she not come to Berwick with you? I would think King James would give her anything she wanted in order to secure that company."

A faint smile touched Stephen's lips. "He would also stretch the law in order to get his hands on it. Bad enough that our marriage meant she kept hold of the Sinclair business. He does not like the thought of a young woman also having a significant military company at her command. So . . ." He trailed off invitingly.

"You're really going to make me ask?" Kit aimed a light cuff at Stephen's head.

His brother deflected it. "And so, as we speak, Maisie is taking St. Adrian's across the border to Carlisle and offering the company's expertise in the coming war to the Queen of England. Once back in Scotland, I shall give King James my resignation as Warden of the Scottish West March. I don't imagine he'll object when he knows what I have done."

Kit whistled, softly, to ensure they drew no attention from any distant guards. "Clever. Is she not afraid James will sequester her business in retaliation?"

"He can't do that publicly without making an enemy of England. He may not want to commit to war with Spain, but he very much wants to marry the Princess of Wales. There is only so far he can go in opposing someone who is now a member of the Courtenay family. Also, Maisie is more clever than even people think her. She has already taken steps to diversify control of the company beyond Edinburgh. And half her board members have left Scotland in the last month to direct affairs from London and Paris."

"And you will command this company?"

"Wherever my wife and the queen wish me. I suspect that will be in the North, will it not?"

"If James is not mustering troops, then most definitely you will be needed in the North. You know that Anabel is trying to draw Philip's forces here first."

"Yes. And I didn't say James would not muster troops. But he also will not commit to their use unless he is absolutely forced to. He is using his mother as a safeguard, hoping Philip wants Mary back enough to not want her executed by Scotland in retaliation."

Kit remembered his time with the two monarchs in Spain—haughty Mary Stuart and inscrutable Philip Hapsburg. Philip might not be in a hurry to get his wife back, now that she had fulfilled her primary function of providing him sons. As well as her secondary function—irritating Elizabeth.

"All we can do now is play out the game," Kit concluded. "The list of things we can control is growing shorter by the day."

NINETEEN

Two days after leaving Berwick to return to Middleham, Anabel's party was intercepted by a courier from the Earl of Arundel. He had come north to Hull in the last month, bringing with him a significant number of armed men. Anabel met Kit's eyes, and sighed inwardly. Time to face the devil and hope she didn't get burned.

They arrived at Hull Castle with as little fanfare as could be managed. To her surprise—and displeasure—Tomás Navarro was already there.

"I was not aware that you had asked leave to come to Hull," Anabel said frostily.

Navarro regarded her with an assurance bordering on arrogance that made her skin prickle. Something ugly was brewing. His words, though, were perfectly correct.

"Your Highness, the Earl of Arundel is waiting above for us."

Perhaps not that correct. An earl waited upon a princess, not the other way round.

Fortunately, Anabel had learned from the best how to assert her position. "The earl asked to see me. It is not for him to decide who will join us. I will send for you when I am ready."

"As you wish, Your Highness. You may find Lord Arundel less . . . amenable than in the past."

She stared at the priest. "We shall see."

Arundel was not nearly as rude as Navarro. The young earl was on his feet when she swept into the low-ceilinged chamber, and he made a proper bow. But he wasn't precisely deferential, either.

"Do you know what you are doing, Your Highness?" Arundel straightened, his light eyes piercing beneath that distinctive widow's peak.

"Meeting with you. Should I be doing something different?"

"You should be deciding which way you're going to jump when Spanish troops land on England's shores."

Anabel inhaled sharply. She forced herself to be still, to take a moment before replying. "My decision is taken. Is yours?" Neither of them were speaking plainly. They were each free to take the other at the value of what they said—or listen deeper, to what they left unsaid.

Arundel shot a look at the closed door, kept his voice low and his words noncommittal. "Do we want to have this discussion now?"

"You're the one who asked me here."

"My center of power, what remains of it, is far south of Hull."

"But your influence amongst certain elements of the North is . . . not negligible."

"Navarro suspects."

"He can suspect all he likes. His influence *is* negligible."

"Not if it's targeted properly."

"If you have something to say, Lord Arundel, say it. Better yet, do something more useful than speak."

Arundel narrowed his eyes. "I dislike Protestants, Your Highness. I dislike Protestant queens. I dislike being told how and whether I may practice the tenets of the True Faith."

"And?"

"And . . ." He drew out the word slowly. "I dislike being manipulated because of my faith. Fortunately for your cause, Navarro has
been even more egregious in his manipulation than you have. And
beneath all the insults from this government, I am English. I have
no wish to see Spanish troops holding London."

"My immediate concern is not Spanish troops in London, but
Spanish troops in Hull. Or Scarborough. Or York."

"That *should* be your concern. I have had word from an . . .
acquaintance in Scotland. The day before yesterday, Queen Mary
was liberated from Blackness Castle by Lord Maxwell. She has been
taken aboard one of the Spanish ships that sailed from Ireland weeks
ago."

"Those missing ships," she said under her breath.

"Quite."

"You're telling me the moment is at hand."

"Very nearly so. Those Spanish ships expect you to welcome
them—if not quite with open arms, at least without a serious show
of defiance. After all, they have Mary Stuart with them. If *you* will
not be reasonable, they have a Catholic queen quite prepared to take
vengeance on the North."

"Do you know where they will land?"

"I do not."

He looked at her guilelessly, and she could not tell if he was lying.
Certainly he seemed to be going to some trouble to warn her. "And
if they land in Hull, Lord Arundel, what will you and your armed
men do?"

"That," he said with a faint smile, "will depend on your actions.
Your Highness."

He would not be drawn further. Anabel left him then, for she was
afraid of losing her temper. She needed to get out of Hull, go somewhere she could think clearly without having to walk the line between truth and lie. Kit was waiting where she'd left him in an
antechamber off the stairs.

"Let's go," she said. "Now, before we can be stopped."

"You think we'll be stopped?"

"I think Navarro might try."

If he meant to stop her, Navarro didn't get the chance. They were out of the castle and beyond the city before most people had any idea she'd ever been there.

"Back to Middleham?" Kit asked.

"Too far. I need to be central, so I can move quickly when needed. We'll go to York. Send couriers out ahead to Middleham, let the council know to meet us there."

But when they reached the safe streets of York, Anabel discovered that the couriers had not been needed. Her council and critical household members were waiting for her at the Treasurer's House inside the city walls.

She didn't have to look far to know why and how.

Pippa smiled serenely, the soft light almost hiding the hollows in her face. "I knew you'd come."

Anabel let out a sigh between laughter and tears. "Let's get to work."

From the moment Kit laid eyes on the newly defiant Navarro in Hull, he'd been aching to fight. He didn't mind battle—what he hated was the long run-up to it, the days or weeks of delay and indecision that left him too anxious to sleep properly and too distracted to concentrate. So while Anabel worked with her council, Kit spent most of his time out and about in the city. York was a pretty place, but it wasn't the splendour of York Minster or the appeal of its narrow medieval streets that kept his attention. Mostly, he was watching the citizens. They were a polite lot—but cautious. If a Spanish army turned up outside its walls, Kit could not predict if York would open its gates in order to keep the peace.

In the event, they didn't have to decide. The city watch had no instructions to keep out recognized members of Her Highness's household, and so, when faced with fifty men dressed as members of

the Princess of Wales's personal guard, the watch allowed them to
pass.

Once the men reached the Treasurer's House, it took precisely
one minute for the threat to become clear. The men were Spanish,
and they carried weapons. Not sufficient to take the city—but more
than sufficient to take Anabel if they wished.

And they did so wish. The Spanish soldiers allowed Anabel the
courtesy of withdrawing with her advisors to a windowless chamber
with only a single door that was guarded from outside. His fists
opening and closing at his sides until they cramped, Kit listened to
Anabel read aloud the message the men had carried. It came from
Tomás Navarro.

Hull has been taken, Navarro wrote. *The city has acquiesced and thus far
been spared violence. To ensure her continuing safety, we require the presence
of Her Royal Highness the Infanta Anne Isabella to join Her Majesty Queen
Mary aboard* La Santa Catalina *anchored at Hull until the city of York is
also safely in our hands.*

"At which point, presumably," Kit said, "you are marched back
into York to a glorious reception from the conquering Spanish
troops and your Catholic subjects. Or, if you prove difficult, Mary
Stuart does it for you." He swore and shook his head. "It's mad."

"Navarro is mad," Anabel said slowly. "Just mad enough to think
this would work. But not so mad as to be unprepared for the worst.
If I don't agree, the Spanish will wreak violence on Hull."

"They would never hurt you."

"They won't have to. I will not let them hurt anyone else in my
place."

"You cannot possibly agree!" Kit yelled.

"It's not your decision."

"The hell it isn't. And I will use force to stop you if I must."

"I will not risk the destruction of Hull!"

Through their clash of temper, Pippa's cool voice intervened.
"There will be no destruction tonight. The Infanta will present herself as requested at *La Santa Catalina.*"

It was difficult to say who understood her first—Anabel, Kit, or Matthew. But it was Anabel whose voice rose the loudest over the instinctive refusals. "Absolutely not. This is not the time for playacting."

"What has all our playacting ever been but a prelude to this moment?"

"You think Navarro will be so charmed by your playacting that he will forgo his threats? Don't be a fool, Pippa. If you deliver yourself into Spanish hands in place of me, all you will have done is bought time for York to panic."

"No. I will have bought time for you to escape and bring York an army to save it."

Kit breathed out as he turned his full attention on his twin. "Stephen," he said, voicing the words held silent in Pippa's mind, clear in his own now that he paid attention. "You have sent for Stephen's troops, haven't you?"

Pippa's smile was as bright as their childhood. "Stephen's troops are only twenty miles off."

"We could send someone else to alert him!" Anabel snapped.

"Stephen needs you to be certain of what to do about the threat. He needs direction."

"*You* could direct him," Anabel pointed out to Pippa. "You could escape the city while I delay Navarro."

Kit felt that his head—not to mention his heart—would split as he listened to the two women he loved best in the world debate which of them would risk her life this night. How, he wondered, did Matthew manage to stand there without protest as his wife offered herself in place of Anabel?

"If you deliver yourself to the Spanish," Pippa said sternly to Anabel, "Navarro will hold a hostage whose worth is great enough to stop the English army in its tracks. Stephen would listen to me, but your other armies? Only you can command them, Your Highness. And only I can buy you the necessary time to do it."

Pippa stepped closer, until the two women were only inches apart. "It will work, Anabel," she whispered urgently. "I have seen it."

There was a weight to those four words, as though Pippa were momentarily able to impress upon the minds of all those present her own peculiar knowledge of what was to come. Kit had no doubt everyone could feel it. For himself, there was something lurking behind that weight, glimpsed through a door left ajar, and he could sense a tumult of other words and other weights. But the moment he turned his attention in that direction, Pippa slammed the door shut against him.

"Who will go with you?" Anabel asked. And as simply as that, assented to this most dangerous plan. Leaving Kit's heart in pieces.

The trick was in the clothing and the bearing. Blessed by nature with a similar height and build, with a bone structure that spoke of blood ties both Boleyn and Plantagenet between them, Pippa and Anabel had some of the physical traits necessary to pass for one another. And those they did not possess—notably their hair—could be manufactured. Since a severe bout of scarlatina several years ago that had necessitated cutting her hair, Anabel had in her keeping several expensive wigs of vivid red-gold. Pippa produced one of them now and, surprisingly, another wig of dark blonde hair with the distinctive black streak that matched her own.

Anabel raised an eyebrow. "You've kept this all these years?"

"Why do you think I had it made?"

"I thought it was to tease the French ambassador eight years ago." Anabel paused, then smiled bitterly. "But then, you always have four or five reasons for everything you do. Even when you were fifteen."

Pippa answered the unvoiced question in her friend's mind. "Yes, I knew it would be needed someday. No, I did not know why." *Not precisely,* she amended silently. She had known even then that it would be for a dangerous purpose.

With the distinctive matter of hair settled, it was then a matter of dress and bearing. Pippa had always dressed well at court, but no one dressed as well as the Princess of Wales. Even when the fabrics were similar, a royal gown had an edge to it. And a gown chosen for a royal surrender must be especially splendid. Cloth of gold, so overembroidered with metallic thread as to be nearly as thick as leather. Silk velvet in a shade of blue-green that moved like water beneath the overgown. A ruff large enough to be ornamental but restrained enough to make riding practical where necessary. Pearls clustered in drops along the neckline and cuffs. With each layer and ribbon and lacing and button, Pippa felt herself being pressed into the royal mold.

They pinned the red-gold of her wig high on the crown and left the rest loose beneath a cap of velvet and satin. The hair was her banner, her safe-conduct to the Spanish ship at Hull. With her would ride Matthew and Madalena. There had been some talk that Navarro would find it odd that Matthew had come, but he cut it off firmly. "Once Navarro sees me, he'll be close enough to see *her* and know she isn't the princess. I'm going."

When Pippa and Anabel were finished, they came together once more, each surveying the other with frank curiosity.

"Do I really look so haughty?" Anabel asked.

"You are being forced to deal with a man who is blackmailing you. I thought haughtiness was a given." Pippa studied her friend, attired in a blue taffeta gown trimmed in navy velvet. It was one of Pippa's favorites, and she had worn it often enough for people to associate it with her. It was disconcerting to see that streak of black in the blonde wig opposite her—a streak that was as much the marker of Pippa as Anabel's red-gold.

That was entirely the point.

"Just remember to be concerned," Pippa advised.

"I won't have to remember that."

It was not the time nor place for more than matter-of-fact farewells. "Be safe, Anabel. And move quickly—I would prefer to spend as little time in Navarro's company as possible."

When they had embraced, Pippa turned to the much more difficult farewell—her twin. Kit knew something vital had been left unsaid in all this. Pippa could not afford to let him know what it was,
or he might hesitate to do what he must.

So she spoke rapidly, with the confidence she'd had years to practice. "It will be raining after midnight," she warned Kit. "Get down
to the river behind the Council House. There's a skiff there big
enough for the two of you. Dress in dark clothing and you won't be
seen."

"Are you sure?"

"Yes."

"Pippa." Kit caught her arm when she tried to turn away. "I don't
like this."

"There is nothing to like. There is only what must be done."

"What are you not telling me?"

She shook free of his hold and put both hands to his face, pulling
it down to look him squarely in the eyes. Those beautiful hazel eyes
that both her brothers had from Minuette—a constant shifting of
brown and green and gold. In his worry, Kit's were darker tonight
than she ever remembered seeing them.

"One thing at a time, twin mine. Get her out of the city. Get her
to Stephen's troops. Alert Lord Scrope. Once those three things are
done, you will know what to do next."

"Don't taunt Navarro, Pippa. He's going to be furious—worse,
he'll be humiliated. He won't like being fooled by a girl, especially
not one he considers—"

"A witch?" Pippa said lightly, but there was a shiver of unease
along her spine. "I may not be the Princess of Wales, but my name
still has value. He cannot lightly hurt me."

"There won't be time," Kit declared flatly. "Lord Scrope and his men
will see to the safety of York. Stephen and I will be coming for you."

"I know." She smiled brilliantly and kissed him on each cheek, to
hide the two words that pounded hard behind her eyes, so desperately was she working to lock them away from Kit's mind.

Too late.

In the event, it was far easier than anyone could have predicted—other than Pippa, who knew that fate had led to this path and it would unfold before her without difficulty. The Spanish guards in York were all strangers, and within two minutes it was obvious they saw what they expected to see: a young woman of twenty-four with a shining fall of Tudor red hair and the bearing of a princess born to two ruling monarchs. Surrounded by guards, the English group rode south twenty miles to Howden, and then took to the River Ouse in a barge hastily converted for the purpose of transporting a royal princess who was something between a prisoner and a guest. The guards were not inclined to be talkative, and Pippa kept Matthew and Madalena close around her to protect her privacy.

By the time they reached Hull, Pippa had herself in perfect balance for what lay ahead. She felt as though nothing could surprise her, nothing shock her, nothing hurt her. She had been born for this. She would not fail.

There were three Spanish ships in port at Hull, the largest with the banner of Mary Stuart flying proudly. There was no question of the English group being allowed to remain on land. The Spanish would want Anabel where they could not only protect her, but remove her swiftly out of English hands if she proved troublesome. The illusion of the princess being there willingly was rapidly vanishing.

At the base of the dock leading up to *La Santa Catalina,* Pippa straightened her back, squared her shoulders, and disdainfully eyed the soldiers arrayed above to greet her—or guard her. Black as grim death in their midst stood Tomás Navarro. Though he had always dressed as a proper Jesuit, in this element he looked . . . more. As though bolstered by the weight of his office when surrounded by men who could enforce his will with violence.

Pippa counted silently as she walked. How many steps before Navarro realized?

One . . . two . . . three . . . She felt Navarro's satisfaction beating in the air, delighted to have brought the proud Princess Anne to heel. *Four . . . five . . .* Matthew's presence behind her was as reassuring as his touch. *Six . . .* Madalena was breathing silent prayers that brushed against Pippa's awareness like moths.

Ten feet away from Navarro, Pippa lowered her arrogant chin a fraction and met his eyes unblinkingly.

The priest opened his mouth to make the Princess of Wales welcome.

And froze.

When Navarro moved, it was with sudden violence that made everyone but Matthew startle. Matthew simply moved very, very close behind Pippa. Not touching, but letting her know he was prepared to sweep her out of reach the moment she wanted him to.

Navarro used one hand to grab her, closing the remaining space between them, and held her hard as fury replaced disbelief. "Witch," he said in English under his breath . . . or perhaps the word began with a harder consonant.

By now the Spanish had begun to stir, their commander striding forward to intervene. "Father Navarro, you must remember that the Infanta is our guest."

"This isn't the Infanta," Navarro snarled. Then, with a visible effort of will, he controlled his temper. He released Pippa, but only to put his hands to her hair and, painfully, jerk the wig loose.

"This," he pronounced, looking from the red hair lying loose in his hands to the tightly plaited and coiled blonde hair that had lain hidden beneath, "is the Infanta's rejection of our kind offer. Seize this traitor and her party and confine them below."

Before they took Pippa away, Navarro breathed a warning into her ear. "It was a mistake to send you."

It seemed to take forever for night to fall. Anabel paced, feeling confined by Pippa's dress and the heavy wig. They had used Pippa's increasingly frequent bouts of illness to explain her staying out of sight,

but really, where else could she be? The illusion of English freedom
still held, but did not change the fact that there were Spanish soldiers
in York, watching the gates that led into and out of the city.

Anabel and Kit were not leaving by a gate. When finally—
finally—twilight bled away into darkness and rain began to fall, the
two of them followed Pippa's instructions to the letter. Out a side
door of the Council House and through the wet gardens to the river.
The skiff was there, and Kit handily and quietly rowed them up-
stream. Anabel's tension, which had been cutting into her head and
shoulders for hours like a vise, eased fractionally the farther west
they got.

It was not practical, nor fast enough, to row all the way in the
dark. Kit found the spot along the riverbank that Pippa had indicated and helped Anabel out of the skiff. Thanks to the rain, it now
had several inches of water in the bottom. Her cloak and skirt hems
were sodden, but she barely noticed the weight or the chill. They
took to horses now, with a young groom who'd been waiting for
them, to ride through the trackless dark to the nearest armed support.

Of all the Courtenays, Anabel had always known Stephen the
least. Unlike Kit, he had been remarkably self-contained from an
early age and never inclined to edge into what might be seen as his
younger brother's territory. But when he met them at the edge of his
camp, torches flaring high now that the rain had paused, Anabel had
never been so relieved in her life. Stephen Courtenay had his father's air of self-possession—a confidence that whatever happened,
he was well able to not only meet it, but match it. After the long day
and night passed in Kit's strung-up company, Anabel found Stephen
refreshingly straightforward.

He wasted no time apologizing to her for the lack of royal comforts in his camp. The three of them met alone in Stephen's tent, a
little larger than those of his men, in order to accommodate the
table and stools needed for communication and council.

His first question was to Kit. "Is Pippa all right?"

Anabel knew that most of Kit's taut temper through the day had been the consequence of intense focus on the thread that bound him to his twin. He nodded at Stephen. "Unharmed. But the masquerade will only last until she meets Navarro. Assuming they reached Hull by sundown, we must anticipate reactions in York soon after the sun comes up. Hopefully no one will think to check on us"—he indicated himself and Anabel—"until the alarm is raised."

"When it is? Tell me about the Spanish forces in York."

The talk turned technical then, not that Anabel couldn't follow the military terms, but the brothers had blood and experience on their side. They possessed the kind of shorthand available not only to family but to men who had fought together. The largest concern, for all of them, was what York itself would choose to do.

Stephen chewed his bottom lip thoughtfully. "Some of the Spanish in York will have to leave the city to try and trace the princess. From what you say, there aren't enough men there to hold the city at the same time. So they leave, and the city has a breathing space before reinforcements can arrive from Hull. The question is . . . will York open their gates to the Spanish?"

"No," Kit objected loudly. "The 'question' is how fast can we reach Hull and get Pippa away from the Spanish!"

"You don't have to tell me that!" Stephen shouted back. "But we have to think of England as well."

"Stop it," Anabel commanded wearily. "We will do both. You know we prepared for this, Kit. I must ride on to Lord Scrope's forces and get them moving toward York."

"It's not safe."

"And leaving York in a skiff was? I must alert Lord Scrope and ride back with his men to York. The city will open its gates to me— and I can ensure they are kept firmly shut against the Spanish." She tipped her chin up. "And Stephen will take his mercenary force as fast as they can move to Hull and get hold of Pippa."

"I'm going with Stephen," Kit announced. It was a measure of his fear for his twin that he would consider leaving Anabel.

It was Stephen who protested. "No. The princess needs protection."

"You have any number of highly trained soldiers at your command."

"And I will release some to attend her, but are you really proposing to put the safety of the Princess of Wales in any hands but your own?"

"But Pippa . . ."

Anabel held her breath. She wanted Kit with her—so badly that it hurt—but she would never put him in the position of having to choose between two loves.

Stephen managed it neatly for her. "I will get to Pippa. You can trust me for that, Kit. Get Anabel to Lord Scrope and then march his army to York as fast as you can. The Princess of Wales must reach the city with armed men before the Spanish, or this war will begin with a major disadvantage to us."

The struggle was evident on Kit's face, but fear and old jealousy and sibling rivalry was submerged beneath the stern sense of duty that Dominic Courtenay had instilled in his children. Kit bowed to the wisdom of Stephen's logic with as much grace as he could manage.

"Give us a dozen men," he said. "And let Anabel sleep for a few hours. We'll leave at first light."

She was the one with the last word, as she nearly always was. "Stephen, if I were to win York and lose Pippa . . ."

"I will bring her back," Stephen promised. "Besides, she has Matthew with her. Anyone who wants to hurt Pippa will have to get through her husband first."

TWENTY

Initially Pippa was kept alone in a cramped cabin below deck. But someone more cautious than Navarro—perhaps someone who knew that King Philip had a fondness for his daughter's friend—must have protested, for within hours Madalena was allowed to join her. She reported that Matthew was being questioned by the ship's captain. That was no worry. Pippa was not afraid of the Spanish military. Professional men were not usually fanatics.

Navarro was another sort of man entirely. Freed now of the need to ingratiate himself with Anabel and her household, his contempt burned bright each time he entered her makeshift cell. It was comfortable enough, for a ship, belonging as it did to the first lieutenant. Presumably Mary Stuart had taken over the captain's quarters. There had been no question—yet—of securing Pippa bodily beyond putting her behind a guarded door. But there was a porthole maybe wide enough for a woman in her shift to wiggle through, and Pippa wagered these men would not guess that she could swim. So could Madalena. If necessary, Pippa would force her to leave that way. She herself would go nowhere without Matthew.

Besides, her hour had come. Now that it was upon her, Pippa met it with an equanimity that, if not perfect, gave a good imitation of being so. She slept through the night, and when daylight came, began counting the hours of her confinement. She simply wanted to get on with things.

She did not flinch when the door opened to again admit Tomás Navarro.

Now free to be wholly himself, the priest was more physically attractive than she had ever known him. There must be women who at one time or another had regretted his spiritual calling. But Pippa knew a lot of attractive men. She was not disturbed by beauty.

"If only you knew," Navarro said softly, "how I have longed for this. To face you as you are, stripped of royal protection. And without any need on my part for a pretense of civility."

"If past encounters were your idea of civility, I cannot imagine how unpleasant you will be now."

He ignored her sarcasm. "In all England, there is no opponent more dangerous than a pretty girl with a serpent's tongue . . . and a witch's charms."

"You underestimate our soldiers, not to mention our navy."

"Princess Anne was meant to be England's salvation. But how could she ever see her true path, with a bastard heretic for a mother and you, dripping your honeyed lies into her ears at every turn? She is stubborn and must be chastised. But you?"

Navarro smiled, the first time Pippa had ever seen him do so. It chilled her to her fingertips.

"'Thou shalt not suffer a witch to live,'" he quoted. "Who am I to gainsay Holy Church?"

"Holy Church says even a witch must have a trial." Not that Pippa liked the thought of the Inquisition, but all she need do was delay. Someone would come for her.

"You have been on trial since the moment I met you, Lady Philippa. Coming here—this little deception of yours—was the final piece of evidence against you. The moment I realized that you kept Princess Anne from doing her duty, the verdict was delivered. You are guilty, my lady. And it is my place to punish the guilty."

"By burning me at the stake for heresy on English soil?"

"You are on a Spanish ship. If I wish, I can send you to Spain for proper punishment."

"But you won't, because once King Philip is aware of my detention, he will ensure I am not harmed."

"I don't have to kill you to punish you. And it will take some time for King Philip to become aware."

Madalena finally made her presence known. In her low, beautiful speaking voice that seemed always to hint of warm skies and fragrant trees, she said in Spanish, "It will take very little time for English soldiers to arrive. Do you think Her Highness would willingly put her dearest friend in danger without a plan to get her back?"

"Then," Navarro said, "we have no time to waste."

He opened the door and summoned two soldiers inside. "Take Lady Philippa above. I want the English to see what happens to heretics and witches."

That did not sound promising. Philippa wished she could see all the steps between now and her final vision. But she had never been able to command her gift so far. She knew the end, but not everything along the way. All she could do was continue to shield Kit from as much of what was happening as possible to ensure he was not distracted from his own tasks.

Before they took her from the cabin, Navarro made her change into something resembling a penitent's robe. Drab grey wool skirt and short coat, with the riding shoes she'd worn. She was momentarily surprised that he ordered Madalena to loosen Pippa's hair from its tight plaits, but then she understood. He wanted that black streak to be clearly seen—the mark of the devil, as he thought it.

They took her off the ship to the courtyard of Hull Castle. There was no gallows present (not that she'd really expected one) nor even a platform, just a cleared space around one of the stone walls. The crowd was restive behind the cordon of Spanish soldiers. Pippa saw the Earl of Arundel near the front; he looked away as she passed him.

Matthew was there. She did not have to look at him to know his hands and ankles were chained. They would never have been able to keep him from her otherwise. She kept her head high and her concentration fixed. Led to the space next to the wall, she saw there were chains hanging from the stone above her head, and she knew suddenly what Navarro intended.

He would strip her to her shift, likely—surely he wouldn't require more than that?—then, facing the wall, her hands would be pulled high above her shoulders and chained so she was held fast. And then he would whip her.

He would do it himself, of that she was certain. She noted that he had also changed for this occasion—the severe Jesuit robes removed to show equally severe shirt and hose. He held the whip, lightly flicking it against the ground as he pronounced her crimes and sentence.

You are making mistakes, she noted as he spoke. Your hatred has made you irrational ... and one thing that will always turn an Englishman's stomach is irrational emotion. Not to mention the circle of foreign soldiers threatening an English woman. An English girl ... it suddenly seemed important for Pippa to make the most of her youth and fragility.

It wasn't difficult to emphasize it when they removed her skirt and short coat, leaving her shivering in only her cambric shift despite the late spring warmth. She could feel Matthew's rising anger and need to act, and so sent to him what comforting thoughts she could manage. She had asked Madalena to keep as near him as she could and remind him not to get himself dragged away or knocked out.

Then there was nothing to do but to divorce her awareness as much as possible from her body. She'd had practice these last months through her increasing illness, and thought herself prepared.

Until the first lash fell. The whip was not barbed, thank the heavens, but it was wicked enough and she gasped aloud at the shock of pain. In her life, Pippa had never been touched with anything but affection. Navarro had specified a dozen lashes. The second fell . . . the third . . .

With the fourth stroke, Pippa's control breached and she could not keep from crying out. The focus she was so proud of deserted her, and only dimly was she aware of the murmur of the crowds, the shouts of her husband ringing the loudest. Navarro struck her a fifth time and she knew she would never remain conscious to the end. Why had this never been in her visions?

Six . . . and then a pause that stretched out so long that Pippa was slowly able to focus on something besides her bleeding back. Voices raised—angry voices—Navarro and . . . who? Not Matthew. And not Spanish. This particular voice was familiar, cultured English, the meaning of the words a jumble through the pain.

Then her arms were unchained and competent hands supported her to the ground. A light weight—a shawl or cloak—settled over her hunched shoulders and that same voice was speaking.

It was the Earl of Arundel. "I will see to her injuries myself," Philip Howard said to a furious Tomás Navarro. "If you try to return her to the ship, I suspect you'll have a riot on your hands. You've sent the rest of the ships and more than half your men to Berwick, and I'm not sure Hull can hold out against a determined uprising. So let me settle everyone's tempers by taking charge of her."

She thought it was in the balance whether Navarro would agree, but even through the fog of pain, Pippa could sense the growing discontent amongst the watchers. And not just the English—the Spanish soldiers were uneasy with Navarro's fanaticism. If he ordered them to resist Arundel, she wasn't sure what would happen.

Clearly, neither was Navarro. He gave in grudgingly, and next thing Pippa knew, Madalena and Matthew had replaced Arundel around her. As lightly as though she were a child, her husband lifted her in his arms and followed Arundel into the castle.

In five years of fighting and commanding in various countries, Stephen had lived through many difficult days and nights. This mission was different. It had the same furious intensity as the summer of 1580, when he and Kit had ridden with Mary Stuart in order to secure Lucette's release as a hostage. Now it was Pippa, deliberately placing herself in peril, trusting to a belief in fate that Stephen himself rejected. He saw Kit and Anabel on their way with two dozen of his best men, then moved the rest of the company east. They rode fast and light, and because they had trained for such things, covered the ground with ease.

In under three hours Hull came into view, with three Spanish ships in harbor. Stephen drew up his company a mile from the town. He did not intend to make an assault unless pushed to it, so he gave his orders and rode alone and anonymously into the city.

There was a small contingent of Spanish guards at the city gate, but Stephen had experience in lying smoothly and got himself admitted with little trouble. They even directed him to the castle, where he had seen the standard of the Earl of Arundel flying. Best to start at the top. Besides his openly displayed sword and the dagger at his belt, Stephen had a smaller knife concealed in his jerkin. He would use it if he had to, even against an Englishman.

He surrendered his horse into the care of a castle groom, who sent a messenger ahead for the earl that an Englishman with information to sell wished to see him. That would at least get Stephen into Arundel's presence without revealing his identity beforehand. Stephen crossed the courtyard, the usual bustle of castle life passing around him, but stopped dead when a conversation caught his attention.

> "*Mad he is, that Spaniard . . .*"
> "*Never saw a priest whip a girl like that . . .*"
> "*Thought her man would rip out someone's arms to get to her . . .*"
> "*Brave thing, she is, for all the priest's talk of witchcraft . . .*"

Stephen strode into the knot of three men talking, and irritation quickly gave way to wariness as they looked at his face. "What are you talking about?" he demanded.

The oldest of the three, a tough-looking Yorkshireman in his thirties, said gruffly, "What's it to you?"

Stephen tried hard to remember that he was posing as a Catholic sympathizer at the moment. "If Tomás Navarro has been reduced to venting his frustrations against a mere girl, that doesn't argue well for our ability to convince the country that we wish only to secure our rights."

The eyes of the quiet two flickered between themselves as the same man replied. "It was all the Spanish, we had nothing to do with it. His lordship himself stopped it and took her away."

"Stopped what?" He prayed that he had overheard that single word wrongly.

He hadn't. "The priest whipped her, here in the yard. Claimed she was a witch. I couldn't see it, myself. Just a woman, and I reckon that priest doesn't think much of women."

Stephen had turned on his heel while the man was still speaking, and he had to flex his hands at his sides to keep from drawing his weapons as he grabbed the first boy he could find inside to take him to Lord Arundel. If he let himself think . . . let their words conjure up a picture . . .

Stephen had seen men whipped before. It was sometimes necessary in a military company. But the thought of his little sister—lovely, mischievous, generous Pippa—beneath the lash of a whip made him want to put his hands around Navarro's throat and choke the life out of him.

Instead, he channeled that fury inward, and by the time he was admitted to Arundel's presence, Stephen had enough control of his temper not to begin yelling immediately.

Arundel looked up sharply at the interruption, clearly prepared to snap at the intruder. But it took only a moment for him to recognize Stephen, and his irritation gave way to alarm. "Leave us," he commanded the boy, who scampered away gratefully.

Philip Howard was a few years older than Stephen, the son of oft-rebel and executed traitor Thomas, Duke of Norfolk. Once a somewhat wild youth, he had been firmly converted to Catholicism in 1581 and had held on to his beliefs in the face of increasing pressure from his second cousin, Queen Elizabeth. His title, inherited from his mother, made him a significant power amongst the recusants.

"By your attire," Lord Arundel said drily, "I assume you did not announce your name. Where did you leave your Scottish company?"

"Where did you leave my sister?" Stephen shot back.

"You've heard." Arundel sighed. "I'm truly sorry, Courtenay. Navarro is . . . unreasonable. With soldiers to back him, he thinks himself invulnerable."

"Where. Is. Philippa?"

"I don't know."

"You gave her back to Navarro?" Stephen ground out, and rested his hand on the hilt of his sword. He could see red at the edges of his vision.

"I did not," Arundel snapped. "She is gone, Courtenay, no one knows where. I took her out of that courtyard and put her in a comfortable chamber here with her husband and the Spanish woman. Three hours later they were gone. I assure you, if you don't believe me, ask Navarro. You'll have to find him, though. The priest is on their trail."

"If you are lying—"

"How do you think they were able to get out of this castle unseen? I ensured they had a degree of privacy and time . . . and they used it to their advantage. I am glad of it. I think Queen Elizabeth dangerously hostile to her Catholic subjects, but I am not stupid enough to take out my anger on a single woman."

Stephen couldn't quite bring himself to thank the man. "I don't suppose you have any idea which direction I should look for them?"

"Not the sea," Arundel said cynically.

Stephen headed for the door, not waiting for more. But he hesitated at the last minute, the fact that there was more at stake than simply his sister returning forcibly to his mind.

"What will you do now?" Stephen asked abruptly.

"Now that the princess has slipped the attempted Spanish snare, and is no doubt well on her way to alert Lord Bolton and his army?" Arundel spoke cynically, but reasonably. "As little as I like this present queen, I have no wish for civil war. I cannot bring myself to support a side I despise, but no more can I bring myself to oppose it with blood. I will, at the least, hold my men neutral, and so you may tell your princess and your queen."

It was as much as they could hope for at this point. Stephen nodded once, in grudging acknowledgment of Arundel's conscience. "Thank you," he at last managed.

Stephen was out of the castle, out of the city, and back to his company as fast as he could move. Splitting the company in three, he sent them in different directions and began to scout the countryside for Pippa—and the man hunting her.

Everything that happened after the courtyard etched itself into Pippa's awareness like a steel-point engraving. A black and white procession of events, stripped of colour and texture, but perfectly clear in detail. Arundel's blunt courtesy trying to conceal his distaste, Matthew's distress manifesting itself in stark lines on his bone-white face, Madalena's gentle care as she bathed Pippa's flayed back.

Through it all, her vision was clear and her thinking sharp. There was pain, but no fear. Pippa knew absolutely that everything that had happened was meant to happen—and everything that was to come was equally necessary. She did not bother herself trying to anticipate events. God would ensure the end.

She slept on her stomach for an hour or two and ate what was brought. Matthew and Madalena had a low-voiced, urgent conversation trying to figure out what Arundel would do next. Pippa was the only one who was not surprised when the earl himself returned to the chamber where he'd left them.

He spoke in as few words as possible. "I tried, and failed, to persuade Navarro to return to the ship. He will not leave the castle without Lady Philippa."

"And so?" Matthew, as he rarely did, rose to his full height. She had never seen him look so much like his intimidating father.

"And so," Arundel rejoined coolly, "Lady Philippa must leave the castle without his knowledge."

"Can you do it?" Madalena asked.

"Give me an hour. I'll quietly have my men get horses outside the city. I know this castle better than the Spanish—I can get you out. But once I do, you'd best ride as fast as you can for safe haven. I will keep Navarro in ignorance as long as possible. But make no mistake—he will come after you."

He addressed that last directly to Pippa. She smiled gently. "I know it," she said. "I am not afraid."

With one nod, Arundel turned to go.

"Philip," she called after him. They had known each other for years, if not especially well. As she'd intended, her use of his name stopped him. And when he looked back at her, his expression had been stripped of its arrogance. He looked like a young man trying desperately to live his religion in an often hostile environment, not always sure of what was right and not overfond of interfering foreigners.

It moved Pippa enough to stand with care and take his hands in hers as she might have one of her brothers. "Thank you," she said simply.

"Be careful," he said in return, then left as abruptly as he'd come.

Matthew worried about her ability to ride, but Pippa assured him she would be well. She did not think he believed her. Just over an

hour later, the three of them had been smuggled out of the castle
and town through low windows and crooked alleys and mounted the
horses left for them. The direction had already been decided by
Pippa—west to the royal castle of Pontefract. They would have to
come at it obliquely to draw off any pursuit, making the distance
perhaps sixty miles. But there were hamlets along the way, and
Arundel had sent them with minimal supplies to make camp.

They'd ridden for four hours and were just thinking of stopping
when Matthew reined in hard and motioned the women to do the
same. A low mist swirled against the ground, hampering sight. But
Pippa heard it at once—or perhaps merely felt the vibration in her
bones. The rumble of mounted men, coming fast and hard.

"Navarro," she breathed out.

Matthew hesitated only a moment. If they stayed on the road,
they'd be caught. There were no nearby manors or churches where
they could make a stand. In that moment of hesitation, Pippa realized exactly where they were and almost laughed aloud. As if the
location was burned into her brain, she could see the stark, unfriendly walls of the abandoned medieval tower they'd come across
just weeks before. Where better to face off against Navarro?

"Witch Willow," she called to Matthew. He swung his gaze at her,
then realized what she meant and subtly adjusted direction.

It was a flat-out run for the tower. Pippa could feel each open
wound on her back and gritted her teeth. She would not be the cause
of their failure to reach safety. By the time Witch Willow could be
seen through the gathering dark, Navarro's horsemen were nearly
within arrow range—a fact forcibly brought home by several distinctive swishes through the air.

Abandoning their horses and supplies, Madalena quickly led the
way up the rickety exterior stairs while Matthew kept hold of Pippa's
arm. An arrow arced through the darkening sky and struck Matthew
in the back, sending his body falling hard against Pippa. Even as he
fell, a second arrow hit him in the arm. Madalena grabbed for him

but his weight was too much for the women and Pippa was driven to her knees halfway up the stairs. The wood groaned and swayed alarmingly beneath them.

Another arrow clattered against the stone above them. "Go," Matthew urged tightly. "Get inside. Bar that door."

"Get up!" Pippa commanded.

Navarro and half his men were off their horses and crossing the ground. Only a hundred feet until the priest reached the stairs.

Matthew gripped her hand so tight her bones cracked. "Run!" he commanded, in the words that had sent her fleeing from him when she was fifteen. The message of the stars, the echoes of her vision. "Pippa, run now."

To hell with the stars. "Matthew Harrington, if you do not get to your feet this second I will walk straight down these stairs and into Navarro's hands. Get. Up."

He got up. With Madalena's help, they somehow managed to get him the rest of the way. Each step was an agony for Pippa, but she set her jaw and kept going. As the first Spanish boots touched the bottom of the stairs, Matthew collapsed on the floor of the tower and Madalena shot home the bolts of the door.

Between them, the women did the grim but necessary work of pulling the arrows out of Matthew. Madalena had managed to keep hold of her pack so they had a little water to clean him as best they could. She tore strips from her shift to bind the wounds that were, blessedly, not bleeding too freely. Then she turned to Pippa.

"Let me see your back."

"I'm fine."

"Pippa," began Matthew, but she abruptly hushed him.

What windows there were in the tower were too high for her to see out of. She'd been listening to the Spanish coming up the stairs, trying to break down the door. Fists, feet, even a makeshift battering ram made little headway. The door was more than a foot thick and barred with iron in two places.

But none of that could stop fire.

Pippa closed her eyes. "They're going to burn us out."

A moment later came another pounding on the door, followed by an unmistakable voice. "Smell the smoke, Lady Philippa?" Tomás Navarro called. "My men have started a little fire. Little for now, at least ... and at the bottom of the stairs. It will consume this old wood fast enough. The door is thick, I know, but fire purifies everything."

They kept silent, since there was nothing to say.

"Here is my offer, Lady Philippa, made this once only. I'm going down now and will wait for five minutes. For those five minutes, the fire will be kept controlled at the foot of the stairs. If you surrender yourself within those five minutes, I will put out the fire. And I will let your husband and the renegade Spanish woman go free. If you do not appear, you all three die together."

They heard his footsteps, good as his word, retreating down the stairs.

There was nothing to consider. Matthew had time only to say, "Don't even think—" before she had unbarred the door and stepped out.

Madalena and Matthew scrambled after her, but she ignored their cries of protest. There was only this moment and then the next. Each moment so clear and perfect that she seemed hardly to be moving.

When she reached the ground, Navarro gestured to his men to douse the flames. She walked directly to him, completely and absolutely unafraid. He gripped her by the arm at the very instant the sounds of more horses galloping at breakneck speed came through the rising fog wreathed around them. Even before Pippa could see, she knew it was Stephen.

She could almost follow the trail of Navarro's calculations. Enemies on horseback, Matthew coming blood-streaked down the stairs like vengeance personified—there was still one thing the priest could do.

Pippa didn't see the dagger. It would not have mattered. She did not flinch when Navarro drove it toward her chest, but he misaimed. Rather than piercing her heart, she felt the dagger catch against a rib.

Before Pippa lost awareness, she performed her last critical act. She dropped every barrier in her mind, loosed every tie of control, and with everything in her heart and soul, reached for the thread that had bound her since birth and sent a call winging across the miles.

Kit.

Kit jolted out of an exhausted sleep in a cold sweat, heart pounding and pulse racing. It was dark before his eyes—all he had was an impression of fog and horses. It looked nothing at all like the inside of a tent.

Kit—a call, a plea, a flood of pain and fear.

In two minutes he was pulling on his boots, shirt thrown on and jerkin unlaced. Because he was concentrating on trying to reach Pippa, to let her know he was coming, Kit didn't notice anyone entering his tent.

Until Anabel spoke, bewildered and wary. "What are you doing?"

"Leaving."

"Now? Lord Scrope's men won't be ready for another hour."

"I'm not going to Hull."

He flinched when she touched him, and forced himself to meet her eyes. He knew she could read the terror in them.

"Kit, what is wrong? What's happened?"

"Pippa." He couldn't speak more yet, had to shake his head to clear his throat. "She's hurt, she's . . . I have to go."

She didn't hesitate. "I'm going with you." And then she did hesitate, long enough to be practical. "Do you know where?"

He did know, the same way he knew Pippa was gravely injured. "Pontefract."

TWENTY-ONE

The only reason Stephen Courtenay didn't kill Tomás Navarro where he stood was because he didn't want to spare time—or thought—for anyone while Pippa lay bleeding on the hard ground. His own men expertly took the Spanish soldiers, and if they handled Navarro particularly roughly, no one was going to complain.

He knelt by his sister and didn't know whether to be relieved that she was unconscious. Better for her, probably.

"I can help," Madalena Arias said at his shoulder. "And someone should see to Matthew. We had to pull two arrows out of him."

Stephen raised his head. "Is he all right?"

She nodded toward the tower, and Stephen saw his brother-in-law coming rapidly to his wife, bloody bandages on his shoulder and arm.

Between the three of them—and, best of all, the Scottish surgeon Stephen had prudently brought with him—they got the wound cleaned. They were just arguing about where to take her when her eyes fluttered open.

"Matthew."

Instantly he was there, then Pippa's eyes turned to her brother. "Stephen," she acknowledged. "Take me to Pontefract."

"That's twenty miles—"

"Pontefract," she insisted firmly. "I shall reach there perfectly safely. I know it."

Stephen met Matthew's eyes and waited. When Matthew reluctantly nodded, he sighed. "You'd damn well better be right," he said grimly to Pippa. "I'm not explaining to Kit why I hurt you any more than necessary."

Her smile was faint but genuine. "I'll be sure to tell him it was all my fault."

They reached Pontefract around midnight. Stephen was not familiar with the castle, but Matthew and Madalena both knew it well, for Anabel had often been here. The governor of the castle met them outside the walls and quickly had Pippa carried to a spacious chamber.

Both Matthew and Madalena went with Pippa, but when Stephen made to follow, the governor touched his arm.

"They're in the solar, Lord Stephen."

He blinked. "Who is?"

"Your family."

Stephen shook his head, certain that exhaustion had made him mishear the man. But he did not retract the surprising statement, and so Stephen followed him, bewildered. And sure enough, there were four people waiting in the solar who he knew perfectly well: his mother and father, with Lucette and Julien. His mother and Lucie paused just long enough to hug him and then followed the governor to the chamber where Pippa had been taken.

Stephen remained in the solar with his father and Julien. "How . . ." he began, and couldn't finish his sentence.

He was suddenly aware of how utterly exhausted he was, and tense with it. His muscles were cramped from riding and subdued panic, and his father must have seen it, because he said abruptly, "Sit down before you fall down. Then tell us."

He told his story succinctly, from Kit and Anabel's arrival at his camp, to his dash for Hull and the subsequent hunt for Navarro and the Spanish on Pippa's trail.

"We were just too late. Another minute earlier—" He broke off. "Navarro got his damage in right before I reached him."

"Where is he?"

"My men are bringing him in."

"Good."

From the way his father pronounced that single word, Stephen thought it was not at all good for Tomás Navarro. He didn't much care.

Again he asked, "How? How do you happen to be at Pontefract? Shouldn't you be in Dover or Portsmouth or even Tilbury?"

"I should always be where my children are in danger. As to the how . . ." Dominic scrubbed his hand through hair the same black as Stephen's, now liberally streaked with silver. "We had letters from Dr. John Dee. Your mother and I, and Lucette." Dominic nodded to where Julien sat silent in this face of family crisis.

For the first time, Stephen looked closely at his father and realized that he was, indeed, growing older. Dominic said flatly, "Dee told us to be at Pontefract on this day. He did not tell us why—only that it was of vital importance. I wish . . . If I find out that he knew what was going to happen and did not warn us, there will be a reckoning."

Every minute spent nursing Pippa was an agony for Lucette. Not because Pippa complained—she could not have been sweeter-tempered. Partly it was the natural protectiveness of an older sister. Partly, it was the nature of Pippa's injuries. It was one thing to tend a person who was ill, another matter entirely when the damage had been wrought by human hands. Once before, Lucette had tended someone deliberately and maliciously injured, when Julien had done battle with his brother. But to see the stripes on Pippa's back and the terrible wound made by a dagger—both injuries done by a supposed man of God—made Lucette's jaw ache from holding her tongue so as not to pour out invectives before her sister.

Those she saved for her husband, in the short spaces when her mother insisted she leave Pippa's bedside to eat or rest.

Her mother, Lucette noted, did neither.

Matthew was also a constant presence, and Madalena a godsend for her calm manner. She would whisper sometimes to Pippa in a soft and sibilant Spanish. And the Scottish surgeon from Stephen's company was a steady and practiced man who spoke bracingly to Pippa when she was awake.

The problem was, Pippa had already been seriously weakened by a prolonged illness that they were only now told was consumption. The surgeon could only shrug when asked how it might affect her healing. But his face was grave. Less than forty-eight hours after being brought to Pontefract, the first dangerous signs of infection were already pronounced.

What frightened Lucette most of all was Pippa's serenity. She tried once to task her sister with the need to fight, but Pippa simply smiled. "I will not go, Lucie, until I have finished."

She would not be drawn further.

They had sent riders to alert Kit, but he arrived faster than they could have hoped. He barely paused to speak to anyone, so it was left to Anabel to explain. She looked wraith-thin from long riding at a punishing pace, and her eyes followed Kit with a queer mix of fear and love as he left for Pippa's bedside.

"He knew," Anabel told Lucette and Stephen. "He woke from a dead sleep—it must have been when Pippa was . . . when Navarro stabbed her. We were on the road in less than twenty minutes. I don't think he's slept, even when we were forced to stop to snatch food and change horses. I have never seen him so . . . inward. As though only his body were moving while his soul was already here with her."

Lucette said roughly, so as not to cry, "Come change, Anabel, and at least wash your face. It will help."

"May I see her?"

"Of course."

Anabel shivered, and Lucette saw beneath the regal princess to the little girl who had come to Wynfield Mote so long ago for friendship. And had found a family.

Gently, Lucette noted, "You are afraid. Why?"

The answer was simple, and devastating. "Because Kit is afraid."

Pippa died as the hush of night gave way to the earliest call of the morning birds. With Matthew supporting her on one side and Kit on the other, God allowed her to slip away peacefully. She was conscious until nearly the end, her breath slight and shallow enough that it took Kit a minute or two to understand when it ceased. Then his mother put her arm around his shoulders. Despite her tears, Minuette spoke clearly. "Come away, Kit. She is gone."

He allowed himself to be passed from hand to hand until Stephen took his arm and led him unseeing through the castle. Dimly, he was aware of his brother talking, but could make no sense of the words. Then there was a quiet, darkened room and a soft bed and someone tugging off his boots, and then only darkness.

An hour later—or two—or possibly a lifetime—Kit woke choking on his own breath. He'd heard that sometimes when people woke after a death it would take a moment for the memory of loss to return, but it was not so for him. How could it be? Even in sleep, part of him had been achingly aware of what was missing. It was as though half his world had blinked itself out of existence.

He felt the unshed tears thick in his throat but could not cry. After sitting with his face buried in his hands for some time, Kit got up in a sudden burst of frantic energy. There was water in a bowl, and he stripped off jerkin and shirt and washed himself as best he could, splashing water through his hair and letting it run down his face in place of crying. Stephen had put him in his own room, and Kit found a clean shirt in a pack at the end of the bed.

Outside the room, he hesitated. He didn't really want to talk to anyone but Anabel, but he didn't know where she had been put. Except that . . . he did. Kit stood still, hardly daring to move for fear of losing it, but where there had once been the silk and diamond tie that bound him to Pippa, there was a slender silver thread pulling at him from someone nearby.

When he let his feet follow his instincts and knocked on the door they took him to, it was Anabel who answered.

She took one look at his face and made an inarticulate sound of distress. She pulled him into the room and closed the door, then guided him to a low couch upholstered in velvet. Sitting as close to him as she could get, Anabel laid her head on his shoulder.

He closed his eyes. "I don't know what to do," he said. "What do I do now? I've always had her, from before we were even born. She . . ."

Kit swallowed against a low sob, then another, and tears found their way from behind his clenched eyelids. "I can't breathe, Anabel," he gasped. "I don't even know how to breathe without Pippa."

He slid from the bench and laid his head in her lap. As he wept, Anabel ran her hands lightly over his hair and his shoulders. And Kit knew that she was the only thing anchoring him to this world.

23 June 1586
Pontefract Castle

It is over. Tonight we laid my little girl to temporary rest in All Saints' Church. There is no time to take her home, no time for an appropriate funeral. But what would that even be? What service—in any religion— could possibly ease our grief? As Dominic wrapped me close while I wept, I had a vivid memory of a similar night thirty years ago. The white gar-

*den at Hatfield, sitting beneath an arbor, sorrowing for the loss of what
would have been our first child.*

I have been lucky, I know that. So few children lost . . .

I do not feel lucky.

But it is Kit I truly fear for now.

24 June 1586
Pontefract Castle

*Public danger makes no concessions to private grief. We woke this
morning—those of us who managed to sleep a little—to urgent riders
from both north and south. From Brandon Dudley, Dominic's chief lieutenant, came word that the Spanish Armada has left Lisbon and is sailing
for England.*

*Even as Dominic and I made plans to make all haste south, an out-
rider came from the northeast coast. Almost twenty ships are rapidly approaching Berwick. Those missing ships from Ireland—including the
three sent away from Hull by the Earl of Arundel. The Spanish intend to
land along the northern border, threatening Scotland so as to pressure
King James to keep his men at home.*

*Stephen has already ridden out with his men for Carlisle to ensure
that Lord Scrope can hold the West, for almost certainly the remaining
Spanish in Ireland will try to land there as well. Lucette returns to Kenilworth to keep the information passing quickly, while Julien will fight
with Dominic. Anabel and Kit will go with all haste to Berwick, to rally
the forces of the East and Middle March . . . and to use whatever means
necessary to persuade King James to lend England his army.*

But first the Princess of Wales will pass judgment.

The trial of Tomás Navarro lasted less than thirty minutes. There
had been a brief discussion about the propriety of Anabel presiding,
but the princess had watched her mother for many years and knew
how and when to exploit her authority.

"I preside over the Council of the North," she said sharply. "It is my prerogative to conduct this trial."

A military trial was swift and efficient. As Stephen Courtenay had already left for Carlisle, his sworn statement was read into the record. It was an accurate and damning eyewitness account of Navarro's cold-blooded attack. *As my company was already sweeping down upon him and he must have known he had been defeated, Navarro's act can only be seen as the most cowardly spitefulness.*

Pippa's public denunciation as a witch and subsequent whipping at Hull Castle was testified to by Matthew Harrington. A man who valued privacy and control, perhaps only those who knew him well could see the anguish beneath the newly made widower's surface.

There was no jury, only Anabel with the governor of Pontefract Castle to offer the appearance of counsel. She had taken care to prepare her verdict in the most damning language.

"Tomás Navarro, you stand accused of unlawful murder. As a foreign agent, you came to England to stir up violence and divide the loyalties of our faithful subjects. When balked of your intent, you most maliciously targeted an innocent woman to bear your displeasure. Your crimes are worthy of death. You will be taken from this hall to the place of execution, where your sentence will be carried out immediately. Have you anything to say?"

The priest had held his tongue thus far, not bothering to conceal his loathing for the princess he had so zealously tried to convert. Now, speaking in English so that everyone present might understand, Navarro declaimed, "Daughter or not, King Philip will punish you for destroying a man of God. He will curse your name for what you do here today."

Anabel contemplated him as she would an unsavory species of insect life. "No," she said finally. "It is *you* my father will curse. In your arrogance and viciousness, you have lost him his war. The fire of resistance has been kindled—and I will see that it burns every Spanish soldier who sets foot on England's shores."

The guards took Navarro to the courtyard, where the executioner awaited with his axe. When the governor had pointed out that hanging was the usual method, Anabel answered, "Hanging is not enough. I want his head."

In their haste, they did not even bother with a platform for better viewing, simply a wooden block set atop a layer of straw.

Anabel insisted on being there, as did the remaining members of the Courtenay family. Whatever else might have been said of Navarro, his faith lent him strength. He removed the cassock of his calling and repeated the Lord's Prayer. Then he crossed himself and knelt. He had declined a blindfold, and did not even close his eyes as he laid his head sideways on the block. Faintly, Anabel could hear him reciting.

"Hail Mary, full of grace . . . pray for us sinners now and at the hour of our death. Amen."

The axe fell as the "amen" ended. Navarro's head, eyes open and fixed, mouth twitching for several ghastly seconds, landed with a subdued thunk on the straw. Anabel felt a sharp pain in her hands, and realized her fingernails had dug themselves into her palms.

She looked at the captain of Pontefract's guards. "Bury him where no one will ever find him again."

When she turned away, it was to speak to Dominic Courtenay. "It is justice," she acknowledged. "But justice is rather hollow. There can never be compensation for Pippa's death."

"No. But there can be meaning to it. Pippa's life and death—make it count, Your Highness."

"I will."

And when every last Spanish ship and Spanish soldier has been routed from our seas and coasts, she vowed silently, I will lay the wreath of victory at Pippa's tomb.

TWENTY-TWO

Elizabeth had never allowed personal concerns to interfere with matters of state. She had faced down assassination threats without retreating behind closed doors, had dared the scorn of her advisors to marry Philip and flirt with France, and had always put England's welfare before that of her own or anyone else.

When Elizabeth received news of Philippa Courtenay's death hard on the heels of the Spanish fleet's maneuvers, it was something of a shock to discover she could not banish the girl from her mind even while she gave orders and plotted for the security of the coasts.

Though Philippa had always been Anabel's nearest friend—much as Minuette had been Elizabeth's—she had also been the most enigmatic to the queen's understanding. Elizabeth had had her personal dealings over the years with Lucette and Stephen and Kit—not always comfortable dealings, but occasions that allowed her access to their innermost workings. But Philippa? Philippa, she felt now, she had hardly known at all.

It was partly these personal issues that brought her this night to Greenwich, where John Dee had been for the last month. If

Elizabeth had a third critical advisor—alongside Burghley and Walsingham—it was Dr. Dee. He had engaged with her when she was a princess and had continued to provide a more esoteric brand of counsel than she could find elsewhere. Walsingham was the cynic, Burghley the pragmatist . . . and John Dee was the mystic.

She arrived by torch-lit barge and was ushered in with little ceremony. Her state of mind did not lend itself to dealing with idiots tonight. In very short order she was seated in Dee's private sanctuary, overflowing as all his spaces were with the miscellany of travel and study and exotic subjects.

"Will Spain land?" she asked bluntly.

"Yes."

"When and where?"

"The stars do not tell me dates and times, Your Majesty."

"If they did, would you have warned Philippa Courtenay of her death?" She hadn't known she was going to ask that.

"Philippa Harrington," Dee corrected mildly. "And she needed no warnings from me. That was one woman who knew absolutely what she was about. England will have cause to be grateful for that before this summer ends."

"If you are going to tell me that I should be grateful for her death—"

"She was the one who encouraged Her Highness to go north, did she not? And she served your daughter well in that wary landscape. That goodwill is necessary for the looming fight. You and your daughter created a pretty picture of estrangement these last years— and Spain has fallen into the trap. They will land in the North. And then England will need all her people, of whatever faith, to fight under one banner. If that fight is won, it will be in no small measure thanks to Lady Philippa's wisdom."

"And the fight in the South? Will I be equal to this, Dr. Dee? Will my sacrifices for England be enough?"

He took her hands in his, a comforting gesture that Elizabeth allowed to so few people these days. "Your Majesty, do you know what

I see when I look at you? I see the young woman I first knew, one with confidence in herself and her country. You were blessed with extraordinary abilities, Elizabeth. As Mordecai said to Esther— 'Who knoweth whether thou art come into the kingdom for such a time as this?' "

As their eyes met, Elizabeth felt chills run through her arms and fingers where he held them. She remembered the first time they'd met: she'd had a queer sense of doubleness, a certainty that as he was speaking to her then, he would also speak to her in the future, guiding her, telling her how to save England.

And here it was. As though he followed every turn of her thoughts—as probably he did—John Dee smiled. "You wish to save England? Then be yourself. That will always be enough for your country."

She left him that night with the assurance she had so desperately needed. Dominic was on his way south to take back his command, and Minuette would come with him.

It seemed fitting that the three of them would stand together at the end.

By the time Anabel's party reached Berwick, she felt as though she had aged several years. Judging by Kit's face, he felt the same. He had lines carved around his eyes and mouth that might never vanish, and a faraway expression that echoed Pippa at her most otherworldly. He had limited himself to only the most necessary communications and shut himself away from even Anabel at night. She herself coped much as her mother would have done—by meticulously anticipating everything that might possibly happen when she reached Berwick. She kept up a voluminous correspondence while on the move and so knew that Lord Hunsdon had reservations about the ability of his March garrisons to stand against a serious Spanish landing.

Within an hour of their arrival, he reiterated that point in a concise manner. "The borders have been underfunded for many years,

Your Highness. I know how stretched the government is, but good-will alone cannot conjure more men or arms out of thin air."

Anabel paced the length of the spartan chamber, meant for war councils such as this. How many times, she wondered, had Berwick Castle seen war? Too many to count, considering how often it had changed hands between Scotland and England. For more than three hundred years violence had stalked Berwick—now it threatened the greatest deluge yet.

"I thought the Earl of Arundel had committed his resources to our side," she said. For that had been the most surprising news along the way—not only had Arundel pressured the Spanish to sail out of Hull once Navarro was captured, but he had then agreed to do more than remain neutral.

"He has, and Arundel comes with several hundred men of his own. His name and persuasion might bring us another few hundred from the Catholics. But the approaching Spanish ships carry at least five thousand men—and they are funded by New World gold. They can afford to land in several places, and we cannot keep all of them from breaking out. And if once they reach the Midlands . . ."

Anabel shut her eyes for a painful moment and grimaced. She had known this moment was coming—despite faint hopes to the con-trary.

With a wry attempt at a smile, she opened her eyes. "I have sent a message to King James of Scotland. I expect any hour a return mes-sage naming a time and place for a meeting. He has five thousand Scottish troops massed along the border. I intend to return from Scotland with those troops."

"James knows his mother is on one of those Spanish ships," Lord Hunsdon warned. "He is afraid of losing Scotland to her."

"If I must," Anabel replied coolly, "I will beg."

James's reply came that evening, naming the day after tomorrow for a meeting in the Scots border village of Ladykirk. Considering the pride she was prepared to swallow, Anabel made no protest at having to cross the border. The English town of Norham faced

Ladykirk directly across the River Tweed and was only eight miles from Berwick. Anabel made the brief trip on horseback with Kit and a contingent of Hunsdon's troops, prepared to sleep at Norham.

Madalena rubbed Anabel's temples that night after brushing her hair. The relief of it made her eyes prick with tears, and after a moment the older woman laid a comforting hand on Anabel's shoulder. She was not Kit, but it allowed Anabel to sleep that night.

He was with her the next morning, and seemed to actually see her for the first time in a week. Looking her up and down, in her severely cut riding gown of dark blue, he even managed a faint smile. "An appropriate blend of dignity and supplication."

"Whatever it takes."

"It will work. I have faith in you."

She crossed the Scots border for the first time in her life, splashing her horse through the shallowest spot in the river with Kit and two guards as her escort. They were met on the bank by royal guards who with little ceremony directed her to the church itself.

The last time she and James had a private conversation, it was his warning at Carlisle to watch herself with Kit. She had thought of him as a boy then. After all, he was a good four years younger than she was. But the king who greeted her today was no boy. Just turned twenty, James carried himself into this meeting with an assurance that he had the upper hand. For once, Scotland had England right where she wanted her—begging a favour.

"Your Majesty."

"You may as well call me James. I will not expect my wife to be so formal in private."

Though it made her uneasy, Anabel nodded. "James. Thank you for meeting with me in such haste. The situation is pressing."

"Please, sit." When they had seated themselves at an angle so that each might watch the other, he said, "We are aware of the Spanish ships and their numbers. Will you be able to hold them at Berwick?"

When one had come to beg, there was no point in being coy. "No. We expect them to land troops not only at Berwick, but at Newcastle. Hull, we think, is adequately defended for the moment. But you must know there are a handful of ships threatening Carlisle as well."

"Since you have a Scots company to help Lord Scrope defend it, I expect Carlisle will stand."

She did not intend to get into arguments about Maisie Courtenay's mercenary company. But it warned her that James was in a prickly mood and not minded to be especially generous.

"James," she said bluntly, "I need your army to protect Berwick."

"And if Berwick still cannot be held—what troops will I then have left to protect Scotland? For that is one purpose of these northern attacks. I know my mother's mind well enough to recognize her hand in these landings. If Berwick falls, at least half the Spanish troops will march straight for Edinburgh."

"Then it is to your advantage to ensure Berwick does not fall."

After a long and nerve-wracking pause of consideration, James said, "I will agree to march my army to Berwick . . . on one condition."

Anabel's relief was almost instantly swamped by misgivings. Somehow she knew exactly what that condition would be. But she was a Tudor princess. The future Queen of England. Nothing came before her service to her people.

She swallowed. "I am prepared to concede to almost any condition you name."

James smiled.

Within an hour of Stephen's exhausted squire bringing her the news of Pippa's death, Maisie left Carlisle Castle with a retinue of those mercenary guards ordered by Stephen to stay with her. Lord Scrope had returned grim-faced from Hull with his men shortly before, with news that the Spanish were sailing to Berwick. This morning reports had come of Spanish ships landing near the Solway. The decision was made to make their stand at Carlisle, which had the benefit of being defensible and also flexible, as it had been besieged dozens of times by the Scottish over the centuries.

Maisie spent a brief, restless night at Penrith and was on the road again by dawn. As her party drew near to Barnard Castle, they were intercepted by her husband.

Stephen was off his horse almost before he reined it in and reached her before she could dismount. She half fell into his arms.

She wished they could sit in silence somewhere and she could comfort him as he had once comforted her in a lonely Irish household after the death of a child. But there was no time. All too soon they had to deal with essentials.

"Tell me about Carlisle," Stephen said.

"Carlisle itself will hold, unless the Spanish decide it worth their while to expend the men and arms in taking the castle. More likely they'll leave a small force behind to keep us penned in behind them while the rest march swiftly to join up with the eastern army. Assuming the eastern army is able to land?"

Stephen made a sound she recognized as displeasure. "Unless James Stuart agrees to intervene, they will land. Anabel has gone to Berwick to beg the use of his army."

"Well," Maisie said practically, "even if he gives it to her, it will take a little time for word of it to come west. I do not think the Maxwell men will join the Spanish in attacking Carlisle without the presence of their lord. But I could be wrong."

His smile was there and gone again like the flash of a fish on a pond's smooth surface. "Not likely, but I suppose stranger things have happened. You are going to Kenilworth?"

"To help your sister coordinate information, yes."

"I wish . . ." But neither of them were sentimentalists, and wishes were for children.

That did not stop Maisie from rising on tiptoe and pulling her husband down so she could kiss him. "It will be all right in the end," she whispered against his cheek. It was what she had said to him four years ago in Ireland. From the tightening of his hands on her waist, she knew he remembered.

Then, as quickly as they had come together, they separated. Maisie set her eyes forward and did not look back.

When Spain's mighty armada was sighted off the Dover coast, sailing inexorably north to the Channel, Elizabeth listened in silence to the report. They had hoped the Spanish would land at Dover itself, or along the southern coasts between there and Portsmouth. But that hope had always been a faint one, and Elizabeth—not to mention her commanders—were far too wary not to make every preparation possible. It had always been a distinct possibility that the Spanish would make a strike directly at London, and so the fort at Tilbury had been hastily reinforced with earthworks and a palisade designed to protect it from foreign troops attempting to land. The old blockhouse fort itself was nearly fifty years old, but it could still employ the deadly crossfire it had been designed for along with the defenses at Gravesend across the river. And to further delay enemy ships, a boom chain had been stretched across the Thames between the two forts.

For all those reasons, it had made sense to make Tilbury a mustering point for England's armies. The problem was, they couldn't be absolutely certain where Spain would land and so had to split their musters. In addition to Tilbury, Dominic Courtenay had a significant army at Southampton and had spared what men he could for the castles at Dover and Portsmouth. He himself rode between camps at an inhuman rate. Not because he did not trust the men who commanded beneath him, but because he took his responsibilities seriously. It was the primary reason Elizabeth had appointed him.

But whatever his gifts and title, Dominic was not the highest power in England. That rested with Elizabeth, and so she deter-

mined to travel from Whitehall to Tilbury and speak to the troops
mustered there to protect London. Both Burghley and Walsingham
protested, but she was unmoved.

"There are moments," she told them quietly, "that every monarch
must rise to. This is one of those moments."

The camp at Tilbury showed bravely against the flat eastern sky.
The neatly dug trenches and sharp palisades were a backdrop to the
multicoloured tents of the nobles and gentlemen and the green
booths to house the regiments, not yet bedraggled by time and bore-
dom. The foot regiments were drawn up in matching coats, with
troops of horsemen in armor behind. Not enough, Elizabeth knew,
to defeat the Duke of Parma if he landed in force—but they would
make Parma bleed for every foot of ground.

As with everything of significance in her life, Elizabeth had prepared meticulously. After disembarking at the Tilbury fort and making a brief tour of the D-shaped blockhouse built by her father, she
changed into a gown of white velvet, a deliberate reference to the war-
rior goddess Athena, and wore a beautiful steel cuirass over the gown.
She could not be a king in armor, prepared to lead his armies' charge,
but nor could she be entirely a queen and hide behind her sex. Elizabeth knew that sometimes the best way to defuse criticism was to
acknowledge it first. So she had crafted her speech knowing it must
bind together the disparate parts of her person to create something
new—a people's queen who would walk amongst them as a symbol
of her willingness to lay down her own life in their protection.

Despite her bodyguards' protests, she left them behind at the
fort. She would not insult her troops with any indication that she
feared the strength of their loyalty. She rode a pale grey horse led by
a young boy, and carried in her hand a gold and silver truncheon.
The sword of state was borne before her by Brandon Dudley, Earl of
Leicester, and a silver helmet rested upon a pillow as though simply
waiting for her to put it on.

There were, perhaps, ten thousand men assembled at Tilbury,

and she passed slowly through them, allowing each to see only her resolution and courage. But behind her controlled face she noted unpleasant truths: the men were poorly armed and even more poorly trained, mostly farmers and craftsmen who were underpaid and underfed. Dominic and Dudley had done their best—which was considerable—but even they could not make skilled soldiers from nothing. If the Spanish landed here in force, Tilbury might easily break. And if it did, then the way to London lay wide open.

Elizabeth let none of her concerns show. Instead, she focused on England's greatest strength—the loyalty of a people willing to defend their homes and way of life to the death. She was here to strengthen them, not give way to fear.

When she had passed through the army, she at last delivered the speech into which she had poured all her faith and hopes and courage.

"My loving people: we have been persuaded by some that are careful of our safety to take heed how we commit ourselves to armed multitudes, for fear of treachery; but I assure you I do not desire to live to distrust my faithful and loving people. Let tyrants fear."

A rousing cheer from the men, as though King Philip and his Papist soldiers could hear the force of their opposition.

"I have always so behaved myself that, under God, I have placed my chief strength and safeguard in the loyal hearts and goodwill of my subjects; and therefore I am come amongst you, as you see, at this time, not for my recreation and disport, but being resolved, in the midst and heat of the battle, to live and die amongst you all; to lay down for my God, and for my kingdom, and my people, my honour and my blood, even in the dust."

She meant every word, even as logic dictated her advisors would employ everything short of force to keep her away from the field. Logic also dictated that they were right—England was more than just land. England—at this hour, at this danger—lived in Elizabeth.

"I know I have the body of a weak, feeble woman; but I have the

heart and stomach of a king, and of a King of England, too, and think
foul scorn that Parma or any prince of Europe should dare to in-
vade the borders of my realm; to which rather than any dishonour
shall grow by me, I myself will take up arms, I myself will be your
general, judge, and rewarder of every one of your virtues in the field.
I know already, for your forwardness you have deserved rewards and
crowns; and we do assure you on a word of a prince, they shall be
duly paid."

She could see in their faces that they believed her. More . . . she
could see that they trusted her. She might be in body only a woman
of advancing age, dressed for show in a cuirass that would not withstand a single sword blow, but she saw in the reflection of their gazes
much more than that. She was Judith and Esther, she was Diana and
Minerva, she was Gloriana.

She was Queen Elizabeth.

"In the meantime, my lieutenant general shall be in my stead,
than whom never prince commanded a more noble or worthy subject; not doubting but by your obedience to my general, by your concord in the camp, and your valour in the field, we shall shortly have a
famous victory over these enemies of my God, of my kingdom, and
of my people."

When the cheers and adulation had died down, Elizabeth retreated gracefully to the fort, where she changed into a riding dress
more appropriate for long distances. From here she would leave the
water and go south on horseback.

Dominic tried to talk her out of it. "You should not be heading
any nearer to the coasts," he argued. "You should be with your government, ready to retreat if needed for safety's sake."

"If I retreat, I give my armies leave to do the same," she retorted.
"I wish to go to Canterbury to make a spiritual appeal. That should
go over well. And it will give you an excuse to force Minuette out of
Dover Castle. Make her come to Canterbury, and I will ensure I
bring her back inland with me."

It wasn't fair to shamelessly manipulate him—but Dominic always made it so easy. At least he had learned over the years to recognize it. "All of which is but to say that you will do as you choose."

"But of course," she agreed smoothly. "That can hardly be a surprise to you after more than fifty years."

He threw up his hand. "Fine. We will go to Canterbury."

"Not you. You are my lieutenant general and you are needed here, or wherever else the Spanish make their stand. I shall do very well with my guards. I will break my journey at Leeds Castle, and then on to Canterbury. As I have already written to Minuette asking her to meet me there the day after tomorrow, I have no time to waste arguing with you unless you wish your wife to be without my protection for long."

"Elizabeth," he said with all seriousness, "do not get yourself injured. I can control the army, but only you can control the people. Don't forget it."

"I never do—not for a single moment." *Which is why I am so very weary.*

She followed Dominic's order for a day and a half. And then, fifteen miles outside Canterbury—after all Elizabeth's years of surviving close calls—Francis Walsingham's worst fears were realized.

A Catholic assassin got lucky.

When Anabel emerged from her private conference with James, she looked subtly different. Kit's observational skills might have become dulled in the days since Pippa's death—as though he could not get used to seeing the world through only his own eyes—but he knew every aspect of Anabel's face and moods. The politeness was surface only. From the curve of her cheek to the elegance of her throat— even the set of her wrists and arms—her human warmth had been extinguished and replaced by the frozen lines of a statue.

Kit shot a suspicious glance at James Stuart, who had escorted her out. The king waited until Anabel was on horseback, then took her offered hand and kissed her fingers. "Until tomorrow," he said.

Then he turned on Kit a look of almost unbearable smugness. *I win,* that look said. Did James think Kit didn't know every detail of the marriage treaty signed more than three years ago? James might have the diplomatic edge, but he would never have Anabel's heart.

Anabel did not speak a word until they had returned to Norham Castle. Then, abruptly dismissing those wanting her attention, she took Kit into the first empty chamber she came to. When she had shut the door on the two of them, she leaned against it with her hands behind her back as though supporting her.

"What happened?" he asked. "Did James refuse his army?" It was the only thing he could think of that would make her look like this—as though every hope of hers had been trampled by careless marauders.

When she didn't immediately answer, Kit rushed to reassure her. "We'll manage, Anabel. With Arundel's open support, and the growing outrage over Pippa—" He had to stop at that, his throat catching. Then he set his jaw and went on. "We may well be out-numbered without the Scots—"

"We won't be outnumbered," she said tonelessly. "The king has agreed to lead his army to Berwick."

"That's . . . Thank God for it." He studied her more closely, then asked shrewdly, "What is his price?"

"There is only one price James will accept."

"You."

She nodded once. "He will lend his armies to his wife, and no one else."

"We've always known that, Anabel. It's not as though it's a sur-prise."

"We will be married tomorrow."

The room spun around Kit, much as it had at Pippa's death, and when it settled he realized that it was, indeed, possible to feel worse. He tried, for her sake, to give Anabel hope. "I doubt the queen's privy council would approve. I know a marriage ceremony means much, but vows can be undone—"

"James has thought of that. He has thought of everything—a good deal more, in fact, than either of us would like. It will not be the vows only. Wedded at noon, and bedded at sunset . . . James Stuart means to make very sure of me."

TWENTY-THREE

When Kit had come to her after Pippa's death, Anabel thought she would never again see anything so terrible as his face in that raw grief. This was very nearly as bad. She watched the colour drain from his forehead downward, until the only thing she could see were his beautiful, bleak, hopeless eyes.

She wanted to go to him, wanted to wrap herself around him and tell him it made no difference, she would never love James, it would always be Kit . . .

But she was trained to self-control. And so, though his childhood had not always shown it, was Kit.

"I see." His voice was new, one to break her heart. "Yes, I can . . ." He cleared his throat. "It will be here?"

"At the church in Ladykirk. I will stay here tonight."

"You will need things—people—from Berwick. If you'd care to prepare a list?"

"I will."

He could not leave while she stood against the door, though plainly he wanted to. Hesitantly, Anabel stepped toward him. "Kit—"

"It's all right. I do understand. Just . . . let me see to what needs to be done. Please."

With all her considerable force of will, Anabel summoned detachment, or at least the nearest image of it she could manage. "Thank you."

She closed her eyes as he passed her, near enough for her to smell the scent of him. Kit always smelled of clean air and open fields and the gardens of Wynfield Mote, where she had first felt the warmth of a family home. He did not linger, but she kept her eyes closed long after he'd gone, knowing that when she opened them, her chosen future would be upon her.

You told me once I might have a husband of my own choosing, she had said to Pippa.

Choices may be made for many reasons, had been the reply. True. If not at all comforting at the moment.

Anabel threw herself furiously into a whirlwind of letter writing the rest of that dreadfully drawn-out day. To Berwick Castle she sent not only a list of necessities for tomorrow but a matter-of-fact explanation of events to Lord Hunsdon. The fact of her marriage was glossed over quickly, in favor of the military situation. Knowing that every hour now counted, Anabel wrote, *King James and I will leave at first light the day after tomorrow to march his men to Berwick.*

It would be none too soon, for when Kit returned he brought Robert Cecil, Matthew Harrington, and her chaplain, Littlefield. The news was dispiriting. Spanish scouts were already beginning to reach shore. Berwick might soon be surrounded.

As long as she had such matters to concentrate her mind upon, Anabel managed well enough. But after dinner, when the long twilight of a northern summer finally slipped into velvety night, all that was left to her were regrets.

No. There was one other thing left to her. One night to do as she wished.

When the castle had gone to bed, she sent Madalena to fetch Kit. When he appeared, an unlaced jerkin thrown over his shirt-

sleeves, he had a distinctly bruised appearance about the eyes. Anabel felt much the same. And though she was no stranger to making
imperious demands, she felt queer and uncertain. Because this was
not a demand . . . and it mattered more to her at this moment than
anything in the world.

"I love you," she said, determined not to waste time on prelimi-
naries. "I will never, in all my life, love anyone as I do you."

"Anabel . . . I love you, *mi corazon,* and no number of Scottish husbands will ever change that."

She was in his arms before she knew it, and when he would have
gently disengaged, she kissed him all the fiercer.

"What are you doing?" he managed to ask, sounding as breathless
as she felt.

She took a step back from the circle of his arms and he let her go.
Reluctantly. And then she found the words that had been tumbling
through her all day.

"Twelve hours from now," she said, "I will wed James Stuart. It is
not the marriage of my heart, but I make it as willingly as I am able.
For England. And when we are married, I will be to him a faithful
wife.

"But Kit?" She raised her chin, determined not to quail. "I am not
his wife yet. Stay with me tonight. Please."

He caught up her hands and pressed them to his lips. "You don't
know what you're asking."

"Is that really the argument you want to make with me?" Even at
the peak of tension, they could not keep from teasing.

"Do you think I do not want to stay? But I love you too well to
think only of myself. In your life to come, I would not have you regret anything."

"Regrets? I do not think there is a soul alive who lives entirely
without regret. Please, Kit. Tomorrow I marry a man I do not love.
Let me take with me the memory that just once in my life I lay with
the only man I will ever love."

She saw his capitulation the moment before he pulled her to him and kissed her with an abandon she'd only dreamed of. She felt wildly, deliciously loved, and knew this would be the finest night of her life.

Princesses did not have experience of a sensual sort—at least, not wise princesses. But any insecurity she might have felt vanished almost at once, for how could she be nervous with Kit? It was the most natural thing in the world to slide her hands through the thick silk of his hair, to keep him pulled tightly to her while his own hands tangled in her red-gold waves. When he pulled away, she made an inarticulate protest and he gently laughed against her mouth.

"I'm not going anywhere," he said. "Not unless you send me away."

She trapped his mouth with her own in a promise that she would not send him away. Then, curious about his intentions, she allowed him to disengage. They were instantly obvious, as his hands let loose her hair and moved to the buttons that closed her robe from high neck to waist. Anabel had spent her lifetime being dressed and undressed by others, but Kit's hands—the graceful, long-fingered hands of his mother—were so erotic in their delicacy she feared her knees would not hold her up much longer.

When he had pushed the robe from her shoulders so it fell in a pool of silk around her feet, and then shrugged off his own unlaced jerkin, she reached impatiently for the cambric shirt that still covered him. Kit obliged her, and drew in a sharp breath as she ran her fingertips down his chest.

"Anabel . . ."

She drew him to her bed in response and arranged herself in what she hoped was a seductive pose.

Kit hesitated. "Are you quite sure?"

She pulled him down in reply, whispering, "Quite sure."

Imagination could only take one so far, and Anabel rapidly passed beyond the limits of hers. How can I ever go from Kit to James after this? she wondered once, and then promptly forgot her future husband.

She learned now that it was possible to be both soft and hard, both gentle and urgent, to allow one's ferocious mind to be drowned by the demands of your own body—and another's.

When Kit eased her up to remove her shift, Anabel said softly, "You will have to teach me what to do."

At that, his hands froze at her hips. "Me? Did you . . . I'm afraid, Anabel, that if you are expecting experience, then you have chosen the wrong man."

She jerked her head back far enough to meet his eyes straight on. "You are never a virgin!"

"I am."

"Why? How? Don't tell me you haven't had women throwing themselves at you since you were sixteen, if not before. I've watched most of them."

"They were never the right woman," he said carefully. "It's always been you, Anabel. Even before I was smart enough to know it. Once I did . . . How can you think any other woman could matter to me?"

She didn't know whether she wanted to laugh or cry. She put her hands on his cheeks and leaned her forehead against his. "My dearest, darling Kit . . . then I suppose we shall learn together."

And so they did. Anabel had always been a quick study—in everything from logic to languages—and this was a lesson her body seemed half to know already. Instinct was an excellent teacher, and so was love. Whatever pain there was mattered little when set beside the overwhelming of her senses that proclaimed she and Kit had been meant for this all their lives.

Kit apologized after. "I'm sorry to have hurt you."

"I don't think it's avoidable—and by far a small price to pay."

With her head on his chest, he ran one hand down her spine. "I may have been a virgin, but that doesn't mean I am completely innocent. Men talk. I think, if you give me leave, I can do better by you in a little while."

"You have all leave with me, Kit—you always have."

In those last, stolen hours of her liberty, Anabel learned much of pleasure and more of joy. It seemed sacrilege to sleep, but they both dozed a little and came awake in the hushed hour before sunrise.

"In my life to come," she whispered, "I will never regret this."

"You have my heart, Anabel. And my loyal service. To fulfill that last, I must leave you now before the castle wakes."

She clung to him as long as she could, but already the weight of the day was settling on her shoulders. If her heart urged her to steal away with Kit on horseback, to lose themselves in one another, her will made her release him and dress as though she had spent the night blamelessly alone.

Kit did not kiss her before he left. Perhaps he knew it would be beyond them both to stop. He simply stared at her, as though committing her face to memory before she appeared again as another man's bride. Then he slipped quietly away, leaving Anabel to count the hours until her wedding.

Be it known to citizens both of Scotland and England: on the twenty-third day of July, the Year of our Lord 1586, at eleven o'clock of the morning at the Church of Our Lady in Ladykirk, Scotland, were wed Her Royal Highness Anne Isabella, Princess of Wales, and James VI, King of Scotland.

   Witnesses: Robert Cecil and Edwin Littlefield

   Marriage solemnized by: Bishop David Bell

Only when Anabel and her witnesses had crossed the river into Scotland did Kit show his face in Norham. He did not want to make it any harder on her than it already was. Or on himself, for that matter. He did not—could never—regret the night, but he also couldn't guess whether it had made things harder or easier to bear.

He had to face her soon enough. There was a stir in Ladykirk and then Anabel and her party reappeared coming back to the river. They were not alone. Next to the princess rode James Stuart, sixth king of Scotland and Anabel's husband. Kit's instinct was to turn away, but why bother? He would have to see them together sooner rather than later, and better to begin now at maintaining a proper distance so as not to upset King James.

So Kit stayed where he was as they reached the riverbank directly across from him. James stepped his horse delicately close to Anabel's, said a few words, then kissed her hand. The Scottish king was dressed exquisitely and expensively in cloth of gold and gemencrusted trim. Next to him, Anabel appeared much plainer in a riding gown of blue-green taffeta and dark navy velvet, hardly fit for a royal wedding. Observers might think it a deliberate insult to James and Scotland—but Kit knew better. Anabel could have made no more meaningful gesture, for the dress she wore had been Pippa's. The familiar blue gown of Kit's twin that Anabel had donned that desperate final night in York when the women parted, pretending to be the other.

Kit felt a surge of relief when he realized only the English were returning just now. As the guards led the princess's—or no, she was properly a queen now, wasn't she?—horse into the water, he felt the eyes of Anabel's husband linger on him.

If James meant to spy out impropriety, he was disappointed. Anabel did no more than nod to Kit as she rode past. But then, her back was to James, so he could not have seen the look she flashed Kit. A look worth any agony of his pride, for it mingled fierce love and the sweetest memories.

The remainder of that day was spent in council and conference. Norham had surely not seen such a concentration of royal power for a very long time, if ever. Kit could only hope the Scots were as busy. Just in case James decided to drag his feet in issuing orders, Kit sent word to his brother the moment Anabel returned that the Scots men of the western March would be ordered to fight with the Carlisle troops.

And pray God we are right, Kit wrote, *and the western landing is not as large as the one we expect in the east. Make Lord Scrope and the Maxwells work together if you have to chain them to one another, Stephen. Because we will need as many men to join us as quickly as we can get them, to keep the Spanish from breaking out in the east.*

Beneath all the work and worry and the still-fresh grief of missing Pippa lurked a superstitious fear of the dark closing in. Tonight, James Stuart would cross the river to be feasted at Norham and then led to his wife's bed to set a seal on their union. Kit thought he could not bear it, not this first night. He would ride for Berwick as soon as the king was on English soil.

An hour before James was expected, an anonymous courier rode into Norham. From the state of both his horse and himself, the man had ridden far and fast. He carried no papers, only a verbal message, which he declined to deliver to any but Anabel herself. Kit might have disputed the matter, except that he knew the courier. He was from Tiverton, a squire long assigned personally to Minuette Courtenay's service.

Kit led the man to the private study where Anabel and Robert Cecil were working in close concert. Madalena took one glance at their faces and let them in.

Anabel looked up, alarm flashing briefly across her face. "The king is not expected yet."

"It is not the king. This man carries a message for you from the South."

Anabel held out her hand, and the courier shook his head. "It was not written, Your Highness, for fear of falling into the wrong hands." He cast a wary glance at Kit, Robert, and Madalena. "Would you prefer to receive it privately?"

"I trust these three with my life," she answered coolly. "What is the message?"

"It is directly from the Duchess of Exeter, and in her words." The courier cleared his throat, and then, obviously quoting, delivered his news. "The queen's party, while riding to Canterbury, was surprised by armed men on the road. In the assault, an assassin slipped through and shot the queen at close quarters with a musket. She was returned to Leeds Castle, where she has continued unconscious for hours."

He faltered, no doubt aware of the numbed silence he'd created. Then he continued in his own words. "Though the musket ball has been removed, it is feared the queen may not ever wake. The physicians will not commit themselves, but Lady Exeter said she has seen their faces and knows how to read despair when she sees it."

In the aftermath, Kit thought he had gone deaf, so quiet was the chamber. He was the first to recover his voice. "When?"

"They were attacked Monday. I left Leeds Castle that evening."

No wonder the man looked ready to drop—he'd ridden four hundred miles in five days.

Despite shock, despite fear, despite uncertainty, Anne Tudor would always rise to what must be done. She must have seen the same exhaustion and dedication in the courier that Kit had, for she said with a valiant attempt at normalcy, "We thank you for your service. Madalena will find you accommodations and food."

When they had gone, Kit looked to Robert Cecil. What were they meant to be saying to the princess? Comfort, or truth?

Anabel took the decision, for truth. "My mother may already be dead. For all we know, another rider is even now on his way north with that news."

"It must not get out, Your Highness," Robert Cecil said urgently. "The queen has held this country together for almost thirty years. We are on the brink of the most dangerous threat to England this century. If it is known—"

"That the country has been left in the hands of a twenty-four-year-old girl? My mother was only twenty-five when she came to the throne." Though Anabel spoke neutrally, Kit could see her eyes were glassy with shock.

"We don't know," he agreed with Robert. "And so we must behave as though everything is as it should be. The queen holding the South, the princess holding the North. The people need that assurance."

"What if I cannot manage to give it to them?" Anabel asked as Madalena slipped back into the chamber.

Kit could not answer, but Madalena did. "You will," she said firmly. "But that is not our immediate concern. Do not anticipate difficulties, Your Highness. Begin at the beginning, and do one thing at a time. We will help you."

Anabel visibly steadied herself, and Kit took the cue. "Right. The first thing we've already noted—keep this information to ourselves. Second, we proceed as planned. From Berwick to Carlisle, the beacons are burning, announcing the immediate threat of invasion. Tomorrow morning, you march with King James to Berwick. For if Berwick falls—"

"It will not fall." She sounded almost herself now. "I did not get married this morning for nothing. I sold myself to Scotland for an army, and I mean to wield it. Nor will I squander Pippa's death. The news of how the Spanish murdered her is spreading like wildfire and swaying the uncommitted to our side. We will fight this war and we will win."

19 July 1586
Leeds Castle

I have never been so frightened as when I reached Elizabeth's bed yesterday and found her unresponsive and already growing fevered. Not even when I surrendered myself to Will, or watched Dominic marched away in chains. Those events, grievous as they were, constituted only a personal disaster. This disaster is England's.

I sent three of my most trusted men with verbal reports—one to Dominic, one to Burghley and Walsingham in London, the last much farther north, to wherever Anabel is to be found.

And now I do what it has so often fallen to me to do—I wait.

22 July 1586
Leeds Castle

Lord Burghley arrived late this evening, looking grey and greatly aged. He has left Walsingham in London to control information; he will do the

same from here. The intention is to preserve the illusion that Elizabeth is
suffering from only a slight injury and continues to direct both the war
and her government. The members of her guard present at the attack have
been sequestered here . . . and there were no survivors left from the enemy
force to tell tales. Every person both entering and leaving the castle is
being most carefully scrutinized. But I am under no illusions—our efforts
will, at best, only delay the news.

She has opened her eyes a handful of times, but without recognition.
The surgeon has removed the ball, but the wound is weeping and red and
her fever is unabated.

24 July 1586
Leeds Castle

As I sit by Elizabeth's bedside, I am often swamped with sense memories
of Hever Castle more than thirty years ago when I performed the same
office for Queen Anne. Sickrooms have a distinct smell, both astringent
and sweet, and physicians still prefer to keep the windows closed no matter
how stuffy a room becomes. I have taken to ignoring their protests and
throwing wide every window I can, if only to ease Elizabeth's fever a little.

I begin to fear that she will never wake. And though I still worry for
the loss to England and the particular grief to Anabel—I confess that my
chief lament is: What will I ever do in a world without Elizabeth?

25 July 1586
Leeds Castle

Tonight, Elizabeth came to her senses for a time. She is weak and still
burning with fever, though Carrie and I have relentlessly scoured the
wound in an attempt to keep it from festering. And though it remains red,
there are no ugly streaks toward the heart or stink of decomposing flesh. It
is only that the fever will not break.

But she knew me when she woke.

Is it any surprise that her first question was not about any one person?
"The war?" she asked.

"No landings in the South. Drake and the navy have kept them well harried."

"The North?"

"No word from Anabel," I assured her. *It is the strictest truth— Anabel herself has not sent word. But the Spanish ships were landing men at Berwick when last I heard, and surely there has been some sort of battle.*

And I have had word about the West from Maisie. There were Spanish troops heading for Carlisle when she left it two weeks ago. Stephen will have been in battle by now. I can only pray my son is safe, and that Carlisle holds.

TWENTY-FOUR

The Battle of Carlisle took place on a late July day of steamy heat and sudden gusts of wind that sent banners changing directions without warning. Stephen and his company were in the van, with Lord Scrope on the right flank and Scrope's son to the left. It was a near classic battle of thrust and repulse. The English had been able to persuade a few hundred Maxwell men to fight with them, though Stephen did not trust them far. There were more Spanish troops than he'd been expecting, but despite the imbalance of numbers, the English were much fresher, not having had the crossing from Ireland to cope with nor the physical and mental drag of having already fought in a hostile country for months.

Stephen and his men broke the center of the Spanish line in a mere half hour. It was hard to escape the conclusion that the Spanish who came from Ireland, at least, did not have their hearts in this fight. Stephen stood tall in his stirrups to survey what he could see of the rest of the field. To his left, Scrope's son was engaged in fierce fighting, but looked to be making gains. On the right, Lord Scrope's flanking attack was in disarray. Stephen left his second-in-command in charge of the van and took a third of his men to aid Scrope against the Spanish.

Except Scrope wasn't fighting the Spanish—not entirely. The officers might have been King Philip's men, but even before Stephen could make out the badges or colours of the enemy soldiers, he could hear a distinctive sound that sent shivers through him: men yelling orders, men screaming in defiance, men who did not speak sibilant Spanish.

Gaelic. Spain had recruited soldiers from their Irish allies.

No wonder they were not giving way before Lord Scrope. The Spanish were fighting, perhaps reluctantly, under orders. But the Irish were fighting for vengeance.

Stephen threw his men into the flank with a few commands, then let himself be swept into the violence. There was an almost physical split that happened in battle, he had learned over the years, so that his body operated best without being slowed by thought. He had worked hard to attain the sort of skill that meant he could still command in such a state.

Finally, under the combined assaults of Lord Scrope and Stephen's mercenaries, the Irish flank shivered and began to splinter. The Spanish officers retreated first, and most of the Irish began to give way as well. But not quite all of them. A tight knot of disciplined fighters held fast, and Stephen set his horse to confront them.

He was nearly upon them, perhaps fifteen men in all, before he recognized the Irish leader. Dark and bristling, the grim face just recognizable despite the blood splashed liberally across it. A face Stephen had last seen on another battlefield, across the sea in Ireland. Cutting through the noise of battle, he heard an echo of the man's voice from years ago: *He is English. No way in hell I'll trust him . . .*

Diarmid mac Briain Kavanaugh. Ailis's husband.

Stephen directed his men to surround the group, ordering them not to kill if possible. No doubt Diarmid would gladly have spent his life here, but some of his men were a little less fanatical. Stephen recognized several of their faces as well.

He knew the moment Diarmid recognized him, for the man swore vividly in Gaelic. Still defiant, despite the fact that he was surrounded and could not resist without condemning himself and his men to death, Diarmid spat eloquently.

"At least you're where you belong this time," he growled. "And not pretending to be on our side."

"Go home, Diarmid. This is not Ireland's fight."

"The hell it isn't! If Spain loses here, they pull out of Ireland and we're left to England's mercies once more."

"Spain *has* lost here, in Carlisle at least. Don't compound the loss with needless death."

"If you're looking to take hostages, you're a fool. We haven't the gold to redeem prisoners, you know that. Better you kill me where I stand."

Stephen dismounted and threw the reins to one of his men. He was not surprised that Diarmid had managed to infuriate him in such short order. Confronting the hostile Irishman, he repeated, "Go home, Diarmid. Our fight is with the Spanish. I have no stomach for killing men I don't have to."

"Don't tell me you don't have the stomach to kill *me*. She's my wife, after all. You'll gladly kill me for Ailis."

"Once, maybe. Now?" Stephen shrugged. "Go home to your wife and your children. Take your men and retreat to the ships. If you move fast, you can set sail before anyone here follows."

He turned away, noting that the other Kavanaugh men had already taken him at his word and were leaving the field in ones and twos.

"Damn you!" Diarmid shouted from behind him. "Did you care so little for her that you can spare me your contempt?"

Stephen did not bother to answer, not aloud. *I cared for Ailis more than I'd ever cared for anyone before. I loved her.*
Then.
Ailis was his past. Mariota was his present and his future. His love

and his hope and the only person he carried with him every moment of the day.

Stephen remounted and wearily set off to help clean up the remains of the enemy. His immediate job was done. Carlisle had held. England would stand in the West.

Plainly, James Stuart had to be told of the English queen's grave injury. For many reasons, not least among them—from Anabel's point of view—that it allowed her to delay the consummation of their marriage.

"I haven't the time," she said plainly as the two of them were closeted alone in Norham. "Or, frankly, the interest. My mother may be dead. Your mother is almost certainly on one of those ships outside Berwick. You shall simply have to take me at the word I gave you in the church today."

James wasn't pleased, but he also wasn't stupid. Another sort of king—another sort of man—would have insisted. She didn't have time? It could be accomplished in very short order. She had other things on her mind? It wasn't her mind he required.

But James was canny and clearly wanted a marriage that would not break down in the first year as had his parents'. So he conceded her point and was only mildly condescending about allowing his army to march on Berwick before Anabel had completely fulfilled her part of the marriage bargain.

He even behaved politely to Kit, who of necessity joined the larger conversation about military tactics. James and the Earl of Arran would lead the Scots; Lord Hunsdon commanded the English forces. But as Hunsdon was eight miles away in Berwick, harrying the Spanish who had already landed, Kit spoke at the moment for the English troops. Mostly those they had stripped from the Middle March garrisons in desperation.

Fortunately the exigencies of the situation kept the men focused on matters other than personal. Only when Kit was dismissed to round up those English troops at Norham and ensure that all was in order, did he spare a personal smile for his princess.

He had his back to James and Arran, so only Anabel could see him. She might have expected a grin and a wink—but instead Kit's smile was as gentle and achingly intimate as his touch had been last night. Almost, she forgot herself.

But only almost. She was the Princess of Wales and the Queen of Scotland. And if fortune continued black—perhaps even the Queen of England.

Anabel was quite certain that no one at Norham slept that night. Already some of the Scottish troops had come across the river. The rest would move rapidly east under the command of Alexander Home, poised to pour across the Tweed next morning and help surround the Spanish outside Berwick. Anabel forced herself to lie down for a few hours, mostly to please Madalena, but in that time she stared into the dark and imagined she was speaking with Pippa.

I married James. Did you know I would do that, Pippa?

I told you I could not see that far.

Right. Because it was after . . . Why are you dead? We need you.

All I ever did was show you what already lay within. You can do this, Anabel.

I don't know that I can.

That was still the fear pounding at the base of her skull when she rose two hours before dawn and dressed for riding. The troops gathered here would be leaving soon, to reach Berwick before the sun was fully up. Anabel would ride well behind them—the most she'd been able to persuade her captains to allow—surrounded by guards prepared to whisk her south and out of danger if needed. Her fallback position would be Middleham, which was built to withstand sieges and battles. She could only pray it would not come to that.

But before the men left, she would mount her horse and ride amongst them. Giving them hope, giving them courage, perhaps merely giving them the symbol they needed to remind them what they were fighting for: their homes and their children, their rights and their hopes. Word of her mother's condition was locked down tightly, but that didn't mean men could not sense the underlying tension beyond just this one battle.

She must speak to them, encourage them, and not for a moment let them see her own doubts and fears. *It is not the men I doubt*, she reminded herself. *It is only myself.*

And then she heard a silent voice in sardonic answer. Not Pippa, this time—her mother. *You are my daughter. There is no doubt of your abilities.*

"Ready?" Madalena asked, after making the last adjustment to Anabel's new dress.

It was not a practical riding gown, because that was not its primary purpose. She would change again before embarking on her careful journey to Berwick, wear something darker and plain. This gown, however, was meant to be seen. It was mostly tissue of cloth of silver woven in a subtle pattern of the double Tudor rose. She wore no jewels save Kit's enameled green panther and her mother's locket ring. Her red hair was loose, caught back from her face with a ribbon of black velvet.

Over the bodice of the gown went a finely beaten and damascened corset of armor that her mother had gifted her—after a similar piece fashioned for the queen. Anabel studied her image, accustoming herself to the unusual strictures of movement, and said, "Bring them in."

Those members of her council present at Norham—Robert Cecil, Matthew Harrington, and the chaplain, Edwin Littlefield—entered with Kit. Both Matthew and Kit were dressed for battle. Though she had always known her treasurer as a man of numbers and finance, his father had been a notable soldier, and Matthew had been raised alongside the Courtenay boys. And he would never forgive the Spanish for Pippa's death.

Littlefield offered a blessing and a prayer upon the endeavour—which he would repeat in a less personal manner for the troops—and then there was no more chance of delay. When she stepped out that door, Anabel must be in perfect command.

Panic rose, its wings beating so hard it threatened to break her bones and fly out. "I don't think I can do this," she found herself saying. And though there were others present, she was speaking to one man only. "I am not my mother, Kit. She would know what to say. She would have prepared it perfectly. But I . . . I am merely lurching from crisis to crisis. What if I fail? What if England falls because I do not know what I am doing?"

"You are not alone. You have councilors and generals and admirals of great experience and greater loyalty."

She didn't say it, but she thought it: *Queen's men. My mother's men. Who fights for me?*

Kit gave her the personal answer she craved. "Stephen will hold the West. My father will hold the South. We will not lose you England."

"And the North?"

"The North will fight for you, Anabel. Pippa saw that. It is why she brought you here. 'I will light the fire, but you will command the flames,'" Kit quoted. "The fire lit by Pippa's death is burning. Command it."

The panic, cowed by his confidence, retreated into a tight knot that she could ignore. "You will stay by me?" she asked.

"Until my very last breath," Kit swore. And added, with a bow of obeisance, "Your Majesty."

SPEECH OF ANNE ISABELLA, PRINCESS OF WALES AND
QUEEN OF SCOTLAND, BEFORE THE BATTLE OF BERWICK

Men of England, I come amongst you today not as a ruler, but as a fellow citizen willing to defend my country with my own blood if necessary. For my blood is England's blood: the blood of liberty, the blood of defiance, the blood of a land that has not failed to defend its shores for five hundred years. We will not fail today, for we fight with the blood of our ancestors as well as our own.

Today, we proclaim that England is not two nations, divided by faith, but one nation, united in a cause greater than our individual concerns: to keep this land free from the terrors of the Inquisition, the contempt of enforced thought, the horror of compelled belief. We may fail often in our attempts to live together, but better to fail with good intentions than to comply in chains.

The North does not belong to Spain. The North does not belong to me.

The North is yours.

And the North is defended.

The English and Scots rode swift and light through the grey dimness in the hour before dawn. The Spanish intent was clearly to seize Berwick as fast as possible so that their ships standing off could disembark more troops at leisure. Lord Hunsdon's orders were to hold the castle but to let the town be taken if necessary. Most of the women and children had been hastily evacuated southwest, away from the coast. England could afford to lose houses and walls.

They could not afford to lose the castle. If they did—and if no English ships arrived to hold back those Spanish still at sea—Berwick would be a strong base for the enemy. The invaders would be perfectly poised to strike either north or south as they pleased.

Kit knew logically that this was not the sole critical moment of the war—his father and the English fleet in the Channel faced a greater threat in both numbers and choice of targets—but if the queen was dead, then England absolutely needed this victory to solidify Anabel's throne.

The army did not hesitate when Berwick came into view, for the orders had already been given and couriers were flying back and forth between them and the town and Lord Home's Scottish forces crossing the border from the North. Kit and Matthew followed their orders and led the small English force toward the water to cut off reinforcements from the ships.

In the three years since Ireland, Kit had fought on a variety of battlefields and in a range of conditions. Today was ideal, fresh and clear and dry. He missed Stephen, but Matthew was a steady and formidable presence who had been trained with the brothers when younger and thus moved and thought in many of the same ways.

The greatest advantage that the border English and Scots held was that they were accustomed to unconventional ways of fighting. Not for them the heavy guns and heavy horses and orderly formations of ritualized warfare. The border riders mounted small, swift, sure-footed horses specially bred to their location. Kit had been so taken by their sturdiness (men swore they could cover a hundred miles a day in time of great need) that he'd adopted a border horse for his own. With Matthew and the Middle March troops, they kept the line of retreating Spanish turned back toward Berwick and the press of the royal Scots troops behind them.

The air was so clear that Kit could see a long way off even without a spyglass, and in brief snatches of calm he watched the fresh Scots arrive from the North. Lord Home had two thousand lances at his command and he used them with skill—sending smaller groups out in forays while he kept reserves in hold at the center. Thus his lances were kept refreshed and could wear the Spanish down. It didn't require a great deal of time.

Though Kit hated to admit it, he knew that the Scottish troops made all the difference today. Left to Lord Hunsdon and the thin garrisons from the Middle March, the English would have required heavenly aid to turn back the Spanish. He was not prepared to call James's aid a miracle, but he could not deny that it served the purpose Anabel had intended. Berwick would hold.

When it became clear that the battle lay decisively with the English and Scots, the only task left was the breaking up of small circles of enemy soldiers. Kit gave command to Matthew and rode to the Scots line nearest him. He intended to seek out Lord Arran and exchange whatever information was needed for the final clearing up. But it was James who hailed him.

Swallowing his pride—and the vision of Anabel in his own arms the night before last—Kit reined in his horse to speak to the king. "The Spanish ships are drawing off. The soldiers left on shore will never reach them, Your Majesty."

"Good. You've done well. Seems my wife was not wrong to give you command of the English Marches."

"She is never wrong." That was a lie—Kit had often taken pleasure in telling Anabel she was wrong over the years—but he couldn't help the instinct to bait James. And won't that be trouble in the future, he thought grimly.

Kit pulled lightly at his reins, to turn his horse and be on his way before he could say worse. But in the brief time they'd been speaking, a Spanish soldier—through sheerest luck—came within range of the king. Despite surely knowing he could not escape, the soldier did not hesitate. He drove his sword straight at the unprotected area beneath the king's left arm.

Moving before he knew it, Kit kicked his horse so it shoved against the king's mount. The other horse startled, moving just enough for the sword to miss the king and catch Kit on his gauntleted arm instead.

The force of the blow dropped him to the ground, and the Spanish soldier moved in with the swiftness of approaching death. With the perfect clarity of a vision—was this how Pippa had seen things?—Kit knew that the Spanish sword would go through his throat before he could move and before anyone else could intervene.

I'm sorry, Anabel.

The soldier thrust . . . and his sword deflected off a swirl of white mist that had not been there a moment before. Except how could something as insubstantial as mist stop a sword? Kit read shock on the enemy soldier's face the instant before he fell from an avenging Scottish arrow.

The mist twisted before Kit—almost danced—until he thought he discerned a shape to it. It couldn't be. Surely not?

A touch of silk against his thoughts, familiar as breath . . . *You're welcome, twin mine.*

Four hours after the first troops had left Norham, Anabel was allowed to approach Berwick. The Spanish had broken and fled before the combined forces of the English and Scots. Those not dead or injured tried desperately to reach the three ships that had landed them. Few of the Spanish made it. With the bulk of fighting over and her army reduced to finding the wounded and imposing order on the victorious men, Anabel took to the ramparts with Lord Hunsdon to watch the three ships retreat from English shores.

From the ramparts they had a clear view of more than just the three ships. The remaining dozen Spanish ships were farther out, holding in their unusual half-moon formation. If that were the only sight, she might have panicked, for the number of soldiers in those reinforcing ships would be too much for Berwick. But remarkably— blessedly—so distinctly that God and nature must wish witnesses to this wondrous, terrible encounter, Anabel also saw a long line of English ships interposed between the Spanish and the coast. The three fleeing ships seemed to hesitate, then swung south to get around the English line that had seemingly appeared from nowhere.

Of naval warfare, Anabel knew only what she had read and studied. She'd never even been aboard a ship at sea, much less one under fire, nor could she imagine the mind that could comprehend such enormous areas of moving water and still manipulate ships—his own and the enemies'—in battle. What sea battles lacked in speed and intimate violence, Anabel could see they made up for with awful grandeur.

The Spanish ships depended on their crescent formation to confuse and outgun the English. It did not appear especially successful. From the water floated the crack of guns and occasional faint shouts, but mostly Anabel watched in silence trying to guess the meaning of what she saw. Lord Hunsdon, who had better information and experience, supplied occasional commentary.

"Their long guns are formidable, but our ships are more nimble—they can swing out of range in a moment . . . We want to break the crescent, that's why all our ships are attacking the left in a single file line . . . The Spanish will want to board one of our ships if they can . . ."

Please, Anabel prayed fervently. *God in Heaven, please let our ships prevail. Send the Spanish threat far from us so we may recover our peace.*

God in His Heaven must have been amenable to English prayers. Without warning or sign of imminent danger, one of the Spanish galleons exploded. Anabel jumped and grabbed Lord Hunsdon's arm.

"What happened?"

"I could not say." He seemed as startled as she was. "I never knew such a thing—the ship was not taking fire, it was on the opposite crescent from our own ships."

More laconically, one of the Berwick captains said, "There's a mighty load of gunpowder on those ships. All it would take is a moment's inattention, a stray spark, the barrels stored carelessly . . ." He shrugged. "It's a wonder more ships don't blow themselves to pieces."

The explosion and subsequent fire on what remained of the galleon decided the battle. All but one of the remaining Spanish ships retreated as quickly as they could from range of the English and began to run. Even Anabel could tell there was little order to the flight. One brave Spanish ship remained, putting off small pinnaces to presumably try and pull survivors from the wreck. She hoped their gallantry would be honoured by her navy.

Half of the English ships put to sea to continue harrying the Spanish, but the remainder anchored smartly offshore, and by sunset their captain was admitted to Anabel's presence at Berwick Castle.

"Your Highness." He bowed, signs of battle showing beneath the hasty wash and change of clothes. "Allow me to present the symbol of your victory this day."

At her feet, he laid the captured royal standard from the wrecked Spanish galleon. Miraculously, it was only singed along the edges. Anabel stared at the crimson silk emblazoned with the arms of the House of Hapsburg. Someone had added King Philip's personal motto to the standard: *Orbis non Sufficit.*

The world is not enough. And therein, she considered mournfully, lay your failure, Father.

TWENTY-FIVE

Elizabeth's physician assured the queen that her survival and comparatively good health was a gift from God—delivered, one was led to suppose, through the hands and mind of the physician himself. Minuette was entirely more cynical. "You're too stubborn to die without knowing how this war ends. Besides, you'd never give Mary Stuart the satisfaction. No doubt you plan to outlive her by fifteen years at least."

But the softness in her friend's eyes belied the tartness of her words, and Elizabeth understood how very frightened Minuette had been.

It was most irritating being confined to this borrowed chamber at Leeds Castle while the war she had so carefully prepared for was being fought. Elizabeth compensated by driving Burghley, her clerks, and the maids to distraction with her unending demands for information and the need to get on her feet once more.

Three days after her fever broke, Dominic appeared sweat-stained and grimy at Leeds Castle. With news.

Elizabeth refused to meet him lying down. Seated in a high-backed chair that provided the support she grudgingly needed, the queen waved away his manners when he tried to make a proper entry and obeisance.

"There's no time for that," she said sharply. "What has happened?"

Minuette stood tensely near her husband, plainly not having been told either. That was only right—for good or bad, any news of import must come to the monarch first.

"Admiral Hawkins and Francis Drake have damaged and scattered the Spanish fleet off Calais. They sent in fireships, which by all accounts worked even better than the most optimistic could have hoped. When the sun rose, only six Spanish ships were still to be seen. And the great galleass *San Lorenzo* had run aground beneath Calais Castle. They say she will never sail again."

Elizabeth did not move. "And what is the current condition of Admiral Medina Sidonia's armada?"

"Scattered and running. Indications are some of them are still stubbornly heading north, perhaps believing they can manage to regroup and ferry across Parma's army. But that is exceedingly unlikely. Unless . . ."

It was unlike Dominic to hesitate over the obvious. Elizabeth finished for him. "Unless the Spanish were successful at taking Berwick and Carlisle and can help clear the way to bring the remnants of the armada and its men ashore in the North."

"Even in that case, there is little chance of bringing Parma's army across," Dominic said firmly. "And without his twenty-five thousand soldiers, Spain has very little hope of holding even the North for long. All reports are that the Catholic English are either fighting for the princess or remaining uncommitted."

Elizabeth drummed her fingers on the arm of the chair, so anxious to be up and doing, hating being confined and having to wait for things out of her control. "All this assumes that the Spanish who sailed from Ireland are not victorious at Carlisle."

"You are right, Your Majesty. This is not outright victory—not yet. But it is the best we could possibly hope for at this point. The armada will not land on England's southern shores. They will not seize London in a lightning raid. And without London, Spain cannot win in the end."

She knew he was right. And she wanted to celebrate. But Dominic himself did not seem particularly cheerful—as if anyone could tell the difference—and Minuette looked nearly as tense as she had before her husband began speaking. Elizabeth knew why, for she felt it, too.

The South was safe. The North? Unknown. And in that large quantity of unknown lay the lives of Anabel, Kit, and Stephen, placed deliberately and squarely in the war's path.

The next thirty-six hours were the longest of Elizabeth's life—except possibly those hours she had spent at Hatfield thirty years ago waiting for word of her brother William's death. Long after dark the next day, a rider appeared with a letter whose writing Elizabeth knew at once.

25 July 1586
To Her Majesty, Elizabeth, by the Grace of God
Queen of England and Ireland

Your Grace,

The North is secured. On Sunday the twenty-fourth of this month, enemy troops came ashore near Berwick-upon-Tweed and attempted to take the castle. Being valiantly defended by Lord Hunsdon, the castle held fast until relieved by forces both English and Scottish.

The enemy was put to flight, including their ships, leaving behind significant numbers of dead and wounded. The cost to our troops was less, though still most deeply felt.

Even as we counted our own victory, word arrived from Carlisle that the combined Spanish and Irish forces that landed in the West have also been most decisively defeated. That word was delivered to us in person by Lord Stephen Courtenay.

The enemy ships that have fled before our English ones are perhaps heading north once more. Certainly they are unlikely to attempt to rendezvous with Medina Sidonia's fleet—not with the bulk of the English navy in their way. We think it likely they are out of the fight for the foreseeable future.

While still ensuring that the North is held in good order, most of our troops will proceed south with all speed to render whatever aid may be needed. We trust Your Majesty will find these provisions acceptable.

I myself will ride directly for London.

Her Royal Highness Anne Isabella

*Princess of Wales and
Queen of Scotland*

Elizabeth and Minuette were both left speechless—by the signature as much as by the content. "Queen of Scotland?" Minuette said, bemused. "When did that happen?"

Because Elizabeth knew her daughter and, more importantly, knew how kingdoms worked, she thought she had the answer. "I expect that James Stuart was reluctant to lend his army unless Anne gave him what he wanted—the binding ties of a church ceremony."

"Then why did she not tell you so?"

"Because how she gained the Scottish troops is of far less import than the fact that she did manage to gain them."

Minuette sighed. "It is a remarkable letter. She could not yet have had word of your recovery, and yet she writes as though she were certain."

"The first requirement of leadership is to behave as though one is in perfect control at all times. Because Anne could not know my condition when she wrote—or what news may have been spread about it—she ensured that no one intercepting this letter would have any grounds for fear or gossip."

"She is certainly your daughter." Minuette shook her head, as though not certain she entirely approved of that assessment. "What next?"

"We continue to guard the coasts until we can discover for certain that Medina Sidonia's armada is scattered beyond recall. There is no point in winning a battle or two if we simply lay down and lose the war for lack of vigilance."

"I meant next for you."

Elizabeth raised a critical eyebrow. "To London, of course. I must be very visibly present to welcome my prodigal daughter on her victorious return to my court."

"With her husband in tow?"

"I wonder . . ."

Only now that Anne had proven she could do what she must did Elizabeth regret it. She knew it was sentimental, but she would have liked her daughter to have had her happy ending.

When one's husband sends a government member to beg his wife's presence for a discussion, one does not expect a pleasant encounter. Anabel nearly said no to Maitland—from sheer perversity—but knew that she should not begin her marriage with more conflicts than could be helped.

Maitland led her to the large tent with the Scottish royal standard flying beside it. Night had fallen and Anabel could scarcely believe that only forty-eight hours had passed since she'd summoned Kit to her bedchamber in Norham.

Not the sort of thing she should be thinking of. Think, instead, that she'd not had an hour's sleep since her wedding service. When Maitland announced her and then withdrew, Anabel noted with some alarm that she and James were entirely alone. Surely he did not mean to consummate their marriage within sight and smell of the battlefield? If he tried, she would shoot him down immediately, and conflict-avoidance be damned.

"Sit, please." James took a seat in a fretworked folding chair and

Anabel took a matching one across from him. It felt . . . adversarial, rather than marital.

She preferred to keep it that way. "I understand you're willing to send half your men south with us tomorrow. Thank you."

"No farther than Leicester, depending on what news comes from the South. If you need them, they are at your disposal. But if your people have already seen off the Spanish threat, they will return to the border."

"Naturally."

He—almost—smiled. Anabel decided James "almost" did a lot of things. "I didn't send for you to discuss the army. We both have capable captains and generals to do that for us. I asked you here as my wife."

She made the offer that she knew she had to make, no matter how it stuck in her throat. "I will ride ahead of the army, heading directly for London. Assuming, as you say, that the news is good." Anabel looked in his eyes—hazel, the same as Kit's, and yet nothing at all alike—and steeled herself for what felt like a much more binding commitment than the few words spoken in the church. "Will you come with me to London?"

"Do you want me to?"

"I have advised my mother of our marriage in the letters I sent today. I am certain she will expect to meet you."

"Are you certain she is still alive to do so?"

"If she is not, then all the more reason for you to ride with me. I will need to begin from a very strong position at this time of uncertainty."

"You are not wrong. If you are indeed England's queen at this moment—and without a visibly royal husband—King Philip would be seriously tempted to redouble his attacks."

"I know."

He leaned forward, as though confiding in her. Thus more casual than she'd ever seen him, he was almost attractive. "I know some things, too, Anne. I know you do not love me. I never expected you to, not seriously. Not that I don't believe we couldn't fashion an affectionate marriage over time. You are practical as well as beautiful, and like your mother, you know how to make the best of a bad situation."

"Are you calling yourself a bad situation?"

The smile this time was fleeting, but definite. It was a surprise to discover he could be teased. "Christopher Courtenay saved my life today. He didn't have to do it. He is a good man. A good man whom you love."

She stilled, within and without. "You are entitled to many things as my husband, but I will not share my most private thoughts on command."

"And that is why I am going to make you an offer. Our marriage remains unconsummated. I propose we leave it as such for now. Tomorrow you will ride south to London and I will remain at Berwick so that I can move quickly in case of trouble in Scotland. I have some few lords who would not mind taking advantage of the chaos to seek their own profit. And then . . ."

"Then?"

"You will send me the first word you have about Queen Elizabeth's condition. If she is dead and you are now Queen of England, I will come straight to you in London and ensure that your succession is secure. And we will fashion what marriage we can manage between two practical people."

"And if I am not queen?"

"If Queen Elizabeth lives, then I will cross back into Scotland and never trouble you again, save as England's nearest neighbor."

Anabel blinked once. Twice. "I don't understand."

"I mean that, to satisfy my own honour, not to mention my pride, I will give you what you are too honest to ever ask me for: I will give you an annulment."

"Why?"

"Because you will not need me then."

"James—"

He stood up. "I imagine your heartfelt wishes for your mother's survival just rose by a hundredfold. You may live to regret it, you know."

"My mother's life? Do you think so?"

"You would never regret the loss of me personally. But perhaps England will regret the loss of Scotland one day."

"Perhaps the next generation will provide a prince and princess more suited to one another."

"Or less stubborn."

He raised her up and kissed her hand, then her cheek. "Farewell, Anne Isabella. Ride safe and pray hard. I will await your message."

Being at the center of a flow of information was only tolerable while there was an overabundance of information. With the sighting of the Spanish ships both north and south, dispatches became briefer and Lucette was left with too much time to worry about the meaning of the messages she was ciphering and deciphering. Julien at least could contact her fairly frequently, seeing as most military dispatches came through Kenilworth, and it was a relief when Maisie appeared direct from Carlisle. A firsthand report from someone Lucette could question gave an outlet for her nerves. Besides, Maisie was as quick-witted as she, and it was nice to have someone who could follow her thoughts without having to spell them out.

And thank God and all His angels that, finally, Felix was speaking to her. As she and Julien had mended the pains in their marriage, Lucette had learned to treat Felix with unfailing kindness and a promise of love if he should want it—without demanding anything from him in return. Save courtesy, which Julien demanded, but Felix was an essentially obedient and well-brought-up child so courtesy was his natural default.

The boy caught himself several times, as though reminding himself of Lucette's sins, and would withdraw back into abrupt silence. But when she had returned to Kenilworth from Pippa's death and burial—alone, as Julien was required with her father and the English troops—she found Felix where she had left him in Nora Dudley's care, and at his most natural. His sympathy was unfeigned. Felix knew what it was to lose family, far more than Lucette did. With her sister's death fresh and sharp, Lucette began to glimpse the depth of pain for a thirteen-year-old boy who had lost more than his share of family. No wonder he was surly.

Except that he wasn't, not any longer. Or at least, no more so than any boy his age. He took to watching her and trying to anticipate what she might need or want—fresh paper, sharpened quills, food brought to her desk so she might not have to disrupt her work too much.

One night, almost a week after returning to Kenilworth, Lucette wearily went to her bedchamber well after midnight to find three roses the colour of sunset skies lying on her pillow. As she wept for the first time since Pontefract, she knew that Felix was going to be all right.

Finally came the alert that everyone in the castle had been waiting for—the dust of riders and floating banners approaching from the North. The entire castle seemed to crowd the walls and courtyard straining to decipher what they could from the sight.

Three white feathers rising through a golden crown . . . a banner of plain gold . . . the lion and torteaux of the Courtenays bordered for the younger son . . .

"Anabel, Stephen, Kit," Lucette breathed, feeling Maisie's hand tighten convulsively in hers. With Nora and Felix at their heels, they raced down the battlements for the gates.

Once there, Lucette loosed Maisie and hung back a little with Nora. Stephen was off his horse almost before he'd reined up and caught his wife as she flung herself into his arms. Lucette and Nora shared a quick glance, amused while each hopeful they might have similar reunions before long.

Even as Kit helped her dismount, Anabel was speaking to Lucette. "May we speak privately?"

Nora tactfully took the hint. "Felix, help me arrange refreshments for the men. Will you be staying, Your Highness?"

"Not above an hour. We must ride straight on to London."

Lucette hugged Kit, conscious of trying to fill a little of the void left by Pippa's absence. "How is Matthew?" she asked as she led them to her private library.

"He's a good fighter, and violence helped exorcise a little of the pain. Having something to do always helps."

With the door firmly closed, Anabel spoke quickly to those members of the Courtenay family facing her. "The North is secure for now. You've had nothing from the South?"

"Not since word of the armada being sighted off Gravelines."

"Nothing from your mother?"

Lucette tipped her head. "No. Why?"

"Two weeks ago Her Majesty was seriously injured by an assassin. The government has been keeping her condition quiet, from the very real fear that she may be dying. That is why I am riding to London as fast as I can."

"To ensure England has a queen prepared to lead," Lucette said slowly, head spinning. England without Elizabeth? She wasn't sure she could begin to contemplate that thought.

"Yes." Anabel hesitated, and shared a look with Kit. A private look that hinted at some deep well of feeling. Then she steeled herself and resumed the mask of leadership. "A queen with a king to support her if necessary. I married James Stuart on July twenty-third."

"I see." Lucette shot a look at Kit, who showed no apparent emotion, and decided to slide over the news without comment. "Can Maisie and I ride south with you? I don't think she'll let go of Stephen and I—"

"Want the earliest possible news of Julien. Of course. One hour," Anabel said.

But it was only a quarter hour later that a rider flew into Kenilworth's courtyard, no banner, no livery, but a face known at once to everyone there. Brandon Dudley, Earl of Leicester, had come home.

They would all have discreetly faded away to allow him to greet his wife, but Brandon said, "I have news for Her Highness."

"News from Leeds?" Anabel asked without any noticeable quaver. Her face was stark, all cheekbones and wide eyes, and Lucette saw how very much the princess would look like her mother when she reached that age.

"Yes, Your Highness. Her Majesty the Queen reports that the Spanish Armada has been greatly damaged and defeated. The remaining ships are running with no sign of an immediate threat to England. Her Majesty desires that you meet her at Whitehall as soon as may be. She also desires whatever Courtenays I may encounter to be assured of the continued health of both Lord Exeter and Julien LeClerc."

"The queen is alive?"

"She is, Your Highness. And she has written to you." From inside his jerkin, Brandon pulled a somewhat battered letter that Anabel accepted as though being offered the Holy Grail.

Lucette drew a deep sigh of relief and shared a smile with Stephen. Then, to her great surprise, the unflappable, often cynical Princess of Wales burst into tears and flung herself into Kit's arms.

What had begun as a desperate dash for London and the possibility of a government left without a queen now became a triumphal procession. Anabel had her mother's instincts for pageantry, but Kit could see that this heartfelt outpouring of love and thanks touched her deeply. It was the first time the princess had been south of Leicester in two and a half years, and Kit thought he could see the tension literally melting from her with each mile.

He was a little dazed himself after Anabel's stunning confession that James would now give her an annulment. Resolutely, he shoved that tantalizing thought into the back of his mind and behaved as he needed to. While most eyes were turned south to London, there were dispatches and orders to be handled behind them in the North.

The Scottish troops on loan from James had left them at Kenilworth, and Kit busied himself communicating with Lord Hunsdon and Lord Scrope about the aftermath along the border.

One day outside London, Kit went through the pack of dispatches and found a single thin letter with just *Christopher Courtenay* on the outside. He did not recognize the writing. Inside, there was no greeting, simply this stark message:

> *If I have relinquished Her Highness only to see her wed another foreign royal, I shall be greatly disappointed.*

It was signed, simply, *James,* surprisingly readable with a flourish at the end. Kit sat with his mouth open for some time, then closed it and burned the letter.

They entered London from the west, along a route thronged with people cheering their princess, their queen, their victory . . . but mostly, in Kit's prejudiced view, their princess. Anabel rode slowly, wearing the same silver tissue gown in which she had rallied her troops in the North. From behind, Kit thought he would never tire of the sight of her straight back and the fall of red-gold hair crowned only with a gold-wrought wreath of laurels.

Kit could only hope that Queen Elizabeth's reception had been as triumphant. Forbearance was not one of her notable qualities.

The gates of Whitehall were thrown wide for Anabel and her immediate party—her privy council and various Courtenays—to enter. Kit stood immediately behind the princess with Robert Cecil. Behind him were Stephen and Maisie, who had hardly spoken to anyone but each other since Kenilworth, and Lucette with Felix LeClerc. Kit had been glad to note the liveliness in the boy's eyes.

Queen Elizabeth appeared beneath one of the arched ways leading to an inner courtyard, and every person present bowed or curtsied deeply. Including Anabel.

At some unseen signal passing between the two royal women, Anabel straightened and walked forward. The others present slowly eased up as well to witness the reunion. When she reached the queen, Anabel sank low once more and kissed the fingers offered by her monarch. The hand gently lifted her until the two women faced one another, mirrors of the past and future.

"Well done, Your Highness," the queen said.

Then Kit saw the queen's expression alter, so that it was the mother looking upon her only daughter. He bent his head, hiding his grin of relief, as they embraced. Decorously, to be sure, but heartfelt nonetheless.

The two women retreated within, to allow for more spontaneous greetings amongst their retinues. Lord Burghley made straight for his son, Robert, at Kit's side, and there were his own parents right behind—still so striking together at whatever age, fair and dark and perfectly balanced. And Julien, taller than the lot of them, swinging Lucette in a wide circle before kissing her so passionately that Kit almost blushed and caught Felix's eye in amusement as he turned away.

It was his nondemonstrative father, surprisingly, who embraced him first. "Well done," Dominic said, before moving on to Lucie.

Kit looked at his mother, her form and colouring and expression so like his lost twin that his heart ached. As always, she understood perfectly. She pulled him down into a tight hug while he wept a little on her shoulder.

Two hours later Kit stood before Queen Elizabeth alone and very curious. Not even Burghley or Walsingham were with her. Still dressed in her ceremonial finery—the ivory damask of her gown nearly hidden beneath embroidered peacocks, her signature pearls dripping from her bodice and sewn into her hair—the queen did not look like a woman who had nearly died two weeks ago. Save, perhaps, for an extra fineness to her hands and face.

She studied him unblinkingly, and Kit could not read a single one of her thoughts.

"Did you enjoy arresting Eleanor Percy?" the queen asked abruptly.

"Rather more than I should have, I expect." He answered cautiously, not at all certain where this was going.

"I wish I could have seen her face." Her face lit up in a mischievous smile very like Anabel's. "I should have locked Eleanor up long ago."

"What will happen to her now?"

"She did commit treason, but I am feeling . . . generous after our great triumph. I shall allow her to keep her life."

"The woman is dangerous," he felt compelled to point out.

"Eleanor will have her life," Elizabeth repeated, "but not in England. For all their bluster, France is enormously relieved that Spain has not succeeded in swallowing up England. Catherine de Medici and her son owe me a favour."

"What kind of favour?" Kit was beginning to enjoy this.

"Being a Papist country, France has any number of convents. I understand it is quite common for noble women of a certain age to retire from the world. Do you think Eleanor will enjoy the peace and solitude of a religious house?"

Kit grinned. "I think a community of nuns will prove immune to her charms. No doubt they will enjoy instructing her in the ways of a virtuous woman."

"Quite." And with that single word, the queen's countenance grew forbidding. Kit felt his pulse quicken.

"I understand," she said, her words like cut glass in the heavy silence, "that James Stuart is willing to forgo his rights as a wedded husband and not seek consummation of the ceremony. He is willing to set Her Highness free to seek another husband. Why?"

"I cannot speak for His Majesty."

"Anne tells me you saved his life at Berwick."

As it was not a question, Kit did not answer. Elizabeth narrowed her eyes at him. "It did not cross your mind to let him die on the battlefield?"

"And leave a kingdom without a monarch? We cannot afford

Scotland in turmoil. And if James had died less than a day after wedding England, there are many in Scotland who would provoke further war."

"I did not think you so wise," she murmured. "Certainly not as a child. As I recall, you were always prone to act first and apologize after. Exactly like your mother. But it seems you have a deep strain of your father's honour as well. I would see your loyalty properly rewarded."

"Your Majesty—"

"Not as you may wish," she cut him off. "The matter of the marriage of the Princess of Wales remains the province of myself and my government to decide. However, since your brother's folly in Ireland, the Duke of Exeter has had no accepted heir to his estates. In the honours bestowed this week upon those who fought valiantly, we have determined to name you your father's heir—and to give you the title and estate commensurate with that position. You shall be Christopher Courtenay, Earl of Somerset."

"But Stephen—" he protested.

"Stephen forfeited such, as he well knows. Besides, he is as stubborn as your mother. I doubt we'll ever pry him away from whatever his Scottish wife wishes. The best we can hope for is to persuade the young Mariota to bring her business to London. Your brother will not be jealous."

His training asserted itself through his shock, and Kit knelt before the queen. "Your Majesty, it is a great honour. One I never imagined."

"That is why it is being given. Every monarch should be served by at least a few men who are not solely seeking their own advancement."

She leaned down a little, so that her voice—even in this empty chamber—would not carry beyond Kit's ear. "And have you considered that only a future duke could be considered a suitable match for a princess?"

On 5 September 1586 the Duke of Medina Sidonia led what remained of the armada into harbor at Santander on the north coast of Spain. Philip had received a surfeit of reports over the last six weeks—reports of victory, of Spanish troops landed in England, of the fearsome El Draque himself captured—reports that had overlapped and contradicted, with the only thing they had in common being a lack of hard confirmation.

Philip sat alone in his secluded chambers at El Escorial, contemplating the wreck of his great enterprise. Medina Sidonia had arrived in port desperately ill, and though he had brought back almost two-thirds of the fleet, many of the ships were good for nothing now but timber. One had actually sunk *after* anchoring in port. And hundreds of the men aboard were dead or dying from scurvy, typhus, dysentery, and even starvation. Philip knew something now of the duke's desperate weeks guiding his flock of ships around Scotland's treacherous north coasts, keeping away from Ireland and the vengeful English who had taken back the territory lost in the last years, surviving storms and simple bad luck.

There had been one piece of surprising news, offered to the king as sign of a miracle: amongst the ships Medina Sidonia had brought back included two of those that fought off Berwick. And on one of those ships came Mary Stuart—hungry, weary, and furious.

Philip had not yet seen his queen. She had gone to Valladolid to recuperate and see their sons. He was not prepared yet for her scorn, for her contempt, for her certain attempts to press another attack against the English. Perhaps it would come to that. Perhaps not. For now, he was only too aware of life's little ironies. For example, the letter that had arrived today from Ambassador de Mendoza—who had left his post in England to serve in France.

Mendoza had been the source of the most optimistic stories in these last weeks, and this letter was no exception. The ambassador wrote that he had excellent intelligence that the armada, having made repairs and restocked food and water in the Orkney Islands, was now sailing south back toward Flanders with twelve captured English ships in tow.

Philip sighed, and picked up his pen. In precise strokes he wrote in the margins of this false report his last word on the Enterprise of England: *Nothing of this is true. It will be well to tell him so.*

Three months after the Battle of Berwick, Elizabeth joined the Courtenay family at Wynfield Mote for the service of reinterment of the remains of Philippa Courtenay Harrington. Her body had been brought from Pontefract with royal honours, the catafalque covered with the colours of both Exeter and the Princess of Wales, and large crowds along the way bearing hushed witness.

The coffin lay in state in the old, unused chapel near Wynfield for the household to pay their respects, and then the service was held at Holy Trinity Church in Stratford-upon-Avon. The mourners exceeded capacity, for Minuette's family was well loved. Elizabeth had ceded her right to be chief amongst the mourners. Instead, she watched the Courtenay family with an attention she rarely paid to anyone outside her council chambers.

They held up well, not that she had expected any different. Anyone trained to be at court knew how to keep their private feelings behind closed doors. And they had each other—a gift of family not to be underestimated. But still, Matthew Harrington looked thin and wan and Pippa's siblings seemed curiously . . . less without her there. Kit, of course, was the worst. But Elizabeth thought he would heal.

Next to her, Anne stood slim and straight, her face giving away nothing of her own loss. Elizabeth considered how she would feel if it were Minuette being laid away beneath stone—remembered the panic that had gripped her when William sentenced Minuette to death—and impulsively she touched her daughter's hand in sympathy.

"I am the resurrection and the life (saith the Lord) he that believeth in me: yea, though he were dead, yet shall he live."

Elizabeth knew the words of the Order of the Burial of the Dead by heart. It was, after all, her own prayer book.

"The Lord giveth, and the Lord taketh away. Even as it hath pleased the Lord so cometh things to pass: Blessed be the name of the Lord."

Pippa's body would lay in the chancel of Holy Trinity, with its abundance of light from the west window and the shards of colour from the stained glass and the whimsy of the carved misericord seats.

"Forasmuch as it hath pleased almighty God of his great mercy to take unto himself the soul of our dear sister, here departed, we therefore commit her body to the ground, earth to earth, ashes to ashes, dust to dust, in sure and certain hope of resurrection to eternal life, through our Lord Jesus Christ."

When the priest had finished the Order of the Burial of the Dead, the Princess of Wales approached the coffin alone. Elizabeth knew her daughter had asked the family's permission to do so, but the queen did not know why.

Kit joined her, handing Anabel a length of crimson silk. Though folded, Elizabeth knew the Hapsburg arms almost as well as she knew her own, and she realized it was a Spanish banner. Taken from one of the ships, perhaps?

Anabel lay the banner on Pippa's coffin, then let her hand rest lightly on the silk, Kit's hand on hers. Though she spoke with her back to the chapel, the words were light and clear. "The banner of victory is yours, Pippa. For it would never have been ours without you."

Elizabeth returned to Wynfield Mote with the family after the service. At long last, on this bittersweet day, she and Minuette walked alone in the rose garden that had seen so much of both misery and joy in their lifetimes.

"How are you?" Elizabeth asked after a time.

"Weary."

"I have no doubt. As always, you are the center that holds all else together. Moving from grief to grief . . . how do you do it?"

"With a great deal of love and a husband who shelters me at day's end. We will be all right, Elizabeth."

The queen was silent for a bit. "I asked Stephen to accept a barony. You know that, I expect."

"I know that he refused."

"Stubborn boy. Still, I have hopes for that wife of his. She is a sensible creature and has agreed to enlarge her branch of the Sinclair Company in London. But first, I understand, they intend to travel to France."

"With Felix LeClerc, yes. At the boy's request, he will spend the next years between Julien and Stephen here in England. But he does have an aunt and cousins in France, and Blanclair will need to be assured of an excellent steward until Felix is of age and returns. Maisie will help with that."

"They will not travel until after her child is born?" For a girl so small, pregnancy was difficult to hide.

"Not until spring."

"So you will be the first to have a grandchild. I expect it will be a boy, simply to complete my defeat."

"Don't tell me that you would have preferred a son to Anabel."

"An imaginary son—which therefore makes him perfect—as opposed to the willful, unpredictable daughter I have?" Elizabeth laughed. "Of course not. Though I expect a Prince of Wales who chose to marry one of his own subjects might be less fraught than will be the case for a princess."

Minuette's breath caught, then resumed. "What are you saying?"

"You know perfectly well what I am saying. I do not want it public just yet, but my privy council has been informed that, as soon as

may be considered proper, Princess Anne will be wed to Christopher Courtenay, the Earl of Somerset."

"Elizabeth—"

"Curious, isn't it, the vagaries of life? If you had married William
like any other impressionable girl would have done, then there
would be no Anabel or Kit at all. But here they are, and perhaps it
was God's intent all along. A sarcastic, cynical intent, to be sure . . .
but perfect for all that. I think even Will would admit the beauty of
your son wedding his niece. That your son is also Dominic's son only
completes the circle."

They walked on in silence, Minuette no doubt thinking about Kit
and his joy. Elizabeth's thoughts were more selfish. England's welfare
was not—would probably never be—completely secure. Philip, his
righteous pride bruised by the defeat, would ponder new attempts
to bring down the heretic nation he considered the world's greatest
threat. Scotland remained independent and thus always on the verge
of being troublesome. Ireland was even more of a mess after four
years of Spanish troublemaking. Anabel would be a very good
queen—but not, Elizabeth trusted, for a long time to come.

This queen had work still to do.

POSTLUDE

Westminster Abbey

25 July 1603

Minuette Courtenay had never expected to attend the coronations of three British monarchs in her lifetime. The first time, she'd been a child—a nine-year-old girl aware mostly that the boy whose birthday she shared had suddenly become the most powerful person in England. The second time, she had been a young woman, marked by fear and grief, watching her dearest friend steadily take her oath as the first Queen Regnant in English history.

Today, she was old. Sixty-seven last month, though she had been remarkably fortunate in her health. If her shoulders and wrists ached in the damp, she could still see to read and embroider, and still had enough mischief and laughter to enjoy her grandchildren. Ten of them living, and all of them present in the abbey on this day.

This day in which Anne Isabella Tudor would take her formal oaths and be anointed the queen she had been since her mother's last breath. *The queen is dead, long live the queen.*

Minuette herself had been with Elizabeth at the end. Summoned from Wynfield Mote in March by a concerned Robert Cecil, she had arrived at Richmond Palace to find her friend obviously ill but stubborn to the last. The queen would not lie down—spending most of her days standing at the window. Minuette did not think it was the landscape Elizabeth saw. She thought it was the past, perhaps the roll call of her dead: Philip of Spain, Lord Burghley, Francis Walsingham . . . and even further back. William Tudor. Robert Dudley. Lord Rochford. Anne Boleyn. The great and fearsome Henry VIII.

By dint of sheer force of will, Minuette finally persuaded Elizabeth to recline on a bed of pillows and coverlets made up on the floor. She stayed there for four days and was finally weak enough that she could be moved to her bed without protest. Beyond her doors, the government hovered, hardly knowing how to behave now that the queen who had ruled them for forty-four years was dying.

And then, as mildly and gently as a lamb—belying all Minuette had ever known of her friend—Elizabeth Tudor died on 24 March 1603. She was sixty-nine years old and had been queen since she was twenty-five.

Minuette straightened her back as Anne Isabella proceeded slowly down the aisle of Westminster Abbey. Like her mother, she could never look anything less than royal. Though just turned forty-one, Anabel retained her slender figure and vivid red-gold hair. Minuette darted a look away from the new queen to the Lord High Constable, a purely symbolic office revived for the purposes of this coronation. Dominic, at seventy-two as reticent as ever, silver-haired and striking, served today only because Anabel had asked it of him personally.

Next to Minuette, Lucette squeezed her hand. She and Julien were on Minuette's right, with their four children beyond, wide-eyed and impressed despite themselves. On Minuette's left were Stephen and Maisie and their equally awed three children. And her remaining son and grandchildren? They would be front and center soon enough.

Minuette smiled often to herself as the ceremony unfolded in the deliberate, formal manner of more than five hundred years of ritual. The Archbishop of Canterbury's call for the Recognition of the Sovereign. The administration of the oath, ending with the monarch's vow: "All this I promise to do. The things which I have here before promised, I will perform, and keep. So help me God."

Then the procession to St. Edward's Chair and the drawing of curtains for the private rite of anointing with oil. After returning to the public eye, there was the ritual robing and presentation of various regalia. Madalena, Anabel's faithful friend and lady for thirty-five years, was today's Mistress of the Robes. Minuette noted the eyes of the Spanish woman's husband upon her—four years after Pippa's death, Matthew Harrington had wed Madalena and they had both served Anabel faithfully in all the years since.

After receiving the orb, the ring, the scepters of both dove and cross, Anne at last received the Crown of St. Edward set atop her long, loose hair. With cries of "God Save the Queen!" it was time for the oaths of fealty.

Though only an earl, and thus subordinate to several of the peers, Anabel's husband was the first to so swear. He knelt at his wife's feet, and Minuette heard the tremble of pride in her youngest son's voice. "I, Christopher Courtenay, the Earl of Somerset, do become your liege man of life and limb, and of earthly worship; and faith and truth will I bear unto you, to live and die against all manner of folks. So help me God."

When Kit rose, he kissed the queen on the cheek, a liberty not allowed her other peers. Save those two who immediately followed their father in offering fealty: fourteen-year-old William, Prince of Wales, and his twelve-year-old brother, George, Earl of Richmond.

Last of all, Minuette's gaze rested upon the youngest member of the royal family. Though two Courtenay granddaughters had preceded her, both Lucette and Stephen had ignored the obvious choice of name for their daughters, leaving it where it rightly belonged—with Kit. And when this baby princess had been born eleven years ago, God himself—or perhaps one of His angels, still watching over her family—had bestowed a mark of favour. For in the vibrant red hair of her mother, the girl bore a single bright streak of gold framing her face.

Princess Philippa Tudor.

ACKNOWLEDGMENTS

Tamar Rydzinski: who changed my life six years ago, and has made each day better ever since.

Kate Miciak: whose edits, wisdom, and good humor are lifelines in times of professional need.

Marietta Anastassatos, Caroline Cunningham, Shona McCarthy, Peter Weissman, Poonam Mantha, Maggie Oberrender, and Julia Maguire: for art and design that makes me swoon from its beauty, for impeccable production and perfection of the text, for enthusiastic publicity, and for taking my every email with good humor.

Matt, Jake, Emma, and Spencer: for being, always, yourselves and letting me be part of your lives. Forgive me my many maternal faults, and know how much I love you.

Becca Fitzpatrick, Pat Esden, and Suzanne Warr: I admire you as writers, and love you as women.

Ginger Churchill and Debbie Ramsay: for being just a text away when trauma hits.

Katie Jeppson: For. Everything. Always. Full stop.

For Chris: Full stop.

For all readers: You are my people. In a fractured and fractious world, reading is an act of defiance that proclaims that understanding and tolerance are values worth fighting for. Fight the good fight.

And for every person who has taken a risk in picking up any of my twisted Tudor books: Thank you. I hope it was worth it.

THE VIRGIN'S
WAR

Laura Andersen

A READER'S GUIDE

Because thou has offended our sovereign the King's grace in committing treason against his person ... thou hast deserved death, and thy judgment is this: that thou shalt be burned here within the Tower of London, on the Green, else to have thy head smitten off, as the King's pleasure shall be further known of the same.

—Duke of Norfolk, pronouncing sentence against his niece, Queen Anne Boleyn, on 15 May 1536

More than ten years ago, I set out to write one book reimagining history if Anne Boleyn's final miscarriage had never happened. A story of a king-who-never-was, of the friends who loved him and broke his heart . . . and of the sister who was left to pick up the pieces.

I'm fairly certain Queen Elizabeth would find both The Boleyn Trilogy and The Tudor Legacy Trilogy presumptuous. I only hope she would not find them insulting. More than a year before any of these books were conceived—the very first time I wondered what might have happened if Anne Boleyn had not miscarried her baby boy in January 1536—I got as far in my thinking as "And if that boy had been healthier than Edward VI, then neither Mary nor Elizabeth would have ever been queen" before mentally recoiling at the thought.

Physics, I understand, posits the Many Worlds theory, in which every permutation of choice and event leads to a timeline split from the one we currently experience. I don't care how many timelines might exist: I cannot conceive of a single one in which Elizabeth Tudor was not Queen of England. On every visit I've made to Westminster Abbey since beginning this series, I pause a moment in the north aisle of the Henry VII Chapel to pay my respects at her tomb. And I offer the same silent plea to this greatest of English queens: "Don't be mad."

Would I meet Elizabeth if I had the chance? Yes. Fearfully and trembling. And I imagine the interview might go something like this:

ELIZABETH: So you are the scribbler who has played so fast and loose with my life and heart.

LAURA: Your Majesty. [Quite likely attempting to curtsey without utter humiliation]

E: Why take so bold a chance?

L: For your mother's sake, at first. Anne Boleyn was in an impossible situation almost from the moment your father fell in love with her. Is it wrong to wish fate had been a little kinder to her?

E: Fate . . . or my father?

L: That is not for me to say.

E: And yet you had so much to say on so many topics of which you can have no knowledge. Walsingham would consider you the worst sort of meddler—the ignorant sort. And yet . . . I admire cleverness. And there are elements approaching cleverness in how you dealt with men like Northumberland. That is certainly a man who would have found a way to get himself executed no matter what world he lived in. And Guildford never had the nerve to carry off plotting.

L: I thought you might not mind the possibility of Mary Stuart's escape. As you were so notably reluctant to condemn her.

E: I did not at all enjoy your implication that Mary Stuart could ever have outwitted me. The situation you created there serves as perfect justification for never marrying. No man to attempt to master me . . . and no child as a hostage to fortune. Though I admit, Anne is not an entirely displeasing imaginary child.

L: May I ask you about Robert Dudley?

E: You may not. That is one liberty too great.

L: If you were to leave your own memorial, what would it be?

E: Perhaps what I spoke at Tilbury in 1588. Not 1586, as you so casu-
ally altered in your timeline. I believe that I fulfilled what I
promised then. Until the last day of my life, I placed my chief
strength and safeguard in the loyal hearts and goodwill of my
subjects, and then I laid down my life, my honour, and my blood
for God and my people.

Despite that fantastical conversation, the truth is we do not have
to imagine what Elizabeth might say about her own legacy. She said
it herself, in a speech to her final Parliament in November 1601.
[Note: Elizabeth often used king and prince interchangeably with
queen to denote her position.]

To be a king and wear a crown is a thing more glorious to them
that see it than it is pleasant to them that bear it . . . There will
never Queen sit in my seat with more zeal to my country, care to
my subjects and that will sooner with willingness venture her
life for your good and safety than myself. For it is my desire to
live nor reign no longer than my life and reign shall be for your
good. And though you have had, and may have, many princes
more mighty and wise . . . yet you never had nor shall have, any
that will be more careful and loving.

In my books, I wrote an Anne Boleyn—and a Mary Tudor—and
a Philip of Spain—and a Robert Dudley—who never existed. But
mostly, I wrote my own Elizabeth. One who did not have to ask why
she was addressed as Highness one day and simply Lady the next.
One who did not have to worry about being the center of plot after
Protestant plot. One who was not arrested at the age of twenty and
taken to the Tower. One who did not have to always wonder whether
she would be executed before her half sister died. One who did not
scratch on the window at Woodstock: *Much suspected by me, nothing
proved can be. Quoth ELIZABETH prisoner.*

And yet, I had to write an Elizabeth who possessed and developed the character traits so notable in her long reign as queen: intelligence, subtlety, practicality, devotion to her people, reluctance to commit to a divisive course until there was no choice, vanity, humour, touchy about her privileges but self-aware enough to know it. What I did in these six books was imagine a different path, different choices, that would bring Elizabeth to essentially the same place in history.

There is a tradition that Anne Boleyn wrote a poem in the days before her execution on Tower Green.

> O Death! rock me asleep;
> Bring me to quiet rest;
> let pass my weary, guiltless ghost
> out of my careful breast.
> Toll on, the passing-bell;
> ring out my doleful knell;
> let thy sound my death tell.
> Death dothe drawe ny;
> there is no remedie.

Despite the story wrought from my imagination, there was no remedy for Anne Boleyn. She died at the command of her king and husband on 19 May 1536, leaving their not yet three-year-old daughter to an uncertain future. I like to think, when I visit Westminster Abbey, that Anne looks with pride on her daughter's memorial, and the achievements listed in Latin around Elizabeth's tomb.

> Sacred to memory: Religion to its primitive purity restored, peace settled . . .
> the Spanish Armada vanquished; Ireland almost lost by rebels, eased by routing the Spaniard . . . and lastly, all England enriched. Elizabeth, a most prudent governor 45 years, a victorious and triumphant Queen, most strictly religious, most happy . . . She died the 24th of March, Anno 1603, of her reign the 45th year, of her age the 70th.

To the eternal memory of Elizabeth queen of England, France and Ireland, daughter of King Henry VIII, grand-daughter of King Henry VII, great-grand-daughter to King Edward IV.

Daughter, I would add, of Anne Boleyn, who took as her motto: The Most Happy. In her daughter, I think Anne would have found all the happiness she could desire.

QUESTIONS AND TOPICS FOR DISCUSSION

1) In what ways does the title of this novel reflect its content? In what ways does it not?

2) *The Virgin's War* is the last in the Tudor Legacy trilogy. What surprised you most? Were you satisfied by the conclusion?

3) Based on your knowledge of Tudor history, what changes would you say made the largest difference in the outcome of the changed course of events?

4) If you had to describe the relationship between Queen Elizabeth and Princess Anne in one word, what would that word be?

5) Throughout the book, it is clear that political relationships and personal relationships are at a dramatic impasse. Which motivation—the political or the personal—do you believe is more vital, either to yourself or to the story?

6) How do the bonds between characters inform their actions? For example, had Anabel and Kit not been in love, do you think she would have wanted the annulment from James so deeply?

7) Pippa stayed away from Matthew for fear of hurting him, and Maisie stayed away from Stephen for fear he could never love after Ailis. Do you think these women took the right courses of action in denying their feelings in favor of practicality? How would their lives have been different if they had followed their hearts?

8) Imagine your favorite character is transplanted into modern times. What would he or she be doing, in his or her career, spare time, et cetera?

9) Both Anabel and Elizabeth make serious sacrifices for what

they consider to be the greater political good. What do you think were the hardest choices these royal women had to make?

10) While Anabel is clearly on the English side, she and her mother pretend that she wavers towards the Spanish—and Catholic— cause. In what ways can you relate to the princess's loyalty to her crown, despite what the other half of her parentage may think about it later?

11) As Pippa imagined as a teenager, she and Matthew most certainly found themselves in terrible danger. What does this say about fate versus free will?

12) How does Navarro's character change from the beginning of the book to the end? Do you ever pity him? Do you hate him? Do your feelings for him ever change?

ABOUT THE AUTHOR

Laura Andersen is married with four children, and possesses a constant sense of having forgotten something important. She has a B.A. in English (with an emphasis in British History), which she puts to use by reading everything she can lay her hands on.

lauraandersenbooks.com
Facebook.com/laurasandersenbooks
@LauraSAndersen

ABOUT THE TYPE

This book was set in Requiem, a typeface designed by the Hoefler Type Foundry. It is a modern typeface inspired by inscriptional capitals in Ludovico Vicentino degli Arrighi's 1523 writing manual, *Il modo de temperare le penne*. An original lowercase, a set of figures, and an italic in the chancery style that Arrighi (fl. 1522) helped popularize were created to make this adaptation of a classical design into a complete font family.

Chat.
Comment.
Connect.

Visit our online book club community at
Facebook.com/RHReadersCircle

Chat
Meet fellow book lovers and discuss what you're reading.

Comment
Post reviews of books, ask—and answer—thought-provoking
questions, or give and receive book club ideas.

Connect
Find an author on tour, visit our author blog, or invite one of
our 150 available authors to chat with your group on the phone.

Explore
Also visit our site for discussion questions, excerpts, author
interviews, videos, free books, news on the latest releases,
and more.

Books are better with buddies.
Facebook.com/RHReadersCircle